Beyond
Aegis

MARION MALDANER

This book is a work of fiction. Any references to historical events, real people, or real locales are used fictitiously. The characters and events in this book are also fictitious. Any similarity to real people, living or dead, is coincidental and not intended by the author.

ISBN: 098977287X
ISBN-13: 978-0-9897728-7-7

In loving memory of Jennifer Acierno Theisen.

ae·gis

noun \ ˈē-jəs \

For Mimi who changed Nathaniel's destiny.
For my beloved parents, Mario and Dirci, my cherished in-laws, Steve and Dottie, and my friends who showed me unconditional support. Above all, for my husband and editor Dave who I love so very much.

Many thanks to Carolyn Whitescarver for assistance and research. Tiffany McIntosh for her contribution and support. Daniel Cancelier, Felipe Szterling, Géssica Falcão, Nathalia Borguesan and Solange Borguesan for their outstanding team work. As well as Kayla, Alicia, Mike, Kelly, Corey, and Rob for lending their talent and expertise.

1

Some people say that omission is the same as lying. If you ask me, some things are better left unsaid. Take this pulse, for instance. This uncontrollable urge to charge into the unknown, coupled with the heavy feeling that I'm no longer the one pulling the strings. It's like gravity, or magnetism. A force of nature. My entire body goes on autopilot.

I take a huge gasp of air and push forward. My heart thumps wildly in my chest, throbbing as if urging me to quicken my pace.

Faster! Come on, faster!

I'm neck-deep, and I mean that *literally*. I'm fighting my way through turbulent water, and for the record I'm not the strongest swimmer. My copilot must not have gotten the memo.

Every fiber of my being is drawing me deeper into the ocean for no plausible reason. It seems like I've been swimming forever, and there is no one in sight. My arms are exhausted, and I'm numb to the cold. I kick my legs forcefully, putting more distance between me and the shore.

Unable to explain why, I don't even pause to consider whether I'll survive this time or not. That's the down side to this pull, not having a chance to think before taking the plunge. It would have been a good idea to toss my cellphone aside before jumping in the water, but it's too late now. I'll try to remember that next time.

I extend my arms to their max with each stroke, well aware that people on the shore must still be staring. It's not every day that you see a five foot eight blonde girl fully clothed darting into the water for no discernible reason. Particularly, if said beach is in Japan. They must think I'm either insane or suicidal, probably both. Good, maybe someone will come to *my* rescue this time.

Behind a massive crest, a tiny pale hand raises up and immediately submerges. The waves slam my body back as I push against the current with decisive strokes. The ocean suddenly becomes more erratic, as if taking claim to the child's life. It's like the closer I get, the more intently it drives me back. But I don't give in, pressing forward with all my might. The little hand doesn't pop up for a second time, and another swell breaks forcefully against my chest. I nearly choke, inhaling a deep breath of pure saltwater.

It's getting dark. Storm clouds are gathering above, hindering my effort to spot the drowning child from the surface. I dive under, but it's no use since I can't see my hand in front of my face through the churning ocean. My eyes sting as I resurface, and I wipe my burning eyes with the back of my hand. From this vantage point all I see is the choppy surf ahead. Back at the shore, commotion begins to build, and two men jump into the water, making their way toward us.

Something solid comes in contact with my running shoes, and I dive down again, swiping around blindly. When my fingers entangle in a head of thin soft hair, panic sets in. I submerge deeper and wrap my arms around a small fragile body, desperately kicking to the surface.

In an attempt to keep both of our faces above the water, I backstroke toward the beach. When my shoes touch the bottom, I drag forward with heavy steps, lifting my knees high like I'm marching up a flight of stairs with a rag doll pressed against my chest. She weighs nothing and can't be older than ten. Her body is limp, head tilted back in an unnatural state, lips slightly blue and eyes wide open.

It doesn't take long before a few people rush toward me in distress, reaching for the girl. I hand the child off to a man who carries her with minimal effort and then follow behind as he makes his way to the shore, watching her wet black hair dangling over his arm.

When he reaches dry land, he lays her flat on a colorful towel. The sight of this innocent little girl in her lilac one piece, stretched out like she might be dead, makes me flinch. Her delicate face and heart shaped lips contrast shockingly with the shade of indigo surrounding her mouth. I get a glimpse at the dead-fish stare in her eyes, and everything becomes too overwhelming to endure.

As a man kneels beside her fragile body and works on resuscitating her, I start walking backward, unable to remove my eyes from her inert figure. Then, I whirl around and speed walk away from the scene.

Crouching on the sand, I take in the commotion and distress from a distance. She's quickly surrounded by a crowd and out of sight, but the image of her face is imprinted in my mind. I focus on tuning out the noise and begin chanting in my head "everything's gonna be fine," over and over again. Until, it finally comes true.

She comes back to life, coughing and gasping for air. With a sigh of relief, I get to my feet and take off running toward the hotel we've been staying for these past few days. A place where Dad, Suri, and I could spend some quality time together before I have to leave Japan.

At the steps of the building, I remove my soaked running shoes and carry them in one hand. It's no use since

I'm leaving a trail of water drops behind. I take the stairs two at a time to the third floor, wanting nothing more than to get out of my drenched clothes and rinse the salt off my skin with a hot shower.

When I get inside, Dad blocks my path blurting out questions, "Where have you been? How many times do I have to ask you to keep your phone charged? Your flight departs in two hours..." He trails off, taking in the puddle of water below my feet. "What happened to you, kiddo?" Dad asks in his concerned fatherly tone.

His question brings back intrusive thoughts, and I shake my head to wave them off. The unexpected sound of thunder coming from outside makes me jump. He faces the double doors that lead to the balcony just as lightning brightens the late afternoon sky and then looks back to me expectantly.

I nervously pull my phone out of my arm band and hand it to my confused dad, "Is there any way we can salvage this?" I ask sheepishly.

He takes the water damaged device in his hands, seeming at a loss for words. A furrow forms in his brow, and I take advantage of his distraction to make my escape. Knowing too well that eventually I'll have to come up with a plausible explanation. But then again, considering the downpour outside, maybe I won't.

"Go get ready, kiddo. We're out of here in twenty minutes," says Dad in a tired voice.

I nod and plant a kiss on his cheek before leaving the room.

Dad shouldn't have worried, though. I reach my departing gate an hour before the scheduled flight. As I pull out my tablet from my backpack an overhead announcement informs my flight will be delayed.

Great!

I gather up my things and approach an airline representative to inquire about my connecting flight and my checked luggage. The smiling agent assures me that everything is under control. I'm going to make my connection with plenty of time. Comforted by her words, I take a seat and wait for the boarding announcement for my flight. Twenty-eight minutes go by before the passengers of flight two thirty-seven are called to board. By the time the plane takes off, we're almost an hour behind schedule and in for a turbulent flight. A connection later, however, the weather appears to clear up and the flight progresses smoothly.

From up here life seems very small. I'm soaring through the atmosphere remarkably fast, and yet the world below me appears to stand still. Through the circular window, the city takes shape between fractured clouds. Just the sight of the endless ocean brings back the vivid memory from the dreadful beach incident. Once again, I'm swayed by the feeling of being overpowered by a force beyond me. I look away in an attempt to clear my head.

As if on cue, a melodic chime sounds over the PA, "Ladies and gentlemen, welcome to Boston Logan International Airport. The time is two twenty-five p.m., and the forecast is partially cloudy with a high of sixty-eight degrees. We request that all electronic devices be turned off until we are safely parked at the gate. Please remain in your seats with your seat belts fastened until the plane has come to a complete stop. Thank you."

The change in pressure causes my ears to pop the instant we begin to descend. The aircraft touches down to the runway with a jolt, and as the plane taxis, the sound of seat belts being unclasped rattles throughout the cabin. After a thirteen hour flight, everyone is eager to reach their destinations. Everyone but me, that is.

Unlike the executive sitting to my left, I remain in my seat until the seat belt lights dim, watching as the other passengers bump into each other and struggle with their carry-on luggage. The aisles are quickly filled with passengers anxious to exit the single hatch of this robotic bird. I delay for as long as I can before even standing up. It's only after the last person passes my seat that I retrieve my backpack from the overhead compartment. Hanging it on one shoulder, I exit the plane and follow far behind the other passengers as we walk through a narrow channel. I'm suddenly self-conscious, standing out in my yellow hoodie and washout jeans as we surround the baggage claim area to retrieve our luggage. After loading it onto a cart, I pass through security and make my way to the terminal exit.

Grandma isn't particularly fond of my hoodie, but I didn't dress this way to annoy her. It just might be the last chance I have for a while. I don't resent her in any way. If it weren't for Grandma, Dad might have enrolled me in a boarding school or something. Dad is all about the acquisition of knowledge, the only treasure that can't be stolen. He's a computer geek, what else can be expected?

So even though Grandma is always on my case to be more "ladylike," and Grandpa starts every other sentence with, "If only you were a boy..." I'm thankful. *Truthfully!*

I love my dad. I sincerely do. He just wants what's best for me. I also understand he can't just abandon his company and leave it's fate in incapable hands. He's needed in Shinjuku, Japan. There was no way around it, not until his partner fully recovers from his bypass surgery at least. In Santa Monica, however, he has a full team capable of running the company's stateside operation without him. It's moving from California to Boston and enrolling in a new school that's bugging me. It's like I'm going back to the start just as I reached the middle. By junior year, cliques have already formed, and I'll probably end up being a loner.

As I approach the inbound passenger pickup, I spot them. They're both here to greet me, my grandparents, Christopher and Melody O'Neill.

"Eliza," Grandma calls out, waving.

Grandpa Chris stands tall right beside her, wearing a charcoal striped suit and looking as sharp as the imposing

US Army general he had once been. Grandma also looks just as I remembered. Blond hair in a chin-length bob haircut, unmoving thanks to an excess of hairspray. Like always, she's dressed in pastel tones from head to toe with layers of pearls hanging from her neck. Today, she's wearing a pale blue bouclé wool suit, which accentuates her eye color.

"Grandma, Grandpa," I walk up to them.

Grandpa is the first one to hug me, kissing the top of my head, "Liz, my sweet girl."

The instant he lets me go, Grandma takes her turn and plants one on each cheek, "It's been so long since we last saw you, Eliza. You're almost as tall as your grandfather!" Her familiar floral scent perfume fills my nose.

Grandpa walks over, taking the backpack from my shoulder. He isn't expecting how heavy it is as he puts it on his own. He feigns a serious tone, "What kind of contraband do you have in here? I hope you're not sneaking any heavy weaponry in from Japan."

I laugh, well aware that he has a room filled with his own private arsenal of antique weapons. No one can tell just by looking at Grandpa who always seems so serious, how playful he can be. He pushes the cart full of my luggage, "You know, Liz, if only you were a boy, I could take you out to the shooting range with my buddies from—"

"Oh, Christopher," Grandma cuts him off, placing an arm over my shoulder. "You'll do no such thing. It's bad enough that David raises her like a boy with all the video games, running, and dangerous sports."

As we make our way out of the airport toward the parking garage, my eyes keep jumping around. Everything here looks so different from Narita Airport in Japan. It's not as crowded, for one, and people walk slower here than they do there. It seems like there are fewer people running against the clock.

When we reach Grandpa's silver Explorer, I try to help him load my luggage into the trunk until he orders me into the SUV, "I've got it, sweetheart."

Grandma follows me inside, handing me a card that reads in bold typeface, "CharlieCard." I flip it over, and look up at her inquiringly.

"It's a subway card. It's for emergencies, keep it with you when you leave the house," she informs me with a smile.

"I will," I say gratefully, unzipping my hoodie and pocketing it.

Grandpa takes his place in the driver's seat, and we're off. I split my attention between light conversation with Grandma and this new scenery that is passing by. As Grandpa stops at a red light, a group of kids about my age cross the street in front of us. I can hear them carrying on from inside the SUV. They look friendly enough and seem happy. I just hope I can fit in here.

Grandma is talking about remodeling the guest room, but I'm feeling jet lagged, and can barely keep up. Until she mentions that she started painting the room two months ago.

"Two months ago?" I turn her last words into a question.

The unexpected answer comes from Grandpa, "Your grandma has been working on it since the beginning of the summer when your father said that you would be staying with us." He looks at me from the rear view mirror and goes on, "Your grandma did a nice job."

"Thanks, Grandma," I reply politely. On the inside, however, I'm taken aback. Up until two weeks ago I didn't even know I would be moving to Boston.

"David shouldn't have kept you until the very last minute," Grandma starts. "Faye got back into town last night. She spent the summer in Colorado with her father. I had to reschedule your uniform fitting three times. Your new appointment is set for tomorrow at eleven since we have to attend orientation a few hours earlier, and..."

My brain stopped processing her words right after she

mentioned the word "uniform." Incapable of hiding the astonishment in my voice, I ask, "Uniform fitting? Do I have to wear a uniform at this new school?"

Seriously. What else did Dad forget to mention?

Grandma shifts slightly in her seat so she can look at me, "It's a private school, of course there's a dress code."

Super!

Dad didn't say anything about the school being private either. Oh no, Dad just said I was going to Faye's school. Very sly on his part. I would expect to wear a uniform if I were going to a high school in Japan, but *here*? Besides, I've studied in public schools for the past six years. Why am I suddenly attending a private school?

As Grandma rattles on, tiredness takes over, and my eyelids feel exceedingly heavy. Grandpa turns right on to their street, and I fight to remain awake. Against his protest, I help him unload my luggage and take it inside.

Grandpa's comment regarding Grandma's decorating talents didn't do her justice. Not one bit. She has transformed the guest room into a modern space that's in stark contrast with the antique classic styling of every other room in their penthouse apartment. Apart from the walls, that is. They're the same plain white.

What used to be a room with barely enough space to move around is now bright, ergonomic, and open. In the center of the main wall hangs a three piece canvas print of yellow tulips. Atop the night stand sits a pedestal shaped alarm clock, and an LED reading light is clamped to the headboard. The bed's platform frame is a pale yellow and the sheets are white with an enormous orange leaf pattern.

"Wow, Grandma," I begin. "This is..." I trail off at a loss for words. "You shouldn't have–"

"Nonsense," Grandma interrupts. "We want you to feel at home while you're staying with us. Besides, this room was asking to be remodeled for decades. Your moving in was just the motivation I needed. We're very happy you chose to live with us while you finish high school."

I choke up, speechless. I rush to Grandma and throw both arms around her, catching her by surprise.

"There, there," Grandma laughs and gently pats my back. "I guess that means you like it."

"I love it. Thanks, Grandma."

"You're welcome, my dear," she smiles kindly at me. "Now, go rest. You must be exhausted after such a long flight."

I nod, thanking her one more time as she excuses herself and leaves the bedroom. Walking up to the window, I gingerly pull one of the two lift cords, and the blinds tilt open. I look down at the view, and I do a double take. I usually come here in the winter for the holidays, when the city is covered in snow. I didn't expect to see the park and its colorful trees at dusk. It's amazing: the kind of view that belongs in a painting or a postcard. It's high enough to get a nice view of the city and the park but not so high that people walking by look like ants.

A yawn escapes, and I close the shades. Opening my biggest suitcase, I remove the items stacked on top of a pair of sweat pants and pull them out. I change into them, take off my hoodie and flop into bed, passing out before my head touches the pillow.

2

A growling sound from within startles me awake. The glowing orange digital numbers on the alarm clock indicates it's a quarter to six in the morning. No wonder my stomach is complaining; last it fed was yesterday on the plane. I must have been more exhausted than I thought. What was supposed to be a nap, turned into a sleep marathon, and I missed dinner.

I dig through my luggage and pull out my aquamarine top, a white shirt and running pants. I change into it and put on the yellow hoodie I wore yesterday. Pulling my hair into a ponytail, I head straight to the kitchen.

Grandpa is up, looking like he's been awake for a while: showered, shaved and wearing a polo shirt. He sits on a bar stool, reading glasses on, with the newspaper spread out on the counter. He has his usual camouflage coffee mug in his hand and takes a testing sip. It must be hot because a little steam is rising from it. He looks up as I walk in the kitchen, setting down his paper and glancing at the clock on the microwave.

"You're up early," Grandpa comments. "Hungry, I suppose?"

I nod, "I lied down for a nap and ended up sleeping through the night. Now my stomach is begging for food."

"Dominika won't be here until seven. We have peanut butter and bread in the cabinet if you still like the stuff. I can make you some oatmeal if you prefer," Grandpa offers, pointing to the left.

"Peanut butter toast sounds great," I say, heading for the pantry.

I set the bread and the peanut butter aside on the center island. Then, I get a plate and drop two slices of bread into the toaster, spreading nearly half a jar of peanut butter on them once they're done.

Grandpa peers at me over his bifocals, "There's juice in the refrigerator."

I nod with my mouth full and fetch the jug from out of the fridge, pouring myself a heaping glass of OJ. Then, I take my plate and sit across from Grandpa. He smiles at me briefly, turning the page on his newspaper. Grandpa isn't the small-talk type, and I eat in a comfortable silence, watching his varied expressions as he takes in the morning news.

Once I finish eating, I rinse my plate and glass, closing them inside the dishwasher. The clock on the microwave reads a quarter past seven in dim green numbers.

"I'm going for a run, Grandpa."

"Sounds good," Grandpa says, without lifting his face from the news.

Back in my bedroom, I grab my sport armband and my iPod, lace up my running shoes and make my way out of the apartment. The morning is still foggy, and the post lights are still on. The weather is chilly, just perfect for a morning run.

At the park's entrance, I stop for a quick stretch. Then, pulling my sleeves up, I break into a nice jog. I slow down as I reach the crosswalk, but I don't have to stop because the cars are lined up at a red light.

As I make my way to the gates, I decide to change my playlist to something a little more upbeat. Maintaining my cadence, I remove the iPod from my armband and look down at the screen just in time to slam headlong into a hooded figure.

The word "BOSS" in light gray is stamped across his chest. The sudden impact dislodges the iPod from my hands, and I swipe at the air around it while stumbling backward. It's unmistakable that his first instinct is to let me hit the ground. But then, it's like he changes his mind at the last second and reaches out to get a hold of me at the same time I reach out to grab his arms for support.

Needless to say that the result of this particular collision is catastrophic. The folder he's carrying escapes from his hands, and an avalanche of papers spill out all over the sidewalk. His iPod hits the ground with a bounce and lands right next to mine. Somehow, he manages to grab my arms, preventing me from landing on my butt.

A sudden vibrant tingling, like a prickling, stirs under my skin where his hands make contact with my bare arms. My face tilts upward, meeting his gaze. His expression goes from annoyance to intrigue. Meanwhile, I'm unable to look away. I'm fascinated. I've never seen eyes so unmistakably blue, even though being overshadowed by his hood. That's when I realize that I'm shamelessly staring at him. So, I try an apologetic smile. It usually works, but then again, I've never smashed into anybody before.

The wind starts blowing his papers all over the place, and I slide out of his hold. I crouch down to gather them, making a pile and placing the papers carefully inside his folder. After a moment, he kneels down to join in, and I dare to speak, "I'm so sorry. If you didn't catch me, I'd have fallen flat on my butt."

What's wrong with me? Did I just say that out loud?

Through the corner of my eye, I steal a glance at him. He's an exceptionally handsome guy, about my age, and appears to suppress a smile before asking rhetorically, "Have you ever heard the saying no good deed goes unpunished?"

I shake my head, "No," holding both iPods in one hand.

He reaches out for his, and I hand it over without looking away from his face. Simultaneously, we both stand up, and I apologize once again. He pockets the device and pulls his phone out of his jacket, plugging the headphones in. Then, he nods and walks away, putting in his earbuds.

He crosses the street, and I replay what just happened in my mind. Still befuddled, I put in my headphones, look down at the device in my hand, and scroll through the playlist. Immediately, I realize that I have his iPod instead of mine. There's a single unnamed album with eighty-one tracks. Curious, I press play.

What on Earth is this?

It's not a song, more like an audio book or a recording. It's also incomprehensible, in a language I've never heard before. I turn it off, feeling weirded out. Then, I look up and see the distance between us increasing as the beautiful stranger makes his way down the sidewalk.

My mind snaps into action, and I step off the curb just as the crosswalk light turns red. An enraged driver blares his horn at me, so I step backward onto the corner and wait impatiently as several cars pass. He's getting further away, and I have to speed walk among the pedestrian traffic to keep up with him. I'm almost running when he turns left on Boylston Street. My mind set on a single goal, getting my iPod back.

As I reach the corner, his dark hoodie is disappearing into the east entrance. I dash after him, deviating from a couple jogging toward me. I dodge a guy on a bicycle and almost step on a little squirrel crossing my path.

Panic sets in as he makes his way to the Park Street station. If I miss which direction he's going, I'll never see my iPod again. Pausing for a split second, I remember the "CharlieCard" Grandma handed me yesterday which is still in the pocket of my yellow hoodie. I pick up the pace when I spot him going down the stairwell. But I'm forced into slow motion as people coming out of the subway block my path.

Keeping my eyes on him, I speed walk around the oncoming crowd and follow him onto the Green-D metro just before the doors slide shut. I want to get closer, but the car is way overcrowded. I'm about to call after him, but change my mind when I notice he still has his headphones on. Besides, I doubt he would even look in the direction of someone shouting incoherently.

He exits at the very next stop, giving me the impression that he knows he's being followed and is trying to lose me. But maybe not since he's taking his sweet time walking toward the blue line. Once there, he leans and rests his head against the wall, waiting for the next train.

When I'm just close enough that he may be able to hear me, a homeless guy sidetracks me by begging for some spare change. I reach inside my jacket pockets and come up with a few bills.

"Sorry, that's all I've got," I say apologetically, handing it to him.

"Bless you, kind girl."

The metro comes to a stop at that instant, and the hooded stranger steps into the car. I do the same, entering through a door closer to me. The car is just as full as the previous one, and he sits near the door facing the opposite direction. I spot an empty seat, beside a heavyset middle-aged man in a suit reading a business magazine. He glances up as I sit, and I stiffen at his scrutiny. The metro departs with a jolt and I hold the handrail to stay in place.

Keeping one hand on the rail, I lean forward ever so slightly and take a peek at the stranger. His head rests against the interior window with his eyes closed. As we reach Maverick station, the lurching prompts him to straighten his head and open his pretty eyes. By reflex, I lean back against my seat out of his sight, which defeats the purpose of getting his attention in the first place. I lean forward once again, but he's distracted by his phone.

At the airport station, he stands up and leaves the car. I get off by the entrance near my seat and look around searching for his hooded head. He's slowly making his way into the airport as if daring me to follow. I don't hesitate, running after him. He steps onto the escalator, and I rush toward him through a crowd of people. I get stuck behind a woman in a pantsuit whose feet are planted on a single step of the upward moving escalator. She's holding a smartphone against her shoulder while digging through her gigantic maroon bag.

At the next floor, I spin around and spot him at a priority check in counter. His hood is lowered, and I catch a glimpse of his dark blond "just-rolled-out-of-bed" hairstyle before getting blocked in again. I dash after him as he makes his way toward the embark area. Not fast enough though, by the time I'm at arm's length, he's crossing security.

An oversized TSA officer wearing his oversized TSA badge throws his arm out in front of me, "Boarding pass and identification, please."

"But, I just," I try explaining, pointing in the direction of the stranger who's rapidly disappearing from view.

"Boarding pass and identification, Ma'am," he repeats, cutting me off in a voice that leaves no opening for argument.

I'm crestfallen as I turn around and make my way back from whence I came. That's not the quick run I had in mind. I didn't even have a chance to say goodbye. *To my iPod, I mean.*

3

By the time I get home, it's a quarter to ten, and Grandma is waiting at the door. She doesn't seem very pleased for whatever reason, "Where have you been, missy? I don't know how much freedom David gives you, but while you're living under this roof you follow the house rules. Being responsible and punctual are on the top of the list."

"Yes, Ma'am," I reply automatically, clueless about what exactly I'm late to.

I just got here. How have I messed things up already?

Then, I remember something she said yesterday on the ride home about orientation. In my jet lagged state, her words were lost to me completely.

"We missed orientation," Grandma remarks, confirming my assumption.

"Sorry, Grandma," I apologize. "I can be ready to go in five."

"It's too late now. But, Faye will be here to pick you up for your uniform fitting in half an hour."

"Right. I'm going to get ready," I agree and begin to back out, catching one last glimpse of her butter white dress and pearl necklaces as I bolt out of the living room. After a quick shower, I change into a pair of jeans and a khaki sweater. I give up towel drying my hair and head back to the bathroom to blow dry it.

"Eliza, what's taking you so long? Faye just called. She's waiting downstairs," Grandma announces from the hall, just as I finish pulling my hair up into a messy bun.

"Coming, Grandma," I reply, grab my crossover bag and rush out of the room.

Outside, Faye is leaning against a black Mustang, her huge sunglasses pulled up on her head. She's looking down at her phone, intently texting someone. I stop dead in my tracks, stunned by her appearance. She looks so different from the last time I saw her. Faye is prettier now. Curvier. Her bangs have grown, and her straight dark brown hair falls in layers down the middle of her back. She's wearing jeans, a bluish green sweater and high heels. It's as though she just stepped out of the pages of a fashion catalog.

Nothing about the girl standing in front of me resembles the Faye with whom I went to summer camps. Back then her parents were going through a divorce, and Dad's company was just getting off the ground. I guess that's why Faye and I got along so well; we were both in transition. Even though we lived on opposite sides of the country, Faye and I stayed friends over the years.

As if sensing my gaze, she looks up from her phone. A perfectly aligned smile appears across her face when she sees me, prompting me to do the same. We used to look like sisters. Same haircut, same height, and the same shade of green eyes. But now, we couldn't be more different. Faye has turned into a stunning brunette, a couple inches shorter than me, while I'm an ordinary blonde with stubborn coiled hair and a skinny boyish body.

She pulls me into a hug and squeals, "I can't believe you're going to Saint Pete's! It's gonna be a blast. Come on, we're running late. School starts tomorrow, and I still need to coordinate my accessories."

"Let's go then," I agree, following Faye and climbing into the passenger side.

She eases the car into traffic, and after a couple of blocks I get the impression she isn't the best of drivers. Plus, this car is a manual, which makes for an unnerving ride. I keep a tight grip on my seat the entire time.

"So, how was Japan?" Faye asks, as a silver car swings around us for whatever reason.

"It was great," I reply. "I was only there for the summer, but it's just how I remembered. It felt like I never left."

"I hear you," Faye says, switching gears.

"Grandma told me that you spent the summer in Colorado. I bet that was fun."

"Nah. Same as ever," Faye says dismissively. "Dad works a lot. I spent most of my summer vacation at the mall shopping by myself. I got to meet his new girlfriend," she shrugs. "She's not much older than me."

I decide to change subjects, "So, have you seen Wellington? Does he go to our school?"

"Wellington?" Faye asks, trying to put a face to the name.

"Wellington Blake," I supply.

"*Right.* Blake," Faye says as if just now remembering him. She sounds a lot like herself, but different at the same time. It's a little disconcerting. Two tiny furrows form between her perfectly arched eyebrows as she continues, "No, he goes to another high school where the program is more focused on music. Last I heard he was planning to get into Juilliard. How about you? Any ideas for college?"

I shake my head no and ask, "And you?"

"I'm going to Harvard, I want to be a prosecutor eventually," Faye replies without a pause.

I'm impressed. Most of my friends back in Santa Monica, or even in Japan, are a lot like me. They have no idea what plans they have for tomorrow, let alone two years from now. I'm leaning toward something in the medical field, but that's the extent of my planning.

Faye brakes abruptly, and I jerk forward, startled out of my thoughts. Then, she switches on the turn signal and reverses the car from mid-intersection. There's an open spot right before the pedestrian crosswalk, and she's reversing into it. She parks right at the front steps of a terracotta brick building that occupies a full block. Undoubtedly, Saint Peter's High School.

Stepping out of the car, my attention turns to a little kid carrying a skateboard under one arm. He looks to be no older than twelve. He has on baggy clothes and his hair sticks out from his Red Sox hat. He's wearing white headphones and starts across the street, ignoring the solid red hand lit up atop the crosswalk indicator. A dark blue car is coming in his direction. It's apparent the driver is distracted, texting on her phone. She doesn't acknowledge the boy at all.

Everything else happens very quickly, I slam the car door shut, startling Faye. Then, without a second thought, I sprint to the crosswalk and lunge at the boy, shoving him out of the car's path. I toss him backward and catch a glimpse of his skateboard flying out of his grasp.

Faye gasps, "Oh G– "

The sound of screeching tires is exceedingly loud in my left ear. In my peripheral vision, the car is plowing toward *me* now. Inexplicably, or maybe instinctively, I leap upward as the front end of the car passes under me. I plant my left foot on the hood and catch myself with both hands on the windshield, kicking off as the vehicle jerks to a halt, and land on my feet. I take a few stumbling steps to regain my balance.

It's only then that I dare to steal a glance at the driver. A wide eyed woman sits frozen in shock as the boy stands up. Without uttering a word, he's running. He drops his board in front of him and coasts down the sidewalk without looking back. The woman erupts from the driver's side door in a panic. In her imminent concern, she steals a glance at the hood, doing a quick inspection for damage. Somehow, there doesn't seem to be a single scratch, or even a dent left behind.

"Should I call 911, do you need an ambulance?" The lady asks in a frantic state.

Faye is beside me in a matter of seconds, "Are you okay?"

"I'm alright," I reply to no one in particular.

The driver doesn't seem very keen on sticking around. She starts backing toward her vehicle as a crowd begins to form, and a line of cars queue up behind hers.

Before getting back into her car, the lady asks once again, "Are you sure you're okay?"

"We'll all be okay if you'd quit playing with your phone while you're driving," Faye replies, standing tall, her voice loud and clear. Apparently, she has no issues with confrontation the way I do.

Grabbing Faye by the arm, I pull her out of the street, "We need to get going, or we'll be late."

Faye follows me reluctantly, and we step onto the sidewalk. At the front steps of the school, I look back. The car is driving away across the intersection, and everything seems to be back to normal as if nothing happened.

"Still coming?" Faye asks quietly, holding the door open.

I nod and follow her into the building. Inside, it's bright with tall foliage decorating each corner and between the reception chairs. Behind the receptionist's desk, a plump middle-aged woman with auburn hair welcomes us. Her name tag reads, "Mrs. Hughes."

"Good morning. We have an appointment with Ms. Wither at eleven," Faye informs politely.

"Year and names, please?" She inquires, pushing a packet of chocolate covered pretzels out of the way and coming up with a spreadsheet.

"We're both juniors. I'm Faye Greenwood, and she's Eliza O'Neill."

"Follow me, please," Mrs. Hughes says, making her way

toward the stairwell.

She leads us up two flights of stairs and then right. We step inside an enormous room which must have once been a dance studio with floor to ceiling mirrors and wall mounted rails. Maybe still is. Ms. Wither is a thin gray haired woman wearing thick glasses, a faculty uniform and a name tag that reads, "Ms. Wither."

"You finally showed up this time," she says between chuckles and asks kindly, "What sizes do you need?"

We tell her our sizes and she disappears into a side door, returning with four paper bags decorated with the school's logo. She places the bags on the counter in front of us, "Who wants to go first?"

I nudge Faye, and she volunteers, stepping forward. She goes into the fitting room and comes back minutes later, handing Ms. Wither one of the bags back and keeping the other. I do the same when it's my turn. We sign a few papers, indicating that we received our uniforms and the care instructions. Then, we're on our way.

On the drive home, Faye smacks her hand on the steering wheel, "I still can't believe that woman."

"Who?" I ask, frowning. "Ms. Wither?"

"No!" Faye says, looking at me in disbelief. "The lady who just ran you over."

"She didn't run me over."

"Excuse me! I was there. She almost crushed you. What were you thinking? Can you imagine showing up at the first day of school in a full body cast?" Faye asks aggravated. "And that kid, he would be dead. You just saved that kid's life."

"I don't know what I was thinking," I say more to myself than Faye. "Maybe I *wasn't* thinking, just acting on reflex."

"Reflex or not, that was kinda awesome," Faye says, sounding impressed. "I don't know how you did it," she pauses to look at me. "Man, I wish I had captured that with my phone. I'd have a million views online."

I shoot her a weary look, but Faye misses it at first. She's back to watching the road. When she finally turns her head, we both crack up laughing.

Faye parks in front of my grandparents' building and says, "I'll pick you up for school tomorrow a quarter to eight."

"Okay. Thanks for everything," I say gratefully, opening the door.

"Don't mention it."

4

My alarm goes off at seven, and I hit the snooze button at least five times before finally giving in. I've been so tired since I got here. It must be this adjusting-to-a-new-time-zone thing. I fling myself out of bed with a yawn, dragging my lazy body to the shower. It does the trick; ten minutes later, I'm back in my bedroom, wrapped in a towel, yanking the retail tags from my uniform's pleated skirt, button down shirt and sweater. Getting dressed in no time, I twist my hair around and hold it up with a clip. One last look at my reflection deflates me, and I fight the urge to bang my head against the mirror in frustration.

Why must I be forced to wear a skirt to school?

On my way out, Grandma insists that I wear the knee socks, so I go back to my bedroom and put them on. Then, I change into my coal knee high boots to cover them. *Hey, there's nothing in the dress code that says I can't wear boots.*

Standing outside the building, I scan the road for Faye's black Mustang, but today she pulls up in a green VW Beetle. She turns the hazard lights on and stops the car in the middle of the street. *Is that even legal?* Probably not, since the vehicle behind her is laying on his car horn. I rush inside to avoid escalating the scene, and the car is in motion before I even close the door.

Faye turns the volume down, "Hey, girly."

"Hey. What happened to the Mustang?" I place my backpack on the floorboard at my feet and buckle my seat belt.

"Oh, I got a couple tickets, and my step-Farrell suggested I get something that doesn't look so sporty. He has a theory that cops like to pull over fast looking cars," Faye replies with a roll of her eyes.

"Step-Farrell?"

"Mother's new guy is named James Farrell, therefore 'step-Farrell.' I don't need a step-father. Last I checked, I have a 'father-father.' Mother hates it, though. She thinks I'm being disrespectful. What-ever," she explains, making a right turn on a red light without stopping. For some reason that I can't fathom, Faye shifts from drive to neutral, and the bug stalls out. She mumbles something unintelligible under her breath, shifts to park, turns off the engine, turns it back on, and we're moving again. She glances at me apologetically, "Sorry about that. It's only the second time I've driven this car. I have to sell my Mustang ASAP, though. We have a little problem with garage space. Your grandma is allowing me to keep it in the parking garage for now, but she said I only have a month to sell it. I'm putting an ad on the school's bulletin board. Mother refused to trade it in at the dealership in the hopes that Ian would take the car and get rid of the motorcycle he bought, but he didn't. Now, she wants to kill him. I told her that she won't need to; the motorcycle will do the trick. She said my joke wasn't funny, though. I think it's funny, don't you?"

I'm about to say "not really," also that the Mustang was cooler. But she just goes on without giving me a chance to reply, "Of course, you know my brother, he will be selling the motorcycle and buying a new car before winter. I told Mother that, and she gave me the evil eye. She is *so* mad. Ian just laughs and laughs, like, 'oh, you worry too much.' He's over eighteen, which makes him an 'adult,' so there's nothing she can do about it. Ian is stubborn that way."

"How old is Ian, now?" It has been more than three years since I last saw Faye's brother.

"He's two and a half years older than me. I'll be seventeen in January so that would make him nineteen. I wanted to sell the Mustang to your grandma at first. But then, she said you just turned sixteen in April and went to Japan before having a chance to take driving lessons. Are you planning to take them soon?" Faye asks as we pull into the school parking lot.

"Not right now, maybe later, we'll see. I'm used to the rail system. Traffic, tolls, parallel parking, not my thing."

We get out of her car and head to what looks like the back entrance of the red brick building we stopped by yesterday. At least it seems like the same one.

As we walk across the parking lot, it's bizarre to see everyone wearing the same outfit. All the girls in their pleated skirts, some even wearing knee socks, and all the boys wearing slacks, white shirts, a tie, and the school jacket. It's like the girls are trying hard to innovate with accessories, and the boys don't care one way or the other, looking sort of geeky.

From the inside, Saint Peter's High isn't much different from my old school back in Santa Monica. The hallways, stairwells, classrooms and the lockers all look basically the same. Apart from the colors, that is. The walls are eggshell white with a thick blue stripe. Bulletin boards hang here and there. All the doors are the same royal blue as the uniform jackets and sweaters. The lockers are also the same hue. I have to admit it looks pretty bright and warm for a hundred year old brick building. Well, I'm not sure if it's actually that old; it's just a wild guess.

Faye offers to walk me to my first class, even though hers is in the opposite direction. I tell her that she doesn't need to, but she insists we have plenty of time. So I agree. The last thing I need is to get lost on the first day of school.

"Catch ya later, 'kay?"

"Thanks," I call out, but she probably doesn't hear it over the chatter of our fellow students loitering in the hall.

Taking a deep breath, I cross the threshold and search for an empty seat. I spot one in the back, close to the window. I'm about to sit down when one of the two girls sitting nearby says in a snotty voice that belongs in kindergarten, "Sorry, but this seat is taken."

"Oh, my mistake," I blush and turn around, leaving the two girls giggling behind me.

Just perfect.

I make my way to the next empty seat on the second row, no window in sight. This time, I ask before sitting, "Is this seat taken?"

The boy looks up from his book, sizes me up and decides I'm not worth his time, going back to his reading.

Rude much?

I let out a sigh and sit down. The giggling in the back turns into laughter, but I try to ignore them and open my notebook. I write down today's date and begin doodling daisies at the bottom of the page. The laughter comes to a stop just as the teacher steps in, and I look up from my notebook. All I have to say is this: Ms. Campbell is not what I expected.

"Good morning," says Ms. Campbell in a soft spoken monotone voice that forces the class into silence. Not because of her authoritative manner, but because it's almost impossible to hear her.

Our instructor is a thirty something year old woman with wiry strawberry blond hair. Her face is pale and covered with freckles. She's really petite, and her wardrobe favors vintage. She's wearing a cardigan skirt, the type Grandma might have worn on her first date with Grandpa. Neither the intonation nor volume of her voice changes the entire time.

It's a wonder no one falls asleep, maybe because it's the first day of class and all.

When the bell rings, Ms. Campbell reminds us, "Those who signed up for Intermediate Drama will also be joining me on Wednesdays after sixth period, starting next week."

Okay, not such an inspiring class, one might say. But then again, I don't really like English, or Drama for that matter.

Next up is Principles of Physics. A few boys are carrying the same physics book that I have, so I follow them. This time I'm early enough to claim a seat by the window. Mr. Wilson's teaching style is the polar opposite of Ms. Campbell's. He has enough energy to run a marathon, although, his weight might be an obstacle. He has a mustache, a head full of gray hair, and eyebrows that connect in the middle. His eyes are huge and greenish blue under his thick bifocal lenses, and he dresses how one expects a private school teacher to dress, trousers and a polo shirt. He speaks fast, but his voice is loud and clear. It seems to resonate through the entire room. He's funny and keeps challenging the students to participate, and I like his class immediately. Time flies by.

"A very clever dude summarized all of classical electromagnetic theory into four simple equations. Can anyone tell me his name?" Mr. Wilson waits, his wide eyes hopeful as he scans the room. "Anyone?"

Before I can stop myself, my big fat mouth is whispering the answer to his question, "James Maxwell."

He takes a few steps toward me, bends at the waist and cups a hand around his ear, "Could you repeat that?"

"Maxwell," I say in a louder tone, making sure this time he hears me, "James Maxwell"

"Indeed, that's the name of our guy, James Clerk Maxwell. That's why we call them *Maxwell's Equations*," he explains to the class and redirects his attention to me, "And your name is?"

"Eliza."

"Eliza?" He checks his clipboard and promptly looks up in astonishment. Pushing his glasses up on his nose, he inquires, "Eliza O'Neill?"

"Yes, Sir," Instantly, I become overly aware of my own voice.

He raises an eyebrow, and since they're linked together, it reminds me of the tilde we use above the letter ñ in Spanish class. If I weren't so nervous about being singled out, I would probably be laughing right now. He touches his mustache, "You wouldn't happen to be related to Dave O'Neill, would you?"

The pressure of suddenly becoming the center of attention makes me slouch down in my chair. The only problem is that I'm too tall for any effective means of hiding.

"He's my dad," I reply in a small voice.

Muffled laughter emanates from my left. A redhead girl along with a few guys are cracking up. Whether on my account or Mr. Wilson's, I'll never know. The other girl in their little group is not laughing, though. On the contrary, she seems bothered by the entire ordeal. She's pretty in an exotic way. She has that unseen type of beauty going on, curly black hair grown down to her waist, manicured nails, and perfectly made-up face. She's the girl who argued with Mr. Wilson at the beginning of class when he mentioned Sir Isaac Newton. *What's her name again?* She catches me staring at her and winks at me.

"I am a great admirer of your father," Mr. Wilson declares for the entire room to hear right at that moment.

"Me too?" I utter with an upward inflection that sounds more like a question than a statement, and the whole class erupts into laughter.

Great! My Physics teacher is my dad's biggest fan.

I look back at the girl who winked at me. She's the only one not laughing. *Kiara,* I think. That's her name. She shoots me a reassuring smile as if to say "just ignore these goofballs."

After being surrounded by my obnoxious classmates for two hours, I'm more than grateful to encounter Faye waiting for me outside the door, and we head toward Advanced Calculus together. She links her arm to mine and we walk in step, taking a shortcut through the cafeteria to the adjacent hall. All the way, she complains about a research paper for her Psych class that she needs to start right away. *I guess that's what comes with taking college level classes in high school.* Her partner, someone called Nate Sinclair, seems to be everywhere and nowhere at the same time.

I gave up long ago trying to interpret Faye's chatty dialect, but the name "Sinclair" does sound familiar for some reason. So, I ask, "What do you mean by everywhere and nowhere? Who is this guy?"

"I mean, everyone I speak to knows of him," Faye explains. "But no one seems to have a class with him. What I can say for sure is that he was not a student here last year, and I would know."

The bell rings, and we enter the classroom, taking the last two empty seats. A blonde girl with hair flipping up at the ends smiles at me, and I smile back. She stands up and walks to the pencil sharpener by the door. She's tiny and curvy at the same time with large blue cartoonish eyes that remind me of Tinker Bell.

"Welcome to Advanced Calculus!" Mr. Hathaway's booming voice is surely audible from the reception area all the way down on the first floor. As he writes on the board, I can't help but notice that his blue shirt has heavy sweat patches under his arms. It's sixty-five degrees outside, and this guy is sweating like an animal. Once he's certain that he has everyone's attention, he briefly reviews Monotonic Functions, Continuity, and Superior Limits. In the next breath, he assigns ten equations from two chapters ahead.

Gee, thanks!

Needless to say, this class goes by even faster than Physics, due to its frantic pace. I don't even have a chance to look at the clock, and it's lunch time.

On the way to the cafeteria, Faye begins, "So, we'll be having cheer tryouts this Friday. The way you jumped over that car the other day..." She lets her voice trail off. "You should totally, totally, go for it. Obviously, you wouldn't even need to try out if it were up to me." She grabs a green bean salad and a bottle of water, placing them both on her tray.

I put a sandwich and a cranberry juice on mine, following her to the register, "I—uh, no. Not this time, I don't think I'll be doing any back flips, or high kicks in a miniskirt."

Faye looks me from head to toe and points out, "It's not any shorter than the one you're wearing right now."

Before I can defend myself, she's walking away toward the lunch tables. Self-consciously, I tug at the ends of my skirt with my free hand, but it's no use. I hurry and catch up to her, just as she reaches her table. Three of these girls are in my English and Physics classes. They're the same ones who thought me hilarious. I nudge Faye without knowing what exactly I want to say. But, she doesn't notice, she's on a roll. She sets her tray down, takes mine from my hands and says to the pixy blonde sitting at the end of the bench, "Slide down a little. *Gosh!* How much room do you need?"

The girl complies, inching herself to the very edge. Faye places my lunch on the table top. I just stand there, staring at them wide-eyed, while Faye doesn't skip a beat. She puts an arm around me and speaks up, getting the rest of the table's immediate attention, "This is Liz O'Neill. Her dad is Dave O'Neill, the famous software engineer that forever changed our cyber world."

Oh, no, not again.

I will for the Earth to open up and swallow me whole as Faye continues, "Liz, this is Francis, Kiara, Alexis, Judy and Anna." The girls glance at one another, trading confused looks. Then, they turn back to Faye who goes on, "Liz just came back from Japan a few days ago. Now, she'll be joining our little group."

I'm starting to wish I had a shovel since the Earth is asleep at the wheel. Maybe if I concentrate hard enough, I can disappear into thin air. Didn't Grandpa tell me about a photo that was teleported from Germany to some other place? Or was it the other way around? The picture materialized again, but it was ripped in half.

I'm yanked from my thoughts of teleportation when the girl on my right says, "That's so cool."

"Totally," the one sitting beside her agrees.

I'm so sure! These two girls were the same ones who told me to go sit somewhere else two hours ago. I don't have much time to dwell on it because the questions start one after another.

"Is it true in Japan, they teach sword fighting, yoga, and martial arts in kindergarten?" asks the pixy blonde.

"Can you write my name in those cool symbol thingies?" asks the auburn hair girl across from me whose name I can't remember.

"My aunt is a model, and she did a campaign in Japan last fall. She told me that they eat fish for breakfast in Japan," says the strawberry blonde from my Physics class.

"Whatever, Fran, it's not like your aunt ever eats," the girl from my English class states, making the other girls fall into giggles.

"Liz is pretty skinny," the pixy blonde states the obvious. *Alexis? That might be her name.* She points her thumb at me, "She might have a sardine for breakfast."

More giggles follow, and before I have a chance to comment on what "fish-girl" just said, more questions are coming from all sides.

"Do you speak Japanese?"

"Isn't it, like, night there right now?"

"Which city did you live in?"

"Like you would know where the city is, you couldn't find Texas on the map in Geography this morning," the girl from my Physics class points out.

"Can you say my name in Japanese?" Girl one asks.

"How about mine?" inquires number two.

"I wanna know mine, too," says fish-girl.

"But I asked first," girl one insists.

I'm getting vertigo. I can't even say their names in English. I don't remember who is who. *Can I be home schooled?* "Your name doesn't change when you go to Japan," I want to say, but don't.

The skinny girl who winked at me in Physics stands up. Just then, I realize she hadn't said a word so far. The noise quiets down instantly, and she finally speaks up, "Are you girls for real? You're worse than the paparazzi. You're gonna scare her off. If you really want to know the answers to all those questions, you need to give the girl a chance to speak."

I give her a shy, but grateful smile. She nods, grinning back at me. Her smile is so earnest that it warms the cafeteria. Only then, am I finally able to sit down. But I barely finish my sandwich because I have to answer twenty questions about my time in Japan.

When we leave the cafeteria, Faye once again is going in the opposite direction. She's heading to Economics. We say our goodbyes, and I leave before Faye has a chance to point out which girl I should follow to Chemistry.

On the way to class, I stop at my locker to switch textbooks. A really cute guy, whose locker is right next to mine, asks, "It's Liz, isn't it?"

I close my locker and look at him wondering what he wants with me, and how he knows my name. Then, I remember the Physics debacle and let my shoulders droop. The animated boy standing in front of me apparently doesn't notice my lack of enthusiasm. He holds his hand for me to shake, "I'm Ben."

Still a little suspicious, but not knowing what else to do, I shake his hand, "I'm Liz," and fight the urge not to slap my own forehead, adding awkwardly, "But you already knew that, so. Nice to meet you, Ben. I guess."

His smile widens, forming dimples on both cheeks, and I automatically smile back.

"Me too, me too," he motions to the stairwell. "You have Chemistry now, right?"

I do a double take, puzzled.

Who's this boy?

He blinks, still waiting for my reply, and I nod.

What else does he know about me?

I'm dwelling about whether or not to ask him when he says, "I'm in your Chem class. We should get going, or we'll be late."

I nod again and follow him. Ben isn't much taller than me, an inch or so, but I have a hard time keeping pace with him while weaving through a barrage of oncoming students. I also miss everything he's saying since I'm more focused on trying not to get run over. When we reach the classroom, Ben notes, "Liz, it's too bad we can't be lab partners. If Greg can't keep his grades up in this class he will be kicked off the basketball team, and we'll get annihilated this year. We're pretty bad as it is."

I just stare at him in bewilderment. He's kind enough to lead me all the way here and now is sincerely apologizing for no reason whatsoever. *Go figure.*

"Hey Liz, over here," the blonde girl from my Calculus class is waving me over. So, I head to her station. "I'm Madison. But you can call me Mattie," she introduces herself. I must look confused because she adds, "I'm Welly's, I mean, Blake's girlfriend. Welly said you would be moving to Boston like two weeks ago."

Mattie and Welly, huh? Wellington will have an earful about that, alright. I knew she seemed familiar. I've seen several pics of the two of them.

I smile back at her, "Hey, I thought you went to the same school as Wellington."

"No, I wish. His school is so much cooler. I go here. I'm also in Intermediate Drama with you. I saw your name on Ms. Campbell's sign up sheet."

"I'm glad you go here instead of Wellington's high school," I say gratefully. "I guess that means I have a lab partner."

"Well, you'll have a pretty bad one for this week. On Monday, I'm switching to Bio. I heard this class is pretty tough. You can still be my partner if you decide to change too," Mattie explains apologetically, making a cute pouty face at the end.

"Sorry, but I'll stick to Chemistry. I'm not that great at it, but in Bio I'm a lost cause."

"At least we both have a partner for now," she smiles, putting her goggles on, and I do the same.

My next class is Spanish II. It progresses in a similar way as my English class. Mrs. Martinez speaks too slowly to be a native Spanish speaker, but she insists she's from Madrid.

Last period is PE, and my assigned locker is right next to a girl from my Calculus class. She's standing in front of her opened locker with her eyes closed. She squeezes the bridge of her nose with her thumb and index finger. I'm about to ask if she's okay when I notice she has white earphones on. They're plugged into the phone that she's holding in her other hand. Her book bag lays abandoned on the tile floor, and she's speaking into the in-line mic.

I hesitate, unsure if I should continue to my locker or give her some privacy. Her voice is delicate and pleasant as she repeats for the third time, "Got it."

One glance at the clock on the wall makes me realize that I have no choice. The class starts in four minutes, and I still need to change. Quietly, I approach my assigned locker. I'm about to open it when something the person on the other line says infuriates her. Her locker slams shut beside me, and I flinch. Grabbing her book bag from the floor aggressively, she stomps out of the locker room without changing into her gym clothes.

O-kay! Good thing I kept my mouth shut.

I change into my blue and white gym outfit, quickly undo my messy bun that's falling apart and pull my hair back into a tight ponytail. Then, I rush outside with a minute to spare.

Faye was telling me earlier that our gym teacher is also responsible for the cheer squad. Her name is Ms. Johnson. So, I'm a little stupefied when I first see her. She's not what I had in mind. Her hair is cropped short and dyed yellow. It has a greenish hue on its tips that must be the result of the swimming pool chlorine. It contrasts badly with her skin. It's also too short for her face, making her plump cheeks resemble apples. Her scrunched up eyes, lack of eyelashes, and her tattooed eyebrows just make her look eerie. Her stocky body looks immovable and intimidating.

She scans her attendance sheet and looks up at us as if counting heads. She doesn't bother calling roll. She just announces in a shouting voice, "It's your first day back, and you all know the drill. It's evaluation day."

I don't know the drill, nor do I know what evaluation day involves. It's my first day at Saint Pete's High, and back at my old school in Santa Monica there was no such thing. Ms. Johnson's grimacing mug and strict voice are a little too scary to raise questions.

I'm silently hoping no one notices me, that I can simply play follow the leader. Ms. Johnson is standing so straight that she seems to grow two feet taller as she marches back and forth with her hands locked behind her back, watching us. I realize we're in a straight line all of a sudden, and we seem to be divided into three groups.

When did that happen?

Ms. Johnson calls, motioning with her right hand, "Group one, two, three."

Apparently, I'm in group one. I relax a little waiting for

her next order, but she only shouts, "Ready?"

The girl beside me bends into a running posture. So I do the same. I barely have time to position myself when Ms. Johnson sounds her whistle, and they dash out. I let out a sigh of relief. If running laps is part of this evaluation, I'll survive. *Or maybe not.*

Ms. Johnson scares the life out of me by clapping her hands and bellowing, "Come on O'Neill, you've got nine minutes and fifty seconds to do your laps."

I'm so startled that I take off without sparing her a glance. She goes on shouting to groups two and three, but I'm so shaken that I don't process her words. I just keep running, easily passing my classmates and getting into lap two way ahead of them. When Ms. Johnson sounds her whistle, everybody in my group stops, so I do the same. Two girls standing nearby ask each other how many laps they did and I start freaking out again. I didn't keep count.

Before I can dwell on it, Ms. Johnson is shouting again, "Group one, on the mat and wait for my whistle."

I follow the two girls, but they just sit down and so does the rest of our group. *Well, sort of.* Some are sitting, others are lying on their backs looking exhausted. Not knowing whether to sit or lie, I kneel.

At the sound of Ms. Johnson's whistle, the girl on my left positions herself and starts doing push ups. I do the same, watching her through the corner of my eye, and mentally keeping count this time. When I get to eight, she's turning on to her back and starting on sit ups. I force myself to do two more before rolling over onto my back. I'm not used to doing push ups and sit ups. Drops of sweat start to form on my hair line as we switch from sit ups to push ups and back again.

So, I'm relieved when Ms. Johnson blows her whistle and calls out, "Group one, two minutes rest and into positions."

I roll onto my back and lean on my elbows, looking around at my red-cheeked classmates. A few of them are lying flat on their backs, breathing heavily. Others are resting on their bellies with their cheeks plastered on the mat, eyes closed. No one is chatting this time, which comforts me a little.

The two minutes feel more like two seconds, and the whistle blasts again. Half of my group stands up right away at the sound, including me. The last thing I want is to hear her shouting in my ear again. The other half doesn't even move. She whistles a second time and a third. The other two groups switch places while my group remains immobilized. Then, Ms. Johnson is marching toward us.

"Up, up, up. She's coming," one of the girls standing nearby whispers.

I wish I knew what she wants us to do. I don't believe anything can be worse than that woman advancing on us.

What is this, boot camp?

She blares her whistle again, "Up, group one! You're almost there. Sixty seconds of jumping jacks. On my whistle. Ready?"

As soon as the few still lying down make it to their feet, she blasts her whistle, and we are all doing jumping jacks. Only then do I notice more than half of my group stops midway through, as well as group two doing sit ups and push ups.

Un-freaking-believable! And here I am killing myself, thinking I have to keep going until she signals us to stop. I'm so annoyed that I finish the stupid jumping jacks. Stopping only after she calls out, "Great workout group one. Take a seat in the bleachers."

Still annoyed, I sit down at the nearest end of the second row. Only after sitting, I notice my entire group is heading to the visitor's side. Too tired to move right away, I choose to stay here until Ms. Johnson calls me back.

Suddenly, a dense feeling in the back of my mind prompts me to look up to my left. The girl from the locker room is watching me. She's sitting a few rows up, still in her uniform, which she accessorizes with black combat boots. Her dark oily hair is propped up into two high pigtails. Her eyes are hazel, and she's sporting a serious skin condition. Being polite, I smile at her. She narrows her eyes and stares at me more intently as if she's trying to read me or something. But, she's probably just lost in her thoughts. I wave, and she blinks proving me right.

I'm about to go talk to this solitary girl when she stands up and walks the other way. Supporting her body with one hand on the rail, she swings both legs over in a single movement, landing a short distance down on the opposite side.

"Miss Parker, where do you think you're going?" Ms. Johnson calls out after her.

The girl, however, just keeps walking away from the stadium as if she couldn't care less. Just then, the bell rings, indicating the end of class. To my complete astonishment group three is still doing laps.

Ms. Johnson starts marching toward me. Maybe she's angry that I'm sitting on the wrong side. So, I stand up to rejoin my group on shaky legs. Too late. She reaches me half way, "O'Neill, why didn't you sign up for the track team?"

I blink nervously. I'm both confused and alarmed. *Where did that come from?* I want to say, "No need to shout, Ms. Johnson. I'm standing right here." But I don't. I barely manage to reply after swallowing a couple times, "I joined Drama."

"That explains the theatrics. Can't you do both?" She asks louder than necessary.

I'm absolutely sure I'm pepper red, and it's not from the exercise. My stammering voice confirms it, "My, um, um..." When I see the words aren't going to come out with her staring at me like that, hands on her hips. I just shake my head, trying to look apologetic. To be honest I still feel a little upset about not joining the track team. That's what I wanted at first. Now, I'm sort of grateful Grandma didn't let me. I make a mental note to do something nice for Grandma.

"What's the matter? *Don't talk too good?* I figured they would teach you kids how to articulate."

"Today's the first day," I mutter.

Ms. Johnson puts her whistle back in her mouth, turns around and blares it. As if just now remembering poor group three. She turns back to me and speaks with the whistle between her teeth, "Well, come see me next semester," making chirping sounds on the "esses."

I shrug, and she looks disgusted by my lack of interest. She orders me to go change and marches away. As her back turns to me, I speed walk toward the locker room.

5

The overwhelming scent of hairspray makes me toss in bed, and I gasp for air. A hand is gently nudging me awake, and I hear my name, "Liz, dear, wake up."

My eyelids flutter open, and I blink repeatedly as my vision adjusts to the bright room filled by the morning sunlight. Grandma's face comes into focus, her bob haircut overloaded with hairspray hovers over me. Aghast, I jump into a sitting position and almost smack my forehead into hers in the process.

"Rise and shine," Grandma says, straightening up. "You slept through your alarm. I really didn't want to wake you. You looked so peaceful, as if you were in paradise."

"It's alright, Grandma–" An irrepressible yawn cuts me off, and I cover my mouth until it ends. "Thanks for waking me."

"Poor baby, I'm going to let you get ready," she pats my hand kindly and leaves the room, closing the door behind her.

Grandma is partially right I suppose. *I was in paradise, wasn't I?* The peaceful part, however, I'm not so sure about. Here's the thing, my dreams are very different from those of the typical sixteen-year-old girl. Mine are always the same. *Well, sort of.* Some factors change, others don't. Like the colors for instance, being able to process coherent thoughts and actions, the weather, the aroma and the texture of the leaves. It's all so vivid. I can grab a handful of sand and let it slip through my fingers, feeling the heat of a summer day or the snow flakes on my cheeks. Also, the moment I wake up, it's like I experienced all those things instead of dreamed about them.

Each time is a different place. I don't recall it ever repeating. Sometimes, they're locations I've never been before, or even knew existed. There are others, in which I recognize or have visited in the past. This last dream was at a beach in Brazil, called Frances beach. An earthly replica of paradise with white powdery sand, warm clear water, and coconut palms. How do I know the place is not a figment of my imagination? Two reasons: for one, I'm not that creative. Second, I just did a web search and the place actually exists.

It's like I said, there's nothing ordinary about these dreams, and it gets weirder. Every single dream has one thing in common: an entirely vacant atmosphere. It might be an empty subway in Tokyo, a vacant football stadium, a deserted beach, an abandoned Japanese shrine, the Taj Mahal in its opulence without a single person in sight...

Well, kind of. I'm not exactly alone in this surreal world. There is always one other person that shows up. His name is Raph. The one and only constant in my cryptic dream world. Raph, with his sky blue eyes, curly blond hair and a few days worth of stubble on his face. Tall and lean like a dancer. He's not as old as my father, probably in his late twenties. The weirdest part is that he never ages, kinda like a vampire. Of course, he's not one. He doesn't strike me as the demonic type of apparition.

NO! There's nothing romantic about it. That would be creepy. Raph is like a big brother, an older cousin, or an uncle. Somebody who's been in my dreams for as long as I can remember. When I was little, he would guide me through the dream world by the hand. When I was younger still, sometimes he would carry me in his arms. Those were the days, playgrounds of peaceful bliss. Now with adulthood just around the corner, Raph seems to have a cryptic agenda. He comes up with all these enigmatic expressions that sound more like warnings than advice. The older I get, the more complex these dreams become. Outright indecipherable.

Once I was old enough to rationalize, I began questioning Raph about the validity of this dream world. Particularly, whether or not they were linked to "the urge" that pushes me into these dangerous situations. Of course, he always manages to dodge the question, just like he does with every other extremely relevant inquiry I may have. Also, the times he humors me with an answer, it makes no sense whatsoever. Not at first anyway, only later, much later. After I've messed everything up, then they're meaningful, crystal clear even.

If only Raph would cut to the chase and tell me what to do... but no, he won't do it. "Vague" is Raph's middle name. *Sigh.* Most girls my age have dreams about hot guys from the movies. I get a guy almost as old as my dad whose favorite line is, "It's against the rules, Liz."

What rules? Beats me.

Last night for instance, Raph laid out several warnings. Did he explain them? No, he didn't. He just spilled them out nonsensically. This one goes something like, "The circle is closing. My shadow casts on you now. Furthermore, beware of the newcomers."

"What circle? What shadow?" Can't tell, thanks to the rules. Don't even get me started about being aware of the newcomers. Last I checked, *I'm* the newcomer. Does he mean I'm supposed to beware of myself?

Arrggh!

It's so messed up. I don't even know where to begin. It's even worse than his last one, "To pull someone from harm's way leaves you in its path." Needless to say, I figured that one out a little too late.

A thought crosses my mind, Raph never mentioned anything about the drowning girl. It's not the kind of thing I can put aside and just forget. *Odd.* I make a mental note to ask him the next time.

But that's not all there is. Right before Grandma woke me, Raph decided he wasn't cryptic enough for one night. No. He revealed another, "In the face of danger come to grips with your fear." I bet he made up this one on the spot. Good thing Grandma did wake me because I might have looked peaceful in paradise, but my brain was spinning way down in purgatory.

The glowing orange numbers on my alarm clock are shouting at me to get a move on. Raph's new enigmas will have to wait. I have school. Besides, Raph usually passes along his riddles a week or so in advance. Probably offering me time to figure it out. *Fat chance.*

Another minute blinks off the digital display, and I scurry to my morning shower, putting my hair up into a messy bun on the way. Not enough time to wash it. I put on my uniform over my barely dried skin and hurry back to my bedroom. Without a second to spare, I sling my backpack over my shoulders, and race down the hall, saying quick goodbyes as I dash out of the apartment and into the elevator.

Just as I step onto the sidewalk, Faye's green bug is pulling up right in front of me. I rush inside, and toss my bag into the backseat. Faye chatters in the same manner she did yesterday the entire ride to school, barely giving me an opening to get a word in.

In the school's parking lot, she pulls into a spot beside a flashy yellow sports car. As we climb out, she whistles, "Who's driving the Lamborghini to school?"

She pauses for a second to admire it. I stare at the car for a totally different reason. The color. It's yellow, my favorite color, the same shade that my favorite hoodie used to be.

Now, it's all faded. The car, however, it's okay, just another sports car if you ask me. I can't tell the difference. She lets out a slow prolonged sigh, and then we're off. We enter the building together and split up. Faye turns left for her AP French, and I go right for *Non* AP English.

The school day goes on uneventfully. No laughter, not even a single joke directed at me. That's an improvement. In PE, we're divided into four teams to play volleyball, rotating every five points. I count the seconds to the final bell. When it finally rings, I follow behind my classmates toward the locker room.

"Hey, Liz," Faye's voice calls from behind. She catches up with me and blurts out in a single breath, "The Yearbook Committee scheduled a meeting at the last minute. It starts, like, right now, actually. Do you mind waiting for me in the library?"

"No worries. I'll take the metro home."

Faye wrinkles her nose, disliking the idea for whatever reason. Then, she pulls out her phone, "Hang on one sec, EJ can give you a ride. He goes to Blake's high school. It's not far from here. I can call him and–"

"It's fine, Faye. I'll be okay. I'm used to the rail system. California, Japan, remember?" I cut her off, taking hold of her arm before she calls EJ, whoever he is.

"I don't know," Faye is unconvinced, looking torn. "You don't even have a phone with you."

"Faye, listen to me. I went to the airport and back by train just the other day without a phone. I'll survive."

"Why did you do that?" She inquires intrigued.

Uh-oh. Me and my big fat mouth. "Never mind that, I'll be fine. You're gonna be late."

"If you say so," she says hesitantly, taking a few deliberate steps backward. "Do me a favor, though? Call me when you get home."

"Will do."

She still looks uncertain as she turns on her heels and

rushes to her yearbook meeting.

As I'm leaving the school building, cutting through the parking lot, a familiar voice calls my name, "Liz?"

"Wellington?" I let out with astonishment dripping from my voice. I didn't expect to run into him at my school. "Hey, what are you doing here?" He looks so different, not at all resembling the boy from last Christmas.

"I came for Mattie. But she forgot to text me about her marching band practice this afternoon," Wellington shakes his head. He doesn't really seem annoyed, but indulgent. Like he's used to it. He shrugs, "No biggie. She's getting a ride with some trumpet player."

"Which way are you headed?" I ask hesitantly. "Would you mind giving me a lift?"

"Not at all," he replies, nodding toward his mother's SUV. "I have to make a quick stop at Dad's bookstore, though. Is that okay with you? If not, I can drop you–"

"It's alright," I interrupt. "I haven't seen the store in years."

Once we're in, he shifts the SUV into reverse and catches me looking at him, "What is it?"

"No glasses," I point out, buckling my seat belt.

He cracks a smile at my comment, and I notice something else, "No braces either."

"When was the last time you were here?" He asks, pulling into traffic.

"Last Christmas, I guess."

"The braces came off right after," he explains. "I got contacts because my cello instructor recommended them. I used to adjust my glasses, pushing them up every time I had to turn the page on my sheet music. It drove him nuts. So, he suggested it to my parents, and they went for it."

"Do you miss your glasses?"

"Not really," he replies. "The funny thing is that sometimes I still catch myself trying to push my non-existent glasses up."

"Your instructor must love that," I catch a glimpse of his phone charging on the dashboard and ask, "Mind if I use your cell? I told Faye that I'd call her when I got home. She sort of freaked out when I said I was taking the subway."

"Go ahead," he consents, eyes on the road, looking thoughtful for an instant. "Oh man! *Faye*. She actually takes vocal lessons at my school, and I see her all the time. But, we never talk anymore."

I dial her number, and it rings several times before going to voice mail, "Hey, it's Faye, don't bother leaving a message. Just text me."

Wellington cracks up, and so do I. After the beep, I leave a message anyway, "Hi, Faye. It's Liz. Just letting you know I caught a ride with Wellington–"

"Blake," Wellington interrupts quietly.

"Right. Blake," I go on. "By the way, this is his phone. So... Talk to you later. Bye."

"She doesn't know me by the name Wellington. Better text her as well," he says the moment I hang up.

I send her a text and put his phone back on the dashboard, turning in my seat to face him, "I noticed that the other day. I wonder why?"

He shrugs, "Her brother, I suppose. He always called me by my last name, and it stuck."

"I didn't know you were friends with Ian."

"We don't hang out as much since he started college, but we're still friends," Wellington clarifies as he parks in an empty spot a few yards from his Dad's bookstore and shuts off the engine. We step out of his car, and I follow him inside.

Mr. Blake's face brightens when he sees Wellington walk in, "Good. You got here just in time. Dora is running late, and I have to run some errands before the bank closes. Do you mind staying until she comes in?"

Wellington turns to me for reassurance, and I give an affirmative nod. Mr. Blake recognizes me then, "Well, if it isn't Liz O'Neill. I almost didn't recognize you with your hair pulled up. You're almost as tall as Wellington here."

"Hi, Mr. Blake."

"Good to see you again," he pats my shoulder fondly. Then, he grabs a black briefcase from the counter and heads out, "Thanks, Son."

"Don't mention it," Wellington replies politely, making his way to the register.

I follow him and sit on a brown leather stool, taking in the two-story rustic bookstore. It's so different from all the big franchises out there. The mixture of aromas between new books and old leather bound first editions fill my nostrils. It's very cozy in here with classical music always playing softly in the background.

The place is well divided and organized. Upstairs, there are the memoirs, auto-biographies, fiction novels, and so on. There used to be two comfortable looking leather couches in the back by the comic book section, and I wonder if they're still up there. Downstairs, the new releases and best sellers are displayed right by the main entrance. In a corner by the register, there are older books, some are even kept in a locked display. They're mostly autographed first editions and imported books.

A girl dressed in black from head to toe stands by the foreign section, her hair pulled up in a tight ponytail. She's probably about our age. She's holding a brown leather hardcover, her violet eyes tracing the lines from right to left. As if sensing my stare, she looks up. Her face is porcelain white, beautifully proportional, the kind you see in makeup ads. She tilts her head to one side and arches an eyebrow inquiringly. Embarrassed for being caught in the act, I get to my feet, "I'm gonna check the graphic novels."

"Second level in the back," he replies halfheartedly, and I glance back at him. His attention is turned to the porcelain girl. She's back to reading, and I hesitate half a second before heading up the stairs.

As I climb the steps, Wellington's low voice calls across the store, overlapping the creaking sound of my footsteps on the old wooden stairs, "You can read Aramaic?"

"No, Cello Boy. I like to look at the squiggly lines," she replies sarcastically.

"Do I know you?"

I can't really tell whether Wellington is being polite, or if he's oblivious to her sarcasm. I stop short, ready to turn around and head back downstairs. The sound of a book snapping shut, followed by a flirtatious laugh keeps me in place, undecided whether to continue upstairs or go back down.

"You tell me, Gorgeous. Do I know you?" She challenges, her voice melodic and seductive.

Definitely, down. If nothing else, for Mattie's sake. But then, he laughs briefly, "You surely don't go to my school. Maybe we've run into each other at Saint Pete's High. My girlfriend goes there."

"May-be," she drags the word into two distinct syllables. A thud, followed by, "I'm taking this one."

Well, well, well, Faye is not the only one who has changed. He has clearly learned how to fend for himself. The Wellington I knew would have choked, the guy behind the counter didn't even stammer. Apparently, I'm the only one who didn't evolve in the past year.

I continue upstairs with soft steps covered by the classical music in the background. Up here things are just as I remember, and I smile to myself, heading to the comic books. After a few aisles, it's safe to say I'm the only one on the second floor.

A chime sound announces someone either just entered or exited the store. It's probably porcelain face girl, leaving with her newly acquired book. *Can she really read Aramaic?* I doubt it. She has no accent which means she's American. But then again, I'm American, have no accent and speak Japanese. I can't read Kanji, though.

Distractedly reaching the graphic novel shelf, I do a double take and freeze. Black sapphire eyes lock to mine holding me in place. If looks could kill, I'd drop dead this very instant. It's like time freezes as our eyes meet, solidifying my entire body. His dark gaze never wavering, never looking away. It's like I'm under a spell, and only my brain still functions. His stare brightens like two blue laser beams, darkening his pupils and lightning his irises.

MOVE! I mentally scold myself to snap out of the stupor I'm in. *MOVE! LEAVE NOW!*

The intensity of his gaze is an indicator that he senses my fear. It's like he overheard my inner battle to escape. His eyes narrow, and the room begins spinning under my feet. Pain spreads over my entire body, throbbing heavily. I feel cold from the inside out as if ice were branching through my veins. My vision clouds into darkness, and a wave of nausea overtakes me.

6

"There you are," a beautiful delicate voice sounds from behind me. Her words break me out of the trance I'm in, and I stumble backward, losing my footing. Gentle hands take hold of my shoulders to steady my balance, and the scent of ginger lilies encompasses me, "Are you okay?"

Blinking in confusion, I shake my head to clear my thoughts. Her hands drop from my shoulders, and she steps into my line of sight. She's smiling inquiringly at me.

"I'm alright," I force a reassuring smile and then quickly look down to my hands, feeling awkward. *What just happened?* I look up at the guy, intrigued. But, now he has a manga book in his hands and flips the page. A crease forms between his eyebrows as his eyes trace the print.

"Are you sure? You look like you're about to faint," she presses, sounding dubious.

"I'm fine," I reply to her without taking my eyes from him. As he frowns clearly puzzled, I note, "You're reading it the wrong way, it's a Japanese manga. You have to start at the back of the book and read it from right to left."

He looks up, making me take an instinctive step back under his dark scrutiny. His expression, unreadable. His gaze goes back to the comic in his hands, and he turns it over. Following my advice, he begins tracing his eyes from right to left, and a hint of a smile crosses his face.

"Mike, I want to show you something," the blond girl pulls him by the arm and drags him away before he has a chance to argue. He closes the manga, placing it sideways atop a row of categorized books, and follows her.

Looking back at me, he blinks, his eerie blue eyes look a bit less frightening than before, but still intimidating. "Thanks for the tip," and with that, his face turns, and he follows her slim figure toward the stairs, her silvery blond curls bouncing all the way.

Approaching the comics shelf, I scan the titles. There's a gap left behind where the manga he held resided. It's a series of sixteen comics. Intrigued, I pick up the book he was reading from the shelf. The cover art features a girl carrying a black bird in a cage. Oddly enough, it isn't even the first one in the series. It's the tenth volume. Maybe he read the previous ones. Then again, probably not, considering he didn't know how to read a manga to begin with. *Go figure.*

"What are you doing here?" The girl whispers almost inaudibly underneath the classical music, tearing me from my reverie.

"Gabe asked me to meet him here," comes his defensive reply. "I do what I'm told."

Careful not to make any sounds, I make my way to the edge of the aisle and take a peek. But they're in between the shelves, out of sight. Curious, I stare down at the pages of the book in my hands and try to listen in.

They're silent for a moment, and then he speaks again, "Call it instinct."

"A bit excessive, don't you think?" She chastises him.

"Debatable. Who knows how long I'd be stuck here otherwise."

"Come," she orders, neither agreeing nor disagreeing with his remark. "We have to go. We need backup."

"Backup?" He inquires. "What for?"

"I just found out we've got company, and strength only takes you so far without wisdom."

"What about Gabe?" He sounds torn.

"Something came up, and he's not coming," she replies simply.

"Perfect," is his disappointed remark.

Their rushed footsteps indicate they're leaving the memoir section, and I quickly hide behind the shelf, nearly bumping into it.

"You know," he begins. "You're becoming almost as antisocial as I am."

"Debatable," she says sweetly. "But, now that you mention it, we really need to work on your people skills."

I stay where I am, part ashamed for eavesdropping on their conversation, part intrigued. *Backup? Are they part of some gang, involved with something illegal?* That's what it sounded like. I barely registered her face, or his for that matter, everything happened so fast. But he's definitely scary enough to be in a gang, I've never been so uneasy around anyone like that before. Considering he can't be more than a year or so older than me, that's saying something. Those eyes, such an unusual color, they were both spooky and alluring. Now, I can't say the same about the girl. She's too sweet, too soft spoken to be a part of anything nefarious, with her pale blue eyes and silvery blond hair, all girly, covered in pink pastel.

The door chimes, and I peek over the balcony. They're leaving the store. I think it's safe to come out now. At the register, Wellington is talking to a woman wearing a graphite business suit. He sees me coming, "Did you find anything good?"

I hand him the manga along with some cash, "Just this one."

"You realize this is volume ten?"

I nod, and he shrugs, handing the money to the woman

who must be Dora. She puts the book in a plastic bag with the store logo and hands it to me along with seventy-three cents in change.

"Ready to go?" Wellington asks.

I nod, following him outside the bookstore and into the SUV. The traffic is light, and in a matter of minutes we're parked in front of my grandparents' apartment building.

"Do you want to come in?"

"Sure, it's been forever since I last saw your grandma."

We climb out of his car and head to the building. He holds the door open for me, and his eyes lock on the bookstore bag, but he doesn't say anything. In the elevator, however, curiosity gets the best of him, "Why did you get this book? Did you read the other ones back in Japan?"

"No. I just liked the cover," I reply.

"It's a cool series," he jumps in. "The main character can turn into a bird."

"That's original," I remark, feeling a pinch of buyers remorse.

Just then, the elevator doors open, and we head to the apartment. Dominika is dusting the living room when we get in.

"Hey, Dominika. Where is Grandma?"

"Mrs. Melody is out running some errands, Miss Liza."

I nod for Wellington to follow me, and catch an expression of slight disappointment in his face. That's one of the weirdest things about my friends. All of them adore my grandma, and she adores them back. She calls Wellington "darling boy," and Faye "sweetie pie." *No comment.*

In my room, I ask, "How is the cello going?"

He sits at my computer desk, "It's going. Mom and I just came back from New York last Saturday. A famous quartet invited me to play with them at Carnegie Hall in a few weeks, and we were arranging things–"

"Whoa! Carnegie Hall?" I interrupt in astonishment. "My friend is a prodigy."

"Not really, Liz. I'm seventeen," he says modestly, looking down at his hands. He opens and closes a video game case for something to do and continues, "It might not work out because neither of my parents can take me. They will never let me go to New York by myself. I should just forget about it."

"Still, absolutely cool if you ask me," I point out, sitting on my bed across from him.

Wellington shrugs and grabs the iPod beside my laptop, turning it on, "What have you been listening to lately?"

"It's not mine," I lean against the head board and hug my pillow. When he looks at me inquiringly, I add simply, "There are no songs anyway, just a long track of non-stop gibberish. I think it might be an audio book or some weird voice recording."

He looks up from the device, "Mind if I check it out?"

I shrug, and he puts the earphones on, pressing play. He looks upward, furrows his eyebrows in concentration, and keeps listening to whatever it is for much longer than I did. He frowns and scratches the back of his head, looking puzzled.

Then, it clicks, and I sit up straight, "It's in Portuguese, isn't it? You can understand it!" I should have realized. I've heard Wellington's mother speaking Portuguese so many times. Not only on the phone with Wellington, but she also watches that Brazilian TV channel starring those over dramatic soap actresses that are always crying and screaming about something.

He takes the earphones off, "What was that?"

"These audio files, they're in Portuguese, right? You can understand them!"

"No. Yes, I mean, sort of," he shakes his head as if gathering his thoughts, just like I do when switching from Japanese to English. "No, it's not Portuguese. It's in Latin, and I kinda understand it."

"Latin? You speak Latin now?"

"I do actually. You know my mom is as crazy about languages as my dad is about classical music. She's a polyglot." I frown at the word, having no idea what that means. He smiles at my expression and elaborates, "Mom speaks five languages: Portuguese, Latin, Greek, Italian, and English. She and Dad made a deal when I was born that he would speak English, and she would speak Portuguese while I was growing up. So I would know at least two languages. I never learned how to write in Portuguese, though. She started teaching me Latin when I reached the third grade. She tried to start with Greek a couple years ago, but I drew the line there. My brain is overloaded as it is. So, yes I know Latin, more than Portuguese even. But this book is really complex."

"Is it a book?" I ask eagerly.

"It seems like it," he replies like it's no big deal.

"What's it about?" I press thrilled that at least one mystery is about to be solved.

"I can't really tell yet," he says, frowning. "There are a few words I've never heard before. But it's mainly about some kind of revolution, a war involving fire and swords. It's sort of captivating."

"Maybe your mom would know the words, do you think?" I suggest already predicting a definitive *no*.

"Most definitely. But I'd rather try on my own first since we have no idea what this book is all about. Besides, if it's some kind of R-rated story, she'll be offended. She will want to know where I got it and so on. Do you mind lending it to me?" Wellington asks.

"Be my guest," I reply simply.

He unplugs the headphones from the device and puts them on the desk beside my laptop. He pockets the iPod, "How did you get a hold of this, by the way?"

"It's a long story, a very awkward long story," heat spreads across my face as I recall the memory. I hope he doesn't press me to elaborate. I'm saved by the bell. Or more precisely, the vibration.

Wellington's phone buzzes in his pocket, and he looks at the screen. He lifts one finger gesturing for me to wait and mouths, "Hold that thought." I nod, and he answers quietly, "Yes, Mom," he pauses, listening patiently. "Not long. I'm at Liz's... no, it's cool. I'll be right there. Love you too, Mom. Okay, bye."

"You have to go," I state the obvious.

"Yep, Mattie is at my place. Her marching band practice must have finished early," he explains. "It's been almost two years since we first started dating, and Mom still can't stand her. She won't get over it. Can you believe that?"

Knowing his mother the way I do, the answer is "yes." I believe it. What I can't believe is that he's defied Mrs. Blake's wishes for almost two years. But I decide its better not to point that out. He must really love Mattie. I smile at his worried face and order, "Go," pointing at the door.

"Okay, okay," he laughs and lifts both hands in surrender, walking backward until he leaves the room. "Later, Liz."

Sitting at my desk, I power up my laptop and check my emails. There's one from Dad titled: Which color?

Hey, kiddo.

I'm replacing your water-damaged cellphone. Need to know: Black or white?

Love you,

−Dad

I write a quick reply.

Surprise me.

Love,

Liz

I know he hates when I do that, but I'm too wound up to make any decisions right now. Anyways, Suri will be the one to decide. She always does.

As I hit send, another email from Dad comes in. *Whoa!* I know he's in Japan and they're ahead of us and all, but still. That's too fast of a reply, even for Dad. I open it.

Hey, kiddo.

You took too long to reply. I ordered it last night. The white one. It'll be there today. You should check your email at least once a day. I hope you like it.

Love you most,

—Dad

P.S. Suri picked the color, she says hi, and that she misses you already.

I write a quick reply.

Oops. Sorry, Dad. I'll do my best from now on. White is cool. I already know I love it, thanks.

Love you too,

Liz

P.S. I knew it :) Miss her too, and hi back.

I click send and lie down in my bed. Then, I turn on the TV and begin flipping through channels. A slow-motion car explosion fills the screen, followed by Kari's voice along with Grant and Tory's laughter makes me pause on the channel. It's obviously a rerun, but I haven't seen this episode yet. Adjusting my body more comfortably between the throw pillows, I watch and try to get my mind off things. I know I have homework to do and riddles to decipher, but after everything that happened today, it's probably best that I unwind a little.

7

Once again I sleep through my alarm. This time, however, Raph has just partial blame. The rest is on me. By the time I finally fell asleep it was four in the morning. I finished all my homework, even the assignments that were not due today. My brain kept going back to Raph's words and I couldn't sleep. I tried deciphering his enigmatic message for hours to no avail.

Today, however, Dominika is the one waking me up. Let's just say, she's not as understanding as Grandma. Not even a bit. She marches into the room clapping her hands loudly and blasts the TV at full volume. Suddenly, sunlight streams into the room.

"Up, Miss Liza, or you're going to be late," she commands me in her Russian accent. I'm on my feet before she finishes speaking, eyes barely open, yawning. Only then, does Dominika turn off the TV.

"Thanks, Dominika," Grandma finally manages to say. "I'll take it from here. Sorry my dear, you wouldn't wake up," is Grandma's justification for letting Dominika scare the life out of me. "Faye will be here any minute, you have to get dressed."

"Okay, Grandma," I muffle a yawn.

Five minutes later, I'm downstairs, eyes bloodshot, still sleepy, looking like a Zombie in a pleated skirt. I hear her coming before I even see the green bug. The car is shaking, the music blasting through the speakers as I enter the car.

At least someone is wide awake.

She lowers the volume, "Hey Liz. I heard your grandma didn't let you join the track team. Bummer!"

"You heard right. Grandma says it's not very 'ladylike' to go running around, sweating like a pig," I reply, quoting Grandma's words.

"You know what she would agree with? Joining the cheer squad," Faye cracks up.

"Ha-ha!" I feign annoyance, by now I'm used to Faye's sense of humor and don't take her so seriously all the time.

"If track and cheerleading are out? What options do you have left? Today is the deadline to enroll in after school electives," Faye informs, sounding a little troubled. Then, as if she just had the best of ideas, "You know what you should totally, totally do?"

I shoot her a look, knowing full well that nothing good follows the words "totally, totally."

"Join the Computer Club. You'd be like a god among men. They might even carve a bust of your likeness and worship it," Faye jokes.

I don't even dignify her comment with a reply.

"But seriously, now. You can always join the Yearbook Committee. I can talk to them if you want me to," Faye offers, abandoning her popular girl facade and switching back to the real Faye.

"Intermediate Drama," I reply simply, bracing myself for the laughing fit.

Faye only seems surprised, "Are you into acting?"

"No," I reply, letting out a short laugh. "But I can do set design stuff. Besides, Grandma approves."

"Not if she knows that you're planning to work

backstage," she points out and glances at me. "Don't worry, I won't tell."

Once again she parks beside the yellow Lamborghini. I'm gathering my things when she notes, "His car is here, I just hope I can find him today."

"If you are planning on hooking up with some guy because of his car, don't tell me. I don't want to know."

"I have two words for you," she pauses. Even though she's a couple inches shorter than I am, she appears to be looking down at me when she adds, "As if."

She shakes her head, closing her eyes momentarily. I feel guilty right away. I meant it as a joke, but I guess she didn't find it all that funny. Faye may care a bit too much about appearances, but she's still my friend. Okay, she hangs out with the mean girls, is the worst driver on the planet and acts ditzy for whatever reason. But in the end, she's been nothing but a good friend to me since I got here. If it weren't for her, I'd still be this year's jester. A loner even. She took me under her wing. If I'm being honest, I don't see why she should. Since I'm pretty sure having me at her table probably knocked her queen bee status down a few notches, regardless of who my father is.

"Sorry, Faye. I didn't really mean it."

"Sure, you didn't," she snorts.

"I'm sorry," I apologize again.

"Uh-huh."

We walk in silence, the walk from her car to the school entrance seeming longer than ever before.

English and Physics go by at the same pace as the past two days. Not Calculus, though. Since I did my Calculus homework around two in the morning I got all mixed up. I did two equations that I didn't have to do, and I left out three that I was supposed to. So, Mattie and I are racking our brains to solve the last equation from our handout assignment that's due today.

Faye is talking with some girl to her left. She's sitting in front of me and offers once again, "Dude, just copy mine. I don't mind."

Apparently, I'm forgiven, "Thanks, but we're almost done."

Mattie shoots me a look that says she could bite my head off for refusing Faye's offer for the third time. Right at that moment, the bell rings indicating the beginning of Mr. Hathaway's class.

His booming voice announces, "Handouts on my desk."

Mattie's fingers tap numbers frenetically in her calculator, and then she finally gets the result "negative two squared."

I write it down and Faye confirms it's right. Mattie stacks the pages in numerical order and drives a staple through them, just as he finishes his announcement for the second time. Then, she freezes. Her big bluish-green eyes nearly pop out of her head, and her pink glossy lips shape a soundless, "Wow!"

As I turn around in my seat to see what's captured her attention, I notice Mattie is not the only one staring. Every single girl in the class has her head twisted like an owl. Except for Samantha Parker, that is. She's looking straight ahead, smirking. Her lips barely curling into a knowing smile, like she has a secret while everybody else is hypnotized by the guy walking in. He's dressed in the school uniform just like all the other guys, but unlike them he looks good in it. I don't know if it's the way it fits him, or his physique, or the devil-may-care way he holds himself, but he looks absolutely gorgeous.

Mr. Hathaway sits at his desk looking at a loss. I'm not sure what astonishes me more: the way this guy just strolls in after the bell, or strict Mr. Hathaway just sitting there without doing anything about it.

When I look back in the boy's direction, he's standing right in front of us, talking to Faye of all people. Then again, a guy that good-looking wouldn't be talking to anyone else now, would he?

Even more shocking is to see Faye so taken aback. In my split second stupor, I missed what he said to her. But now, Faye hands her pink Blackberry to him, blinking up speechless. He punches in a series of numbers and gives it back to her, "Thanks. See you around."

"O-kay," Faye sounds as astonished as the rest of the class.

Then, he glances down at me and a hint of a smile crosses his face. In that brief instant, it hits me. I've seen him before. It's the "BOSS guy," the one who has my iPod. Without a word, he turns around and heads out confidently, like he's his own *boss*. When he passes the teacher's desk, he says all casual, "Hey, Mr. Hathaway."

As if it were the most normal thing in the world, coming and going as he pleases.

"Mr. Sinclair," Mr. Hathaway nods. "Will you be gracing us with your presence next week?"

"Sure thing," and with that, he steps out the door, leaving our class in utter silence.

Once our visitor is out of sight, our teacher tries to salvage his authority. He keeps us busy for the remainder of the class. I'm anxious the whole time. I want to talk with Faye and ask about this Sinclair kid who has my iPod. I remember her mentioning his name on the first day of school. *What was it? And what about him?* I really need to start paying more attention to Faye's chatter. One never knows when it might be useful. Right now for instance, she holds the key to retrieving my iPod.

Mr. Hathaway assigns another set of ten questions which are due tomorrow. This teacher must love grading homework, or something.

Seriously, doesn't he have a life?

As I take notes from the board, Mr. Hathaway retrieves a paper slip from someone standing at the door and calls out, "Miss Greenwood, your presence is required at the director's office."

Faye looks surprised, but she doesn't question it. She gathers her things and leaves the classroom.

At lunch, Faye's cafeteria crew says her dad is in town for business and wanted to have lunch with his only daughter. It's a good thing they're too distracted by tomorrow's cheer tryouts to pay me any attention.

When the final bell rings, I rush outside the main building into the school parking lot and call Faye. She picks up on the first ring, "Hey, girly. You read my mind. I was just about to call you."

"Oh!" I exclaim, caught completely off guard. I take a few steps forward and lean against the brick wall.

"I kind of need your help. Remember that research paper I told you about? The conscious versus unconscious mind."

"Um!" I mumble. *Gee! I really, really, should pay more attention when she talks.* I clear my throat, "What about it?"

"Well. My co-writer just emailed me all the research he did on it. We are pretty much covered on the theoretical part, but we need to experiment. So, I've chosen you to volunteer. Can we stop by at your place around fiveish?" When I don't answer either way. She clarifies, "It's for my Psych class," she pauses suddenly and then blurts out, "Oh shoot! You don't have a ride home, do you? I completely forgot. I'm a terrible person! That's probably why you called me in the first place. I'm on my way back right now. It'll take–"

"It's alright," I cut her off, straiten up and begin walking toward the station. "That's not why I called."

"I can be there in ten," Faye sounds as guilty as I did earlier this morning, ignoring my words altogether.

"I'm almost to the station," I stretch the truth. "Don't beat yourself up. Just go do your thing. I'll see you at five."

It does the trick. Faye says cheerfully, "Cool. See you then."

As I'm putting my phone away, a male voice calls out, "Liz, wait up."

It's not Wellington this time. I spin around to see Ben jogging toward me, dimples forming in his cheeks. His smile is contagious, just like yawning. You can't help but do the same.

"What's up?" I ask when he reaches me.

"Not much," he replies, catching his breath. "Coach canceled practice, so I'm heading to the station. And you?"

"Same here," I pause to correct myself. "Sort of. Leave out the canceled practice part."

"Gotcha," he laughs briefly. "Which way are you going?"

"Green line, Beacon Hill. You?"

"Same train, opposite direction, Somerville," he replies, switching his backpack to his other shoulder. "I heard Mattie is dropping Chemistry."

"Don't remind me."

He laughs before saying, "You'll be okay."

"Yeah, right."

"There's a transfer student starting in a week," he informs. "Greg and I will sit close to you and help out in the meantime."

"Thanks," I smile gratefully. "How do you know that?"

"He's joining the basketball team. Coach just mentioned his name today. Everyone is freaking out about losing their positions to him. As far as we know, he could be some kind of star point guard at his former high school."

"Huh," I exclaim. "That's good news, I suppose."

"He might be bad news, you never know. His name is Michael Price."

"Michael Price," I repeat his name softly.

We enter the station and head downstairs. His train is coming to a stop as we reach the platform and he steps in, "See you tomorrow."

"See ya," I reply, and the doors slide closed.

Inside, Ben holds the rail with one hand and gives me a single wave just as the train departs. It takes about five minutes until my train comes around, and another fifteen until I'm finally home. The first thing I do is take a long shower, washing and conditioning my neglected hair. After changing into a pair of old beat up jeans and a mint cream hoodie, I take my time blow drying my hair.

Sitting crossed legged on my bed, I begin working on my homework. By the time I get to my Calculus equations, my hair is twisted into a bun with a pencil sticking through it. My brain refuses to keep going, and I surrender, taking a much needed break.

8

I'm checking my email when Dominika pokes her head in the doorway and announces, "Miss Faye is here with a very beautiful boy."

"Thanks Dominika. You can tell them to come up," I stand and start gathering up some stuff that's misplaced.

Dominika nods, leaving the room.

Just as I finish piling up my books, Faye walks in. To my surprise she's not in her cheerleader uniform. She's wearing jeans, a dark green sweater and high heel boots. As always, perfect hair and makeup, looking like she's just stepped right off a runway. This time, she brought a model along with her.

I can't believe the Sinclair guy is here, standing a few steps behind Faye. Dominika was right. He's a very beautiful boy, with his piercing blue eyes and sun-kissed tan. Everything about him is picture-perfect. The symmetry of his face is absolutely impeccable. He's slim, but proportionally well defined, as if he were carved and molded by the hand of a master sculptor. His well fitting casual designer clothes just enhance his visual appeal. He's also taller than I remembered, taller than Faye in her five inch heels. His eyes meet mine, and I catch myself once again wondering if he recognizes me. The answer is probably yes, but I'll wait for *him* to mention it. No matter how much I miss my iPod, the embarrassment is too high a price to pay. Besides, his iPod walked out the door with Wellington yesterday. *How am I supposed to explain that?*

As if reading my thoughts, a knowing smile crosses his face. It's official. He should be in the *Guinness Book of World Records* under the category most beautiful person. Not liking the way my thoughts are headed, I turn my attention back to Faye, "Why didn't you tell me the guy from *Resident Evil* would be coming along?"

Faye seems confused by my question. Of course, she would be. Faye never played *RE4*. Wellington did. She glances at the Sinclair guy, who now carries a weary look in his eyes. She runs her hand through her hair and turns back to me, "*Resident Evil*, do you mean the movie?"

"No, not the movie, I mean the game." Noticing that Faye still has no clue what I'm talking about, I stop and wave it off, "Never mind."

Faye opens her mouth to speak, but he cuts her short, "What are you saying? Do I remind you of some kind of demon?"

His question makes me chuckle, "Not at all, I mean Leon Kennedy. He's the character rescuing the president's daughter from zombies in Spain..." I trail off, knowing full well that neither of them are following me. My cheeks start to burn, and I'm certainly blushing.

"Zombies, huh? The by-product of humanity's self-destruction," he remarks thoughtfully.

"How poetic!" Faye cuts in impatiently. "Are you two done with the nerd talk? The clock is ticking. Liz this is Nate, and Nate, Liz."

Keeping his smile in place, he says in youthful innocence, "I think we've met before, haven't we?" He knows all too well that we did and goes on as if testing me, "I could swear we've run into each other... but I may be mistaken."

If he expects me to admit that I'm the girl who slammed into him face first in the park, it's not gonna happen. Not in a million years. He'll have to say it. He raises an eyebrow quizzically. *Oh, great.* My expression must be mirroring my thoughts.

Faye breaks up our staring contest, "We better start, we have a lot to do."

Nate glances down at my unfinished Calculus handout and offers, "Do you want to copy my assignment before we start?"

"No, it's alright. I'll do it later," I reply, a little too fast.

"You know, it's not cheating if you don't get caught," Nate explains in a quiet voice.

"Let's just go ahead and do your little experiment," I try to talk my way around the whole cheating thing.

"Is she always like this?" Nate taunts. "Little Miss Perfect?"

"The answer is *yes*," Faye replies bluntly, turning to face me. "Okay. To start, we need you to have a clear mind, or it won't work."

"I'll try. I guess," thinking about clearing my mind requires me to think of what not to think about. Is it even possible to clear one's mind?

Faye and Nate look at each other. Nate shrugs. Faye pulls out my white chair and orders, "Sit!"

"Yes, Ma'am." I reply, sitting down.

Faye rolls her eyes, "Come on, take this seriously. This assignment is ten percent of this semester's grade." She sits on the edge of my bed facing me and explains, sounding like a PhD, "We have been researching and converging theories about human brain functionality in its unconscious state, and revealing its full potential in that state. Research indicates that we use a mere fraction of our brains' potential at any given time. By tapping into the unconscious mind, a person will have the ability to answer questions that they wouldn't be able to answer while fully conscious. That's our theory in a nutshell."

Faye hands me a stack of papers covered in graphs with squiggly lines, and pie charts. She goes on explaining their idea regarding the conscious versus unconscious mind. I try to keep a straight face, but it's getting harder and harder as Faye continues to elaborate on their hypothesis.

Nate remains completely silent throughout Faye's speech. I'm tempted to peek over at him, but don't. Mostly, I wonder if he shares the same ideas, which he probably does since they're working on this project together. As if in tune with my line of thought, Nate contributes in a light and serene voice, "Theoretically speaking, this can be confirmed through trials. We put some questions together, mainly the random type. Incidental knowledge of events heard or seen in the news, on the radio, and so forth, which we believe the brain may have retained, except it can't be readily accessed consciously. But, we believe the unconscious can."

It's clear that Nate not only shares Faye's idea, but strongly reinforces it with concepts of his own. Also, it's good to know that he can speak without mocking, teasing, or being coy.

Faye breaks my train of thought, "And that's where you come in."

Understanding overtakes my conscious brain. I sit up straight and raise both hands frantically waving them in front of me, like a stop signal, "Hang on there! Did I miss something? Or are you two planning to hypnotize me? I thought you were going to ask me questions, or give me a Rorschach test or something like that."

They exchange looks, and before they have a chance to comment I stand up, "Not gonna happen." I don't care that Faye is my only girlfriend in this town. Or how cute Nate is. I'm not letting the two of them hypnotize me.

Nate detects my defiant tone and implies skeptically to Faye, "I thought you said she didn't believe in psychology or hypnosis."

"She doesn't!" Faye exclaims at the same time I say, "I don't!"

"Then, what are you afraid of?" Nate asks through a laugh.

"Listen," Faye starts, feigning patience in her voice. "We'll ask you a few questions and document your answers. Then, you'll be placed into a trance. We'll ask you the same questions and see how many answers you get right. That's all. We'll wake you up afterward. Don't you trust me?"

"Right now, I kinda don't. You guys sound like a couple of mad scientists," I say honestly.

Faye proceeds with her preparations ignoring my grievances all together. She lifts the top page on what seems to be a medical chart and scribbles something illegible. Then, she pushes a button on a voice recorder speaking closely into the mic, "Patient: Eliza O'Neill, age: 16, non-believer"

I sigh and drop back down into the chair with a thud. I decide to play nice for Faye's sake. *How bad can it be?* It's not going to work anyway.

The questions range from obscure references involving politics, celebrity news and sports trivia. Aside from the celebrity stuff, Grandpa would be great at this. I, on the other hand, scored a solid F+.

All the while, Nate takes notes and makes observations. Faye sets down the recorder on my bed with the microphone facing us. From her pocket, she produces a green stone pendant. It hangs from a thin silver chain. It's disc shaped, and a little larger than a quarter in diameter. A cryptic design decorates its center, some kind of pyramid within a flower inside a square with loopy edges. She begins speaking in a soothing voice, positioning the pendant right in my face. I pull my head back to keep from crossing my eyes, and she backs up a few inches. I'm not sure if I'm supposed to follow the swinging motion with my eyes or look past it. My vision blurs, my eyelids keep fluttering, and I have to fight the urge to blink.

After what seems like hours, my eyes start watering. I'm still trying to focus on Faye's words, "Sleepy. You're feeling very sleepy. Clear your mind and relax…"

In the background Nate suppresses a quiet laugh, and I crack up.

"Liz, come on!" Faye sounds exasperated. She turns to Nate who is now laughing outright and gives him a one handed shove. Faye tries to scold us, but starts laughing mid-sentence, "You guys, this is supposed to be serious." She composes herself briefly and insists, "Okay, guys. For real this time."

Two attempts later, Nate points out, "Maybe we should just write down that it doesn't work."

Annoyed, Faye offers him the amulet, "Here, I think you should try."

He doesn't take the object, dismissing it with a wave of his hand, "It's clear her brain is not responding to that thing. Let me try another approach." He takes a knee at my feet.

Oh man, now my mind will never get clear.

He locks his gaze to mine, and I blink a few times by reflex, swallowing hard. He's so close that I can smell his cologne. He maintains eye contact, his expression serious and commanding. Even closeup, he's flawless. He's right. He doesn't need an amulet. His blue eyes are hypnotic enough. From this distance, they have a painterly appearance, like a mixture of light and dark shades of blue over a turquoise primer. If I focus just right, I can see my reflection swimming in his irises. It's as though I'm drowning in his presence. I'm so enamored, drawn in and enthralled that I have tunnel vision, forgetting there's a world behind me.

Out of the blue, I hear clapping. I'm startled and jolt backward, blinking repeatedly.

Nate stands up, "We're done here."

"But it didn't work," Faye whines. "She got all the

answers wrong again."

"Maybe our questions are just bad. Hell, I've never even heard of the vice-president of Finland."

All the while, I'm feeling dazed. Trying to make sense of what they're saying, and getting nowhere. So, I ask, "What just happened?"

"Mr. Gorgeous here, hypnotized you without using the pendant," Faye explains sarcastically.

I blink again, *"No way."*

"Yes way," Faye lets out. "You were under for about ten minutes."

I'm speechless. I can't wrap my mind around it. *Me? Hypnotized?* It's surreal.

Nate closes his notebook, peering out the window. He looks back at Faye, "We have our conclusion."

"And that is?" Faye asks, unconvinced.

"Does it matter? We did the assignment," Nate states confidently.

Faye crosses her arms in exasperation, "Yes, it does matter. I don't know about you. But I don't wanna go through the motions here. I intend to get into Harvard."

"Undesired outcomes aren't necessarily incorrect," Nate concludes and starts packing his things into his book bag. Indicating, whether Faye likes it or not, he's leaving.

Faye sighs, surrendering. She begins gathering her things and follows after him. At the door, she stops, "I better catch up with him. No one knows if I'll find him again. I'll call you. Thanks for your help."

"Okay, I guess," I reply, and she leaves the room. My mind is in overdrive. I still can't remember a thing from the ten minutes I lost. All I can seem to recall is Nate's piercing blue eyes.

9

It's finally Friday, and by the looks of it, a cloudless sunshiny day. I scurry to my morning shower and put on my uniform. Tomorrow, no school. I can run in the park, go watch Denzel Washington's new movie, play video games all day...

"Eliza, breakfast is ready when you are," Grandma calls out from the hall, bursting my bubble and bringing me back from fantasy land.

Sigh.

Not wanting to put my towel dried hair up, I smooth it down the best I can. Then, I coat it with a thick layer of leave-in conditioner and fix my long curls into a messy side-braid. I don't bother with makeup. I just apply a thin layer of sunscreen and cherry Chapstick. I unplug my new iPhone from its charger and tuck it inside my pocket, hanging my backpack on my right shoulder as I head for the dining room.

Grandma is writing in her leather itinerary that she carries around all the time, and I take the seat across from her. Grandpa is sitting at the edge of the table, his head hidden behind a newspaper as usual. *What year is it?* Seriously. These two need some technology.

"Morning Grandma, Grandpa," I say, grabbing a

cinnamon muffin.

Grandma looks up from her planner, "Eliza, don't you look nice this morning."

Does she mean the hair? I wonder to myself, touching my side-braid self-consciously.

Grandpa looks up from his newspaper and sets his tea down, peering at me over his bifocals. He frowns, "Why, Melody, she's in her school uniform, looking exactly as she did yesterday."

I almost choke on my muffin and take a sip of milk. Grandma waves him off dismissively and Grandpa shakes his head, going back to his article.

"Thank you, Grandma," I reply politely.

She nods in acknowledgment and takes a sip of her tea, going back to her writing. Just as I finish eating, Dominika walks in, "Miss Faye wants you to meet her downstairs."

"You better hurry, she doesn't know how to parallel park," Grandpa notes, not looking up from his paper.

Grabbing my backpack from the floor, I head downstairs. As I step outside, I scan the street for Faye's green bug. To my surprise, Faye pulls up in the black Mustang again. She lowers the passenger side window and leans over, "Hey, girly, wanna ride?"

I climb in, and she takes off. I'm itching to ask about Nate Sinclair, but how do I do that without seeming too eager? As I buckle my seat belt, I engage in a more subtle topic to start, "So, the black stallion is back."

"For one last ride," Faye says thoughtfully. "I found a buyer yesterday. Kiara told Dwayne, who told Blake, who told Ariel Price, who contacted me–"

"Whoa, that's a lot of telling," I tease.

"I know, right?" Faye laughs briefly. "So, I was at Blake's school yesterday afternoon when she called. Dwayne had already given her the sales pitch for the Mustang. We closed the deal for the asking price, and I'm gonna drop it off with her brother after school. All the paper work is done. Mother is impressed. I did it, I sold the car. So, you're coming with me. Is that cool with you?"

"Sure. Why not?"

"Sweet!" Faye says cheerfully, pulling over a few yards from the school building. "I talked to him on the phone. We'll drive to his place right after tryouts, deliver the car, and he'll drive us home."

When am I going to learn to listen first before agreeing to do stuff? Too late now. So, I say, "Just text me after the tryouts."

Faye is retouching her makeup, but she pauses and looks at me, "Why? Come watch the tryouts, you'll have a blast. You have my word."

"I don't know about that."

"Come on Liz, you can't say it isn't fun to laugh at other people's misfortune," Faye challenges, putting away her lipstick.

We climb out of the car, and I want to say that I don't think it's funny, considering I find myself on the receiving end most of the time. But I don't. Instead, I just cave in with a shrug.

"So, you're coming!?" She asks with a burst of energy, just as the bell rings.

"Meet you there," I reply gloomily, heading to English. I never got a chance to ask about the mysterious guy who has my iPod. And now, I'm forced to sit through cheer tryouts. *Super*.

As I make my way to English, I catch myself looking for Nate Sinclair, finally understanding what Faye meant on the first day of school. It's like he doesn't even go here. But then again, it's not like I'm scanning the halls, or peeking through classroom windows. Because I'm not. *Really.*

In Calculus at Mr. Hathaway's roll call, I survey the class, but he's obviously MIA. As I do so, that girl from PE, the one who insists on being called "Spark," narrows her hazel eyes at me. From then on, she spends the remainder of the class stealing not-so-subtle glances in my direction. Her shoulder length black blue hair is braided into two parts, and she's wearing a beret. I have to admit, she has an offbeat style. Neither goth nor punk. It's kind of artsy, unique. I'd attempt to be friends with her once again if it weren't for the bad vibe she's broadcasting. When the bell finally rings, she gives me a pointed once over as she walks by, and my entire body shivers.

"Careful Liz. Prozac chick's got your number," Faye jabs at me once Spark is out of earshot.

I laugh, taking the plunge, "So, did you catch up with your Psych partner yesterday?" There, that's innocent enough. *Or not,* since Faye is now watching me closely with an inquiring expression on her face. Silly me trying to fool Faye of all people. I blurt out, "Hey, it's not everyday I get hypnotized, you know? How did he do that?"

Score! That seems to convince her.

"Beats me," she shrugs, wrinkling her nose. "He surely did a lot more research than I did. He's the one who gathered most of the material. Nate Sinclair is so full of himself. He single-handedly wrote the paper. When I complained about it, he had the audacity to insinuate I was into him. *As if...* Then, he emailed me the assignment as if it were a done deal. Worst of all, I can't knock it. It's impeccable, a well deserved A+."

By the time she's done talking we're sitting down at the lunch table. Today's gossip revolves around this afternoon's cheer tryouts, and which girls are clearly not gonna make the cut. I tune them out, picking the mushrooms out of my pasta. I don't care about how nutritious they are, I refuse to eat fungus.

Running into Ben at my locker after lunch is becoming routine, and we walk to Chemistry together. Today is Mattie's last lab, and she's bubblier than ever. As a result, we're the first to finish it.

Ms. Johnson's mind is on the tryouts, so we hang out in

the bleachers as the boys throw a ball around. I work on my Spanish homework, enjoying the early afternoon sun. Kiara sits beside me, working on her Physics assignment and sighing a lot.

"I really don't get it," she shakes her head. There's a tone of disbelief tinting her voice.

I look at her notebook, and frown. Her homework is done, "What don't you get?"

"Not Physics. Them," she nods in Spark's direction. Beside her is none other than Nate Sinclair, texting on his phone. Kiara tilts her head to one side, admiringly, "Just like Beauty and the Beast, but backward."

"Nate and Spark?" I whisper to myself. As if he heard me from all the way across the field, Nate looks up from his phone and catches me staring at him. For half a second he just stares right back at me and then stands up. He says something to Spark and begins to descend the bleachers. Panic sets in, he's making his way toward us.

"Is he coming here?" Kiara voices my thoughts.

To my relief and Kiara's disappointment, he isn't. He's heading to the locker room. I steal a peek at Spark through the corner of my eye. As expected, she's staring straight at me. So, I busy myself gathering my things. In the back of my mind an eerie question arises, "Is that why she looked at me that way in Calculus today?" *No, it can't be.* She couldn't know just by looking at me that I couldn't get him out of my mind since yesterday. Because of the whole hypnosis thing, I mean. Not because...

"Nate Sinclair is beyond hot," Kiara echoes my thoughts and I look at her in shock. She shrugs, "What can I say? He has a nice behind."

I laugh at the sound of that and tuck my notebook into my backpack. Putting it on, I stand up and follow Kiara toward the gym. I'm intentionally slowing down with each step as if I'm a sloth riding a turtle.

"Come on Liz, those long legs of yours can move you

faster than that," she stops, waiting for me. When I catch up, she links her arm to mine, half walking, half dragging me. Still, I manage to delay us a little and we reach the gym just as the third girl leaves the floor.

Kiara reads my apprehensive expression, "It's fun. You'll see."

Fun.

I spot Alexis waving at us, and we walk up to sit beside her in the middle of the third row. I take the seat beside Alexis and Kiara sits to my right. Faye is the captain of the cheer squad. So, she's sitting in the first row along with two gym teachers. She spots us and shoots me an inquiring look, arching an eyebrow at me. *What now?* I know, I'm a few minutes late. But I made it here, didn't I?

One of the teachers is Ms. Johnson, the second one I've never seen before. They whisper to each other and take notes as the girl performs her routine. We applaud politely as a petite brunette girl stands from her grand finale. She smiles and high steps off the floor in excitement. Then, she immediately starts crying all over her friends in the second row.

Alexis volunteers to fill us in on what we've missed, "There are two open spots on the senior squad and she's the best one so far. We'll see how she compares to the next twelve. The first one doesn't have it. Ms. Johnson is very strict. The second girl fell on her head, butt to the air. You missed it. It was hilarious."

I force myself to smile at her sweetly. *TWELVE? Seriously?* There are still twelve other girls waiting to jump around chanting, "Go Egrets! Go Saint Pete Egrets!" I really need to learn how to walk slower.

Four girls are on and off the floor in the space of sixteen minutes. It turns out, Faye and the teachers can interrupt them mid-performance if they mess up. Kiara explains that they have a total of five minutes each, but if they won't make the cut why waste time. I think it's mean since these poor girls must have spent hours jumping around just for this moment. But I won't complain since I can't wait to get out of here.

A spunky little thing steps up. She's so tiny. I think she's doing good, but they stop her in a matter of seconds. Maybe I just don't have a critical eye for this. I turn to Alexis inquiringly, "What happened?"

"She must be a freshman," Alexis informs plainly.

"And?" I ask for clarification, looking from one girl to the other.

"Anyone can tryout, but there's an unspoken rule. Upperclassmen only," Kiara elaborates, clapping politely.

The next one starts with, "Ready? Okay!" Which is enough for me to send her packing. She spells out the school's team name one letter at a time E-G-R-E-T-S. She does a little jump, followed by a cartwheel.

Her routine is cut short by an abrupt call for, "Next," from Ms. Johnson.

"Thanks, Linda. We'll let you know what we decide," Faye patches things up with a little more tact.

The next two perform similar routines. I just now find out that Alexis isn't a cheerleader. Apparently, she's here for the sideshow. She keeps cracking up. According to Kiara, none of them qualify, and she should know, she's on the squad.

That's when an exceptionally beautiful girl walks in. If looks count, which they obviously do, this one qualifies by appearance alone. The tall and slim Asian girl, with accentuated curves, stands apart. She's pale white, as if her skin has never caught a single UV ray in her entire life. Her black hair is waist-length with a few red streaks and her pale blue eyes look unreal. Her features are all gracefully proportional, with heart shape lips and a delicate nose. Unlike the previous girls, she's not wearing a skirt. She's wearing the school gym outfit, shorts and a t-shirt. Still, even wearing the gym uniform the contours of her body puts the competition to shame.

"Oh my," Alexis whispers beside me. "And here I thought Kiara was an exotic beauty."

Kiara doesn't seem to appreciate Alexis' backhanded compliment. She straightens in her seat and smirks, "Let's see if she's any good."

"Zoë Fairchild, we're ready when you are," the teacher on the left informs, managing to sound impartial.

She kicks off a sequence that makes my jaw hit the floor, opening with a toe touch jump split about six feet off the ground, and lands perfectly on her toes. She throws the pompoms way up in the air, does a double back flip, spins and still manages to catch them. She drops the pompoms to either side, does a triple front hand spring and returns back to the same spot with a double gainer. She finishes in a floor split between the pompoms. Somehow, she's able to slide from a split position back to her feet in a single motion without the support of her hands.

For a brief moment, you can hear a pin drop. Then, she takes a bow. For the first time, since I entered the gym this afternoon I genuinely applaud. A few guys from the basketball team are cheering from where they stand in the doorway to the gym. They're whistling and shouting, "Woo-ho!" and "Yeah!" Just like a bunch of high school guys.

"That's it. Thanks girls for trying out, better luck next year," Ms. Johnson calls out, standing up unceremoniously.

Faye looks at the other teacher at a loss. The teacher just shrugs and leaves Faye sitting by herself. Faye takes a few seconds to recover and walks up to us, "I guess we know who made the squad." She turns to me, "Come, we need to get going."

I stand up, say bye to the girls and walk with Faye to the parking lot. By the time we're off school property, it's half past four. When I point that out to Faye, she says dismissively, "Chill, there's not much traffic. We'll get to Revere Beach before five."

Revere Beach? That's on the other side of town. Or is

that another town completely? The only thing I know about the area is that my dad's best programmer, Ken, has a place there.

Half an hour later, Faye parks in front of a five story building and climbs out of the car. I do the same, scanning the area. It's nearly dusk. Across from the boulevard is the beach, the sea looks agitated and dark. Apart from a few runners and a couple walking their dog, the place is deserted.

A tall guy who must be Michael starts walking toward us, calling out, "Faye?"

Faye's expression is pure "*oh*," and she whispers too quietly for him to hear. I almost miss her words myself, "If Revere Beach was Olympus, he would most certainly be Zeus."

Gee! Exaggerate much?

To me, the boy walking up to us is just an ordinary guy, a lot like all the other guys in our school. His posture and the way he carries himself reminds me of Nate. But he's not nearly as handsome as Nate, that's for sure.

Michael walks with the confidence of a guy who could take down anyone effortlessly. Which is comical, since he can't be older than Wellington. He's definitely much more imposing, though. It must be his eyes, they're downright creepy. Some freaky dark blue color, even though it's late afternoon and cloudy, no one could mistake his eyes for black. They're a discernible dark blue as if they had a light source of their own refracting from inside. That's when it hits me. He's the guy from the bookstore, *Mike.*

Faye walks up to him, "Hey, you must be Ariel's brother."

He nods in confirmation, "I'm Michael."

"Faye," she replies.

Faye takes him in, and her brow furrows, "You and Ariel are so different from each other."

"That's an understatement," he replies meaningfully.

She laughs, "You sound just like me talking about my

brother Ian." Faye remembers me standing here and adds, "This is Liz."

"We've met before," Michael turns his dark gaze to me, his lips curl up into an almost smile. "She gave me tips on how to read a manga."

"Oh," Faye faces me, eyes narrowing.

"We were not officially introduced. Pleased to meet you, I'm Michael Price."

"Me too," I nod. "Liz O'Neill." Since we're giving surnames.

"Okay, then," Faye jumps in. "Here are the keys. You know how to drive stick, right?"

"In theory," Michael replies, reaching for the keys which Faye pulls back out of his reach.

Weirdly, he closes his eyes and presses the bridge of his nose, one hand left outstretched.

"I think he's kidding," I attempt. He seems the type of guy who'd drive a stick-shift for some reason.

"Are you?" Faye inquires, arms crossed.

"I can guarantee, I'll get the two of you home safe," he opens his eyes, looking straight at Faye, hand still extended. She hesitates a split second, studying him carefully, and then hands him the keys. Michael climbs into the driver seat, I get into the back, and Faye rides shotgun. He starts the engine, presses the clutch to the floor and switches from neutral to first gear, stalling the engine.

Faye freaks out, "Oh shoot! You really don't know what you're doing, do you?"

He ignores her, repeating the process. Amazingly, he does it without a problem, and Faye sighs in relief. When Michael releases the clutch and accelerates, the car jerks, but stays in motion.

Faye's voice is easy-going as she teases, "When was the last time you drove a manual?"

"Trust me, you don't want to know," he replies, making Faye uneasy. She just looks out the window to avert the awkward situation.

After a few blocks, we find ourselves in a traffic jam. The light hasn't even turned yellow at the intersection of 4th and Everett when Michael hits the brakes. It isn't an abrupt stop or anything. He does it right, slowing the car down to a halt behind the solid line. But the other drivers, probably trying to get home from work, don't appreciate his cautious driving. Some motorists change lanes almost causing a crash and roar past us. Others simply forget to remove their hand from the horn.

"What did I do wrong?" Michael asks in a patient voice, glancing at Faye.

"Actually, nothing, it's just…" Faye trails off and runs her hands through her hair. She tucks her overgrown bangs behind her ears, looks at Michael and then adds, "People don't usually stop at yellow lights around here. They should, but they don't. So, if you want to avoid the noise, the swear words, the honks and prevent a car crash you have to do the same."

When the light changes, Michael seems distracted by the screeching late afternoon traffic, and the Mustang bucks wildly before it lurches forward through the intersection.

"Clutch, first to second," Faye squeals a few times before he does it. Which in my opinion does nothing but make Michael even more apprehensive. My heart thumps hard in my chest. *How did I get myself into this situation?*

Without warning, the lurching evens out and he begins to pick up speed. He shifts from second to third on his own, which is good. *I think.* Faye glances down to confirm that he's in third gear. Suddenly, the rear end of a public bus occupies the entire view out the front windshield and Faye acts on reflex, jamming her foot on the floor panel hard. I hear one of her heels snap off. My assumption is confirmed when she lets out, "Shoot!"

Clueless, Michael looks over at her, asking, "What was that?"

"My shoe," she wines, looking at him who's looking at her instead of the road.

From the back seat, I point and yell, "Look out!"

A crazy cab driver changes lanes, cuts us off and then slams on the brakes. The angry honking and varied forms of swearing becomes overwhelming. I rub my eyes. I could be home right now watching TV, surfing the web, or doing anything else.

Michael slows down, and signals to change lanes, but no one is letting him in. An irritated lady yells through her window as she passes by, "This isn't driving school? Get off the road!"

Faye opens her window, raises her fist and gives a one finger salute to the driver yelling beside us. Michael is visibly losing his composure. All the shouting, cursing and noise seems to be getting to him and his knuckles turn white as he grips the wheel.

"Just pull over," Faye insists, undoing her seat belt.

Instead, Michael punches the gas and swerves around the traffic blocking the turn lane. He flies through a yellow light and drifts the car around a sharp corner.

Faye is fighting with her seat belt, as she shouts, "What-the–"

Whatever she's about to say is muffled by the sound system which blasts to life in full volume. Michael swings the Mustang into the right lane, maneuvering in and out of a line of cars, and takes the ramp to US-1 South.

I hold my seat in a death grip and glance at Faye. Her expression is one of shock and disbelief. The way he handles the car with such aptitude and confidence indicates the obvious, Michael knows how to drive. I can tell Faye wants to shut off the music and confront him about it. But, I think she won't risk it since we've just entered a toll road, so instead she leans back in her seat, crossing her arms.

We exit the highway, and he turns left leading us back downtown. Faye looks outraged, and I don't know what to make of it. I try to angle myself to get a glimpse of Michael's expression in the rear view mirror. He seems calm enough, eyes forward, focused on the road.

Faye, however, looks affronted. Her expression tells me that she is not going to put up with any of this. I already hear her voice in my mind, "I don't give a *shoe* about how foxy he looks. People just don't go around clowning me like that. Who does he think he is?"

I can see myself saying, "Zeus, maybe?" and earning a killer glare from Faye. Smiling at the thought, I look out the window. Faye catches my eye through the side mirror. Her expression is one of pure discontent, and I just shrug.

A couple songs later, Michael is parallel parking on the road behind Grandma's building, claiming the spot right in front of Faye's green Beetle.

How on Earth does he know where I live?

The music turns off with the engine, and Michael gets out of the car. I do the same. Faye stays inside, looking straight ahead, arms crossed against her chest. She's visibly steaming. He walks up to the passenger side and opens her door. I stay put and lean against the car, waiting for the nuclear explosion.

She shoots him daggers instead, asking, "What kind of game was that?"

"My apologies," he replies simply.

Who actually speaks like that? "My sincerest apologies, milady." *Is he mocking her or something?*

Faye doesn't notice his unusual reply and growls in indignation, "Why?"

I don't blame her. I'm almost as annoyed as she is, and I was only along for the ride. Still, not believing how much I misread Michael, I study him closely, waiting for the wave of lies that ought to follow. But it doesn't. He just looks down at his feet, considering what to say.

"Please accept my apology," he finally says meeting her eyes. "I should have let you drive."

Vague much?

He keeps eye contact the entire time, a half smile crossing his lips. In my mind hovers the thought, "clever, clever, boy." He's not lying or telling the truth. To be honest, I think he's a heck of an actor. I wonder if he's in the Drama Club. Probably not, I decide. He doesn't seem the type, but neither do I.

It's clear that his words mollify her a bit, and his dark blue killer gaze does the rest. Faye lets out an exasperated breath, "It's fine. I just don't know if the ringing in my ears will ever subside."

Faye gets to her feet, almost falling sideways in the process. Michael catches her instinctively. After all that happened, she must have forgotten about her broken heel. *I certainly did.* She swears under her breath and groans. Then, as if remembering Michael is supporting her, she looks up apologetically. He seems lost as to what he should do next, and Faye looks at her green bug parked a few steps away, "Just help me to my car. I have a pair of ballet flats that I use to drive."

He guides her, and I follow behind them. When she's sitting in the driver seat with the door opened, Michael asks, "I'll be off then, will you be alright?"

"Sure," Faye replies, putting on her left ballet flat.

"Okay, then. Thanks for everything," Michael waves goodbye, jingling the keys in his right hand.

"Welcome," Faye replies with a dismissive wave.

"Good night, Faye," he says, turning around and heading to his car. He glances at me as he passes by and nods, "Liz."

I just stare as he gets inside and drives away. I turn around to look at Faye who is wistfully watching her black Mustang disappear around the corner. The roar of the engine can be heard long after the car is out of sight.

"How on Earth did he know where I live?" I ask under my breath.

Faye doesn't seem to hear me as she blinks out of her

trance. Finally taking notice of me, she asks, "Do you want me to drop you in front of your building?"

"No need, I'll just cut through the garage. Thanks anyway."

"Are you sure?" She insists, biting her lower lip and looking torn.

"Sure. It's fine. Don't worry about it," I reassure her, turning on my heels.

I head toward the garage and hear the door of her car closing. Two beams of light project my shadow against the brick wall of the building. Then, the darkness of the starless evening falls over me as she drives away, slowly for once.

10

It's getting dark. A gust of chilly wind hits me, and I fight the urge to shiver. I'm still in my pleated skirt which doesn't help at all. I need to remember that I live up North now where night falls earlier and it's much colder than it is during the day.

As I walk down the dim alleyway, a black cat jumps out of a dumpster and scurries off in the opposite direction.

"Where is your red hood, Liz?" Nate breathes down my neck, making me jump almost as high as the black cat did.

I yelp, and my heart skips a beat, "You shouldn't sneak up on people like that."

"You're sort of jumpy, did you know that?"

"Even Dalai Lama would jump if you were to creep up on him like that," I point out.

"Sorry, I didn't mean to scare you," Nate apologizes.

"Yes, you did," I look up at his handsome face.

"Well, kinda," he admits, flashing me a playful smile. "Don't pretend you're not thrilled to see me."

I refuse to engage in this conversation and just go on walking. He keeps step with me, and I turn at the sidewalk toward my building, "Bye, Nate."

"Liz," he calls after me.

My name coming from his lips is so alluring that I can't help myself. I turn around to look at him. *What can I say? I'm a glutton for punishment.*

His smile widens, "Do you really need to go?"

I pull my phone out of my pocket and see how late it's getting.

"Or is it past your bedtime?"

Of course, he can't leave his mocking personality behind for longer than two seconds. I should seriously turn around and leave. *But who am I kidding?* That's the last thing I want to do. Maybe I wasn't hypnotized yesterday, maybe he cast a spell on me.

I take a step toward him, lift my chin and say, "No. It's just too cold to be hanging around outside."

"Not when one likes the cold weather. And if you think it's that cold, what are you doing out here?" Nate asks nonchalantly. "Where are you coming from?"

"Nowhere in particular, and how about you?" I reply, still not knowing why I'm lingering here.

"Ditto," Nate extends a gloved hand to me, inviting. "What would you say about coming with me? We can grab some dinner. My treat."

I study him carefully. My inner voice is screaming for me to get away and go upstairs, but part of me wants to take Nate's hand and dare to do something different for a change. Hesitantly, I put my hand in his, and he clasps it tight with his gloved fingers.

The streets are illuminated only by the post lights and sparsely lit apartment windows. Nate turns left at the corner and we follow the sidewalk for a couple of blocks. He's been holding my hand the entire time. No guy has ever held my hand before, and even with a layer of material separating our hands, it feels too personal somehow.

Nate's eyes are fixed straight ahead. There's a hint of amusement in his expression, but his thoughts seem to be elsewhere. We come to a stop at the corner and wait for the crosswalk light to change. He looks down just in time to catch me shamelessly looking at him, and his lips quirk up.

We walk two more blocks before I realize where he's taking me. I come to a halt, forcing Nate to stop as well. We're almost in front of The Scythe. There's a line of people snaked around the corner, waiting to get inside. It's a restaurant/bar with live music so loud you can hear it from the street. A place where college kids go, not high school kids like us.

Nate looks at me inquiringly, "Is there something wrong?"

"We can't get inside The Scythe. Well, I can't at least. I'm only sixteen," I reply in a rushed voice.

Nate just laughs that charming laugh of his, "Don't worry. You're with me."

Yeah, right.

Unless his dad owns the place, they're just gonna tell us to go home and come back in a few years.

As we approach the entrance, a hulking security guard is manning the front door. He seems to get bigger the closer we get to him. He's wearing all black and his stretched earlobes are adorned with two silver shower curtain rings. I slow my step, falling behind, and Nate gives me a tug. The guy just nods, and we walk straight past him. No questions asked.

"Who *are* you?" I ask over the loud electronic music.

"Nobody," Nate answers dismissively.

"Nobody? Yeah, right. As if a *nobody* would be able to sneak a minor into a renowned place like this one without ID," I'm almost shouting over the loud music, following him upstairs.

"It's only dinner," he gestures for me to sit at a booth wedged in a dark corner, but I just stare in amazement. The dark booth is lit by exotic candles shimmering blue. Laser lights draw geometric patterns, which project along the walls and ceiling. The whole place has a dark retro vibe. The décor is exotic but not as Gothic as I expected it to be, given its namesake. The people here vary from middle-aged business men to punk rock college kids. Still, I'm the only one in a pleated skirt, that's for sure.

I look up at Nate, "Are you sure it is okay to seat ourselves?"

Nate gives me a half smile and motions for me to go first. This time, I shrug and sit down. It is not like they will be letting me back in anytime soon.

What do I have to lose?

The high backs on the booth dampen the sound a bit. Either that, or I'm already starting to lose my hearing. Nate removes his gloves, placing them at the edge of the table. He looks up, catching me staring once again, and that amused knowing smile is back. I'm still perplexed about how he got us in here. But I doubt I'll get a straight answer, so why bother asking.

"I'm Nate Sinclair, just like I said before, and I am nobody," he finally says. My face is probably tattling on me, and my theory is confirmed when Nate supplies, "But my sister *is* somebody. Her name is Lill."

I'm astonished. *The supermodel? No way.* I look for similarities between them.

Nate notices my reaction and says in his usual mocking tone, "We don't look alike. We don't get along either. So, please spare me and refrain from asking for her autograph."

I know who she is, but I'm not a fan. I tuck my lower lip under my teeth to refrain from saying, "Look at me. Do I seem the fashion obsessed type to you?"

The waitress appears at our table asking, "What would you like to drink?"

Once again, Nate motions for me to go first and I say, "I'll have an ice water with lemon, please."

"I'll have the same, thank you."

She hands us two closed menus and walks away. I look from the menu on the table to Nate, "I believe she forgot to leave us flashlights."

Nate suppresses a chuckle by covering his mouth with his fist and then speaks, "Open it, and you'll see."

I do, and he's right. I can read it because the letters on the menu are freaking glowing. The menu is a computer tablet. My eyes are adjusted to the dark atmosphere, and it hurts just trying to read the stupid thing.

I look up at Nate and ask, putting a smile on my face, "Are we in the future or something?"

It seems that Nate didn't hear me over the loud music, and he doesn't look up from his phone.

I try again, louder this time, "Any suggestions?"

Nate's menu sits closed in front of him, which gives me the impression that he's a regular here. He looks up from his phone. Then, he speaks in a voice almost inaudible in this infernally loud place, "If you're feeling carnivorous, I would suggest the *Tenderloin a Chateaubriand.*"

I can't remember the last time I had red meat. I lived in Japan for five years mostly eating fish and vegetables. In Santa Monica, Suri lived with us, and since she's strictly vegan, we both ended up becoming herbivores by association since she did most of the cooking.

"Sounds great. Now we just need the waitress back," I shout to an amused Nate.

"I got it," Nate touches his *menu-tablet.*

Is he doing what I think he's doing? *Yep. We live in the future.*

The waitress slides by, dropping off two narrow glass bottles along with two thick frosted glasses with lemon slices wedged into their rims. I scan the room, feeling more than slightly uncomfortable. Then, I take a sip of my imported artesian water, probably shipped here from Norway, atop trillions of gallons of the cheap stuff.

Nate closes the menu and looks up, "Do you want something a little stronger to drink?"

I shake my head, "No. No. I don't drink. *Do you?*"

I stare at his eyes, expecting a lie. But he deviates from answering by asking me another question, "Aren't you tired of gazing into my eyes yet?"

I'm blushing without a doubt. I can feel the heat on my cheeks. So, I challenge, "Would it kill you to play nice for a change?"

"Not sure. I never put it to the test. Besides, you wouldn't like me if I were nice. You're surrounded by boring nice people every day," Nate replies confidently.

"Who says I like you?" I ask, lifting my chin, proud that my voice didn't tremble.

"Your eyes give you away," Nate flashes me a knowing smile.

Right on cue, our main course arrives. The waitress places our plates on the dark table, and I poke at the steak with my fork. A fount of red juice issues from the cylindrical cut of meat.

"Give it a try, trust me. You won't regret it," Nate says, taking a bite from his own.

I cut a tiny slice from the outer edge. Then, I quickly bite it off the end of my fork, before changing my mind. I chew slowly and stop, looking up at his expecting expression. Nate is right. This is freaking terrific. I start sawing off a larger bite this time.

"See, you can trust me," Nate takes a sip of his water.

I doubt that, but since I'm busy chewing, I just shrug.

"Tell me something, Liz. What's your obsession with eyes?" Nate asks, resting his silverware on his plate.

Not knowing what to make of his question, I go with a straight answer, "Suri always said the eyes are the window to the soul."

"A lot of people say that," Nate remarks. "The question is, does she believe it?"

His words catch me off guard. So here I am, waiting for him to ask me who Suri is, or make one of his sly remarks. But no, he challenges me with another question. Suri is highly superstitious and has many unconventional beliefs. I consider for a moment before answering, "She probably does."

"How about you?" Nate presses.

I involuntarily look straight into his eyes. He looks down, shaking his head in amusement, and jokes, "You won't find an answer there."

"Really?" I challenge. "So, why did you look away? More importantly, does that mean you believe it?"

He takes longer than I expect to look back at me. When he does, I answer his question, "I do."

"So do I," he says simply.

Nate suggests the crème brûlée, and I agree without hesitation. After dessert, unsurprisingly, he doesn't need to summon the waitress for the check. She approaches from thin air and hands his black credit card back, making me wonder, *when she got his card in the first place.* He puts it back into his wallet and stands up.

He waits patiently as I slide out of the booth. Then, he takes my hand, clasping it with his fingers. This contact, skin to skin, catches me off guard. Apparently, I'm not the only one. Nate tenses beside me and looks away. By his reaction, I expect him to let go of my hand, but he doesn't. He tightens his grip and begins to lead me downstairs. His hand feels strong against mine, and the tingling current runs right through me, making my heart thump wildly.

Downstairs, he stops at the door and takes hold of my arm gently. I pause to look at him. He takes off his coat and places it over my shoulders. Truly grateful, I slide my arms in and wrap it around my body, smiling at him. He places a hand on the small of my back and leads me out of The Scythe.

On our way home, Nate says apologetically, " If you're too cold, I can hail a cab. I didn't want to drive because it's impossible to park around here on a Friday night."

"I don't mind walking. I'm used to it. I don't drive."

Nate raises an eyebrow at me quizzically, "You're joking? You don't drink, don't cheat and don't drive. What *do* you do?"

I notice the usual teasing tone in his voice mixed with a hint of disbelief. How embarrassing and annoying, not him, me of course. I'm so dull. *What do I really do?* I do all sorts of stuff, just not lately. After a minute of thought, I reply, "I play video games, run in the park and apparently sneak into night clubs with boys I barely know."

"Exciting, isn't it? Taking risks, someone has to push you into new experiences," Nate's tone is animated.

"Is that what you're trying to do? Push me?" I inquire dubiously as we cross the intersection.

"I'm just pointing you in a new direction. Trying to make you choose dare instead of truth for once," Nate justifies slowly crossing the street beside me.

"Is that so?"

"Live life every single day, make it count. You have what? One hundred years, maybe less. What is the point of living in fear, without taking risks?" Nate challenges. "Someone once told me, 'Live every day like it's your last because one day you're going to be right.'"

"Interesting," I let out thoughtfully. "Tell me one thing, what were you really doing outside tonight?"

Nate looks at me, "I told you before. Enjoying the chilly evening. I don't spend my time looking out at the world from above."

"You'd rather stalk high school girls through the alleyway and then invite them to dinner," I deadpan.

"Exactly!" He laughs, stopping in front of my building, and I start to shrug out of his coat.

"I'll get it back from you next time," Nate holds up his hands to stop me.

I take it off and hand it to him anyway, "Thanks, it wouldn't be easy to explain where it came from to my grandparents."

"Fair enough," he folds the coat over his left arm. "See you around, Liz."

"Bye, Nate," I say, heading up the stairs.

11

Running in the park on a cold Saturday morning is invigorating. There are only a few passers by, and I'm able to set my own rhythm. So far, I've only come across a woman walking her tiny Shih Tzu, an elderly couple speed walking and a man jogging in the opposite direction who reminded me of my dad.

I kick it up a notch, despite the fact more and more people are showing up with every lap. The chilly breeze feels nice on my face. The wind whispers through the few curls around my ears that have escaped from my ponytail. My legs charge in approval, almost like I'm floating. I get a second wind and go for another lap.

Boston is sublime in September. The park is still green, but the signs of fall are starting to emerge. The leaves are fading into a yellowish orange and falling from their branches down to the walking path. Dry leaves crackle below me as my feet hit the ground. The weather is so perfect that I close my eyes for a split second, inhaling deeply. As I approach the gates, I slow to a walk and make my way home.

Back in the apartment, I immerse my entire body in the

bathtub until only my head floats above the water. My mind keeps visiting last night's dinner with Nate at The Scythe. The entire ordeal still seems odd to me, but like he said, thrilling nonetheless. My mind can't wrap around why someone like Nate Sinclair would waste a Friday night with someone like me. It's atypical. I dunk my head all the way down until I'm totally submerged. Then, I surface, wiping the soapy foam from my eyes with a towel.

Get him out of your head, Nate Sinclair runs in a different crowd from yours. A tiny unrealistic part of my brain argues, "Not quite, you're sitting at the cheerleaders' table lately." Except Nate doesn't hang out with the popular kids. He's never even at school for that matter. When he is, he hangs out with that girl *Spark*.

Pulling out the drain stopper, I step out of the bathtub and wrap myself in a towel. I wipe the fog from the mirror with my hand and take in my reflection. The long-legged girl staring back at me silently disagrees, "Nate was just being polite." There's a flaw in that line of thought, Nate isn't Ben. He doesn't fit the nice guy persona. He said himself, nice is boring. I frown at the mirror and leave the bathroom, switching off the light.

Peering into my closet, I wonder what I should wear to this lunch date with Faye and company. She made it clear, these were not the wannabes from the school lunch table. She said Kiara may come along, but she wasn't sure.

Deciding on a marshmallow white sweater, I put on a pair of light skinny jeans. My sweater has a crochet pattern, and I need to wear something underneath. I step out of the closet to grab my lacy white tank top from the corner couch and hold it against me to see if it matches.

"Your tan is to die for," Faye's voice scares me back into the closet.

"Faye, a little privacy. Gee!"

She cracks up, "Dude, don't be such a prude. There's nothing you have that I don't."

I put on my sweatshirt, buttoning it down as I step out of the closet, "You scared the life out of me."

"Sorry. Your grandma let me in," Faye says between laughs.

Slightly annoyed, I redirect the conversation, "Where are we going?"

"We're going for Japanese," Faye replies, sounding a little too enthusiastic.

"Japanese?" I ask, hoping she didn't choose the place on my account.

"Of course, I want to know how far off they are. No better way to tell than having a person who just spent the last three months eating the real thing," Faye explains her logic.

Half an hour later, we're entering a Japanese restaurant in downtown Boston. The interior is modern with dim lighting, and the sushi bar extends from wall to wall. A few guests are lined up on aluminum stools eating and watching Sushi chefs busily crafting rolls.

Faye scans the room, looking for her friends. Since I have know idea who we're meeting, I can't help. She nods toward the stairwell, "Let's check upstairs."

I follow her to the dining area. The table tops are made of tinted glass and seat six. There's the largest lucky bamboo arrangement I've ever seen placed in the corner. I keep glancing around, but I still don't spot any familiar faces.

"There they are," Faye points to a table on her left.

When we reach them, I recognize Ian. He looks remarkably different from how I remember him. Ian's light brown hair is long now, as long as Faye's. Both Greenwood siblings have the same thick, straight, shiny hair, the kind that seems to be immune to weather conditions. One can tell they are related, but they don't look much alike. Faye is drop-dead gorgeous. The type of girl, men of all ages turn to look at, regardless of what she's wearing. Ian is okay looking, right down the middle. His eyes are blue, he has a square jaw and a wide smile. He's also quite tall. One of the few guys I know that would still be taller than me if I decided to put on heels.

All in all, Ian is just an okay looking guy. But, for some reason that I can't fathom, girls go crazy over him. It must be his easygoing personality. Ian is as popular as his sister, also as genius as she is. Faye said he's starting his second year at Yale, studying to be a Biomedical Engineering Researcher. Just like my mom was.

Faye sits down beside Ian, and I crack a smile when the other boy sitting at the table stands up and pulls out the chair for me. I nod appreciatively at him as I sit down and he gives me a crooked smile. His looks are a little unusual. His skin is truly pale, paler than Ian, almost as pale as Faye. Except while EJ has a pinkish complexion, Faye is porcelain white. His hair is dirty blond, wavy and short. His eyes seem to be hazel, or maybe honey brown, I can't really tell because of the lighting. He's also very skinny, or maybe it's his choice of clothing that gives me that impression. He's wearing a v-neck shirt, jacket, and a pair of dark jeans that cling to his body.

"Liz, you remember Ian," Faye points at her brother. "Don't get thrown by his hair."

"Long time no see, O'Neill."

"Hey, Ian."

"The one pretending to be a gentleman is EJ, good luck finding out what his initials stand for," Faye eyeballs him.

"Faye-Faye, I'm nothing but a gentleman," EJ feigns hurt, placing a hand over his heart dramatically.

I laugh.

Faye rolls her eyes, "Yeah, yeah. Whatever you say EJ, whatever you say."

A third guy approaches the table speaking in a familiar rusty voice, "Hey, you guys made it. Finally!"

To which Faye responds defensively, "We had a hard time finding a parking spot."

I turn my head toward the voice and say in surprise,

"Dwayne?"

"What-the-?" He exclaims, looking at me. "Blondie?"

I know Dwayne from back in California. His older brother lives in Santa Monica, more precisely right next door to our house. He's always visiting his brother on holidays, summers and spring breaks. His brother is in his early thirties and is something of an athlete. He's into all kinds of sports, just like Dwayne. That's how he and I became friends and started hanging out a few years ago. Dwayne is all muscle. For as long as I've known him, he has kept his head shaved. He looks like one of those fighters from that UFC fighting show that Dad always watches. Except Dwayne's ears and face are not deformed like those guys. His face is cute and all in one piece. In my opinion though, Dwayne's smile is his prettiest feature, followed by his light brown eyes always gleaming with energy.

"How do you guys know each other?" Faye seems confused for a change, at the same time Ian asks, "How do you know O'Neill?"

"Back in Santa Monica, Blondie was the girl next door... *literally,*" Dwayne replies to both of them. He turns to Faye, "Where is Kiara?"

"She couldn't come," Faye says apologetically. "Family stuff."

"Then, I guess we're all here. I'm starving. Are you guys ready to order?" Ian asks, waving the waiter over before we have a chance to respond.

We all order different drinks, along with California rolls. And here I thought we came to this place to test the authenticity of its cuisine.

"Are you really gonna leave us short handed, Brit?" Dwayne asks, the moment the waiter is out of earshot.

"I can't," EJ sounds clearly resigned.

"Dude, you're such a pansy," Ian contributes to EJ's discomfort.

"I can't believe you're gonna chicken out," Dwayne

pumps in.

"I am not chickening out," EJ contests. "I can't. My folks are coming all the way from London. I can't just say 'sorry Mum, Dad, but I had plans. See you next time.'"

"Excuses," Dwayne scoffs.

"What are we talking about now?" Faye asks, unaccustomed to being left out.

"We're going rock climbing tomorrow and EJ is a chicken. Do you wanna take his place, little sis?" Ian asks, redirecting.

"Sure. I'd love to go hang from the side of a mountain. But, I just got my nails done," Faye replies sarcastically.

"Listen mate, I'm not a–" EJ pauses, considering, and then continues, "You know what? Just forget it, keep running your mouth."

I can sympathize with EJ. I felt the same way a lot this week at the lunch table. Faye's friends love to single me out.

"Blondie here can climb. This chick doesn't mess around," Dwayne suggests to my dismay.

I've been rock climbing before, but it's been a while. "I don't know," I reply hesitantly, not sure if I'm up to it. In the back of my mind, Nate's words come back to taunt me, "Choose dare for a change."

But I don't have a chance to decide, EJ does it for me, "Brilliant! It's settled then."

"Sweet!" Dwayne says to no one in particular.

"Grandma would never let me go. She didn't even let me join the track team, and the only risk there is scraping my knee," I point out.

"No worries there," Faye scoffs. "She adores Ian."

I shudder at the very thought of rock climbing tomorrow. It's been so long, and I'm really not up for it. EJ mistakes my nervous trembling for cold and takes off his jacket, placing it around my shoulders. His kind gesture brings Nate back to my thoughts, until the smell of cigarettes hits me, that is. I fight the urge to wrinkle my nose and manage to

smile instead, "Thank you, EJ."
  "You're welcome, love," Comes his gallant reply.
  Oh Gee!
  The waiter finally comes back, bringing our Sushi rolls.
But now, my appetite has been replaced by anxiety.

12

I wake up before dawn. My heart is pounding fervidly in anticipation. I've been tossing all night, anxious, lost in a dreamless sleep. Sitting up in my bed, I switch the LED reading light on. The alarm clock shows it's five in the morning.

Ten hours have past, and I still can't believe Grandma agreed with this rock climbing thing. She was all, "Of course, Ian. She'd like that. Wouldn't you, Eliza?"

I just don't get it. It's Grandma. *My grandma*, the one who said I couldn't join the track team for no plausible reason. Now, hanging with two guys in the literal sense is okay. Not a problem at all. Does she think I'll be some damsel in distress, and either Ian or Dwayne will be my knight in shining armor?

Gee, I hope not.

Deciding to get ready, I unset my alarm clock and stand up. No reason to sit around. I change into my cargo pants, basic navy top, and a charcoal jacket. With more than a half hour to spare, I begin braiding my hair in a high double French ponytail to keep my mind off things.

Just as I finish, Ian texts me: *We'll be there in five.*

I grab my sunglasses, strap my backpack on and go downstairs. As soon as I step outside, Dwayne is parking his white Jeep in front of the building.

"That's what I call perfect timing," Ian says lamely.

"Dude, She's not Faye. She knows what five minutes means," Dwayne remarks and says to me, "You're gonna dig this place, Blondie. The rocks we hit before don't even compare to this, the view is amazing."

As we get onto the highway, I wonder, "What am I getting myself into?" The drive is long and we stop for breakfast halfway. Pancakes by unanimous decision. Then, we're off again. By the time we get there, my battery is almost dead. I have only ten percent to spare. My fault, I played *Prim* on my phone the entire trip while the boys talked about last night's UFC fight, basketball and protein supplements. I leave my phone under the seat in Dwayne's Jeep and climb out of the back.

Before we head down the trail, we stop to rent some climbing equipment. Well, I do. Dwayne and Ian brought their own stuff. After a short hike, we reach the bottom of the climb. It's a route of three slabs. The anchors and bolts look kinda new to me which is a relief.

The preparations begin, we start racking up, strapping our harnesses on and making sure everything is tight. Then, we're off, with Ian in the lead. I follow next, and Dwayne comes last. It's a short slab, clearly a warm up. Before we can even feel it, we're at the first ledge. I stretch my neck from side to side and work my shoulders.

"Long climb ahead," Ian whispers to the rocky view. As if the range may change position or fall over at the sound of his voice.

The rocky climb towers over as if daring us to go on. Behind us, the meadows and trails are still hidden among a wall of trees. Dwayne reaches our first stop a few seconds after we do. He runs his hands over his shaved head, grinning wide. We stand in silence for a while, recovering and drinking water. The morning is dry, and the sun seems to be smiling at us.

After a few minutes break, Dwayne brings his wrist close to his face and reads the time, "It's a quarter to eleven. We better get a move on, if we want to finish this route."

"No arguing with that. Do you want to take the lead?" Ian puts his backpack on.

"Cool. Let's do it," Dwayne says rolling the rope on his arm.

Ian just nods and turns to me, "Are you good to keep going?"

"Sure," I shove my water bottle into my backpack's side pocket and check my climbing gear.

Dwayne starts his climb with confidence and skill. It amazes me how much better he's gotten since the last time we climbed together. Beside me, Ian also stands admiring Dwayne's progress before following after him, and we begin our ascent in a faster pace than before.

Ian is keeping it slow on my account, so I don't get too far behind. I get the impression that he's afraid I may slip any second. I'm not sure if I'm touched by his gesture or annoyed. Before I can make up my mind, Ian shouts, "Slow down, man! If we're trying to reach the top, that's not a good pace."

I look up and Dwayne is farther up than I expected him to be. Ian is right, he's going a little too fast. Among the three of us, Ian is, hands down, the most experienced climber. On the ride here Ian said he's been rock climbing for more than five years. Which makes him the expert since both Dwayne and I started a couple years ago.

Looking up again, I gasp. Dwayne heard Ian, *alright*. He's stopped, with his arms hanging free, only his feet and the rope are supporting his weight. I desperately shout, "Don't do that!"

"What? This?" Dwayne jokes locking his fingers behind his neck. He looks down at me, seeing what must be pure fear plastered on my face. He gets a grip on a rock and turns back to me, apologizing, "Sorry, Blondie. That was reckless."

I let out a sigh of relief and overhear Ian mumbling under his breath, "You think?"

We continue ascending. Dwayne has slowed down, and I push myself to keep up with them. By the time we reach the second peak, I'm almost breathless, sweat drops forming on my neckline.

From up here, we can see beyond the trees, the meadows, and the trails. The view is mind-blowing, and the quietness of it all is pure bliss. Dwayne and Ian sit down, and I do the same, taking in Mother Nature. All I can hear are the sounds of birds interlaced with our own ragged breathing. The midday sun hits us merciless, brighter under the dissolving clouds.

Dwayne lays back on his elbows and looks up at the sky. He inhales deeply, grinning, "I'll definitely miss this weather, the breeze, and all the climbing this fall."

"Nah. If I know you well enough, which I certainly do, by the end of winter I'll get you hooked on hockey," Ian says all chill as usual before taking a sip from his water bottle.

"Good luck with that," Dwayne laughs. "I can't picture myself sliding around on a sheet of ice."

Ian turns to me, winks and then adds, "O'Neill here is the one who will need luck."

"Why is that?" I ask him puzzled.

"You'll be going to school every single day with my sis. You'll need luck, patience, and anything else you can get to pull that off. Faye is a force to be reckoned with," Ian explains, sounding dead serious.

I can't help myself. I laugh, and so does Dwayne. He's right. I can't imagine anyone going against Faye, but she's awesome too and has been nothing but kind to me so far.

"Faye is cool," I manage to say once I stop laughing.

"I don't know. How do you feel about human pyramids

and pompoms? I don't give it a week before she puts you on the squad," Ian feigns concern.

The mental image makes me flinch, and he smiles, "That's what I thought. You'll need more than luck," he pauses and redoes his low ponytail. "O'Neill, you'll need a miracle." Wide eyed, I stare at him through my sunglasses. He just pats my head as if I were a little child. Then, he stands up and stretches his arms, ending the subject.

The image of me shouting, "Be aggressive, be, be aggressive," turns my stomach, and I try shaking my head to erase it. Ian smiles and offers a hand to me. I take it, and he pulls me to my feet. Dwayne also stands up, and as if reading my mind he says in a cracking falsetto, "Go team!"

I just glare at him, but he doesn't notice. So, I turn and admire the amazing scene one last time before facing our final climb. Dwayne gives a low whistle beside me catching my attention, and I whirl around.

"Okay, O'Neill. Here is your chance to back out. We can always take the trail down," Ian points to the dirt path on his right.

I visualize the climb, it's studded with rusty looking bolts. I get the impression that most people opt for the walking trail when they reach this point. I'm confident that I can do it. Sure, it will be tough, but I can manage. Once my mind is made, I glance from Ian to Dwayne and ask, "Dwayne?"

"Ian, it's too late to punk out, bro. EJ would give us an earful if he heard we made it all the way up here just to back out at the last minute," Dwayne replies with a bright grin, not taking his eyes from the challenge ahead of him even for a second.

"Who cares what EJ thinks. He didn't even show up," Ian points out, emptying his water bottle in one last gulp and placing it in his backpack. He waits and waits. When we both remain quiet, Ian lets out a long breath, "Alright, let's climb then."

Dwayne doesn't need to be told twice, he starts rolling his rope around his arm right away. I double check my harness, and Ian tests the carabiners. He checks mine next and turns to Dwayne who's checking his own gear. As if sensing Ian's gaze, Dwayne looks up and gives his "OK."

Dwayne is the first to start climbing. He looks back at us on his way up and says playfully, "I'll meet you guys at the top."

Ian smiles broadly and looks at me one more time, sounding doubtful, "Ready, O'Neill?"

I hesitate a split second before nodding. Ian waits until I finish tightening my gloves and then takes off climbing. I follow suit, constantly checking my ropes as I ascend. We move up in a slow steady climb, but I get the impression that Dwayne is way ahead of us already without even looking up.

Drops of sweat are dripping from my forehead, and I start to feel uncomfortable as we climb higher and higher. Not even the steady breeze makes me feel any better. We have a good way to go, but it seems like I've already climbed twice the distance since our last stop.

A wave of fatigue hits me forcefully, and my brain screams, *"Slow down!"* That's when Ian digs in, making a thud sound, and I look up at the same time Dwayne looks down. Ian makes a time-out gesture with his hands. Dwayne nods, adjusting his position. I keep climbing until I close the distance between Ian and I. Then, I stop as well.

Ian looks down at me. His expression is on edge, almost as if he sensed my discomfort moments ago. A double wrinkle forms between his eyebrows as if he were trying to make sense of something.

"I thought you were closer. I heard you asking us to slow down so clearly," Ian finally says, sounding puzzled.

"Huh?" I ask stupidly, trying to remember if I even said it out loud in the first place. I must have, or the altitude is making Ian hear things.

His furrow deepens. I inhale and exhale deeply, taking

advantage of our little break to recover, "I'm alright now. We can keep going."

He doesn't seem convinced, and I give him a reassuring smile. It works, his face lightens up a little. Ian signals Dwayne to go on, and we're off again. We're less than a quarter from the top of the slab when a jolt of energy shudders my entire body, sending me into high alert. A distant crackling sound comes from above, and my eyes turn immediately to Dwayne. As he moves his left foot from the rock face, I hear the cracking sound again. That's when I see the stone under his right hand shift ever so slightly.

It's a loose rock. Dwayne has a grip on a loose rock, and he doesn't realize it. My first instinct is to scream "watch out." But, it's too late. He's already prepping to anchor to the next bolt. If the rock gives way, he's going to fall.

My inner pulse shifts me into autopilot. I pull test my rope, and swing my body to the right, lowering myself down about three feet. Then, I grip a recess on my right and adjust myself.

"O'Neill, what are you doing? Are you out of your–" Ian's sentence is cut short as Dwayne cries out.

A shower of rocks fall from above as Dwayne loses his grip and tumbles down the rock face. Bracing myself, I throw my right arm out a split second before he passes by. Reaching for whatever I can grasp, his shirt, harness, rope, anything.

Dwayne desperately claws at the wall, and I manage to grab his wrist as he plummets past me. He takes hold of my upper arm, with one hand at first, then both, clamping on for dear life. I'm not prepared for the forceful impact from the momentum. My shoulder pops, and I yelp in pain. Dwayne struggles to regain his leverage, causing me to lose my footing.

A terrible pain jolts my ankle as my left foot locks into a fissure while my right foot slips from the rock face, dropping us both a short distance. I'm almost upside down when I manage to unlock my left foot with another yelp, and we are both sliding down against the rocky surface for several seconds. My rope finally catches us, and we're suspended about ten feet from the ground.

"HANG ON!" Ian shouts from above us. "I'M COMING DOWN!"

Ian starts repelling toward us, but it's too late. The rope comes undone, and we're free falling. I close my eyes, and Dwayne is screaming below me. Dwayne hits the ground, and I land right on top of him. It knocks the wind out of us both, and he gasps loudly, followed by a groan of pain.

My entire body is in agony. I'm beat, scratched, and broken. Summoning what's left of my strength, I roll off Dwayne and open my eyes. Ian is making his way down in double-time, and I'm about to ask Dwayne if he is alright, when he speaks in a raspy voice, "You just saved my life, Blondie." He's facing up, eyes still closed as he whispers, "Thank you."

"Did I?"

Ian reaches the ground with a thud. Drops of water sprinkle on my face, and Dwayne swears loudly. When I open my eyes, Ian is standing up above us, the sunlight behind him, "Stay still. Try not to move." Ignoring Ian's words, Dwayne sits up and kneels over me. Ian kneels on my other side, asking, "What hurts?"

"Everything," I reply with a wincing laugh and elaborate, "My ankle, mostly. My shoulder feels wrong."

Dwayne leans over and rolls up my cargo pants to examine my ankle. He curses under his breath and stands up, inhaling deeply.

"Is it that bad?" I ask, not wanting to look.

"Let's just say you won't be joining the cheer squad," Dwayne half jokes.

I laugh despite myself, lifting my arms to cover my face from the blinding sun, and wince in pain.

"Should we call for help?" Dwayne suggests, all torn up.

Ian has his phone in hand and shakes his head, "No signal out here."

"Stay with her, and I'll go get help," Dwayne insists.

Ian shakes his head again, "It'll be faster to just carry her down the trail."

"Right. I'll do it," Dwayne volunteers, kneeling beside me again.

"No. I got her. Plus, I'm the only one here who is in one piece," Ian bends down to pick me up. He places an arm under my knees, the other around my back, and lifts me from the ground. "Hold on to me," Ian says kindly when I flinch in pain. I do as he says, tightening my good arm around his neck.

Dwayne places a backpack on each shoulder, and Ian carries me in his arms. We make our way down the trail, none of us speaking. More than once, I catch Ian studying my face, unspoken questions swirling in his aqua blue eyes. He never puts a voice behind them. Nonetheless, I know what he's thinking. Many times, I've silently asked myself similar questions, but I still have no answers. So I close my eyes and focus on the sound of our foot steps and labored breathing. Proof that we're still alive.

13

When we arrive at Boston Medical Center, my grandparents are waiting for us impatiently. The paper work is complete, but to Grandma's distress we have to wait along with all the other sick and injured people populating the waiting room. All the while, the paramedics in their dark blue jumpsuits push around rolling gurneys.

Everything looks very sterile. The flooring is light beige, and the walls are plain white. The unmistakable hospital smell fills my nostrils. It's a mixture of chemicals, latex and cafeteria food. Just like the last hospital I was in, the offensive odor overloads the place.

Eventually, a nurse in teal scrubs leads us to the examining room where I change into a blue paper gown. She drapes me with a cute lead apron in order to x-ray my leg. Once that's done, I'm wheeled to another room where I'm subjected to further examination.

After what seems like forever, Dr. Huston finally comes back to read the verdict: a dislocated shoulder, a fractured ankle and minor abrasions. Then, he gets on with resetting my shoulder. No pain killers, or elephant tranquilizers for that matter, could ease the excruciating pain of this procedure. A pain that's here to stay, apparently. And my cast? *Pink.* Grandma helped me pick the color.

Dr. Huston lays out his recommendations, "You should stay on bed rest until Thursday's appointment. Avoid putting weight on your ankle. It might heal by itself, and there will be no need for an operation."

Grandma thanks him, and we're cleared to leave. Ian pushes my wheelchair out to Grandpa's SUV, and Dwayne leaves with his parents. He doesn't just look tough. He *is* tough. Aside from a few minor scratches Dwayne leaves the accident unscathed while I look like someone who tried to bathe a bobcat.

By the time we get home, the pain is almost unbearable, and I'm nauseous. Faye is nowhere to be found, and Ian volunteers to carry me inside, scooping me into his arms like I weigh nothing. He lowers me gently into my bed and adjusts the throw pillows under me. Ian is trying his best to get me settled, and here I am feeling unsettled.

Good thing Dad is on the opposite side of the world. There's a thirteen hour time difference and Grandma is too polite to wake someone in the middle of the night.

And yet, she does just that. Call my Dad, I mean. Now, he's freaking out, wanting to book the first flight from Japan, "Are you Okay? What happened? Mom said you fell rock climbing." Dad's voice is agitated and sounds far away as if coming from the end of a tunnel.

"Dad, relax. I'm alright. By the way, I didn't fall. Dwayne did," I try to calm him down and recount everything that happened for the third time in the past hour.

"Oh, wow. Is he okay?" Dad asks in a tormented voice.

"He's fine, I'm fine. Grandma should have waited to call you until it's actually morning over there."

"She did the right thing. Eliza, I'm your father, waking up in the middle of the night and worrying about you is in the job description," he explains in a commanding voice.

"Is David still on the phone?" Grandma asks, entering my

bedroom.

"Grandma is back," I inform Dad.

"Let me talk to her. Take care, kiddo. Do what the doctor says."

"Will do, I love you, Dad."

"I love you most," he replies, and I hand the phone to Grandma.

She heads out, speaking, "David, yes. Dr. Huston said..."

Ian slides my computer chair closer to my bed and sits down, "We need to talk." I meet his gaze and wait for him to elaborate. He does, "What you did up there breaks the laws of physics. You weigh nothing," Ian pauses, fixing his gaze on me, "Dwayne is almost two hundred pounds. He's solid muscle, built like a brick. The way you caught him, it's physically impossible. It's almost as if you knew that you wouldn't get hurt."

"If you haven't noticed, I did get hurt. Hence the pink cast," I nod toward my busted ankle.

He steers the conversation to a completely out of the blue topic, "What do you know about your mother?"

"*My mom?*"

Amanda Layne O'Neill, *aka Mom*, was a medical researcher renowned by her peers. A scientist who died too young. To be honest, that's about all I know. I'm told that I have her hair and her eyes. But, that's where our resemblances end. I look a lot like the women on my father's side of the family. Plus, all the memories I have from her are the ones captured in photos. The worst part is that I don't feel all that bad about not knowing her. Then, I feel terrible for not feeling bad. It's all very confusing. I know I should miss her at least, and then again maybe I shouldn't.

How can you miss someone you have no memory of?

I was four years old when my mother died. From what I've heard I was with her at the time, and my own survival was mere luck. We lived here back then, but like I said, I was too young to recall. It's like my memories come to life afterward. I remember flying with Dad to a really crowded place where the words coming from everyone's lips didn't make any sense to me. I have memories of meeting my dad's partner, Daisuke, his wife and his two kids for the first time. We would play together without understanding a word. I remember sitting in a big chair beside Dad while he typed away for hours on his computer.

As I grew up, I was home schooled by an American tutor and also learned that what sounded nonsensical at first were real words with real meaning. Then, Suri came along, and we slowly became a family. We couldn't be any different from one another, but we have one thing in common: we care for each other. Not long after Dad's corporation launched, the three of us moved back to the US where Dad opened his office in Santa Monica. Which is where we lived up until the end of my sophomore year.

Focusing back on Ian, I say, "I don't know that much. I know she was a scientist, a medical researcher, the kind of stuff you're into."

"Dr. Amanda O'Neill made groundbreaking discoveries in the study of DNA."

Here is the thing, when people start talking about my mother and how great she was. I feel pretty uncomfortable, like fate was tricked and took her instead of me. I'll never live up to her standard. I don't understand genetics. I'll never find the cure for anything.

"What does my mom have to do with any of this?" I decide to cut to the chase.

"Everything," Ian replies promptly.

"How so?" I'm confused. Mom died twelve years ago.

"Don't you see? You might be the consummation of her research," Ian explains, his aqua blue eyes shining in excitement.

"*Whoa*, did you take some of my pain medicine?" I ask, unnerved by his remark. I'm starting to see that the Greenwoods siblings are more alike than I thought. *What exactly is he trying to say?*

"Let me prove it to you," Ian urges. I open my mouth to contest, but he presses on before I can speak, "It'll only be between the two of us. I can do it myself. All I'm asking is a sample of your DNA. I admit it's a long shot. But what if your mother did alter your DNA configuration? What if your enhanced strength, speed and reflexes are just a side-effect?"

Faye's voice comes from the hall, "Thanks, Mr. O'Neill. I know my way to Liz's bedroom." The clip-clop sound of her heels against the hardwood floor precedes her arrival.

Hearing his sister's voice, Ian adds, "You don't need to give me an answer this exact instant, but think about it."

I blink up at him, considering his words. Just then, Faye walks in with Nate in tow. My eyes widen, and a thousand questions cross my mind, ranging from, "What on Earth is Nate doing here?" to "How awful do I look right now?" I'm in pj's, wearing a pink cast and unsightly scrapes adorn my bare arms.

Faye comes to a halt a few steps from my bed. She glares at Ian as if he's to blame for my present condition.

Ian ignores her and stands up, looking at me, "Let me know what you decide." When he passes by Faye, he adds, "Five minutes. She needs to rest. I'll be in the living room." He leaves without even acknowledging Nate's presence.

I, however, can't take my eyes off Nate. *Why is he here?* He barely knows me. Nate is probably just another guy lovesick over Faye.

"Really? What a pitiful excuse for a big brother," Faye complains, breaking my train of thought. She's just glaring at the empty doorway. Turning back to me, she asks, "What happened?" My gaze involuntarily returns to Nate. Faye rolls her eyes, "This goofball was downstairs when I arrived. I told him that you had an accident, and he just tagged along uninvited–"

Nate cuts in, "If it weren't for me, you wouldn't be seeing her until tomorrow. Mrs. O'Neill needed some persuasion." He walks toward me and sits at the chair Ian was in.

"Maybe she didn't want me to come in because *you* were with me," Faye contests, sitting on the edge of my bed. "Kiara told me you saved Dwayne's life. What really happened?"

I close my eyes, taking in a deep breath as a wave of nausea sweeps over me, followed by a bout of vertigo. The pain just doesn't go away. I wish I had the strength to clear things up with Faye, but I just can't. I'm exhausted. My entire body aches, and the pills I took back at the clinic are useless. All they did is make me puke.

"Liz, you're killing me here," Faye presses, oblivious to my discomfort.

"Faye, can't you see she's in pain?" Nate reprehends in a low soft voice.

"Are your meds wearing off?" Faye stands up. "Is it time for another dose? Maybe I should get your grandma."

I open my eyes and shake my head no, wincing from the movement.

Faye apologizes, "I'm sorry. We'll let you rest. I'll stop by tomorrow after school." She turns to Nate and orders, "Let's go."

"Go on. I'll be a minute," Nate replies, not moving.

Faye looks at me, inquiringly, ready to grab him by his white shirt collar if I say so.

"It's okay," I reply in a small tired voice.

Faye hesitates at the door, her lips pressed into a thin line. Then, she leaves, wishing me to get well soon.

As the sound of her heels on the tile floor fades down the hall, I turn to Nate, "Thanks for checking on me…" I trail off, in too much pain to continue.

Nate leans his chin on his clasped hands. His expression is neither one of concern or pity. He looks intrigued, but also pained. Meeting my eyes, he asks, "How bad is it? Did…" Nate trails off when I close my eyes, fighting another wave of vertigo. He inquires, "Do you want me to leave?"

"No," I reply a little too fast, and my eyes blink open. I swallow and elaborate to an amused looking Nate, "I mean, unless you need to. Your company is sort of calming."

"Really?" Nate asks, studying me closely. "That's new. Is there anything you need? Some water maybe?"

"I'm all set. Thanks," I reply in a soft voice, starting to believe that he must be a hallucination. Probably another side-effect of the pain killers. *What else could explain having Nate right here, watching over me?*

A hint of a smile crosses Nate's lips. He reaches for my hand and touches it gently, "You know... I told you to live a little, not get yourself killed."

Despite the pain, I laugh and then wince at the agony caused by the slightest of movement.

"Try to sleep, it will help," Nate starts making small circles with his thumb on the top of my hand, slowly and very gently. "I'll stay with you until they kick me out."

I don't know how much time passes as I watch his blue eyes, feeling the warm touch of his hand. But eventually my eyelids start to feel heavy, and I fall asleep.

When I wake up, Nate is gone and Dominika is arranging my breakfast atop my night stand. French toast, a glass of water with no ice and yet another orange bottle of pills with my name on it. I eat the food, but refuse to take the tablets. Now, she's on my case about it. I explain that I have a high pain threshold, and narcotics do nothing to help in the healing process. But she won't have any of that. Only when Grandma walks in and says it's okay, she stops trying to shove them down my throat.

It's not that I fear taking medication or anything. Pharmacophobia has nothing to do with it, as Faye suggested. It's just that, except for the unpleasant side-effects, I can't really feel any difference. The pain is still there. Maybe my body is immune to medicine.

Grandma checks on me several times throughout the day.

She comes up with excuses like going over my school schedule and telling me about this new oil painting class she's taking. Grandpa stops by, and we talk about the time he broke his leg. Also, about how back then a hamburger was a dime and people would go see a movie for a quarter. They *so* need to bring that back.

I officially become Dominika's first priority. She stops by my room every five seconds. She brings me food, brings me drinks, brings me snacks, brings me more drinks, checks if I'm feverish, adjusts the pillows under my leg...

When she reappears at my door for the fiftieth time today, I sigh. But to my relief, Faye is with her this time. She's bearing my homework and seems happy to bring me up to speed with all the gossip at school.

"Cheer practice begins tomorrow and Kiara is in one of her down phases. She said that she'll be watching from the sidelines this year. So, it's going to be up to me and Ms. Johnson to come up with a routine," Faye lets out a loud sigh and says sarcastically, "I just can't wait."

"What's up with Kiara?" I ask, adjusting myself among a pile of throw pillows.

"Dwayne," Faye replies bluntly.

I just look back at her, frowning.

She shakes her head, "Sometimes I forget you weren't here last year. Dwayne goes to Blake's High School now, but up till his junior year he went to Saint Pete's. He also played for the SPHS basketball team. That's how Kiara and Dwayne started dating. They've been off and on since then."

"Why the ups and downs? Dwayne is cool, and so is she."

"Dwayne is immature and reckless. It drives Kiara crazy. She asks him to keep his feet on the ground, he doesn't, and they fight," Faye explains. "This time is a little more serious, as you know."

I nod, wince, and the conversation goes on. She mentions the hypnosis paper that she had to present alone. Apparently,

Nate was MIA again. After half an hour, Faye looks bored. I'm sure she won't be able to handle being trapped inside this room for much longer. I'm about to tell her that she can leave when Dwayne and EJ walk in.

"Hi, love," EJ walks up to me, leans down and kisses my cheek. I don't know what's worse, the smell of cigarettes or his cologne. The kissing my cheek part... I grew up in Japan, and we barely shake hands there. All this touchy chivalry EJ lays on makes me pretty uncomfortable.

"Feeling better today, Blondie?" Dwayne asks, sitting by my computer.

"Well, better than yesterday. Worse than tomorrow, I hope," I reply honestly.

Faye takes the cue to leave, "I'll stop by again tomorrow, girly."

"Bye, Faye-Faye," EJ says, which must be some kind of inside joke.

"Time to return to your queen bee affairs, Your Highness," Dwayne teases with a whimsical bow.

Faye sticks her tongue out at them, waves at me, turns on her heels and sees herself out. Dwayne and EJ crack up. I fight the urge to smack them with a pillow for making me laugh. Well aware that if I do, it'll freaking hurt. The three of us talk for a while. Then, Wellington and Mattie show up, and suddenly my bedroom reaches maximum occupancy. All the company takes my mind off the pain. Until Grandma comes around, that is. She asks politely for them to come back tomorrow, saying that I need my rest and that I've had enough excitement for one day. And with that, I prepare myself for the dullest evening ever. Grandma could get a part time job with the TSA. Nobody's getting past her.

I try killing some time by doing my school assignments. But there's just so much homework one can endure when your *everything* hurts. I put my homework aside, turn the TV on and start watching a movie that I've seen a hundred times before, bored as one can be.

"May I come in?" Nate asks, leaning against the door frame.

"*Nate?*" I voice in complete astonishment, muting the TV. "Sure. Yes. Please, come on in."

He suppresses a smile on my account and walks up to me. Stopping just out of arms reach, "How was your day?"

I completely miss his question, spacing out. Once again, I can't believe he's here. It's just not the kind of thing that happens to me. I've always had male friends because I'm into video games and sports. Cute guys like him, however, don't give girls like me a second look, let alone a second visit.

Today he's wearing dark washout jeans, a slim fitting button down shirt and a lightweight cobalt jacket. A few strands of his dark blond hair fall over his blue eyes as he looks down at me, still waiting for an answer to a question I missed.

"I'm sorry. I was distracted," I apologize, feeling idiotic. "What was that again?"

"Your day?" Nate asks, sitting down in my computer chair across from me. "How was it?"

"Oh, boring, but not as bad as I thought it would be," I reply honestly and ask, "And yours?"

"Just as uninspiring," he replies, handing me his phone. I blink up at him, confused, and he asks, "Is this the game? The one you mentioned the other day."

I hold his phone and immediately see that he's got the right game, smiling to myself. I can't believe he still remembers and cares enough to download it. Then again, I shouldn't read much into it because I'd do the same thing if someone compared me to a game character, or anyone for that matter. I touch the screen and the intro sequence flashes on. I watch in its entirety and look up at him, smiling widely.

Nate breaks into my thoughts, "So? Is that the one?"

"That's him."

"Do you want to play?"

"I'll try. But the controls must be different."

"Go for it," he says, standing up. He slides the chair closer, sits down and leans over.

Nate is so close that it makes me nervous. His familiar alluring scent envelopes me. My hands start to tremble, and I hope he doesn't notice. I tap the screen to skip the cut scene that has been repeating over and over again. Then, I tap through the menus until the game begins.

"Zombie at six o'clock. Behind you! *¡Detrás de tí, imbécil!*" Nate mimics the zombies on the tiny screen, once he starts to catch on. I'm eaten several times, but I finish a few stages before the battery dies. "Do you still think I look like him?" He asks when I hand his phone back.

"What do you think?" I redirect his question.

"He kind of does. But I'd rather think that he's the one that looks like me," he mocks.

I don't have a chance to either agree or disagree because Grandma walks in, seeming surprised by Nate's presence. She says politely, but sternly, "I forgot you were here. Sorry, dear, but she needs to rest. Doctor's orders. Stop by again tomorrow."

"I will. Have a good evening," Nate replies politely. He stands up and slides the chair back into place. "Take care, Liz. See you around," he looks at me one last time before following Grandma out of my room.

After he leaves, all that occupies my mind is how many hours I have until my appointment on Thursday afternoon. It's a total of sixty-two hours, fifty minutes and twenty-three seconds, twenty-two, twenty-one, twenty...

14

When you're home from school, every day seems exactly like the one before. That's how my entire week has gone. It's been a game of patience being baby-sat like an infant by my grandparents and Dominika. My friends have been coming by less and less. It's like they've agreed to stagger their visits, alternating days. Except for Nate, that is. He comes by every day. He even signed my cast along with everybody else.

"*Nice catch, Blondie,*" from Dwayne.

Kiara wrote, "*Get well soon,*" with an emoticon smiley face.

Wellington drew a bass clef and a few notes, and Mattie wrote, "*Break a leg!*"

EJ wrote his initials in big block letters.

Ian signed, "*Get better,*" along with his name underlined twice.

Faye wrote her name in swirly letters and spent the next hour drawing flowers, butterflies and hearts all over the place.

Nate signed his name, "*Nate.*" Just like that. *Nate.* No block letters, no drawings, no nothing. Just *Nate.*

Fortunately today, just as I hoped, I'm losing the pink nightmare. Dr. Huston is impressed, "You did great, Miss O'Neill. Generally, adults follow the recovery instructions but don't heal very fast, while kids heal quickly but don't sit still long enough to recover."

"Well, that's because they don't have Mrs. Melody O'Neill as a Grandma," I point out.

He laughs at my weak attempt at a joke and writes me a note excusing me from PE for the entire month. I'm also supposed to avoid walking too much for another week. Maybe now Faye will quit nagging me about joining the cheerleader squad. *Bummer!*

Cast free, Grandpa drives us home, and we walk in the door just in time for dinner. After stuffing myself with Fettuccine Carbonara, I head to my room just as I'm told and finish the last three questions of my Calc homework. Then, I gather my things and put my notebook inside my backpack. I set my alarm for seven a.m., change into my cupcake pajamas and brush my teeth.

Computer tablet in hand, I head outside through the dining room onto the penthouse balcony. The evening is chilly. A light breeze blows ever so slightly as I slide the doors closed behind me. The balcony area is uncovered with a straight shot view of downtown Boston. It's about as wide as the living room. There's a fountain in the middle that they turn off in the fall and back on again in the spring. Two comfortable padded all-weather seats face outward, and two little trees in each corner add some color to the place.

The evening lights are enchanting, or maybe it's just a side-effect of being locked indoors for almost a week. To the left, a hundred foot fall separates our balcony from the adjacent building. The space between the two balconies is pretty narrow, and nobody seems to live next door. If someone does, they never step outside.

Our balcony is situated about half a floor up from the roof access area, and I sit on the partition wall, poking at my tablet screen. I log on to Skype, but Dad is still offline. It's seven forty-five p.m. Which means eight forty-five a.m. for him, and he's late.

A noise near the roof entrance below catches my attention, and I look in the direction of the sound. Two glimmering eyes the size of pearls are looking back at me. *A rat maybe?* I tilt my head to one side, and lean forward for a better look, but the image on my tablet changes and Suri's crooked smile appears on the screen.

I smile back at her, "Hi Suri, how are you?"

"I'm fine, running late as always. Your dad will be here in a minute. I heard about your little incident. All better now?" Suri asks kindly.

"I'm alright. Today, Dr. Huston gave me clearance to walk and even go back to school. How about you? I miss you guys. Dad mentioned the two of you would be traveling this weekend."

"I miss you too, sweetie," Suri's voice is kind and modulated as usual. "We're leaving this afternoon, and I can't wait. The weekend can't get here fast enough. All and all, everything is good, busy like always. You know how things are over here. Sometimes, I think time goes by faster on this side of the world. Oh, here he is. Nice talking to you. Can't wait to see you on Thanksgiving. Bye now."

"Byeee!"

"Hey, kiddo. I heard you're back on your feet. That's good news," Dad pops up on the screen.

"That's right, all better. Well, almost. I have one last checkup, a week from today. I'm also excused from PE and can't run for a couple weeks. But other than that, I'm okay," I reply happily.

"Good. Try to stay out of the hospital from now on. The reason you're in Boston is to finish high school, not to sit around in bed," he half jokes.

"I'll do my best. Mattie and Faye have been dropping off my homework assignments. So, I should be all caught up."

Dad says something in reply, but his words are lost on me. Because at that moment, a girl appears through the roof access door, letting it slam behind her. She's dressed in dark skinny jeans and a really tight black hoodie, her dark shoulder length hair blowing around in the wind. She pauses for an instant and lights a cigarette. Then, she makes her way to the guard rail, taking a long drag. When the girl reaches the edge, she flicks her cigarette down without bothering to extinguish it. She lifts one leg over the rail and then the other, climbing onto the outside ledge of the roof.

Dad is still speaking, but I stopped listening to him a while ago. Never taking my eyes from the girl, I whisper, "Dad, I gotta go. I'll email you later, okay?"

I power down my tablet and place it on the ground. Switching both legs to the roof's side, I carefully drop down and land on my good foot. I shift my weight and quietly walk toward her.

A cold breeze blows a few curls into my face, and I take deliberate steps forward toward the rail and gently speak trying not to startle her, "Are you okay?"

She turns to me, "Where the hell did you come from?"

I just stare back at her, afraid to speak again.

Her eyes narrow, "Never mind. Forget I asked, just get out of my face."

"Okay, as you wish," I pretend to leave, but the moment she looks away, I climb onto the outside of the rail and stand tall beside her.

Carefully, keeping hold of the balcony rail behind my back, I take a few steps sideways until I'm at arms length from her. *Hey, Dr. Huston didn't say anything about not climbing around on the side of a building.*

There's a moment of hesitation on my part, a furious inner struggle. Without looking down, I breathe deeply and whisper, "Pretty view, huh?"

Glaring at me, she asks skeptically, "You're still here? Why don't you get lost?"

I continue, "You're not the only one who appreciates heights." The girl stares at me in disbelief. She blinks a couple times, like by doing so I may simply disappear. I speak again, trying to sound matter-of-fact, "You know the chances of dying from jumping off a building are not as high as you might think."

She closes her eyes in disdain and puffs some air through her mouth in irritation.

I just keep talking, "You might become a vegetable or a paraplegic. Can you imagine lying in bed all day, depending on others to take care of you?" The girl turns her head and glares at me. Not once have I taken my eyes from hers. I go on, "I'm sure you must have a good reasons to be on this side of the rail. You're also very brave. I'm certainly not that brave." Her scowl intensifies, but I just keep talking, rushing the words out, "I usually ask myself, 'what's the worst that can happen?' If I can live with it, I go for it. If not, I try something else. I most certainly cannot handle being a vegetable right now."

She gives me a twisted smile and speaks unexpectedly, "Well, I have a good reason now. Getting you out of my sight. Go play the hero with someone else."

The girl turns her head and looks down once again. Making me wish I had called the police before rushing into this. What do I do if this girl actually decides to jump? No, no, no. I have no time for that now, and I need to think fast. Should I try reverse psychology? Better not risk it. Or should I? "So it's settled, we jump. On the count of three?"

She looks back at me as if I've lost my mind. I don't blame her. I'm on the ledge of a building in cupcake pajamas and kitty cat slippers. I try smiling at her, but it's obviously a mistake.

She shrugs, "Whatever," and with that, she lets loose her grip and falls forward. With one arm locked on to the rail, I instantly reach out and grab the girl by her hoodie, before her feet leave the ledge. She squirms in my grip, yelling,

"Let me go, you freak! You're choking me."

"Seriously, a second ago you wanted to die, and now you want to breathe? Stop struggling, you're gonna get us both killed," I shout back, wondering how in the world I'll get this crazy chick back up by myself.

We're so dead.

She ignores everything I say and keeps pulling away from me. I tighten my grip on her hoodie and deepen my lock on the balcony rail. The situation gives me a flashback from last Sunday's rock climbing ordeal, and it makes me wonder if I'll be so lucky to survive this time. *Maybe I cheated fate last week, and now my number is up.* Come to think of it, my number might have been up since Mom died.

All of a sudden, the girl stops flailing, and I see what she is up to immediately. She's trying to unzip her jacket. My benign temperament reaches its limit, and I snap. My voice sounds foreign to my own ears as I say with spellbinding authority, "Stop it now and look at me!"

Astonishingly, she stops moving and meets my gaze with a perplexed, almost dazed, expression on her face. She's staring straight into my eyes, like she can't do anything else.

What on Earth did I do? No time to think now.

A pink glow appears out of the darkness, glimmering brightly. My grip on the rail loosens, and I start to blackout. Just as I'm falling unconscious, my eyes catch a wave of silvery blond hair in a blast of wind, and a familiar pair of pale blue eyes gaze straight into mine. Then, I'm out.

I open my eyes to a wide empty hall. *Another hospital?* There's a stretcher left abandoned up ahead. The doors are open, but I don't hear the sound of ill patients, nurses, doctors, or the rhythmic beep of vital sign monitors. That's when I realize I'm sitting in a wheelchair, wearing a white hospital gown. No scratches or bruises remain on my arms, and I'm barefoot. This place seems sanitary enough, but I still choose to wheel myself toward the light, rather than stand up and walk on the cold floor.

"Come to me, Liz," an alluring low voice orders.

A long pause. All is silent.

"Liz, what's taking you so long? Just follow the light," the voice insists.

More silence.

"Focus, Liz. Follow the light," the soft spoken voice repeats.

I pause at an open door and peek inside. There are two empty operating tables, some wires, tubes, and an infusion pump. The waste disposal is opened and filled with syringe wrappers and bundles of gauze. I turn away and start to wheel myself toward the light again. Stopping once after passing a few doors, beside a tipped over oxygen tank, I hesitate. *Maybe I shouldn't follow the golden light.*

"You're not dead, Liz. Just follow the light. Hurry, we don't have much time," the familiar voice speaks inside my head.

"Raph?" I ask aloud, and the sound of my voice echoes down the empty hall.

"It's me. Come along."

I wheel myself faster toward the brilliant glow and into an empty waiting room. A place I've been before, the reception of Boston Medical Center. Raph walks in wearing a spotless white coat with the stethoscope hanging around his neck, carrying a chart in his hand.

"Dear Lord, I'm dead," I voice, getting goosebumps all over my arms.

"No, Liz," Raph smiles. "For the third time, you're not dead. Listen to your heart beat, you're alive. What gives you the impression that you're dead? You never thought about death before."

"I don't know. I can't remember. Maybe it's this place. Why are we in a hospital?"

"You tell me. You brought me here," he replies, taking a seat across from me.

"Does that mean that I'm the one who chooses the

place?" I'm intrigued by his words.

"Sometimes," Raph replies, leaning back in the chair. "Other times it's me. It usually happens when I can't reach you as fast as I need."

"Hmm!" I wonder aloud. *Why here?* Especially considering all the beautiful places I've been.

"I'm wondering the same thing," he points out, reading my mind.

I gasp, "You can read my mind."

"I wouldn't call it mind reading since it's not something that I can control. I would say it's telepathy. You can block your thoughts if you want. I believe sometimes you do," Raph explains, and I'm too astonished to speak. He goes on, "But as I said before, we don't have much time. So, tell me: what have you done?"

I blink in confusion, "What did I do?"

"I have no idea, Liz. But you sure did something. I could sense the disturbance all the way down in South America."

"Disturbance..." My voice trails off in sudden realization. *"Wait! What?* You were really there, then? Does that mean you *are* real, you're not just in my dreams?"

"Yes. I am real, but I'm also in your dreams," Raph clarifies without thoroughly explaining. But, what else is new?

"You know what, Raph? Now you're just trying to confuse me again. You can't be both."

"Why not? You are," he says matter-of-factly.

"That's different."

"How so?" He asks, crossing his legs and leaning back, now genuinely looking like a doctor.

"I don't know, it just is, okay?" I utter foolishly, not knowing what else to say.

"Okay. But Liz, try to stay with me, enough sidetracking. You still haven't told me what you did since we spoke on the beach," Raph inquires, resting his hands on his lap with his fingers clasp together.

"That was almost seven days ago," I point out. "Approximately one hundred sixty-eight hours, give or take a few. Do you really want me to tell you everything I did? You just said we don't have much time."

"You have a point," Raph agrees. "Tell me what you would consider out of the ordinary."

Gee, let me see! I saved my friend from falling to his death on Sunday, I think before I can stop myself. Then, I remember he can read my thoughts, listen to, or whatever he calls his "mind reading" thing. I shouldn't give him answers. He sure never gives me any. He does give me riddles. He gives me plenty of those.

A suppressed laughter tears me from my thoughts, "What else, Liz? Tell me what you did an hour or so ago?"

I rack my brain, but everything seems fuzzy. I can't really remember. Raph stands up all of a sudden, startling me. He kneels right in front of my chair and takes hold of my hands. As if prompted by his touch, the memory of what took place on the roof flashes back in my mind all at once. My chest tightens, and I think I'm going to hyperventilate.

"Calm down, Liz. Breathe. Keep in mind that you're dreaming. Inhale and exhale, " Raph attempts to calm me.

It helps a little, and I blurt out, "There was a girl, crazy hair, too much eye makeup. I think she was trying to kill herself. She was going to jump. No, she did jump, and I let her go. I think I blacked out. Oh no, I killed her. Raph, I let her die. She's dead, and it's my fault. I should have called 911. I wasn't even supposed to be out there on the balcony. That means I died too. *I'm dead.* That's why you brought my memory back, isn't it? I remember the light, the silvery blond hair, the pale blue eyes, right before I blacked out. I'm dead, so, so dead–"

"Liz, for the love of all that's holy," Raph cuts in. "You're not dead."

"But–"

"No buts," he interrupts. "Our time is almost up."

"Okay, okay, what's the riddle this time?"

He lets out a quiet choked laugh, "No, Liz. No riddles this time. I just want you to be careful. Take it easy. Stay indoors as much as you can. Wear your earphones when you go out, listen to some music."

"Huh?"

"And Liz, one more thing. Promise me. If you ever cross that girl's path again, don't talk to her, just walk the other way. Forget it ever happened."

"I promise," I give him my word. Even though I'm more confused than ever and have no idea what he's talking about. I don't even own an iPod anymore. It's not the first time Raph asked me to promise him something. After all these years, he's someone I know I can trust, so if he tells me to promise, I'll do it. No questions asked.

"Oh Liz, if only you would listen to everything else I tell you," Raph remarks in a wistful voice.

Now, I'm annoyed, and I say so, "If I understood your parables, I sincerely would follow your advice. I'm not good with riddles. By the time I understand what they mean, I'm in a recovery room."

"And not even then..." Raph trails off in the same nostalgic tone. He straightens up as if suddenly aware of something and gets to his feet.

"What is it?" I ask, still puzzled and now also intrigued.

"He's here, I have to go," Raph sounds distant.

"Who?" I take hold of his arm, knowing that he's about to vanish.

Raph looks down at me, and a kind smile lightens his face, "The messenger," and with that, he disappears into thin air, leaving me alone in this dream with yet another riddle: *who on Earth is the messenger?*

15

I jolt awake. A distorted heavy metal guitar, and a screaming voice juxtaposed with a vibrating buzz loops continuously.

Is that my phone?

I sit up and rub the sleep out of my eyes. My TV is on, a rerun of MythBusters is playing on the screen. *Odd.* I don't remember leaving it on. I don't remember going to bed in the first place. I rummage around the bed for the phone. Instead I find the remote and turn the TV off.

Where is it?

I dig through the sheets looking for the phone. When did I ever download that ringtone? Maybe it's under the bed. Not under, beside. Nestled between the throw pillows on the floor. I dive toward it and I'm baffled to see Ian's grinning mug staring back at me on the display. At least that explains the unexpected rock and roll. He probably downloaded the song himself when he punched in his phone number that day at the Japanese restaurant.

"You owe me two bucks," I answer the phone with a tired voice. To my bewilderment the voice coming from the other side of the line is not Ian's, but his sister's.

"When it's Ian calling you pick up," Faye teases. "And

here I thought you were into Nate Sinclair. I killed my battery trying to reach you all morning. But no, O'Neill can't bother to answer my calls. And Ian owes you two bucks for what exactly?"

"Faye?" I ask drowsily, still confused.

"Who else?" Faye laughs. "You thought it was my hotshot brother, didn't you? Sorry to disappoint you, my dearest injured friend. But it's just me," she pauses for emphasis, sighs and continues, "I know exactly what you're thinking..."

Does she? Good, because I don't.

I muffle a yawn and force myself to focus on what she's going on about, "Ian doesn't have classes on Friday this semester. He stopped by the school today to take me out for lunch. He's cool that way sometimes, but only sometimes. Most of the time Ian is a pain in the neck. By the way, he wants to talk to you, something about DNA. Which is pretty weird if you ask me. Didn't you say you're terrible in Bio? What's up with that?"

"*Ian? What?*" I ask, muffling yet another yawn. "*DNA?*" I usually have a hard time comprehending what Faye is saying fully conscious, when I'm half asleep it's hopeless.

"Yes Ian, last I checked he's the only brother I've got. Thank goodness, heaven knows one is more than enough," Faye says playfully. "What's wrong with you?"

"I just woke up, that's what's wrong. The ringtone woke me."

"No kidding. Are you a bear now? You go into hibernation mode when it gets cold," Faye jokes. "You sounded alright yesterday. Then, you weren't downstairs this morning, and when I called the house your grandma said you took some pain medicine last night..."

Horror seizes me. I'm suddenly awake. I spot the medicine bottle and the half empty glass of water on my night stand. My head is spinning. Holding the phone against my shoulder, I pick up the bottle and twist off the cap. I dump the tablets on my comforter and mentally count them out. *Nine.* There are nine tablets. I pour them back in the bottle. So, I'm not going crazy. I didn't take any pain medicine. That's not why I overslept.

"Liz?" Faye calls out.

"Hey. I'm alright. Just a little confused, that's all," I reply and stand up. Taking a seat at the desk, I power on my laptop.

"Confused? About the oversleeping part?" Faye asks with a chuckle.

"I'm not sure, about last night, I mean. I don't know. It's a blur," I pause in mid-sentence when I open a reply email from Dad.

You scared me out there for a minute. I'm glad it was just a rat. Later, kiddo. Good night and don't let the bed bugs bite.

Love you most,
– Dad

A rat? What rat? I immediately check my sent messages box. Nothing. Now Faye is going on about prescription pain killers. A weird nagging feeling settles in, and I tune her out, searching for Ken on my laptop screen. He's among the green icons and I click on his username.

LIZARD96: Ken?

KOKEI999: Yo!

I can always rely on Ken for tech support. He not only works for Dad, but he's also a distant relative to Suri, which technically makes him family. When I got my first computer, I'd always ask Dad for help. One day he was too busy with something else and asked Ken to debug my laptop. He did it faster than I thought possible without bothering to explain what he had done. From that day on, any troubles I had with software, viruses, lost files, and so on, Ken was my guy. He could figure out anything, and that was putting it mildly. I always thought Ken was wise beyond his years. Then again, he couldn't be that young since he'd been with Dad's company for almost a decade. He hasn't changed at all, though. He appears to be in his mid-twenties. But I bet he's in his thirties and just looks young for his age.

LIZARD96: How do you explain a reply from an email you never sent?

KOKEI999: I can't, but I can check.

LIZARD96: Thanks.

While I wait for his reply, I tune back to Faye, "I'll probably stop by around fiveish so we can work on the Calc assignment together."

Only Faye can make a leap from talking about prescription pain killers to school assignments in less than a minute.

"I heard Nate Sinclair visits you every day. What's that about?" Faye asks suddenly and then she elaborates, "I know he lives next door, but still–"

"Wait?" I cut her off. "What do you mean he lives next door?"

"You didn't know?" She asks, sounding genuinely surprised. "We walk by it every day," Faye pauses and then continues in an annoyed voice, "You're trying to sidetrack me. Let me tell you in advance it never works. Back to Nate, don't even try to deny it."

I sit up straight as Ken's chat box pops up, blinking on my screen.

KOKEI999: Sorry, no can do. Not from here at least.

LIZARD96: If you had my laptop, could you?

KOKEI999: Probably.

LIZARD96: When can I bring it to you?

KOKEI999: LOL... last I heard you were on house arrest. Mandatory downtime, for believing that you're Peter Pan.

LIZARD96: Sort of, I have clearance to go back to school, so... and, Peter Pan?

KOKEI999: Believing that you can fly, like Peter Pan. Too old of a joke, I see. Never mind, I'm at a coffee shop nearby. I'll be by in five. How does that sound?

LIZARD96: Sounds terrific, thanks Ken.

KOKEI999: TTYL.

"Liz?" Faye calls out. "Spill it! What's up with you and Nate?"

"There's really nothing to say. He stops by, helps with my Chem homework, and we engage in casual conversation until Grandma comes around to kick him out."

"Nate Sinclair helps you with homework?" Faye scoffs from the other side of the line. "You're being too dense, even for your standards."

"What's that supposed to mean?"

"It means you're totally oblivious about boys' interest in you. EJ, my brother," Faye explains. "It's like you don't even care. I was beginning to believe that you play for the other team. I even considered setting you up with Alexis. Until last Sunday, that is. The way you looked at Nate when we walked in..." She trails off. "I don't know how I missed it before."

I don't even know where to begin. EJ is the kind of guy who throws around his gallant chivalry hoping to get lucky. Ian only seems to be interested in my DNA. But, setting me up with Alexis takes the cake. Is Faye out of her mind? Even if I played for the other team, "fish-girl?" Really?

Gee! Maybe we'll share a sardine for breakfast.

Unaware of my astonishment, Faye goes on, "Nate stopping by every day is a big sign that he digs you, add personal tutoring and it's official. The guy is head over heels."

"Yeah, right."

"Nate Sinclair doesn't do homework," Faye lets out, sounding exasperated just by having to explain it. "He isn't the type to do anything out of pity either. You're always trying to see the best in everyone. Nate Sinclair doesn't do nice. He's the male version of me. As polite as necessary, selfish as can be. He has his own agenda."

"Faye, come on."

She continues, "My point is you have the hots for the guy, and he obviously has the hots for you. Just let your hair down, wear a tighter shirt, and some lipstick. Then, enjoy your one-on-one time—"

I cut in, completely appalled, "Faye? Nooo."

"You know what? If you don't get it, you'll never get it, just forget it. So, anyways..."

I tune her out as Ken walks in, covering the phone's mic, "Hey, you got here fast."

"I was right around the corner," Ken looks around for my laptop, "Where is your baby? I don't have much time before Mrs. O'Neill decides to call the cops on me."

I laugh, knowing full well where Grandma is coming from. Ken is in a pair of low waist ripped designer jeans, a white long sleeve shirt that hugs his slim body, tracing the contours of every muscle in his arms, abs and chest. His signature beat up black leather jacket flung over one arm, and he wears several spiky looking silver rings on his long fingers. A couple of thick aged-silver chains hang from his neck, and on the shorter one hangs a black Kanji pendant. He told me once it means, "crazy people."

As usual he has his orange tinted computer eye-wear on, framing his Asian features and making him resemble a dragonfly. His shoulder length black hair is still wet which makes him look even more imposing. Until he smiles back at me, that is.

I point, "Over there."

He throws his jacket on the desk and sits at the chair. As he touches the track pad, the screen comes to life. I lean in for a better look. He cracks his knuckles, his fingers hovering over the keyboard. Then, he looks over his shoulder at me, "Really? You're going to breathe down my neck the whole time."

"Can I watch?" I ask in a small pleading voice.

He lets out a resigned breath, "Knock yourself out." Turning back to the laptop, he starts typing. In a split second, the computer restarts and a black screen comes up. The text appears and disappears too fast to read. The only sound in the room is the clicking of Ken's fast fingers on the keys. Without taking his eyes from the screen or stopping even for a second, Ken says, "When I asked you not to breathe down my neck, I was kidding. Please breathe. I can't do CPR."

I let out a breath that I didn't realize I was holding.

Ken scoffs and mumbles something incoherent. The monitor blinks back to life, and Ken turns around, "And I'm done."

"What did you find out?" I ask anxiously.

"All I can tell is that the email was sent from your laptop around midnight. It was probably left behind in your outbox and auto-sent. I wouldn't worry about it," Ken explains, sounding like he truly means it.

"Thanks anyway," I reply quietly, unable to hide the disappointment in my voice, and then add meaningfully, "Especially for coming all the way out here. I appreciate it."

He stands up and grabs his jacket, "Don't mention it." He looks down at my kitty cat slippers, and a few wrinkles appear across his forehead, "I need to teach you about e-security one of these days."

"How about you teach me some stealth ninja martial arts instead?" I ask hopefully, already knowing the answer.

His expression goes sober, but his words are not what I expected, "Get your dad to agree and I'll do it."

"*Really?*"

Ken throws his arms into the air and lets them fall to his sides, "Why not? As long as Dave agrees. But for now, I'm out. Can you hear it? The sirens are getting closer." Ken points a finger at me and says in a serious commanding tone, "You behave and stay out of trouble. But, just in case, try to remember that I'm only a few minutes away. Just text, email, call, smoke signal, or a thought, whatever. Just reach me."

I nod and wave goodbye, watching him leave the room. My attention goes back to Faye who is saying, "...and obviously Nate Sinclair. Then, I'm going to the Red Sox game with Henry Cavill."

Whoa! What?

"What was that about Nate?" I ask in confusion. And isn't Henry Cavill the guy from *Immortals*?

"I should have mentioned Nate's name before. Girly, you got it bad. Apparently, not even smashing face with Logan Lerman and skinny dipping with Matt Lanter were enough to catch your attention, but *Nate Sinclair* did the trick. Good to know, when you space out on me, I'll just drop his name and have your attention back," Faye says smugly.

"*Logan Lanter who?*" I have no idea who she's talking about now.

"Dude! You're unbelievable. You're the only girl on the planet who doesn't know who those two are," Faye replies, laughing again.

I'm about to say that I usually don't watch the kid's channel, but stick with my trusty excuse, "Japan, remember?" I unquestionably need a new one.

"Never mind that," Faye exclaims from the other side of the line. "Seriously girl, you really need to stop tuning me out. If you would pay attention, you just might learn a thing or two." Before I have time to say anything else, Faye adds, "Ian is back. See you at five." And then, she just hangs up.

Sigh.

Putting my phone down, I rack my brain to remember the names she mentioned. Then, I do an internet search. When images of them finally pop up on the screen, I do recognize both of the guys. They're pretty cute. A dumb thought crosses my mind, "Nate Sinclair is cuter."

Darn it. Faye is right. I've got it bad.

I'm about to do a search for the name "Nate Sinclair" when I hear his voice, "May I come in?"

I mash the backspace key and lower my laptop lid discreetly. As I turn around on my seat to face him, I nudge the TV remote off the edge of the desk and it hits the floor before I can catch it. The back cover and the batteries fan out across the room. Just as I get to my feet, Nate is collecting the pieces and reassembling it.

He hands it to me, "Here."

I take it, accidentally touching his hand and feeling my cheeks blush. Embarrassed I let go of the controller, and he puts it on my night stand. *Thanks a lot, Faye. I'll never be able to act normal around this guy ever again.*

I swallow and look up at Nate. He's absolutely breathtaking as usual. He's dressed very casual for a change, wearing jeans and a white jacket. His expression is searching, pure bewilderment as if I'm a crossword puzzle he is determined to solve. When I don't say a thing and just stare dumbly at him, he breaks the awkward silence, "You seem better."

"Yes. I'm better, much better," I reply, sitting on the edge of my bed.

"No pink cast," Nate remarks gesturing to my leg.

I want to curl up and die right now. Not only am I acting weird, I'm still in my cupcake print pj's with kitty cat slippers.

He catches on to my embarrassment and adds, "You heal pretty fast."

"Good riddance," I breathe out, happy that our conversation is getting back to its usual routine. "I don't know how much longer I could stand that thing. It was just a fracture, my leg wasn't snapped in two or anything."

Nate seems to consider it. He slides the computer chair closer and sits down, studying me.

"What are you thinking?" I ask intrigued by his unusual behavior. I hope Faye didn't say anything to him.

"I don't think you want to know," he says, sounding more serious than the situation implies.

Oh, great! She did talk to him. I swear I'll never forgive her if she said anything. I hesitate for half a second before blurting out, "Please."

He leans closer, resting his elbows on his knees, and then inquires almost in a whisper, "Can I ask you something?"

I'm sure if I try to utter anything this exact instant, I'll stammer, or even worse choke. So, I nod my head in reply.

He meets my eyes and asks, "Why do you do it?"

His question is vague, but at the same time it couldn't be more clear. Somehow, I know exactly what he means by that. I could say truthful words while telling a lie, avoid replying altogether, or maybe throw him another question. Something in his eyes, the expecting way he's looking at me, makes me go with honesty, "It's just something I do."

He waits for me to elaborate, and I whisper more to myself than to him, "The intention of the seed,"

"Come again," he asks, leaning even closer.

I swallow hard, "A long time ago, I read somewhere once, something like: if there were no fruit, we'd still have the beauty of the flowers. If there were no flowers, we'd still have the shade beneath the leaves. If there were no leaves, there's still the effort of the stem. If there were no stem, we revere the intention of the seed."

A distant look seems to take over his face, so I go on, "I can't change the world, but I can be a seed and make my life worthy in someway."

Now, I've done it. He lowers his eyes, looking down at the floor. A half second later, he confirms my assumption by getting to his feet and making his way out. At the door, he pauses and drums his fingers on the frame. Then, without looking back, he says, "I've got to go."

"I'll walk you," I offer hopefully.

"No, Liz. I'll see myself out," and so he does.

Frustrated, I stand up and head for the kitchen. My unexpected presence scares the life out of Dominika, who happens to be preparing a tray of food for me. I insist on eating at the kitchen counter, she insists I eat in my room. In the end, she wins and I head back to my cell, carrying a sandwich in one hand and a grape juice box in the other.

16

The sunlight is streaming in through my opened window and casting a shadow on my periodic table printout. I'm sitting in bed, trying to get a grasp on this lab report that's due tomorrow. But I just can't seem to focus at the moment. Nate hasn't come around this weekend, not since he walked out on me Friday. I'm completely lost without him, Nate makes this stuff seem so easy. Even knowing that I shouldn't care, part of me misses him so badly that it hurts, almost as much as my past injuries. I just wish I could take back whatever it was that I said to scare him off. But then again, I shouldn't have to change who I am to win some guy's approval.

I didn't even dare to mention it to Faye, knowing exactly what she would tell me, "Way to go, Liz! Brilliant move, play the deep chick type with the hot guy."

I try to focus on my Chem lab, but it's just no use. Annoyed with myself, I stand up and walk to the window. The park seems to be chanting, "Come outside, come outside." It's beautiful out there, sunny with a soft cold breeze. But, I'm incarcerated in my bedroom. I close the window and return to my lab report. When an hour has passed and I've barely finished the first question, I give in. I pile up my papers, stand and go looking for Grandma. It's time to put my foot down. She can't keep me locked inside forever.

My moment of courage falters when I find her outside on the balcony, sitting in a chair. I blink a couple times in confusion. *So help me, she's reading!* Not that Grandma never reads. She does, all the time. But she's reading an e-book on a mini tablet. I notice for the first time the reading glasses, she usually doesn't wear them. At least, I've never seen her wearing them before now.

I must have spaced out because I hear Grandma's voice, "Eliza, you're doing it again. Don't just stand there with your mouth open. You're going to catch a fly."

I press my lips together but my eyes don't seem to obey my brain's commands, they keep staring at the device in Grandma's hands.

"Eliza, now you're gawking," Grandma reprehends.

"Oh, sorry," I apologize.

"I guess you want something, what is it?" Grandma asks, seeming mollified by my apology.

So I dare to say, "Okay. I should avoid walking, but a few blocks won't kill me, will it? I mean, it's not like I'll be spending a full afternoon on my feet, I'm just asking to spend a few hours outside in the park to breathe some fresh air. Maybe then, I can finish this Chemistry lab report."

"Why don't you join me out here on the balcony? There's plenty of fresh air and sunlight. You can have a seat right next to me," Grandma suggests.

"Oh, never mind," I say, making an about-face.

"Eliza," Grandma calls me as I'm about to cross the threshold.

I turn hesitantly, hoping she won't insist for me to stay on the balcony with her another afternoon. It's impossible to get anything done with her making comments about what she's reading every other minute.

"You can go, my dear. Run along, but be back before sunset and don't wander around too much. Just sit at a park bench or under a tree, okay?"

I throw my arms around her and kiss her cheek. I'm elated, "Thanks, Grandma."

"Now, there," Grandma pats me on the back. "You better not go skipping around, take it easy on that ankle."

I spin around, "Don't worry, I'll be back before the sun goes down."

"Bring a snack," Grandma calls from outside.

"Will do. Later, Grandma," I reply and rush to grab my lab manual and notebook. I'm out the door before she has a chance to change her mind.

Outside, the day is as refreshing as I hoped. It's amazing how much the scenery can change in the space of a week. The color is slowly fading from the trees and everyone is starting to dress in thicker layers. The sun is breaching through the leaves and shimmering the letters on my lab manual instructions, as I highlight answers sitting crossed legged under a tree. The fall wind comforts me, and a fat squirrel hovers around, begging for a pecan.

"Did you finish that one already?" I ask the cute animal and rest the highlighter on the book, fishing for another one in the pack of mixed nuts. "Come get it, don't be afraid. You did it just a minute ago," I hold the nut by its edge as the little creature hesitantly makes its approach. Once it has the pecan in its tiny hands, it flees a few feet away to eat it, watching me the entire time. I laugh at the fluffy thing, take hold of the highlighter and go back to reading.

"You talk with animals, how adorable," Nate's mocking voice is unmistakable.

I look up from my book, and there he is as gorgeous as ever, the sunlight cascading over his dark blond hair like a halo.

"Don't you know that it's impolite to eavesdrop?" I ask, feigning disapproval.

"My bad," he apologizes, lifting both hands as if giving up a right. "I didn't mean to intrude on your little man-versus-wild scene," Nate pauses, clicks his tongue, and goes on mocking, "It was just so cute."

"Charming," I exclaim, feeling provoked.

He flashes a smile brighter than his usual, suggesting his mission is accomplished. Then, he glances down at the book sitting on my lap.

"It's Chemistry. I have a report that's due tomorrow morning," I explain, noticing his eyes locked on my lab manual.

"So you *do* have a character flaw. You leave things for the last minute. I would have never guessed," he feigns surprise.

"Well, if you stick around long enough you'll see I have tons."

"I might take you up on that," he sits down beside me.

Faye would slap my forehead for me if she were here. Then, she would roll her eyes for good measure, as if to say, "You're hopeless." But seriously, how can I make sense of her advice? It's worse than Raph's. "Be flirty, but not slutty. Direct, but not easy. Be friendly, but not clingy. Be mysterious, but not..."

Yeah, I get it, find an equilibrium. But where is the middle ground?

Her answer: *You'll know.*

So, maybe I do deserve a smack on the forehead or a roll of the eyes because I have no idea. I'm hopeless.

As his eyes meet mine, I'm absolutely sure that I'm goggling at him. But I just can't stop myself from doing so. His presence is compelling enough to silence a room, stop traffic, or maybe even cause a cease fire without any effort on his part. When he lays on the charm like he's doing now, it's hard to keep in mind that he bailed out on me.

"I've been thinking about our talk the other day and I owe you an apology," he says as if sensing my conflicted feelings. "I'm not very good with apologies. So, here goes nothing," he pauses, running his fingers through his messy hair, making it worse, and somehow looking even cuter. He lets out a breath, as if what he's about to say might kill him, "Forgive me, Liz. The way I left on Friday, it was just plain inconsiderate."

Little does he know his apology was accepted before he even uttered it. I try mastering Faye's flirty confidence, "Maybe."

"Maybe means yes," he replies, back to his usual self. He shifts my lab manual slightly to read it. "So, what's up with the procrastination?"

I laugh despite myself, "The procrastination, as you put it, is nothing but a bad habit, putting off stuff I dislike."

"Like Chemistry?" He inquires, still sounding bemused.

"And Biology," I add for no reason.

"And I heard a rumor you're planning to get into the medical field? How are you gonna pull that off?"

I look up at him, wanting to let out, "Does everybody in this town make it their main priority to know everything about the new girl, Eliza O'Neill?" But, of course I don't. Assertiveness is among one of the many qualities I lack.

I just shrug, "Well, I'm still undecided."

"What makes you consider this field?" He asks engrossed.

I think about it, giving a short pause and really considering his words, "I like helping people. It would be nice to be qualified to do so."

Nate looks me straight-on, "I'm afraid I'll have to offer you some tough love then. If you really want to head in this direction, you'll not only need to finish those questions, you'll also need to grasp the concepts. Since I'm partly to blame, allow me to help you. Or would that count as cheating?"

"No. I don't think so. I'm supposed to have a lab partner–"

"Okay, then," Nate speaks before I have a chance to finish my sentence. "What's the next question?"

I pull the worksheet out from under my textbook. I'm about to hand it to him, but I change my mind at the last second, giving him a chance to back out, "You don't have to."

"I insist," Nate reaches for the stack of papers. When I hand it to him, he says, "Besides, your 'squirrel-friend' is back for another nut."

The poor little creature is hovering around with bugged out eyes. So, I feed him a cashew and go back to my notes. I've already answered four of the ten questions. Nate, however, manages to find the answers way faster than I can.

After a few questions, I suggest, "Maybe you should become a doctor or even a pharmacist."

"Nah. Too much work. Just because I'm good at Chemistry doesn't mean I enjoy it," he replies dismissively.

"Do you want to be a lawyer? Maybe a prosecutor like Faye," I press for a little info on this mysterious intruder who insists on helping me with my school work.

His reaction catches me by surprise. Instead of considering it, or simply saying no, he cracks up, like my question is the funniest thing he's ever heard. When he finally answers, his reply is not far off from my thoughts, "No. No Law School for me. I hate laws. If it were up to me all law would be abolished."

I study his face for a very long time and he stares right back at me. When I make up my mind, I say, "I don't believe you."

"Don't you now?" Nate asks in a playful voice. "Which part? The one that I'll never be caught dead in Law School, or the anarchy part."

This time, I don't skip a beat, I say flat out, "The second one, of course. You're not an anarchist. Not by a long shot. I think you like having some ground rules. Sometimes you may wish they weren't there, but nonetheless you like having rules so you can break them."

The expression that crosses his face says I hit the jackpot.

Here is the thing, I'm well aware that I'm not as clever as my dad, as talented as Wellington, as beautiful as Faye, or book smart as Ian. But I'm great at reading people. I still don't know what good that does me. I'll probably be six feet under before I figure it out. *Oh, well...* still, I can tell without missing a beat when someone is telling the truth or not.

Nate is lying through his teeth. He's a great liar, I give him that much. I have a feeling he can fool almost anyone. He might be able to lie his way to the top for all I know. But the split second change of his expression shows me I just shattered his facade. Maybe I should have joined the Chess Club instead of Intermediate Drama. Except I don't know how to play chess. Of course I don't know a thing about acting either.

"So what do you suggest I go for, Miss know-it-all?" Nate asks sarcastically.

I guess I touched a nerve. I didn't mean to, but he pushed me with his bravado. I reply tentatively, "I'm no psychic. I can't see into the future. Most of the time I know even less about the present."

"But you've got me all figured out," he states cynically.

"Not even close," I say with a chuckle. "But I will soon enough."

"We'll see about that," Nate leans back. "Let me know when you've got it."

His nonchalant attitude triggers something inside me and the million dollar question is out before I can stop myself, "Why do you keep coming around?"

He makes a *tsk-tsk* sound with his mouth, "Isn't that obvious?"

"Not quite," I reply, managing to mask my annoyance at his smugness.

"To spend time with you," he deadpans, and so help me, Nate means it. He really does. The truth of his words are unmistakable, it's stamped crystal clear in his eyes.

Attempting to follow a piece of Faye's advice, "Be

enthusiastic, but not exuberant," I look down to hide a smile. Apparently, it works because Nate lets out a deep breath and I can feel the weight of his gaze on me.

"You don't believe me.".

I do believe him. I don't understand his reasons, but I'm not about to point that out. I don't think I could, even if I wanted to. Right now, my tongue feels tight and if I try to speak I'll probably mumble something unintelligible.

Nate takes my silence for disbelief and elaborates, "You're like Pandora's box. I'm allured to peek inside, even though I know what happens if I do."

I look up at him, meeting his blue eyes once again. In the sun light they looked even more vibrant. He's too distracting, too handsome for his own good, too charming and intelligent. One doesn't need my dad's IQ to figure out that it's too good to be true. Only in fairy tales does Prince Charming go around singling out girls like me. I shake my head unconvinced.

"The one time I tell the truth and she doesn't believe me," he laughs, looking up at the blue sky as if he can't handle the absurdity of it all.

"No. I believe you, I just..." I trail off, deciding against what I was about to say. I've already said more than I should. I shake my head again and add dismissively, "Never mind."

"You're killing me here, Liz, please elaborate, I beg you," Nate says dramatically.

I decide to ignore him. So instead of answering I fish out another nut and hand it to the greedy squirrel, leaving Nate staring anxiously at me. When I look back at him, he's still waiting for an answer.

I shrug, "Maybe some other time."

"You're saying that you'll tell me, just not today," Nate sounds hopeful and adds as a second thought, "You know, I'm still confused whether you want to get rid of me or keep me around. It's like you're having this epic inner struggle every time you're near me."

"Yeah, because we hang out all the time. Including today makes a total of what? Eight times?" I mock, sounding a lot like him.

"Eight and a half by my count," he replies, studying my reaction.

Of course he would count the embarrassing collision incident. I make a mental note to call Wellington when I get home so I can retrieve Nate's iPod. In an attempt to sidetrack him, I look down at my almost finished lab report. The last question involves some calculations to find the pH of the solution and the ionic net equation for the reaction. Nate lets the subject drop and leans in close, and together we solve it faster than expected.

With my lab report complete, I gather my stuff. Nate stands and offers his hand to help me up. I take it. His hand feels warm to the touch, and that tingling sensation spreads from my hand, down my arm and deep into my chest. Too soon, he releases my hand leaving a phantom awareness of his touch behind, and we walk together toward my building. At first I have the impression he's walking me home, but when he stops at the steps of the building before mine, I say idiotically, "This isn't me. It's the next one."

"I know," he snickers. "But I live here."

And of course, I blush, turning as red as the corvette parked across the street. "Later, then," I blurt out, looking down at my feet as I head toward my building.

"See you around, Liz," he replies simply, and I hear his rushed foot steps against the stairs.

17

It's easy to forget that life goes on whether or not you're there to observe it. My classmates have already fallen into a daily routine. They're now divided into sub-cliques, the students who pay attention, the ones who pretend to pay attention, the hide and text kind and the sleepers. Evidently, Nate has maintained his MIA status. I wonder if his parents know he skips so much.

At lunch, Faye's wannabes have too much to gossip about to notice I'm back. Such as: Saturday night's party at Joshua's house, whose folks were out of town. I just keep to myself until the bell rings and follow the procession of students through the hallways.

Ben is at his locker, flashing his dimpled smile, "You're back!"

I smile at him, switching books, "Yep. I'm here."

"I heard you jumped off a mountain," Ben leans against his locker.

I close the door and face him, "So I keep hearing."

Ben laughs and straightens up, "Come on, or we'll be late for Chem."

We walk to class together and then sit at our separate

stations. Mattie is gone, and my new partner isn't here. Ms. Olson begins the class with a review of pH solutions and ionic net equations. Then, she gets us started into what she calls a "dry lab." I spend the entire class reading and re-reading the instructions, figuring out what exactly I'm supposed to be doing.

By the time the bell rings, I'm nowhere near finished. As a result, I'm running late for Spanish. I take the stairs down two at a time, dodging students going in the opposite direction. That's when I feel my shoelace tug from under my left foot and stumble, head first. My Chemistry book escapes my grip as I reach out for the handrail. Strong arms wrap around my body and stop me from cracking my forehead on the floor. Once again, my face is plastered against his chest, and I find myself immobilized in his arms.

"One foot in front of the other, Liz," Nate jokes.

"Thanks," I reluctantly let my hands drop from his arms. "My ankle isn't keeping up."

"No worries, I'll always be there to catch you when you fall."

"Come, Nate. We have Chemistry," Spark says, thrusting the Chem book into my chest.

I wrap my arms around it at a loss. *Where did she come from?* It's not like anyone could miss her. Today, she has her jet black hair braided into a faux-hawk, revealing her unnatural blue highlights.

"Learn how to tie your shoes," she says before stomping up the stairs.

"See you around, Liz," Nate lets go of my waist and follows her up the stairwell.

I kneel to tie my shoe and then head to my Spanish class, wondering whether Spark is into Nate or if she's just the jealous type of friend. Mrs. Martinez seems to attribute my tardiness to my busted ankle by default. She's not so understanding about my poor Spanish, though.

Since I'm excused from PE for a whole month, I'm

supposed to go to the library until the end of sixth period. I waste another forty-five minutes trying to interpret the Chem lab report. The entire time, I keep hoping Nate will show up, but he never does. I blame him for my shortfalls in the subject. It's tough to concentrate when he's not around and impossible when he is.

When the final bell rings, I leave the library to meet Faye in the parking lot. She rattles on the entire ride home, but I tune her out, too tired to keep up. After she drops me off, I do my homework, have dinner with my grandparents, email Dad and head to bed.

I wake up the following morning to the same routine. Except for the encounter with Nate, I haven't seen him at all. I saw Spark plenty of times, though. I still don't know if she's always glaring, or if it's just when I'm around.

Today, the classes seem to drag on forever, and Faye is awfully quiet for a change. I never thought I'd say it, but I miss her nonstop chatting. Most of the time, I don't have much to say and just listen to someone who actually does. It's awkward to walk to lunch in complete silence.

I'm about to ask what's up when she blurts out, "Shoot! There she goes." Then, she detaches her arm from mine and dashes after Ms. Johnson, leaving me to fend for myself with her cafeteria crowd. *Thanks a lot, Faye.*

I turn around deciding to skip lunch all together just to be met with Kiara's smiling face, "Thanks for waiting."

Actually, I wasn't. Out loud, I say, "What's up?"

"You know, this and that," she replies vaguely and hands me a lunch tray.

I get in line with tray in hand, scanning for something edible among all the bunny food on display. I look back, but Kiara is nowhere to be found. Alexis is standing behind me where Kiara had been a second ago. She gives me a closed lip smile and grabs a side of celery. I pay for my unappetizing cheese pizza and hesitate whether or not to wait for Alexis, deciding to do the polite thing in the end. We walk to the table and sit across from each other. Judy and Anna follow right after, sitting on either side of Alexis. Then, we all concentrate on our meals in a miserable silence. I take a tiny bite and slowly chew the rubbery thing.

That's when Fran walks in and throws an open tabloid magazine on our lunch table, asking in a snotty voice, "So, is that why your father dispatched you here all the way from Japan?"

I barely have a chance to read the headline, *"Enigmatic software designer Dave O'Neill gets engaged–"* before Alexis snatches it from the table. She starts reading the interview and the other two girls sitting on each side of her hover to get a peek, their eyes flying over the article.

Of course, I knew my father was getting engaged. I'm the one who helped him pick out the ring. My question is how the US tabloid found out about it from the other side of the planet. I've got to hand it to them. They're good. It's not as if they had an extravagant engagement party or anything. Besides, they even traveled out to the countryside to celebrate in isolation.

I look at the salad bar line, searching for Kiara. But she isn't there yet. I scan the cafeteria and spot her talking with some guy at the entrance.

"Girl, you're Dad is hot," Judy points out. "How old is he?"

"Can't you read? He's in his mid-forties. He looks about the same age as my aunt's boyfriend," Fran says, rolling her eyes.

"He's probably older though. Her aunt's boyfriend, I mean, not your dad," Judy delivers this last part looking at me. Then, she turns back to Fran and asks, "Isn't your aunt's boyfriend some sort of Canadian actor?"

"He's probably all Botox like Tom Cruise," Alexis points out and bites a celery stick loaded with ranch.

"Totally," Anna agrees, taking a bite of her Caesar salad.

"Yeah, except Tom Cruise eats placenta to look younger,

not Botox," Judy clarifies, turning the page on the magazine.

I'm about to take another bite, but instead let the pizza slice drop back on the plate.

"That's disgusting!" Fran exclaims, putting her fork back into her Greek salad plate.

"Totally," Anna agrees, wrinkling her tiny nose. It makes me wonder if she knows any other word.

"That's not true," Alexis says defensively.

I think it's over now. Their short attention span will probably lead the conversation down another tangent.

My hope is short lived, Judy rotates the magazine and points at the picture of Suri and Dad, squealing, "OMG, Fran. You're right. She looks so young."

The photo takes up almost the entire page, and it's one I've never seen. They're wearing the same clothes they wore at last year's Christmas Party in California. So this picture must be old. Suri is in a silver cocktail dress, and Dad looks sharp in his graphite suit. He has his arm around her, and she's looking up at him with a big smile on her face. It's a very nice photo.

Note to self: Pick up a copy of the magazine for Suri.

I'm sure she'd love the picture.

"Is that why you left? Because your dad is gonna marry this Matsuri girl who's practically your age? The two of you don't get along?" Alexis asks, apparently sympathizing with me, or maybe she's empathizing. I don't know.

Suri is not my age. She's actually old enough to be my mother if she got pregnant when she was my age, that is. But, hey? It happens all the time. Besides, I love Suri. She's one of the best people I know. I wish Dad had proposed earlier. Suri is practically the mother I never had.

"Hello! She didn't leave. Her dad threw her on a plane. She's lucky if you ask me. My cousin was sent to a boarding school after her dad shacked up with a twenty-something," Fran remarks in her know-it-all tone.

"Totally," Anna chimes in, taking a sip of her diet soda.

I close my eyes and massage my temples with my fingertips. No point in even trying. It's not like they'll actually listen to me. It's my first day all over again.

Please, somebody save me! Get me out of here.

For a moment, I believe my wish is granted because silence falls over the lunch table. I open one eye and then the other. No, I'm still in the cafeteria, *alright.* But they have an expression of total astonishment on their faces, and their eyes are staring past me.

Nate's voice projects over my head, "Sorry to interrupt. You girls seem to be in the middle of something here," he pauses glancing at the open magazine on the table and raises his eyebrows. "Anyways, I need to borrow Liz for a moment."

I look up at him and blink. When I remain unmoving, he shoots me a look that speaks louder than words, "I thought you wanted out of here. This is me trying to get you out of here."

"Sure," I get to my feet.

He flashes his devil-may-care smile, and the girls appear to be struck dumb. He grabs my tray and says, "Enjoy your salad, ladies."

I follow suit as he makes his way toward the nearest exit. He stops and mercilessly disposes my untouched meal into the trash receptacle, tray and all. I feel the weight of the girl's eyes on my back, but I don't turn around. Spark stands a few feet away from us, and of course she's glaring at me. It makes me wonder what I did to deserve such spite. She's never even talked to me. Maybe she dislikes Faye's crowd, and I'm getting caught in the crossfire. I wouldn't blame her if that were the case. I attempt to smile at her as we pass by, but Spark's glare intensifies. My smile fades. Oh well, I'll just have to get used to being disliked.

I don't know what makes me do it, but I take hold of Nate's hand. His head turns at once to look at me, a quizzical expression crossing his face. Embarrassed, I unlace my fingers to let go of his hand, but Nate tightens his grip and leads me out of the cafeteria. I follow close behind, trying to keep pace with him. We almost make it to the door when he comes to a halt, and I slam into him.

"Back off," Nate orders in a low voice.

I step back, ready to apologize when I notice he isn't talking to me, but with Zoë Fairchild of all people. Her straight black hair hangs loose over the waistband of her pleated skirt. She's even prettier up close. Her blue eyes are so pale that they're almost transparent under the cafeteria lights. Zoë has a tight grip on his arm, and her posture says Nate isn't going anywhere. His expression is one of slight annoyance while hers, on the other hand, reflects pure rage.

Now, this is awkward. She must be an ex or something. I try freeing my hand from his, unsuccessfully. *Fine.* If he doesn't mind neither do I. It's not like she's glaring at *me* after all. But in the back of my mind, I'm afraid this incident will come back to haunt me. Her athletic spectacle at tryouts are still a vivid memory. A person has to be exceedingly tough to perform like she did. I clearly don't wanna be on her bad side.

A sudden pain hits me, like the pounding of a migraine, but in reverse. Instead of having the pressure pushing in, it's pushing out, and *darn* it hurts! I bring my free hand to my forehead and press down on my temples. A second later the pain subsides, just as abruptly as it arrived.

A shadowy movement on my left catches my attention, and I turn to look at it. Spark is marching in our direction. Her eyes glued on us. Her disapproving scrutiny says accusingly, "I told you so." An unlucky freshman boy steps into her path, and she sends him stumbling over a trashcan with a stiff shove. It looks like she's about to jump Zoë.

Nate and Zoë are oblivious, the staring contest between the two of them is still on. As if just now sensing Spark charging ruthlessly toward us, Nate shakes his head ever so slightly. Not looking away from Zoë, he laughs with a hint of sarcasm and says reprehensibly, "Now, now. If there's something you wanna say to me, just speak up. Let's hear it."

"You're walking a thin line here, Nathaniel," her threatening tone is effective even through her sugary voice.

Nathaniel? So, that's his name. It suits him.

"That's what I do best," Nate replies with a hint of amusement and challenges, "Besides, I'm not the one who changed the course of things, am I?"

"Watch it," she confronts him, lowering her voice. Somehow, it sounds even more threatening than before.

Zoë peeks at me and turns her head toward Spark. I do the same. Spark's eyes are still locked on us, but now she's just standing there motionless.

"Lighten up, *Z*," Nate says in his cocky way. "Just let go of me and go cheer for the Egrets."

Zoë releases his arm more briskly than necessary. With her eyes still locked on Nate's, she advises me, "Do yourself a favor Eliza, stay away from him." Then, she brushes by me without another word.

I'm dumbfounded. Before I can even think what to make of it, she's gone, and Nate is leading me out of the cafeteria.

Outside, Nate releases his grip and whirls around to face me. He places both hands gently on my cheeks. My first thought is that he's going to kiss me right here and now, disregarding the few kids walking by and the total PDA. This isn't how I pictured my first kiss. It feels wrong. Especially following the confrontation with who I presume to be his ex.

As if that weren't enough, two girls choose that instant to pass by us with their arms linked. One of them glances back as they pass and whispers something in the other girl's ear and then they both giggle. I'm about to take a step back, but stop myself when I notice that kissing me must be the last thing in Nate's mind. He looks concerned and appears to be scanning my eyes. He says something under his breath that I miss. I'm lost in that familiar tingling sensation, when he lets his hands drop from my face to my shoulders, asking, "Are you okay?"

"No," is my mental answer, but I don't voice it.

"I'm sorry about what just happened," Nate apologizes vaguely.

I blink off my stupor and finally reply, "I'm fine." I nod in the direction of the cafeteria and ask, "What was that about?"

"Zoë?" He waves it off, dismissively. As if he couldn't care less. Then, he elaborates for my benefit, "She's just having some trouble in paradise. That's all." He watches my doubtful expression and invites, "Walk with me."

Nate strolls down the little trail leading to one of the many entrances of our school. He's confident that I'll follow him. Of course, he's right, and I do. We walk side by side at a snail's pace in silence until curiosity gets the best of me, "Is she your girlfriend? Ex? Should I be afraid?"

"Zoë?" He laughs briefly. "No. Not a girlfriend, not an ex, not even a friend. She just dislikes me, and you have nothing to worry about. Zoë is okay," he pauses, looks straight into my eyes. "Can you keep a secret?"

"I guess," I say hesitantly.

"You guess?" He challenges.

"What do you want me to say? Cross my heart and hope–"

Nate doesn't let me finish, cutting me off, "Be careful with what you say, words are more powerful than you think. Once said, they can never be taken back. Your thoughts, they're yours and yours alone. Well, most of the time."

"What do you mean by that?" I ask in puzzlement.

"Life is like yin and yang, it's a balance of opposites. It all depends on what you believe," he explains, making me even more confused.

"Huh," I exclaim stupidly.

"Do you believe in mind powers?" He asks, stopping for

a second to look at me.

I open my mouth to say a flat "nope" and stop myself. My mental plea to get out of the cafeteria comes to mind, and the way Nate came to my rescue completely out of the blue. I shake my head. *That's ridiculous, impossible even.* Or *is* it? It's like what Wellington always says, "Nothing is coincidence."

Nate smiles at me and runs the back of his fingers down my cheek, "Come on, or you'll be late."

The feeling lingers where his fingers brushed my skin and stays with me as I walk bedazzled down the hall. It's only after he's long gone that I remember he never told me the secret. The sound of the bell snaps me out of my stupor, making me realize that if I don't rush I'll get a tardy in Chemistry. I dash toward my locker almost running over the same freshman boy Spark threw in the trashcan.

"Sorry," I call back.

Ben is shoving his Chem book inside his backpack when I reach my locker. He kindly waits for me to find my book. He's so polite. I smile at him and try to rush. The last thing I wanna do is to make him late along with me.

Mrs. Olson is watching the clock, waiting for the final bell to sound when we walk in. I head over to my empty station and sit down, feeling solemn from lack of a lab partner.

Spanish class almost puts me to sleep today. Mrs. Martinez keeps going on and on about a movie we will be watching in parts. It's called Don Quixote. I wish I could speak Spanish as fluently as I speak Japanese. I'd tell Mrs. Martinez that she's not supposed to spoil the movie, and to just play the darned thing already.

After my Spanish class, I go to the library and sit down in my usual spot, wondering how Nate manages to miss every class and still remain enrolled in school. As if once again summoned by my thoughts, he appears out of nowhere and takes a seat across from me.

"Where did you come from?" I ask, looking up at him.

He responds by placing a book on the table. The title reads, *"Chemistry Concepts and Problems,"* which tells me that he just came from aisle D.

"Can I see the lab you're working on?" Nate asks, opening the book.

I nod, digging through my papers. I find it stuck between the Don Quixote handout. I pull it loose and hand it to Nate. In return, he slides the open book toward me, "Go over chapter two, part one. I'll solve the equations for molar mass."

Fifteen minutes later, I have no doubt that we beat some sort of record here. All the questions are answered, and I'm not afraid to bet they're all correct.

"Come on, let's get out of here," Nate's invitation catches me by surprise.

"I can't," I blurt out regretfully, wishing I could.

"Of course you can. You're excused from PE, and we just finished the lab report. You don't need to stay here," he presses and leans over the table, letting his thumb slightly touch my pinky finger. Nate's voice is almost a whisper, and I catch myself leaning closer to hear him.

The librarian disagrees and lets loose an exaggerated, "Ahem!"

He lowers his head hiding a chuckle and squeezes my hand, pressing the issue, "Come on, Liz."

"I'm sorry. I wish I could. I really do. But I made a promise to some people I really care about that I stay on track and out of trouble. I can't break a promise," I let my hand linger under his touch a second longer, before pulling away. I open my Calc notebook and pick up my pencil. Mentally kicking myself for being such a coward. Nate is right. It would have taken me ten times longer to finish my lab report. I have an alibi, but I just can't do it. I simply can't lie.

"Do you really think I'm trouble?" He challenges.

"I don't *think*, I'm sure," I reply bluntly.

He lets out a laugh and runs his fingers through his dark blond hair. The librarian shushes him, and he mouths to her, "Sorry."

This time he's the one to surprise me. Nate pulls out his own Calculus assignment and starts working on it in silence across from me. I just stare at him for several seconds.

So, he does own a notebook.

Stalling my pencil in place, I watch him as he works on his equations and performs all the calculations in his head. I keep gaping at him up to the moment his hair falls over his eyes, and as he brushes it away he catches me staring. I expect him to confront me, or throw me one of his mocking comments, but he doesn't. He just stares back at me for a few seconds and gives me a knowing smile. I open my mouth to speak, but he mimics the librarian giving me a quick, "Shh!" pressing his index finger to his lips. Then, he dives back into his assignment.

We work in silence until the bell rings. That's when I decide to ask, "You weren't in class today, how did you get the assignment?"

"Of course I was, you were just too distracted to notice me. I'll remember to say *hi* next time," he stands up and puts his cross-body book bag on.

Instead of leaving like I assumed he would, he waits for me until I finish gathering my things. Once I zip up my backpack, he grabs it from the desk and hangs it over his left shoulder. Then, he holds his hand for me to take.

"What are you doing?" I ask undecided whether to take it or not.

"Proving you wrong," he replies simply as if that answers everything.

I decide to play along, ignoring his vague nonsensical answers. Who can blame me? If a drop-dead gorgeous guy voluntarily spends his time trying to convince me that he's not as bad as he actually is, I would have to be really dense not to let him, wouldn't I? So, I take his hand and follow him out of the library.

When we reach the parking lot, Nate stops all of a sudden. I have to press my lips together so my jaw won't hit the floor. Faye is locked in a deep kiss with a blond boy whose back seems very familiar. Instead of trying to identify the guy, I choose to look away. Nate is not as courteous. He clears his throat loudly, and they break apart.

Faye turns around and finally notices us. I'm not sure who's more surprised, me for catching Faye with Ben or her for seeing me with Nate. Come to think of it, it kinda makes sense. Faye is the head cheerleader, and Ben is the captain of the basketball team. The thing is, I never see Ben as the basketball star he is, but as the friendly locker guy.

Nate's expression is one of pure amusement as the situation keeps getting more uncomfortable by the second. Faye decides to break the awkward silence, "Liz, this is my boyfriend, Ben. Boyfriend, this is Liz."

"So, what are you guys up to?" Nate asks casually.

"I have to get to practice," Ben explains. "I was just keeping Faye company while she waited for Liz."

"Since you're here, I guess we can go," Faye pauses, hesitating. She looks from me to Nate and back again, "Unless?"

"No, she's all yours. Liz has prior commitments," Nate replies sarcastically.

Faye shrugs and plants a quick kiss on Ben's cheek, "Call me after practice."

"Sure thing. Bye, Liz. Nate," Ben waves and turns around, heading toward the basketball court.

"Let's go then," Faye makes her way to her car and I follow, bringing Nate along since he's still holding my hand.

When we reach Faye's green bug, he gives a little squeeze before letting go. He puts my backpack in the backseat and pulls his key fob out of his pocket, "See you around."

To my total disbelief, it's the yellow Lamborghini that lights up when he presses the button. Both doors open at once, and from where we stand it seems like the car has spread its wings and is about to take flight.

"I knew that was yours," Faye says unsurprised.

Nate drops his book bag on the passenger seat, "Of course," he flashes his dazzling smile at us. "What else would I drive?"

"Insufferable arrogant prick," Faye snorts, just loud enough for Nate to hear.

I nudge her playfully, "Hey, be nice."

"Humph!" She opens the driver's side door of her car.

There's no doubt he heard her, but it's like he couldn't care less. Nate gracefully moves around his car, climbing in. He honks goodbye, and I wave as he drives off.

18

Finally, I've mastered the power of invisibility. Call me, Eliza *Copperfield*.

I've been saying "excuse me," "pardon me," to two boys from the basketball team talking animatedly for the past minute, and they're still blocking my path. It's no use, I just have to squeeze my way through.

I'm compressing myself between the row of seats and the two giants in my English class when Judy pulls me by my backpack, "Sit here."

She does it so abruptly that I hit my elbow on the corner of the desk. Who would guess? Just a few weeks ago, she wanted me as far away as possible, like I had rabies or something. Today, she wants me sitting near her so badly that she's physically assaulting me. She doesn't even let me settle before she turns in her seat and squeals, "He talks to you?"

By *"he"* I know she means Nate Sinclair. *He* is the only boy who talks to me at school. Well, Ben does too, sometimes, but something tells me that she wouldn't be so jumpy about that.

Apparently, I took too much time to answer her because she goes on, "OMG! He's a god! He's probably the hottest guy to ever live." I guess I'm not the only one thrown by his looks. I scoff, and Judy snaps out of it, asking, "Do you know who his sister is?"

I don't even try to answer. I just hang my bag on the back of my chair. As expected, she continues, "Lill Sinclair, like *the* 'Lill Sinclair.' She's this supermodel/actress. Her twitter feed has like a zillion followers from all over the world. She has her own place in New York City and she's only eighteen. She's like a generation goddess. Have you met her yet? Do you think her hair is natural?"

She blinks up at me, expectantly. Apparently, this last question I was supposed to answer.

What was that about her hair? Better play it safe... I shrug.

That's all the encouragement she needs to keep going, "I think it is, but Kiara says no one has hair that red. So it might not be, especially since she doesn't have any freckles. My hair is auburn, and I'm covered from head to toe in them."

"I've heard of her," I note in the hopes she'll stop going on and on about Nate's sister.

"Did he introduce you?" Judy rattles on. "Is she cool? I bet she's the coolest chick ever."

"No. Maybe. Nate doesn't really..." I trail off. I was about to say "he doesn't get along with her," but it seems private somehow. So, I backpedal, "Nate is his own person. They're two different people. How does having a runway model for a sister make him a god?"

"Because of that thing about gods by *sibliation,*" she explains nonsensically.

"You mean *association,*" I suggest.

"They're siblings, so I do mean *sibliation,*" she retorts in a "duh" type of voice and rolls her eyes at me.

English is not my best subject, but I'm pretty sure Judy just made this word up on the spot. I'd give her an "A" for confidence, and a "C" for creativity.

I shake my head. But before I have a chance to utter a word, she cuts in, "You think I'm exaggerating, don't you? So hear me out. Nate is never in any of his classes, never, like ever. Do you want to know why?"

I nod and lean in. She has my full attention now.

"Because he's a *Sinclair*," Judy explains. "The school is so grateful to have 'Nate Sinclair' in it's student body that they don't even care what he does, as long as his grades are good. Plus, the school's art program received a hefty donation around the same time he showed up. That's just how private schools work, they love donations and they love to drop names. I heard that from Anna. She volunteers at the admissions office."

Her comment bugs me, and I jump to his defense, "Still, he's not just a name, or money, or Lill Sinclair's brother. He's an individual. Maybe Nate would be better off if he didn't have to carry the weight of others expectations."

Judy looks at me, blinks, seems to consider it and scrunches her made-up face in confusion. I have the impression she will just turn around and ignore me from now on. But she surprises me with a reply, "You're talking about Shakespeare. You mean, like that line about a rose called by any other name would still have the same aroma."

"Yeah," I exclaim before I can process what she said.

She shakes her head vehemently, "No, it doesn't work that way. Nate wouldn't be the same, he'd be a totally different person. A name makes all the difference, it's like a name brand. If you finished the book you'd know that Juliet was wrong, and the name *did* matter. Believe me. I read it and know what I'm talking about. She was suffering from adolescent delusion if you ask me. She was under the impression that true love would trump their names, which turned out to be a load. Because guess what? *Spoiler alert!* She was wrong, and in the end she shot herself."

"Wait, *what*?" I ask confused.

"Whatever," Judy rolls her eyes again. I swear she does it

so often that one of these days they'll get stuck looking back at her brain. She concludes, "They both die. Therefore, a name is more than a name. Anyone who says otherwise is just fooling themselves."

"I have called thee by thy name; thou art mine," A low male's voice says beside us.

"*You*?" I look up at Michael in dismay.

Judy's reaction is uncharacteristic. For once, she's at a loss for words and just stares up at him.

"Hello, Liz," he sits at the desk beside me, puts his textbook on the table and elaborates, "Your friend is right. A name carries with it a certain power."

"Okay, Plato," I mock still unconvinced by either of them.

"Not Plato. *Isaiah*."

"Huh?"

My confusion frees Judy from her reverie, "Hi, Isaiah," she giggles and introduces herself, "I like your name. It's different. I'm Judy, by the way."

I fight with all I have not to crack up, but I'm failing miserably. It turns out, Michael is a better person than I am because he refrains from laughing. A smile curls his lips upward for once as he introduces himself, "Pleased to meet you, Judy. I'm Michael Price. No nicknames, just Michael, if you will."

"Michael it is," Judy beams at him.

The second bell rings, and Ms. Campbell walks in. Michael turns in his seat to face her along with the rest of the class. Aside from Judy, that is. Before turning around, she narrows her eyes and gives me an exaggerated once over.

You don't have to be a mind reader to know what she's thinking. Just look at me, no makeup, no jewelry, hair pulled up and nails that have never been done. Then, look at her, wearing earrings that perfectly match her necklace, which matches her bracelet, which matches her book bag. Her shoulder length auburn hair is perfectly styled with the layers flipping up at the ends. Her nails are painted in the same glittery tone as her lipstick, which complements her lilac eyeshadow, accentuating her hazel eyes.

After sizing me up, she wrinkles her nose, "Are you a hot boy magnet or something? Or do you put out?"

Unable to stop myself, I give her a cartoonish shrug and reply simply, "Maybe it's just the O'Neill name legacy."

Judy turns around with a *humph.* She's not used to hearing me talk back. To be honest, neither am I. It feels good. Beside me, Michael suppresses a laugh disguised as a cough, just loud enough to get a few girls to notice him.

Right then, Ms. Campbell greets in her flat voice, "Good morning."

We open our textbooks and Ms. Campbell continues her didactic monologue. It's safe to say only the boys are paying any attention to her class. The girls keep shifting in their seats, dropping objects and tossing their hair. They're all stealing glances at Michael every chance they get.

Gee! He's just a guy.

And right now, he looks decidedly uncomfortable and seems tense, almost rigid at his desk. Nothing like the guy who walked in speaking so confidently with us a second ago.

I turn my attention back to Ms. Campbell, but it's hard to follow along with all this fidgeting going on around me. I'm utterly lost. Her words may as well be in Latin because I have no idea what she's saying.

A wave of dizziness hits me, and I recoil in my seat. I swallow hard and close my eyes in an attempt to diminish this strange feeling. It keeps coming and going incessantly, and I concentrate on my breathing. When the vertigo finally subsides, I slowly open my eyes.

Inexplicably, I turn my face automatically to my right where Michael is sitting. He's pale by nature, but right now he's beyond ashen. Deathlike. It's like his color has abandoned him altogether. Michael's eyes are closed, and he's resting his forehead against the desk. By the erratic way his chest raises and lowers with each intake of air, it's clear he's having a hard time breathing as well.

Concerned, I nudge Judy. She discreetly turns in her seat facing the wall and then mouths, "*WHAT*?"

I nod in Michael's direction. She shifts to look at him, frowns, and turns back to me, mouthing, "So?"

"I think he's gonna pass out," I whisper.

She looks back at him and comprehension finally dawns in her glittered mind. Her hazel eyes become gargantuan, and I insist, "We have to do something."

She presses her lips together, moves her book bag to the other side of her desk protectively, and then her arm shoots up. Ms. Campbell is not used to students interrupting her lectures and looks at a loss for an instant, just staring at Judy's raised hand. Then, she blinks as if her mind just switched off the autopilot and asks in a patronizing tone, "Yes, Miss Carlton?"

"I think Liz needs to go to the nurse," Judy replies to my utter disbelief.

What is she doing?

I shrink into my desk as much as I can manage, letting my ostrich legs extend under Judy's chair.

Ms. Campbell looks at me, "Are you sick, Miss O'Neill?"

I swallow hard, and my cheeks get warm under the scrutiny of the entire class. When I just shrink some more without saying anything, Judy digs her triple strap platform heel into my foot. I yelp loudly and flinch in pain.

Judy speaks up, "Maybe someone should walk her to the school nurse. It looks like she's going to purge."

Please, she didn't just say that.

Right about now, the invisibility trick would be fantastic. I'm looking down at my lap, sensing all eyes on me. Michael's included. Nate's words from our first encounter come to mind, "No good deed goes unpunished."

"Yes, Mister...?" Ms. Campbell trails off.

"Price. Michael Price," he supplies. "Shall I accompany

her?"

"Yes, please," she replies, sounding relieved.

A shadow is cast from above and I look up. Michael is standing beside me, his complexion turning into a pale bluish green shade. Maybe he's asthmatic, or has allergies, or whatever. He needs some air, *immediately*.

I get to my feet and make my way out of the class, ignoring everyone else. Michael follows right behind me. All the while, I look down at my feet. Neither of us acknowledge Judy when she whispers, "You're welcome."

In the hallway, Michael straight asks, "Why did you do that?"

He can't be serious. The guy looks like he will fall flat any second. Annoyed from all the embarrassment Judy just put me through, I repeat her words to him, "You're welcome."

He doesn't say anything else, and I quicken my pace, wondering which hallway takes me to the school nurse. We're almost to the end of the empty hall leading to the stairs when Michael comes to a stop. He leans against the wall and slides down into a sitting position.

"Oh-no, no, no!" I gasp, rushing back to him.

He closes his eyes, and I have no idea what to do. I'm debating whether to leave him here and call for help or not, when he speaks slowly, "I am not going to faint, or get sick for that matter. I am just worn out. It's been too long."

Michael looks up at me. Even his eyes are paler than usual. It's like his black sapphire gaze faded out into blue topaz just like the rest of him. I'm sure he's going to lose consciousness any minute. I can't leave him here.

"Come on, you're not making any sense. We need to get you to the nurse," I look around, trying to figure out which way we should go.

When he doesn't make any effort to move, I speed walk a few steps left to where the hall splits and scan the area. I spot the nurse's office a few doors down and I rush back to

Michael. Kneeling beside him, I grab hold of his hand. He flinches and yanks it away.

A chill runs through my veins and I shiver, standing up. I don't push it. The guy looks like he'll drop dead any minute. My head is spinning. I don't want to abandon him here on the floor, but I need to get the nurse.

"What is it, Michael?" asks a delicate voice coming from down the hall.

"Zoph," Michael begins and pauses, pinching the bridge of his nose. Then, he tries again, "Zoë."

Zoë speed walks toward us, her long black hair seems to flow like a dark river with her rushed steps. Her face is serious, filled with affectionate concern.

"He needs to go to the nurse," I remark as she approaches us. My voice is strange to my own ears. It's somewhere between shaken and worried.

Zoë kneels beside him, "Thanks, Liz."

"You are encouraging her," Michael complaints in a low voice, almost inaudible.

"Don't mind him. He's in a bad way right now, but he's grateful beneath his brooding personality. You can get back to class, I'll take it from here. Thanks again," Zoë smiles widely.

"I am more than grateful. Thank you, Liz," Michael looks at me with bloodshot eyes, catching me off guard. This guy is a roller-coaster, he's all over the place.

"It's nothing. Are you sure you'll be okay?" I ask in concern. "I can rush to the nurse and ask for help."

"I will," he replies simply with a half smile on his face.

"Don't worry, he'll be alright. I'll make sure of it," Zoë reassures, flashing me a pearly white smile.

I nod. Hesitantly, I turn around and head back to class. I'm reluctant to open the classroom door since I'll have to walk past all the eyes. Just as I pull the door open, the bell rings, and an avalanche of uniformed students rush past me. I stand there holding the door opened until Judy walks out.

To my surprise, she has her book bag strapped across her body and is carrying my backpack on one shoulder.

She spots me, "Oh good! You're here. I was afraid I'd have to carry *this* around all day."

"Thanks," I remove my bag from her shoulder and put it on mine. We part ways, and I head to my next class.

At lunch, the hot topic is that Michael went home after only twenty minutes on school property. Rumor has it he's suffering from food poisoning. I barely touch my overloaded lasagne, picking at the ricotta cheese. Part because of the gross discussion going on, but mostly because I'm bracing myself for the inquisition that ought to start any minute.

Miraculously, it never does. Our lunch table comes to the conclusion that Michael is pretty hot when he isn't turning green. Once that's established, the gossip steers to Zoë, the newest member of the cheer squad. Apparently, the breathtaking *Zoë* is Michael's girlfriend. In a rare occasion of agreement at the table, they come to a consensus that no one stands a chance against Zoë. No girl in this school could make him look away from her. No one but Faye, that is. All eyes turn to Faye who is distractedly chatting with Kiara.

She notices and frowns at us, "*What?*"

The girls squirm in their seats, and Kiara comes to the rescue, "You guys are right. Faye might stand a chance, if she were interested, which she's not. So, stop obsessing with the hot new couple and get a life of your own."

Kiara rolls her eyes and turns back to Faye, the two of them picking up where they left off. The girls go back to their salads, engaging in a new topic, like the good minions they are.

Whoa! Kiara has been tuned in to us while talking to Faye? I'm impressed. I have a hard time keeping up with just Faye, a parallel conversation is out of the question. But I guess with all the lunches Kiara spent at this table, it must be like a sixth sense she's acquired. Plus, I could attribute it to the fact that Faye tends to dumb it down a few notches around her wannabes.

As we leave the cafeteria, somehow, I engage my cloaking powers again. This time it lasts throughout both Chemistry and Spanish. It only wears off after fifth period.

"Liz," Nate calls as he enters the library, catching my attention and that of the librarian at the same time. He winks at her as he passes by her desk, grabs a chair and straddles it backward, "I hear that I've got some competition."

"*Competition*?" I repeat confused.

"The new guy," he supplies, resting his chin against the back of the chair.

"You mean, Michael?" I ask still puzzled. He nods, and I rephrase Judy's earlier comment, "Don't worry, the girls still think you're a god."

"*Hardly*. Besides, that's not what everyone's saying. I heard you pretended to be sick so Pretty Boy wouldn't be tagged as the guy who hurled in English class," he pauses and stares me straight-on, waiting for a reaction. He shrugs and imitates Ms. Campbell's monotone way of speaking, "I don't blame him, though. It's hard to keep your breakfast down in her class—"

"That's not true," I cut in, finally recovering from his shocking news. "I can't believe people are saying that. It's all Judy's fault. She's the one who said I was sick in front of the entire class. I had no other choice but to walk him to the school nurse."

"So, Judy framed you," he uses my own words against me.

"When you put it like that... I don't know. He was super pale, like he was about to faint. I asked Judy to do something, and you heard the rest," I volunteer in her defense.

"So, I *do* have competition," Nate presses on. "You were watching him."

"Nobody is competing for anything, especially not for my attention," I scoff, shaking my head. "Are you pulling my leg or something?"

"No. I just didn't expect you to be so cozy around him, that's all," Nate feigns nonchalance.

I'm dumbfounded. *Is he jealous?* It's laughable even to consider it. He *can't* be serious.

"Michael was unwell," I repeat, failing to hide the exasperation in my voice. "What would you expect me to do? Let the guy fall to the ground? What would you have done?"

"Nothing," he replies bluntly and quickly reconsiders, "No—scratch that. I'd film it and post it on YouTube."

"No, you wouldn't."

"Believe me, I would," he states in a tone that doesn't leave room for debate. It's clear he means it.

"Why all the hate?" I ask rhetorically, still doubtful he'd do such a thing.

He shrugs dismissively and throws me another hideous question, "Do you like him?"

"No," I blurt out without thinking and immediately try to mend my reply, "I mean, I don't like or dislike him. I don't even know him." Nate smirks, and I add, "He got sick. That's all there is. Why do you even care?"

"You're right. Let's just drop it," he stands, spins the chair one-eighty and sits down again. He pulls out the handout from Calculus homework and begins working on it.

I pretend to do the same, discreetly stealing peeks at him. He seems ticked off. I can't tell whether it's with me or with Michael. Once again, Nate solves one question after another without the aid of charts, or a calculator. It's fascinating. Not only is he easy on the eyes, but he's also a brainiac.

"Liz, stop gawking at me like I've sprouted wings or something. It's Math, not rocket science. There is only one right answer," he doesn't lift his head from his calculations.

My lips curl up in a half smile at his smart remark, a constant reminder that he's far from perfect. I go back to solving equations and don't dare to look up again. Not until the bell rings, that is.

Nate guardedly places the handout and his mechanical pencil in his book bag. He stands up and hangs it across his body. I shove my notebook, handout, calculator, eraser and pencil into my backpack. I zip it closed and get to my feet.

He's conspicuously suppressing a smile as we leave the library, and I fight the urge to ask why. He saves me from further embarrassment by breaking the silence, "Are you heading home or hooking up with Faye at the school newspaper?"

"Neither, I have Drama class," I wait for his answer, ready to be mocked.

Nate comes to a complete stop, and I indulgently do the same, waiting for the punchline. But, he just asks in a surprised tone, "Drama? *You?*"

I nod and start walking again. He shakes his head and gets back into step with me. When he doesn't say anything, I inquire in bewilderment, "No smart comment?"

"Nope. Just unexpected, that's all. You don't strike me as the acting type."

"You're right, I'm not. I'll probably be working back stage. They always need people for that."

"Why did you choose Drama, then?" He asks just as we reach the classroom. "Why not something else, like shop or track?"

"My grandma doesn't approve," I shrug.

"Do you always do what you're told?" He challenges, leaning against the door frame.

"No comment. I don't wanna give you another reason to call me a goody-goody. Later Nate," I open the door, forcing him to straighten up.

"See you around, Angel Girl," Nate teases and gracefully walks down the hall.

Of course, he must always have the last word. I go inside where most of the students are already sitting in a circle. Ms. Campbell is among them. She catches sight of me, "Helen!"

"It's Eliza," I correct, gingerly closing the door behind me.

"Come join us, Miss O'Neill. Please, take a seat," Ms. Campbell gestures for me to sit.

"Yes, Ma'am," I walk to an empty spot beside Mattie.

"Hi," she mouths, and I give her a tiny wave.

It turns out Drama class is sort of fun. For now at least, I'm not sure I'll feel the same when we actually start performing. Ms. Campbell conducts several warm-up games. We're now in the middle of what she calls the rain game. In this particular one, she rubs the palms of her hands together making a swishing sound, and we join in mimicking the sounds of a thunderstorm. Next, we do a read through of a scene from *The Tempest*. I have to admit I like it. Even her voice is much more dynamic than in her English class, as if this is her calling in life.

On our way out, Mattie suggests, "You should ride with Welly and I. The school newspaper meeting goes on for another hour."

"Are you sure?" I ask, not wanting to be the third wheel.

"Of course," Mattie links her arms to mine and leads me toward the parking lot, not giving me much of a choice. "Don't you live right next door?"

"More like the same block," I clarify just as we climb into Wellington's mother's SUV.

"Hey, Liz," Wellington greets as I slide into the backseat.

"Hey," I reply distractedly, busying myself with the seat belt.

"Hi, babe," Mattie says, giving him a quick peck on the lips.

"Clarinet lessons with Mrs. Shawn?" He inquires, turning on the engine.

"Yep. Until five," she pulls a jacket out of her backpack and puts it on. "I'd say we should all hang out after, but I know you have to practice."

Wellington just nods in agreement and throws the car into

reverse, easing into traffic. Mattie's remark is a solemn reminder that tomorrow he'll be traveling to New York with Grandma, and I'm not going. I still can't believe it. When his mother didn't want to let him go alone to New York City, Grandma offered to chaperone. Now, my best friend is playing Carnegie Hall, and I'll only be present for the last of his three performances. That's unfair, cruel even.

Wellington turns the hazard lights on and pulls over in front of an unfamiliar building. It must be where Mattie takes her private lessons. She says good-bye and quickly climbs out of the car, her clarinet case swinging at her side. She leaves the door open, and I switch to the front seat.

"Are you excited?" I ask, buckling my seat belt.

"Terrified, actually," He replies, changing lanes.

"Don't be. They wouldn't invite you if they weren't sure you could do it. Their good name is on the line, you know?"

"Not helping, Liz," Wellington tightens his grip on the wheel.

"Sorry. What I'm trying to say is that you'll do great. I've never met anyone who plays cello like you do."

"Do you know someone else that plays cello?" He challenges, peeking at me with the corner of his eye. When I don't reply, he laughs, "That's what I thought. So, did you convince your dad to let you come?"

"No. When I brought it up again last night, he said there's no reason to watch a performance of Pachelbel's Canon in D on a cello more than once."

"He's right, you know," he laughs for whatever reason.

"Faye is going, though."

"Faye?" Wellington sounds intrigued, his laughing fit ending abruptly. There's a spot in front of my building and he takes it. He kills the engine and shifts in his seat to look at me, waiting for some sort of explanation.

I shrug, "She volunteered to take my place."

"Faye Greenwood? Ian's sister?"

"The one and only," I assert.

"And she wants to see me play?" There's a hint of incredulity in his voice.

I understand his doubts, Faye doesn't strike me as the classical music type either. So, I tease, "Actually, she doesn't want to miss out on a New York shopping spree—"

"And will be watching me play by default," he cuts in, shaking his head in amusement.

A black car with tinted windows maneuvers an outstanding parallel parking job right in front of us, catching our attention. The driver steps out, promptly making his way around the car to open the back door. Then, a girl about my age gets out of the car, dressed too formal for her age. She has her dark-brown hair pulled up and wears an ivory business suit that reminds me of Dad's thirty-year-old assistant back in Santa Monica. She stops beside the driver, and a second girl steps out.

Wellington lets out a sharp breath. I'm speechless, staring at none other than Lill Sinclair. Even with her red curls pulled in a high ponytail and the gigantic sunglasses hiding most of her face, she couldn't be mistaken for anyone else. A third girl gets out of the car, almost like a clone of the first with the exception of being a brunette. Then, Lill Sinclair makes a beeline straight into Nate's building with the two girls tagging along. The driver closes the car door and returns to the driver's seat.

"Is that who I think it is?" Wellington asks.

"It's her, *alright*. Lill Sinclair, her brother goes to my school."

"Wow! And here I thought she was all Photoshop..." He trails off and says again, "Wow."

19

Is this Saint Pete's High? It certainly doesn't seem to be. Today happens to be casual day, and it's like I just walked into a fashion event. The girls are all made-up, sporting their expensive brands and designer boots. The guys are not so flashy, mostly wearing retro shirts and beat up jeans. I get the impression that while the girls are overcompensating, the guys are taking it a step down.

Faye is a no-show. She flew to New York with Grandma and Wellington this morning. It's safe to say she'll have enough outfits for a year of casual days when she gets back. Why is it that the girl who barely talks to him is the one who gets to see all of his performances?

Grandpa and I are joining them on Saturday to see his closing act. I wish I could have gone with them, but Dad's answer hasn't changed. I've already missed too much school.

So, that's why I'm sitting in Calc, listening to Mr. Hathaway's thunderous voice explain the Chain Rule, while my friends are in the Big Apple. I keep stealing glances at the clock on the wall, counting down the seconds. I'm ready to tear out of here the very moment the bell rings. My mind is set, I'm going straight to the library. Faye is out, so I'm not obligated to sit with her lunch bunch.

When the bell finally sounds, I make my escape. My mind is so busy calculating the most efficient possible trajectory to the library that I don't notice Nate is giving chase, until he takes hold of my arm and spins me around. I blink up at him in confusion.

Where did he come from? He was definitely not in Mr. Hathaway's class.

His hand slides from my forearm to my palm, and he pulls me in the opposite direction, "This way."

Taken by surprise, I follow him through the school halls, down the stairs and outside to the parking lot. We come to a stop at his flashy Lamborghini, and he opens the hood of his car, which turns out to be the trunk. He lets go of my hand and removes my backpack. Before I have a chance to ask what he's doing, he drops both of our school bags inside and closes it. Then, he presses his key-fob and the doors open, "Hop in."

I just look at him, bemused. "I can't," I finally manage to reply, "I've already missed too many classes."

"You won't be missing a thing. Besides, I'm saving you from another forty five minutes of Don Quixote," Nate points out and gestures for me to get inside. "I guarantee we won't get busted. Hop in."

I hesitate. Nate has a point. I probably won't be missed. Still, I've never ditched a class before, not without a valid excuse anyway.

"You realize I'm holding your backpack ransom," he challenges, feigning seriousness.

I stare at him for a second longer, then drop into the passenger seat in surrender. He grins widely and rushes to the driver's seat. Both doors lower, and we're off.

"Where are we going?" I ask as he takes a right on red.

"Not far," Nate replies, withholding the specifics.

I've been hanging out with Nate enough to know that

when he gives a vague answer that's all I'm going to get. So, I don't bother pressing for details.

After a few turns, it seems like we're heading home. Now, I'm officially starting to freak out. What if Grandpa sees his car? Like its driver, it's hard to miss. What if Nate is taking me to his place? What then? And what if his parents come home? Does Nate even live with his parents? Judy said his sister has her own place, but she's eighteen.

"Relax, Liz. We're almost there," Nate seems to sense my distress.

"How old are you?" I blurt out, catching him by surprise.

"How old do I look?"

Faye said he's a senior, but he can't be eighteen, unless Lill is his twin. Judy would have mentioned it if that were the case. I give it a try, "Seventeen?"

"Look and see," he offers his black leather wallet to me. The tiny white star on its bottom left corner tells me that it might be some kind of ritzy brand name. Curiosity gets the best of me, and I take it. His driver's license reads Sinclair, Nathaniel, no middle name. He was born September, 21st, 1995.

Yep, he's seventeen.

I hand it back to him and he pockets it. At the sight of an empty spot on Beacon Hill, he signals and performs a perfectly aligned parallel parking job.

"You're good," the compliment is out of my mouth before I can stop myself.

As a reply, he smiles and the doors fly open. We climb out of the car, and Nate pops the trunk, producing a picnic basket and a big yellow blanket. He takes my hand, and we walk in silence toward the park. Nate gets us set up at the base of an enormous orange oak tree. He places the straw-woven basket down and lays the blanket neatly on the grass.

"Please, have a seat," Nate kneels and throws the lid open.

"Um," I reply, distracted by the scenario unfolding before

me.

"Liz, relax."

I sit down on the blanket across from him at a loss for words. He fetches a couple bottles of strawberry-kiwi juice and three plastic containers from the basket. Two of them hold tiny finger sandwiches, and the third is filled with black and white cookies.

If Nate is trying to win me over, it's working.

As if reading my mind a sly smile crosses his face, "Bon Appétit."

"This is so nice, thanks," I say lamely, smiling back at him.

"Eat first, thank me later," he jokes.

I pick a sandwich from its container and take a tiny bite. Nate twists the cap off a fruit drink, hands it to me and then throws a piece of bread to a white duck standing right beside a sign that reads: *Do not feed the birds.*

"Are you being kind to animals or just trying to break the rules?" I inquire playfully.

"I'm just looking out for my fellow feathery friend here," Nate tosses out another crumb.

"Oh really, what's his name?"

"Let me ask him," Nate turns back to the hungry duck, "What's your name, bro?"

The duck quacks right on cue.

"Well, there you have it," Nate replies, feigning seriousness.

I crack up laughing, and Nate joins in after a short pause. It's a perfect day. The sky is bright blue and almost cloudless. The chilly breeze is canceled out by the warmth of midday while sunlight peeks around the branches of the ancient tree standing over us. I've lost track of time sitting here with Nate enjoying the exquisite fall weather, and eventually catch myself watching him in the foreground of the beautiful scenery. The wind keeps blowing his dark blond hair into his face, and he brushes it away with his hand. *Don't do it, don't fall for him.* I try to convince myself. *It's stupid, and you know it.* But, I have a feeling it's a little late for that.

Shortly after, we load everything back into the car and go for a walk. Nate takes me to the Public Garden, and we rent a swan boat.

"Now tell me, was I right or was I right?" Nate asks, slowly pedaling in a rhythmic pace. "Isn't this better than Don Quixote?"

"Is this what you do when you're not in class?"

"I have no idea what you're talking about," Nate replies with indifference.

"Sure, you don't. Why do I even bother asking questions?"

"Because maybe someday you'll get your answers," Nate says in that way of his.

"Yeah, yeah. Ignorance is bliss and all that."

"This from the girl who didn't answer *my* question yet," Nate scoffs. "Liz, even you have to admit this is better than being stuck in the library."

"Of course it is. It's such a beautiful day and you've been so sweet. Still, it's not right to bail out on school."

"Right and wrong is overrated," Nate declares as we pedal down the lake. "Besides, no need to be so responsible all the time."

"You sound just like my dad's girlfriend," I start and then correct myself right away. "I mean, fiancé. Next, you'll be telling me to live life to its fullest because I might be reborn as a ladybug."

"Do you believe that?" Nate asks, focusing entirely on me now.

"I don't even know what that means," I reply. "Suri is a very spiritual person. She's into all that new age stuff."

"Well, what *do* you believe?"

I consider his question: *"what do I believe?"* My family is not very religious, Mom was a scientist and Dad encourages me to find my own answers. Suri has tons of beliefs, but Dad is always telling her not to brainwash me.

"Nothing and everything," I finally say. Nate arches his eyebrow enquiringly, and I elaborate, "Just like a spark that spreads into a fire, there's a little bit of truth in every belief and a lot of euphemism surrounding it."

Nate doesn't give me one of his smart remarks, and his expression is unreadable as we pedal back to the dock. We step off the swan boat and walk toward the bridge. Just past the halfway point, we stop to take in the view. I think about asking him if we can snap a picture of us together, but stop myself. The last thing I need is photographic evidence that I skipped school today.

Below us, an elderly couple sits on a bench holding hands, and a college girl leans against a colorful tree enthralled in her paperback. Down the walkway, a group of young mothers steer their baby strollers toward the north gate. Nearby, a father teaches his daughter how to ride her bike without training wheels. He follows behind her holding the bike seat with one hand while the other is busy wrangling her little brother by his panda bear leash. The scene reminds me of the time when Dad taught me how to ride a bike at Yoyogi park in Japan.

The little girl looks adorable in her pink helmet, although she seems frightened. She keeps begging her dad not to let go, without realizing he already has. She's so focused on her pedals that she keeps swerving left and right.

Suddenly her little brother breaks free and dashes toward a baby duck. The father rushes to catch the little boy calling, "Come back here, Parker!"

The girl on the pink bike looks around at the sound of her father's voice, moving the handle bars along with her head and turning the bike toward the lake.

Without thinking, I take hold of the lamp post and swing myself into a jump nearly missing the sidewalk below. I reach out just in time to grab the screaming girl by her pink jacket, preventing her impending fall into the cold dark water. Her bike hits the sidewalk ledge, flips into the lake, and she starts crying just as I set her back down on her feet.

Almost immediately, her father has his son in one arm and is running toward us, breathless. He kneels beside his daughter, picking her up in his free arm instantly. Before he even acknowledges me, I'm taking the stairs back to the bridge two at a time.

Nate is waiting for me at the top, his expression surprisingly blank. He places an arm around my shoulder as if nothing had happened and starts leading me toward the street. When we reach the sidewalk where his car is parked, Nate steps in front of me, forcing me to face him. He's about to speak when my phone chimes from inside my pocket, and I pull it out to check the message.

It's from Ian. Since the rock climbing incident, Ian has been texting me nonstop, all hours of the day and night. The message is always the same: *Did you change your mind yet?*

My answer is always: *No.*

This time, I text back: *When?*

Looking up at Nate, I ask, "What were you going to tell me?"

Nate doesn't have a chance to speak because my phone lights up, along with that loud heavy metal ringtone blaring. He throws his head back and lets out an exaggerated breath, clasping his hands behind his neck. Then, he leans against his car and motions for me to go ahead.

I press answer and raise the phone to my ear.

Ian is talking before I can say *hello*, "Is there any chance you can come here, like in a few hours or so? Take the train here, and I'll drive you back. Or maybe ask Faye to give you a ride. Wait. It's Thursday. Faye's in New York. I can call EJ. He won't mind. He'll get you here and back in no time," he says all in one breath as if by giving me a second to think I might reconsider.

"Hang on just a minute, Ian," I cover the phone mic and

look up at Nate. His face carries a thousand questions, and I hesitate. There's no way I can ask Nate for a favor right now. I shake my head and raise the phone back to my ear.

"Ask away, Liz," Nate says, stopping me. He notices that I'm wavering and presses on, "The answer is yes."

So I blurt it out, "Is there a chance you would drive me to Yale and back? I'll pay for your gas."

Nate straightens up and pulls the keys out of his pocket, "Let's go, then."

Uncovering the mic, I tell Ian, "I've got a ride, we're on our way. I'll call you when we're getting close."

Then, I hang up and ask Nate, "How long does it take to get to Yale from here?"

"That depends on how fast we're driving," Nate pauses considering his words and adds, "At the lawful speed limit about two hours."

I look down at the clock on my phone. It's half past three. Grandpa will flip if I'm not home by seven.

"What is it?" Nate breaks into my thoughts.

"Not enough time," I reply glumly.

Nate holds his hand out for the phone, and I oblige. I hover nearby as he scrolls through my contacts, stopping at Grandma. He commits the number to memory with a short glance, hands the phone back to me and clicks the doors open.

"Hop in," Nate says and lowers his tall figure into the deep bucket seat without waiting for my reply.

I follow suit and the doors lower automatically, encasing us inside. I shift in my seat and look at Nate. He has his phone in his hand and is touching numbers on the screen keypad. He hits send and presses the phone against his ear. Then, as if remembering I'm still here, he raises his index finger perpendicular to his lips with a soft "Shh!"

I give him a single nod.

The call connects, and he starts, "Hello Mrs. O'Neill. It's Nathaniel Sinclair." There's a pause, and he continues,

"Terrific. Thanks for asking, and yourself?"

Another extended pause. If I had long nails, I'd be biting them right now. *Is he out of his mind?*

"I'm glad to hear that. I apologize for disturbing you, but Mrs. Sinclair has been eager to meet Eliza for quite some time. She's asked me to invite her for dinner tonight, and I thought I should run it by you before making a formal invitation," Nate explains in a low charismatic voice. He pauses for an instant, and politely cuts in, "Dinner is served at seven, so we'll have her home before nine." It's silent for a moment, and then he says, "Absolutely, I'll have her call you. She'll be delighted," he pauses. "No. It will just be Mrs. Sinclair and I."

He listens quietly for what seems like forever, and then his lips curl into a smile, "Sure, I'll do that," he stops, waits patiently and assures, "Of course not, it's my pleasure. Sorry about the short notice. Thank you, Mrs. O'Neill." Nate listens to her reply and then he finishes, "I'll make sure to pass on the message. Thanks again."

He hangs up. I'm expecting him to look at me and offer some kind of explanation, but he doesn't. He dials someone else instead.

"Hey, *Mom*? Do me a favor. Call Liz's grandma and confirm she'll be joining us for dinner," he speaks into the phone and instantly seems exasperated by her reply. Her voice is loud enough to be overheard, but not enough to be coherent. After what seems like forever, he cuts in, "Could we please talk about this later? She's sitting right beside me." This time he cringes at her reply, pressing his lips together.

I try to tune in the other side of the conversation and catch a single sentence, "*FINE, give me the number.*"

He recites it from memory and ends the call, "Thanks, *Mrs. Sinclair.*" Nate hangs up before his poor mother has the chance to reply. Then, he turns and looks at me, wearing a smug expression.

I'm too dumbfounded to speak and just stare right back at him in utter disbelief.

"So, Yale?" He looks at my astonished face and starts the engine before I retrieve the ability of coherent speech.

The car roars to life, and Nate merges into traffic. I clear my throat over and over again, but it's no use. Ms. Johnson would be *so* proud of how my articulation skills have improved since the first day of school.

"I can't believe you lied to my grandma like that," I groan. "No one lies to my grandma and gets away with it. I'm toast. She'll ask me twenty questions about your mother, and I've never even met her."

"You'll be fine," Nate reassures me, shifting from forth to fifth.

I ignore him. I still can't believe he convinced his mother to lie on his behalf. *Who does that?*

"Tell me, why exactly are we going to Yale?" Nate asks, keeping his eyes on the road.

Since he went out of his way to do me a favor, the least I can do is tell him the truth about Ian's DNA theory. So, I do.

Afterward, Nate inquires, "Let's see if I've got it right. Your friend's brother believes that your late mother altered your DNA, transforming you into a mutant superhero. Was this before or after you were born?"

"When you put it like that it sounds really dumb."

"It's not dumber because it can't be. It's the dumbest idea I've ever heard, and that's saying something. You don't buy it, do you?" Nate asks and changes his mind before I have a chance to answer, adding, "No–scratch that. Of course you do, or we wouldn't be driving to Yale."

"Honestly, honestly, I don't. But I can't come up with anything else, so, why not?" I shrug. "And if he's wrong, he'll get off my case."

Nate seems unconvinced, but refrains from teasing me for a change. Instead, he suggests, "How about some music?"

20

Sitting at a tall science lab table with my legs dangling over the edge like a four year old, I keep asking myself, "How do I get into situations like this?"

My hands are trembling, not because it's cold, nor is it due to a caffeine high. No. My hands are shaking like this because I'm really starting to freak out. I'm not sure if I actually want to know the results of this test.

In an attempt to calm my nerves, I take a slow deep breath. *It's no use.* I try focusing on all the high-tech equipment locked in this bright facility. I don't really know what a DNA test entails, but they sure have a lot of machines in this place.

Ian's voice brings me back into the moment, "Let me ask you, O'Neill," Ian starts, digging through a cabinet drawer. "When did you first notice your mutant abilities?" Half joking, at least I hope.

Ian shrugs into a white lab coat over his street clothes and pulls his long hair into a low ponytail. He snaps on a pair of blue latex gloves and approaches carrying a small acrylic box. The way he looks in all that medical attire does nothing to change the lab rat sensation rapidly growing inside me. It actually kicks it up a notch.

I still don't know what to make of his theory. On one hand, I don't want to believe that my mother would experiment on her own child. On the other, it would explain a lot. My height for one, I'm as tall as most of the junior guys in my school. If I'd dare to wear Faye's platforms or high heels, I'd tower over them. Then again, my grandpa is tall, and Dad is even taller. My mom was short though, shouldn't that even things up?

I wish I understood genetics better. I mean, shouldn't I have an IQ of 200 or something? I'm the sum of two very intelligent people. But it seems like I can't get my GPA above 3.0. My good grades in physics and math are always canceled out by an abysmal performance in English and Chemistry. Then, there's my strong immune system which may just be the result of being indoctrinated into Suri's vegan life style. I attribute the quick thinking and reflexes under life threatening situations to the video game industry.

My PE evaluation report indicates that I set a new record at the track on the first day of school. But, it's not as if I have super human speed or anything. I've just had a lot of practice, that's all. I've been running with Dad since I was seven. I also ran with Ken a lot which may explain my speed. Add long legs to the equation, and there you have it. From what I've read online, the human land speed record is 27.9 mph. *I can't run that fast, I don't think.*

Now, Ian may have a point on the strength account. I have no explanation for that. *None.* The only strenuous activity I've ever performed is rock climbing. So, yeah. Maybe Ian could be onto something here with his crazy gene modification theory. But if that's the case, all I have to say is: *"Really, Mom? Gee, thanks! Couldn't you enhance my neural capacity index, or at the very least my cup size gene?"*

Ian is staring at me with an amused expression on his face. I've spaced out and probably missed something he just said.

"Sorry," I apologize. "What was that?"

"I wonder how you do that."

"Do what? Space out completely? It's one of my super powers," I joke.

"You have no idea, do you?" Ian crosses his arms and cocks his head to one side.

I frown, he lost me. But, what else is new? Having no answer I just shrug.

"Come on, O'Neill. Let's get this party started," Ian says, still laughing.

He sits on a metal stool by the counter and I take the one next to him. He opens the DNA testing kit for the sample collection and turns, "I already know the answer, but it's standard procedure to ask. Did you drink any coffee, or use tobacco products in the past four hours?"

"No, not in the past ever."

"Good girl," Ian teases. "Do you know anything about the procedure?"

"You'll be collecting samples of my spit," I reply wisely.

"Right, you could say that. But I'm talking about the actual process," Ian explains, curbing my short lived moment of wisdom.

"No clue."

He nods and takes an individually wrapped cotton swab out of the acrylic box, "It's easy. I'm gonna swipe this cotton swab against the inside of your cheek. Got it?"

I give him a nod.

Ian tears the tab off a sterile package and removes the cotton swab from a clear plastic cylindrical case, "Open, please."

He places the swab against my inner cheek and rolls it back and forth. Then, he carefully places it back inside its case and repeats the procedure on the other side. He seals the last sample, "I can explain to you what tests I'm planning to run. If you're interested, that is."

"No, thanks," I quickly reply.

"Do I bore you, O'Neill?" Ian challenges skeptically.

"*Who?* You? *Never.* Genetics is just to complicated for my super average brain. So, your expertise and the test results will suffice. Thanks, Ian."

Ian removes his gloves and trashes them, laughing in disbelief. He disposes the used material and goes back into the other room to store my DNA sample. Then, he returns, removing his lab coat, and hangs it on a hook by the door, "¡Vámonos!"

"Lets," I agree, following him out of the lab.

As we walk down the covered sidewalk toward the parking lot, I ask, "So how long do you think it will take for the results, like seventy-two hours or something?"

"Who do you think I am? *Dexter?* I'll need more time than that, O'Neill," Ian replies with a brief amused chuckle.

"What did I tell you? I'm terrible at Bio," I apologize.

We continue down the side walk and into the parking lot where Nate is leaning against his car, looking bored out of his mind. It's like I'm staring at one of those sports car magazine covers. Just replace the plastic model in a bikini with a hot guy in two hundred dollar ripped jeans.

I say his name softly, but somehow he hears me, turning his head in our direction. Ian and I both stare for a brief moment. I'm mesmerized by Nate while Ian is fascinated by his means of transportation.

Nate slowly straightens up and asks, "All done?"

"Is this the friend you mentioned?" Ian asks, sounding incredulous.

"Yeah, this is Nate. Nate, this is Ian," I introduce as he approaches.

Ian offers his hand for Nate to shake, but Nate doesn't seem to notice. He starts heading toward the driver's side, pressing his key-fob. The doors fly open, and Nate says, "You're Faye's brother. We've met before."

"Later Ian, let me know what you find out," I say,

pausing at the car door.

"No prob," Ian's expression changes ever so slightly when he faces Nate, and he urges, "Drive safe."

"Will do," Nate replies surely. He cordially waves at Ian and gets inside the car.

I wave goodbye, following suit and the doors slide closed. Ian stands by as Nate eases his way out of the parking lot. He sounds a double beep of the car horn. One last wave from Ian, and we're off.

21

"Why did Nate drive you to Yale?" Faye asks dubiously. She lies on her belly atop one of the two queen size beds, her legs swinging back and forth. A plate of grapes that she ordered from room service sits half eaten in front of her.

"Because Ian asked me too."

"I got that," she sounds annoyed, and I don't blame her. I blame her brother for opening his big mouth and telling her that we were there in the first place. Now, she's pumping me for answers, "What nobody can explain is *why* you had to go all the way to Yale to begin with? And with Nate of all people..." Her voice trails off at the end.

It's Ian's theory, his experiment, I'm just the test subject here. I'll leave it to Ian to explain *why* he thinks I'm a mutant freak, "You'll have to ask him. I'm terrible with biology. I was just there for a DNA sample."

Faye narrows her eyes at me unconvinced, "Yeah, right. Because my brother couldn't find any other willing girl at Yale to volunteer, could he?"

I shrug, and she shakes her head. Then, it's like something just occurs to her. Faye flips to her side and props herself up by her elbows, facing me, "OMG! You skipped school, didn't you? You were ditching class with Nate Sinclair when my brother called."

Thanks, Ian. Why must guys be so obsessed with sports cars? If Nate drove any other vehicle, we wouldn't be having this conversation. I bite the inside of my cheek, knowing that anything I say will dig the hole deeper.

"Unbelievable," Faye laughs. "You skipped class for Nate Sinclair," she shakes her head again, still laughing a little. Then, she tilts her head to one side as if analyzing me while I patiently wait for her diagnosis. "It's just a face you know," she blurts out eventually and looks me straight-on. "I would get it if Judy or Anna were so into Nate Sinclair, but you..." She trails off, popping another grape in her mouth.

"He's more than a pretty face," I jump to his defense.

Faye scoffs, "He's a piece of—"

"*Faye!*" I cut her off.

"What? I was going to say work, piece of work."

"No, you weren't."

"No, I wasn't," she admits.

"He's not that bad," I add defensively.

"He's worse than bad. Nate makes my brother look like the Pope."

I know Ian has never had a serious girlfriend, but I've heard all about the trail of broken hearts he has left behind. Nate is nothing like that. He doesn't even talk to anyone, apart from me and that Spark chick. I choose not to say anything and steal a grape from her plate. It's unexpectedly sweet. So, I grab a second and a third.

Faye shakes her head, clearly amused, and presses on, "Girly, you're too caught up... You'll ignore anything I have to say on the matter. He owns you. You're just too enticed by his looks and charisma," she lets out an exasperated sigh. "But don't worry, I'll be your shoulder to cry on once the spell is broken."

I copy her sigh pointedly, no point in arguing with her.

Faye holds a grape carefully between her thumb and

index finger, admiring it intently. Then, she says thoughtfully, "Beauty is like a grape, sweet and perfect... But remember, it'll eventually become a raisin."

A double knock at the door sends Faye leaping out of the bed to answer. She opens the door and motions with her hand, "Come on in, Blake."

Wellington enters the room, seeming uncomfortable, and stops only a few steps in. He's in black suit pants and a white button up shirt, the first two buttons undone. His suit jacket is folded neatly over his arm and he's carrying an aged leather bound book in his hand.

Faye closes the door and comes to stand beside him. Her eyes fall to his hand, and she wrinkles her nose, "You brought a book? I thought you were on your way to rehearsal."

Wellington shifts his weight from one foot to the other and looks down, as if just remembering he's holding a book. He shrugs, "I have a Latin test on Monday, and we have a long break between rehearsal and the performance. It's a good way to get my mind off things."

"*Latin*? Who takes Latin these days? Isn't it considered a dead language? When are you ever going to need that?"

He smiles shyly and taps the book in his hand.

I jump to his rescue, "Sit down, have a grape."

"Thanks, but I need to get going. I just stopped by to pass along a message from your grandma. She asked me to tell you that you guys are leaving at seven sharp."

"Got it," I say with a smile. "Good luck tonight."

"He doesn't need it." Faye surprises us both by adding, "Blake knows his stuff."

If Wellington seemed uncomfortable before, now he's visibly embarrassed. He looks down at his feet, "Thanks, Faye. Um... See you guys tonight."

"We'll be there," I assure him.

He nods, turns to leave, and Faye walks him to the door, "Later, Blake."

The moment she closes the door, I chastise her, "Could you make Wellington any more uncomfortable?"

She walks to her bed, flops down on her back and faces me, "By complimenting him?"

"Not that," I pause, crossing my legs under me, "Picking on him about a book."

She rolls her eyes at me and reaches for the controller. I get to my feet with a sigh. *Faye will be Faye.* She flips through the channels and stops on a runway special or something of the like, shooting me a sideways look. I squint at the TV and sit back down on the bed, lending my undivided attention.

On the screen, Lill Sinclair strolls across a catwalk. I can't figure out what she's wearing. It's one of those intricate designs that no one would be caught dead actually wearing on the street. Her hair is a wave of long red curls cascading with each step she takes. It's difficult to resist her allure, something about her makes it impossible to look away. She's perfection with a forest fairy gleam and an imposing confidence a lot like Nate's. It's the only similarity between the two of them that I can pinpoint, though. Truth be told, Lill and Nate couldn't be any more different from each other in appearance. I'm beginning to wonder if she's his half-sister, or stepsister maybe. She's pale and delicate with features resembling a porcelain doll while Nate's are perfectly symmetrical, strong and masculine.

Faye chuckles, breaking me out of my trance. I ignore her and lean against the headboard. Faye doesn't say anything, she just turns the volume up, and we both watch without a word.

When my grandparents, Faye and I arrive at Carnegie Hall three hours later, Mr. And Mrs. Blake are waiting for us in the main lobby. It turns out, Wellington's mother managed to leave her College seminar a day early and flew straight to New York. So, his father had Dora supervise the last few hours of the book signing to meet Mrs. Blake at the airport. Now, they're both here to surprise Wellington on his final performance, and we head to our reserved seats together.

It's strange seeing Wellington perform in this fancy auditorium as part of an ensemble. All the other times I saw him playing, it was in smaller events. It was always him and his cello, sometimes a violinist would string along. Tonight, he looks so grown up, performing with these old dudes. It's like he aged ten years in the past hour. He shines under the lights, and their performance is extraordinary.

I'm lost in the dreamy notes of Bach's Cello Suite Number 1, when Faye's whispery voice declares, "I'm head over heels in love with him."

At first I take it as her grandiose commentary on his musical proficiency, but one look at Faye's expression tells me that she isn't joking. *Nope.* Faye is dead serious, and her next words are even more frightening, "You've been one of his best friends *like* forever, can you set us up?"

"No!" I deadpan, forgetting for an instant who I'm talking to. Nobody dares to be so forward with Faye. Not unless they're looking for a smack down. I brace myself for the onslaught, but she holds back. Faye just studies me carefully as if trying to understand my motives. Wellington has a girlfriend, that's my motive. I know the concept must be lost on Faye since, from what I've heard, she doesn't stick with a boyfriend for longer than a month. Still, she ought to know the difference, Wellington and Mattie have been together for almost two years.

Faye finally asks, sounding intrigued rather than annoyed, "Why not? Do you like him or something? What about your blind crush on Nate Sinclair?"

"No, that's not it," I reply honestly, totally ignoring her comment about Nate. First things first. "It's just that Wellington has a girlfriend."

"He does?" She whispers, seeming sincerely confused all of a sudden.

She can't be serious.

Wellington is always picking Mattie up at our school. It's hard to believe she's never seen them together. I'm the new one in town, not her.

"You're punking me, right? You can't say you've never seen them together," I reply quietly in total disbelief

"Nope. To tell you the truth, I might have past him a thousand times without noticing. He looks entirely different from how I remember. If someone mentioned Blake's name three days ago, I'd picture another person completely. You have to admit he's changed. Not only is he more mature now, but he's also hot."

"Faye, snap out of it," I cut her off before she can go any further and repeat my earlier words, emphasizing each one of them very slowly this time, *"Blake has a girlfriend."*

Faye blinks out of her daze. She seems just as confused as I usually am in Spanish class. Feigning nonchalance, she inquires, "Who is she?"

I don't like the sound of that. It's obvious Faye never acknowledged Mattie's existence until now. It's best to keep it that way. So, I omit that she's in our Calculus class, and answer vaguely, "I don't believe you know her. She's in my Drama class and plays the clarinet in the marching band."

"How fascinating," Faye replies, sounding bored. "I know a lot of people, what's her name?"

"From the marching band?" I ask, attempting to postpone the inevitable.

"Try me," Faye challenges.

"Her name is Madison."

"What? Fatty Mattie?" Faye squeaks, prompting the woman beside her to shoot us a well deserved glare.

I clamp my mouth shut, appalled. I've known Faye for years and never heard her say anything so mean about anyone, ever. Her wannabes speak in that manner all the time, but not Faye. Indifferent, yes. Most days, Faye strolls the school halls as if the world revolves around her, completely self-absorbed, but I never took her for heartless.

"Don't look so horrified, you know it's true," Faye lowers her voice and rolls her eyes in resignation.

"No, it's not!" I disagree, still aghast. "I think she's adorable. She's also really nice."

"Well, the Elephant Man was nice," Faye voices in a mocking tone.

Faye is way off base. Mattie is actually pretty cute, with her blue anime eyes and blond hair. I whisper back, "By the way, Mattie is not fat. She's curvy."

"So are you gonna set us up, or not?" Faye asks insistently, disregarding everything I just said.

"*HE HAS A GIRLFRIEND*," I hiss in the loudest possible whisper I can muster. Just then, Ben crosses my mind. Faye's gorgeous boyfriend, with his dimples and award winning smile. I add in frustration, "And wait? You have a boyfriend."

"No, I don't," Faye replies simply.

I scowl at her.

"I broke up with Ben two nights ago," Faye clarifies.

"Two nights ago you were here in New York..." I trail off as it sinks in and then chastise her, "You didn't. You wouldn't be so cruel to breakup with Ben over the phone."

"He'll live," she waves me off. "Actually, I texted him," something in my expression gives her pause, and she considers, "Hey, don't judge. He asked me out by text message. So, it's fitting to end it the same way."

I slouch in my seat, wanting nothing more than a way out of this love quartet. Faye is giving me a migraine, and I never have migraines. I massage my temples, "Just leave me out of this, please. I'm begging you. Madison is cool, and I like Ben even more. Neither of them deserve whatever it is you have in mind right now."

"As you wish," Faye disregards and adds almost inaudibly, "Just wait and see, someday he will be mine."

I groan and slouch even further down in my chair, feeling

crummy about poor Mattie who is sure to go down in flames without knowing what hit her. Faye smiles at me mischievously before turning her attention to the musicians on stage. It's sad to know Wellington's virtuoso performance won't be the most memorable event of the evening. When I think back to this night years from now, I'll remember Faye's bold declaration in my ear, and the overdressed lady scowling at us.

I'm so annoyed and beat after this unending day that when Grandpa says he's heading to the hotel, I offer to come along. Faye volunteers to stay behind with the Blakes and Grandma to wait for Wellington. I momentarily debate whether I should stay or go, deciding to leave with Grandpa in the end. Whatever scheme she has in mind, it's not like she can execute it with his parents around. Besides, what could happen with Grandma as chaperone?

22

"Say, Faye, who's Mr. October?" Fran asks, sliding her lunch tray onto the cafeteria table.

"Nobody," Faye peels off the lid of her zero fat, zero sugar, zero taste Greek yogurt.

"No lucky guy this October?" Fran presses skeptically.

"Not this month, not next month, or ever again. I've found what I was looking for, no reason to keep trying other flavors," Faye shoves a spoonful into her mouth and impressively doesn't make a face.

"So, what's this new flavor?" Kiara sounds amused.

"Vanilla mint," Faye replies dreamily.

"Can I quote you on that? I have room in my school paper column," Fran asks, overloading her salad with blue cheese.

"It's your funeral," Faye shrugs and takes a big gulp of water, probably to wash it down.

"Who is he?" Kiara cuts in curiously.

"He'll remain unnamed for the time being," Faye pauses and looks straight at me. "He's taken."

I look down and stir my watery soup. Just then, Alexis, Judy, and Anna join us. Alexis slides her tray beside me and asks, "What's the meaning of '*Wa ka ra na i?* '"

"I don't know," I reply, grateful for the change in subject.

Judy lifts her chin smugly, "What did I tell you? Not Japanese," she rolls her eyes at Alexis and elaborates to the rest of us, "Zoë can't be Japanese. Her last name is Fairchild. They were just–"

"Oh, it's Japanese *alright*," I cut in, exceedingly interested now. "'*Wakaranai*' means *I don't know* in Japanese. Who was Zoë talking to?"

"Michael Price," Alexis replies, wearing a smirk.

Michael is back, fully recovered from his food poisoning episode. Without the bluish complexion, his good looks compensate for his temperamental personality, at least according to most of the girls in the halls of Saint Pete's. Let's just say one needs to keep their eyes peeled not to get run over by his admirers when he passes by.

I take a peek in Michael's direction, he's staring intently at Faye. She's oblivious, engaged in conversation with Fran and Kiara.

Out of nowhere, Faye turns to look at him and then stands up, "Be right back, guys."

All eyes are on her as she walks up to a waiting Michael Price and follows him outside without a word exchanged.

"No flipping way," Fran blurts out. "Is he vanilla mint?"

"It can't be him. Zoë is hot and all. But she sure wouldn't be sitting there so confident while her boyfriend so casually walked out of sight with Faye," Judy points out, wrinkling her nose in confusion.

"Definitely not Faye's vanilla mint. Zoë even smiled at Faye," Alexis notes in accordance. "She's totally cool about whatever is going on between them."

"Totally," Anna agrees.

Kiara raises an eyebrow at me inquiringly. I just shrug, clueless. Then, I go back to work on my MSG flavored cup o' soup before the other girls have a chance to bombard me with questions for which I have no answers.

Faye never returns to the lunch table, and I carry both of

our trays to the trash receptacles before heading to Chemistry.

Surprisingly, Ben acts normal when we meet at the lockers. His dimply smile is not so dimply today, but other than that he seems to be taking this breakup ordeal pretty well.

We part ways at the door and I start setting up the lab station. Not long after, Michael sits next to me, and I try to initiate a conversation before class begins, "How are you feeling?"

One look at him makes me regret my question. After what seems like forever, he replies with a simple, "Fine."

He must be embarrassed about the incident. I shouldn't have brought it up. In search of something to do, I open my notebook and begin doodling beakers and test tubes on the left corner of the page. This could get very awkward, considering he's my newly assigned lab partner.

Michael is also in my Spanish class and looks mostly bored the whole time. When I walk to the library, he follows two steps behind me without saying anything. Then, he sits down across from me, pulls out his notebook and works silently on his homework. I just stare at him, confused as one can be, not daring to force the small talk a second time.

A few minutes before the final bell, Greg drags Michael into some kind of basketball huddle outside the library. Michael is visibly annoyed and reluctantly follows him. Once they're out of sight, I gather my things and leave.

Half way to the parking lot, Mattie calls out, "Hey, Liz, wanna a ride?"

Before I can say "no, thanks," she is beside me, wrapping her arm around mine like a chain link. Right away, she starts drilling for info, "Do you know why Faye broke up with Ben? Is it because of Michael? Do you know if they got together this weekend?"

Thanks to Wellington, I'm spared from Mattie's game of twenty questions. He hops out of the SUV when he sees us coming and opens the passenger door for Mattie.

Unaccustomed to his sudden act of chivalry, she lets out, "Oh, wow, thanks."

He closes the door behind her and faces me, "What did you say to her?"

"What do you mean?" I ask at a loss.

"About Faye and I."

Comprehension dawns, but I don't have time to chastise him because Mattie rolls down her window, "What's the hold up?"

"It's nothing," he replies without looking at her and opens the back door for me.

I point back at the school building, "Maybe I should wait for–"

"Just get in," he cuts me off, and so I do.

I place my backpack beside me and fumble around for the seat belt. The entire time I sense Mattie's eyes on me, but I don't look up. I really wish I were anywhere else, but Wellington is my friend, and Dad always says, "Friends don't turn their backs in a moment of need."

The SUV starts forward and I reach for my water bottle to keep my hands busy. I open the lid and take a big gulp. Just as I do Wellington blurts out, "I kissed Faye."

A geyser of warm spring water mists the back of the seat and I start coughing.

"What did you just say?" Mattie asks deliberately.

Wellington immediately appends, "It was unintentional, and it's not gonna happen again."

"*Unintentional?* Did you fall into her mouth or something?" Mattie inquires cynically.

I launch into a coughing fit, unable to believe my ears. *When did that happen? Before or after our little talk?* I cough some more.

"When?" Mattie's voice is contrite.

"Well," he hesitates, scratching the back of his neck. "Last Saturday."

"And just now you felt like sharing," it's a statement, not a question.

"It's not something I could tell you over the phone," he rationalizes.

She shifts in her seat to look at me, "And you knew."

I didn't, but I might as well have. Faye was clear of her intentions, I just didn't expect it to happen so fast. I shake my head vigorously, still coughing.

"She clearly didn't," Wellington cuts in. "Can't you tell?"

Has he lost his mind? This is not a good time to be a smart aleck, Wellington.

He realizes his mistake too and apologizes, "I'm sorry."

"For what?" She snaps. "Sucking face with the queen bee, or for not telling me before."

"Um... Both?"

"Aaaarrrgggghhh!" She fumes, and I feel terrible for her.

"Say something," Wellington pleas in a small voice.

She puffs out her cheeks and jabs on, "What's there to say? You got hot and heavy with Faye on your big weekend. Hooking up with *her* of all people."

"Can you please tone it down?" His voice carries a hint of impatience as he repeats, "It was only a kiss."

"How could you?" Mattie's voice hits an all time high. "She's such a heartless bit–"

I open my mouth to defend Faye, but Wellington beats me to it. He shoots Mattie a "cut-it-out look" and lowers his voice, "If you're gonna hate someone, it should be me, not her. And definitely, not Liz. It's my fault, blame me."

Now, he's done it.

"You're defending her," she yells and grips the door latch. "Stop the car, let me out."

"Chillax, we're almost there."

Mattie presses her lips into a tight line, her eyes filled with tears as she turns away, facing the window. Wellington turns the music on, but the melodic piano does nothing to break the tension. After a block, Mattie is climbing out of the car before we even come to a complete stop.

"What time am I picking you up?"

"Don't bother!" She slams the door behind her.

Wellington takes off, the SUV wheels screeching in complaint. I brace myself, not knowing what to do or say. I've never seen him like that before. He slams his hand on the wheel and turns the volume up. The music seems to calm him, and the car slows down. The entire drive home his eyes remain on the road, and I keep my questions to myself.

When he pulls over in front of my building, I mumble, "Thanks for the ride."

I grab the handle to open the door, and he speaks in a choked voice, "Sorry to put you in the middle of all that."

"It's alright," I turn around, but he's looking straight ahead. I hesitate before adding, "A little advice, though. Next time you need a mediator, pick someone neutral to the matter."

He faces me, "That was never my intention, I wasn't going to say anything until after. But..." He trails off and lets his forehead drop against the wheel. "I can't seem to do anything right lately."

I don't know what to say to that. So, I just sit here debating whether to stay or go. I'm about to leave when he speaks again, "She'll never forgive me."

His statement catches me off guard, and the words are out before I can stop myself, "Isn't that what you wanted?" It sure seemed like it by the way he handled things.

"No. Of course not," Wellington says without a pause, looking at me as if he couldn't believe I would suggest such a thing. "I'd never..." He trails off and scratches the back of his neck. "I've never even looked at another girl since I started dating Mattie. I don't know what got into me."

"Well, you ripped off the band-aid," I point out and sigh in sympathy.

He goes on, "Faye is unique, she's brilliant... To me, she's the prelude from Bach's Cello Suite No. 1," he pauses, taking in my confused expression, and a sad smile crosses his face. "What I'm trying to say is that Faye is perfection," he lets out a long breath, clearly torn. "But, there's Mattie. Just because a drop-dead gorgeous girl is into you out of the blue, doesn't mean you'll give up someone you care about. Plus, Faye will ditch me the moment someone more interesting comes along, and it's only a matter of time. I just hope Mattie forgives me."

"I don't know what to say."

His smile is forced, "You don't have to say anything. Thanks for hearing me out."

"Any time," I reply before leaving his car and watch as he drives away.

I go upstairs, head straight to my bedroom and pull out my homework. Just to put it away minutes later, unable to focus. I grab a charcoal pencil, my sketchbook, and head outside. Then, I sit in my usual spot on the ledge of the balcony and resume drawing the adjacent building from where I left off.

By the time I finish, the sun has changed positions and the shadows are cast across the edifice. Instead of closing the sketchbook and heading back inside, I catch myself turning to a blank page and drawing again. Not a building this time, but a person.

I've never drawn someone from memory. But somehow, it's as though he's sitting right across from me. I picture him in a way I've never seen before. In my mind, Nate sits on the edge of his balcony. One of his legs hangs over and the other is propped up on the ledge. Pressing the charcoal into the paper, I trace a vertical line, creating the wall his back rests against. From there, I work on his back and shoulders, his neck disappearing in the collar of his button down shirt. I shape his hair and head with sketchy lines and then begin to trace his profile.

Taking a deep breath, I work on the shape of his lips and with perfect precision run my thumb gently above his eye before tracing his eyelashes, shading in his features until I'm sure that I've captured his essence. I'm so focused on my drawing that I don't feel a presence hovering over me.

"I didn't know you could draw," Faye's unexpected voice startles me, and I jump. Faye gasps and grabs my shoulder.

My sketchbook flies over the balcony's edge, the pages fluttering like a wounded bird all the way down. We're so high up that I don't even hear it hit the ground.

"Faye," I get on my feet, feeling a little shaken. "Don't sneak up on me like that!"

"I'm so sorry," Faye apologizes, her voice cracking at the end.

"It's okay. I'm alright."

"I'm not," Faye's voice trembles, and her hands are shaking. "I swear I saw you falling." I pull her into a hug to reassure her, and she hugs me back. When we break apart, she goes to the edge, "Your sketchbook is down there somewhere, but I can't see it from here."

"Let's go get it," I motion toward the door, and she follows me.

We comb the alleyway for my sketchbook to no avail. It's getting dark, and we call off the search.

Back upstairs, we head straight to my bedroom. Faye gets more and more uneasy by the second, so I ask, "What's eating you?"

"I need to tell you something, and you're not going to like it."

"You kissed Wellington."

She frowns, and her shiny lips open, "That's not what I wanted to–" Her phone starts ringing, cutting her off mid-sentence. Michael's face fills the screen. She sighs and mumbles, "Man, this is gonna get annoying." Then, she answers it, "Chill, you've got my word. I just–"

She sits down on the corner sofa, crosses her legs and listens to him impatiently. I sit on the edge of my bed across from her. She shakes her head and runs her fingers through her hair. Faye seems worked up by whatever he's saying. She catches me watching her, and rolls her eyes, "You won't have to. Okay, bye now."

"What was that about?" I ask the instant she hangs up.

"Just Michael," she waves him off.

She's definitely hiding something. *I wonder what?*

She looks quizzically at me, "Why did you say I kissed Blake? I mean, how come you didn't say Blake kissed me?"

I decide to play along, "Ok, so Wellington kissed you."

"How did you find out? We were backstage, just the two of us. He told you, didn't he?"

I stop myself just in time from revealing that Wellington confessed to Mattie, and I just got caught in the crossfire. If I did, Faye wouldn't leave me alone until I gave her a full report on it. So, I shrug.

She takes my silence as disapproval and gets defensive, "It happened, okay? I didn't plan it. His mother sent me to go fetch him. You don't believe me, ask Mrs. Blake. It must be nerve-racking to play in front of so many people, because I walked in, and he pulled me into a hug. Next, we were kissing. It was the sweetest kiss ever. His lips are so gentle and soft. I've never been kissed like that before. He tastes like—"

"Vanilla mint," I cut in. "I was at the lunch table today, remember?"

"Did you know he has gold flecks in his brown eyes?" She asks in a dreamy voice, a dopey smile crossing her face.

I shake my head and sigh, "I've never been that close to him before."

Faye sounds lost in her own bubble as she goes on, "Me neither. And that smile of his, it's captivating, when he smiles he truly means it. Don't even get me started with those strong arms. I still can't believe we actually kissed. It's too bad his conscience got to him. But that's when I realized he's not the kind of guy who would ever cheat on me. I'm unquestionably in love with him."

"Oh brother!" I murmur to myself, and she dares to accuse me of having a *blind crush*. At least she kissed the guy. But then again, Nate doesn't have a girlfriend. Not that I know of. I scoff, "Why is that? Is it because he actually 'has' a conscience and opposites attract?"

"No," she breaks out of her daze, annoyed by my comment. "Because of the way he did it. He could have just pushed me away, made a scene, or played innocent. But he didn't. He handled it like a true gentleman. He must have been conflicted by the situation, but he put that aside because he was concerned about my feelings. When he finally pulled away, he did it gently. He said that he admires me, among many other things. And he apologized, like a gazillion times. So, it's not like he led me on or anything. But, here's the best part. Not once did he mention that he had a girlfriend. Liz, he said he was flattered, holding me in his arms until I was ready to let go—"

Her phone rings again, and she glances down at the screen before answering, "Hey Brit, how's it going?"

To me, she mouths, "It's EJ. Gotta go, catch you later, 'kay?"

"'Bye," I mouth back.

She hangs her purse on her shoulder and waves goodbye.

I stare at the empty doorway long after she's gone, wondering, "What's going on in my friend's brilliant mind?"

23

Wednesday afternoon. It's like the student body of Saint Pete's High has been abducted by extraterrestrials and replaced with alien clones. The ones I interact with daily, I mean. It's the only way I can explain everything that's happening.

More than a week has past and things have changed a lot. The rumor about Faye and Michael hooking up soon died out, but she has been acting weird since then. Particularly around Nate, if before she disliked him, now she despises him. She isn't subtle, it's like she wants him to know he's unwelcome when she's around.

Nate isn't his usual self either. He has attended every one of his classes this week to everyone's surprise. He's also around the cafeteria during lunch with Spark. I wonder what's up with those two. He talks to me more casually. Maybe he's had enough of my "angel girl" behavior as he calls it. He hasn't stopped by the library even once, but for that I hold Michael as the culprit. It's clear those two have a grudge against each other, I just can't put my finger on it.

The wannabes appear to be in sync with Faye's mood, and it's pretty odd not hearing them defaming anyone during lunch. Even *I* got a break this week. Lately, their topics revolve around the Halloween dance which is weeks from now, the game from the weekend before, and the season finale of *Gossip Girl.*

Ben is back to his old self, dimply smile and all, clearly over the frigid way Faye cut him loose. I can't say the same about Mattie. Wellington is still trying to straighten things up with her, but Faye's presence is a constant reminder of his betrayal. At least she's talking to me again, just not like she used to. Sometimes, I have the impression she blames me for the way things turned out. Sometimes, I do the same.

Now, we're doing this zip-zap drama game, and Mattie keeps messing it up. She seems devastated and crestfallen. Her puffy eyes are evidence of hours spent crying, and it's all Wellington's fault. He could have broken the news more gently. But then again, I guess there's no easy way to admit that you cheated. To top it off, Faye is turning guys down left and right, proof that she's waiting for Wellington to come around.

Sigh.

Ms. Campbell calls for a semi-circle. Today we're reading through excerpts from *A Midsummer Night's Dream,* another piece by William Shakespeare. Which makes me wonder if there are any other playwrights out there.

Michael Price is in almost all my classes, including this one. He's sitting directly across from me and will be reading the part of Puck. As I stare at him, I just can't get over it. It's just a plus one to the oddities that surround me lately. Michael doesn't seem the drama type, and his expression concurs. He looks incredibly bored and annoyed. But, he's sticking to it, lack of enthusiasm and all.

After the bell, I stay to help Ms. Campbell put the room back together. I'm supposed to meet Faye and Kiara in thirty minutes for this volunteer gig they're organizing. Faye says volunteer work looks good on college applications.

While stacking chairs in the back corner of the room, I overhear a quiet argument taking place between Michael and Zoë.

"Michael?" Zoë says his name in an inquiring way as if expecting some kind of explanation.

"We both know my angle is irrelevant. I shall do what I am told," is Michael's candid reply.

"Enough with the '*shall*' Michael, it's the twenty-first century. Nobody says that anymore," Zoë remarks bluntly.

There's a pause, and I try to spot them as I continue helping Ms. Campbell.

"Share what's in your mind, Michael," Zoë presses on.

"We do what's asked of us," Michael pauses and then adds reassuringly, "I'll stick with it until the end, you don't have to worry about me going rogue."

Are they rehearsing for some part? This doesn't sound like Shakespeare.

"Shut off the lights on your way out, please," Ms. Campbell calls from the door.

"I will, Ms. Campbell," I reply distractedly.

"Something's bothering you, and I need you to tell me what it is," Zoë's tone is one of plea.

They must be exceptionally close since I'm hearing them clearly. But somehow, they're nowhere in sight.

"Michael?" Zoë insists.

"Zophiel, it took me days to recover. We're falling way behind here," he pauses.

Zophiel? Is that her name? I wouldn't have guessed.

"Go on," Zoë probes.

"Let's just say that throwing a ball around can't be of any help," he finally blurts out.

Huh? I thought he was this basketball MVP back at his old school. Now, he wants to quit the team? This guy never fails to surprise me with his strange behavior.

"We need to blend in here," Zoë explains calmly. "This might take a while. It could literally take a life time. I don't believe she's in imminent danger. I really don't know what game he's playing. He's either purposely delaying, or he's unsure. Either way, we still have the upper hand. She's not afraid of you, and he barely approached her the entire week. If only you could shadow her full time... Nobody would dare to get near her."

"It's not a bad idea," Michael sounds hopeful for the first time.

"But it is. If we did that, any doubts they may have would vanish. One missed step..." Zoë trails off.

"I still think we're at a disadvantage here."

What on Earth are they talking about? Who is "she," Faye?

"I don't," Zoë contests thoughtfully, "You made an ally who's cooperative, and surprisingly she's keeping her mouth shut."

"I knew she would. Her mind is unique, and she can be a great asset to us," Michael reassures.

"Like I said, keep her from interfering and I see no harm in it," Zoë replies. "It's always wise to have a backup. Even though, we have no reason for concern just yet. So far she talks to you and smiles. She doesn't seem bothered by having you around. She even helped you to the school nurse the other day."

Wait! What? Are they talking about me?

Now I need to know where they are. It's almost like the voices are coming from the ceiling. I pull back the curtains, but there's no one behind them. I open the door and peek down the hallway. It's all cleared out, except for a maintenance guy mopping the floor.

"Nathaniel is not stupid. He's already figured it out," Michael's words stop me in my tracks.

Without question, they're talking about me and Nate. Just when I thought things couldn't get any weirder... Unable to hold my tongue any longer, I call out, "Michael? Zoë? Where are you guys?"

Only silence answers my call. I wait for the voices to return, but they don't. Eventually, I grab my backpack, hit the lights on the way out and make my way to the volunteer gathering.

When I enter the room, I'm taken aback by the number of kids they were able to assemble in such short notice. I guess being popular has its perks at times like this. Scanning the group, I spot Michael Price among them. He's alone, Zoë is nowhere to be found. Part of me feels like I should walk up to him this very moment and demand to know what's going on. *Who am I kidding?* I'm no Faye. I'd never confront him in a room full of people. *Or would I?* I start toward Michael, but Ben Nolan gets there first, which makes my decision for me. They strike up a conversation right off the bat, and I leave an empty seat between Michael and I, just so I'm not tempted to do something stupid and embarrass myself in front of half the school.

I'm awestruck when Nate shows up at the meeting. Since when does he care about aiding the community? What's more, he takes the seat between us. That's so "un-Nate-like" I'm not sure how to react.

"Thanks for saving a seat," Nate says in a low voice.

"Um... Sure thing."

Faye calls for our attention, and Kiara kicks off her spiel about the volunteer work we'll be performing the second Saturday of the month, starting in November.

"What will we be doing exactly?" A guy's voice from the back corner cuts in.

"I was thinking something along the lines of visiting a hospice, a retirement home, or maybe a hospital," Faye suggests.

Students start nodding in agreement and Nate chuckles beside me, catching my attention. Nate looks smug, as if he's keeping a priceless secret.

Faye frowns and looks straight-on at Michael, "That's all I got, Mike. But I'm open to suggestions."

Wait! What? Did I miss something here?

Michael is as silent and self-absorbed as ever. He barely seems to be breathing since Nate sat beside him. So, what on Earth is Faye going on about?

I remove my eyes from Nate and look around the room. The other students seem to be as confused as I am. Even Kiara seems thrown by Faye's words. I keep telling Faye, she has too many extracurricular activities on top of her AP classes, something's got to give. She's losing it.

All eyes jump from Faye to Michael, expectantly. As usual, he's uncomfortable under the spotlight and tightens his grip on the armrest. Moved by his discomfort, Judy steps in, "Do you feel awkward around sick people? I usually do. So I totally, totally understand."

"Totally," Anna notes beside her.

Judy is willingly attempting to help someone. *What did I tell you? Alien clones.*

"No, Judy. That's not the case," Nate puts a hand on Michael's shoulder and announces sarcastically, "Pretty Boy here doesn't like to hang around impending death."

I fight the urge to elbow Nate in the ribs. *Seriously, does he have to pick on Michael every single chance he gets?*

"Hands off," Michael says between clutched teeth.

"Just telling it like it is, bro," Nate removes his hand, but not before giving a little double pat on his back.

Michael leans forward and suggests in a gentle tone, "How about an orphanage?"

"That's a great idea," Kiara agrees.

"There's one about twenty minutes from here," a brunette sophomore says, looking down at her smartphone.

"There's one in Cambridge. My sister volunteered there her senior year, they're always looking for extra help," Jonathan from my Physics class suggests.

"So, is everybody cool about volunteering at an orphanage?" Faye asks.

Some students nod, others say "yes," and in the end, Faye

wraps up the meeting with a unanimous decision.

As I hang my backpack on my shoulder to leave, Nate offers me a ride home. Before I can accept, Faye is pulling me aside, "You're riding with me."

"It's fine, Faye. He lives right next door."

"No, Liz. You're riding with me," Faye insists.

I'm about to cave when she turns to look in Michael's direction at the other side of the room. She presses her lips together into a thin line, never removing her eyes from his. Then, she closes her trembling hands into two fists at her sides, and her voice drops an octave, "Whatever," before walking away.

"What's up with her?" I bristle at Faye's behavior.

She's so mad at me that her hands are shaking. I've never seen her like this before. I'm debating whether to stick around through cheer practice or catch a ride home with Nate, when he says, "She's on to me." His speculative eyes fixed on Faye's retreating back.

I can't stifle my scoff, "You think?"

He narrows his eyes at me as if pondering my remark. Then, he shoots me one of his most radiant smiles before offering his hand, "Come on, let's get out of here."

It throws me off for a split second, but I quickly recover and take hold of his hand, allowing him to lead the way.

"What have you been up to?" Nate asks as we drive. "We haven't hung out much lately."

"What happened to you?" I blurt out. "Did you finally get caught, or just decide to be responsible for a change?"

"You've been busy with Pretty Boy lately. I didn't want to intrude," Nate brushes off.

I just look at him. *Really? That's his explanation.* He senses my gaze and peeks at me as he switches gears. A puff of air escapes my lips in exasperation and I urge, "Why the sudden change of heart?" I study him closely, waiting for any reaction. His manner remains the same, but the tension is tangible.

"You saved a seat for me," he replies noncommittally.

That's not exactly what happened, but I decide to drop it. I missed him this past week. I don't want to push him away, just when he's coming around.

As if reading my thoughts, Nate takes my hand and squeezes it reassuringly. I close my eyes, savoring the feeling. Just then, he pulls it away to change gears, and its absence hits me more forcefully than ever. Nate parks in front of my building and shuts off the engine. We're home.

I unbuckle my seat belt, "Now, that was fast."

"It's a Lambo," Nate laughs briefly. "I'd hope it makes better time than Faye's bug."

The door raises beside me, and I chuckle, "Don't let Faye hear you say that." Then, stepping out of his car, I add, "Thanks for the ride."

"Don't mention it."

I start heading toward the building and hear the little blip as he locks the car. I've taken only a couple steps when Nate calls after me, "Hey, Liz." I turn around, and he asks, "Are you happy?" That came from nowhere. I must look confused because Nate presses on, "Would you consider yourself a happy person? Content?"

Where is he going with this? Am I happy?

"Most of the time," I reply honestly. "Why do you ask?"

He shakes his head, "Just forget it. It's my evil manipulative side rearing its ugly head."

"Huh?"

"What can I say? Old habits die hard," he spins around and strolls to his building.

"Are you?" I call after him. "Happy?"

He pauses and looks at me over his shoulder, meeting my eyes, "Hardly ever."

My heart tightens inside my chest, and I want to reach out to him. But his mask is back in its place, and he's walking again, "See you around, Liz."

As he takes the stairs, I wonder what he meant by "evil

side." What kind of inner demons can bring him such sadness? And what does Faye know that she isn't telling me?

I dash inside, charging toward the elevators, "Hold the door, please!"

The newly weds from the floor below ours smile kindly at me. The doors close, and I push my button, smiling sheepishly back at them. It takes what seems like forever to reach my floor.

As the doors slide open, I rush into the apartment, heading straight to my room. Without hesitation, I pull my phone out of my pocket, and call Faye, pacing back and forth as it rings. A glimpse at my alarm clock tells me that she's probably still at cheer practice, but I let it ring anyway.

The line clicks, and after a short pause Faye speaks, "Liz?"

I can't help but notice a hint of edginess in her voice. *Is she that worried? What's going on here?* I brace myself not to sound overeager, "Hey, Faye. Did I interrupt your practice?"

"No, we're still warming up. What's the matter?"

Where do I begin? I can't just blurt it out, it's better to invite her over.

"Liz?"

"I'm here. Can you come over after practice?"

"Why?" Faye sounds skeptical.

"I need to talk to you."

"It's about Nate, isn't it?" Faye inquires knowingly. I hesitate, and she takes my moment of pause as a "yes," saying, "Liz, I can't talk about it. I swear to you, or maybe I shouldn't do that either..."

Now, I'm the one starting to get worried, "Faye, what's going on?"

"I really wish I could tell you," Faye replies. "I just can't."

"But I need to know," I press. "What did you find out about him? You used to like him before –"

"Oh, no. I never liked him," she cuts in. "And you're better off not knowing. Even if I told you, I don't think you'd believe me. Do you want my advice?"

"Do I have a choice?"

"This time, yes. You do. So do you want it or not?"

"Sure," I surrender, hoping that maybe she'll let something slip.

"There are a zillion guys out there. Give someone else a shot, EJ is cool, he always asks about you. Let me think..." She trails off, mumbling to herself. "My brother is too old and he's all the way at Yale. There are all these cheese balls in our school," she pauses before letting out. "Ben! You should go out with Ben. You like Ben. I'm calling him right now, and–"

"Stop it!" I almost shout. "I'm not going out with Ben, or your brother, or EJ. I'm not even going out with Nate. We're just friends, and I wanna help him."

"I know you always try to see the best in people, but you can't help Nate," Faye sounds resolute. "I don't think he can be helped. Just get over it, okay? Nate is bad news."

Now, I'm the one annoyed, "Faye, how can you say that? You barely know him. He and I have spent a lot of time together lately. He has a good heart, nothing he has done can be that irreversible. What is it? Is he on drugs? A felon? A cyber-stalking serial killer?"

"Don't even bother, you wouldn't guess in a million years. I'm really sorry Liz, but I can't tell you."

"Because you promised Michael you wouldn't."

Silence.

Jackpot!

"Fine, I'll ask Michael myself," I press on.

"You do that," she agrees, and there's something in her tone. *Relief?* Then, she hangs up.

What is Nate's dark secret? What did he do that's so unforgivable? Would Nate tell me himself? Or would he just distance himself from me? Above all, can I trust Michael?

24

I probably slept an hour last night, thinking of ways I could approach Michael in the morning. Now, I can barely stay awake in Ms. Campbell's lecture let alone execute any of my strategic ideas.

When the bell rings, I do the unthinkable. I follow him. I'm almost to the third floor when I'm finally at arms length and manage to tug at his jacket, "Michael, wait."

He turns and crosses his arms, waiting for me to speak. His posture almost makes me retreat without a word.

What was I thinking? I can't even look him in the eye, how do I expect to confront him? And is this the appropriate place, here at the stair landing between the second and third floor? I better make a decision, because Michael is patiently waiting as students dance around us to get to class.

He waits a few seconds, just to see if I'm going to say anything. When I don't, he asks, "Do you want to go somewhere else?"

"Physics is downstairs," Nate's voice stops me from answering. He takes the remaining steps toward us and stands beside Michael. We both look at Nate, and I suddenly feel the guilt of going behind his back. "The mighty Michael inviting Liz to skip class. Do go on, this I've gotta see," Nate drawls in his familiar sarcastic tone.

The second bell rings, but none of us move. Michael drags his hand through his hair, like he's going to tear it out in frustration, and his expression grows pensive. He aims his dark gaze at me, and I realize then that he's allowing me to decide. Leaving no doubts that if I ask him to ditch class and come with me, he'll do just that.

I look up at Nate, his posture is nonchalant, but the unfathomed mixture of emotions twirling in his painted blue eyes betray him.

How did I end up here?

If I go to Physics with Nate, I'll miss my opportunity to get Michael alone. If I ditch class with Michael, he'll tell me the truth, but then Nate might never talk to me again.

I look from one guy to the other and back. Standing side-by-side like they are right now, it's like they're brothers, same height, same imposing demeanor and same lean physique. It's like they're two poles of a magnet, different sides of a coin, like day and night.

My lips part with a sigh, and I turn around. Choosing neither of them, I take the few steps down and make a beeline to the ladies room. I rest both hands on the sink counter, letting my head drop.

Why do things never go as planned?

Now, all I've managed to accomplish is being late to Physics. Let's just hope Mr. Wilson's admiration for Dad inspires him to cut me some slack.

I twist the handle of the faucet, letting the water run over my wrists and hands to calm my nerves. I lift my head and look at the reflection staring back at me. Who *is* this girl? Certainly not me. She looks flushed with purple rings under her eyes from lack of sleep. The hair is a dead giveaway. It's me alright. The bird nest on top of my head is unmistakable. I don't bother fixing it. I just wash my hands, turn off the faucet, dry them and throw the crumpled paper towel in the trash on the way out.

When I step out, Nate is leaning against the wall.

"Whoa!" I jump back.

He straightens and hands me a yellow slip. I take the card from between his middle and index finger, frowning at the note. It's legitimate, justifying me from being late. It's unmistakably Ms. Campbell's loopy handwriting and signature. I look up at him with a question at the tip of my tongue.

He doesn't give me a chance to muster it, and remarks cynically, "So, you and Pretty Boy were skipping class together."

"Could you please stop calling him that?" I beg grumpily. I'm annoyed. It must be the lack of sleep, because I can't seem to stop myself, "You calling him that doesn't even make sense, you're prettier than he is. Besides, I wasn't, I didn't..." I let my voice trail off, unable to explain my actions.

He arches an eyebrow quizzically at me, and I look down at the paper in my hand. It's not like I can tell Nate my reason for pursuing Michael. He's gonna like it even less if he finds out what I was planning to ask. I keep staring at my feet, hoping for some hall monitor to show up and shoo us away to class. But apparently, that only happens on TV.

"Careful, Liz. You're flirting with death," Nate breaks the silence, and I look up at him, frowning. He just spins around and walks in the opposite direction.

I waste a split second trying to make sense of his words before defending myself, "I wasn't flirting with Michael, if that's what you mean."

Nate turns, walking a few steps backward as he winks at me, "Sure, you weren't." He whirls back around and makes a left at the end of the hall, going heaven knows where.

I stare at the yellow slip in my hand, sigh and start walking toward Physics. I press my nose against the little window, not knowing what to do.

Mr. Wilson sees me and opens the door, "Don't you think you're a little early for tomorrow's class?"

I'm too tired and wound up to respond to his joke. The class thinks it's funny, though. I hand him the note and he motions for me to come in. He picks up where he left off, and I ask myself, "why did I bother?" I should have headed straight to Calc. This class is almost over, and my brain is not absorbing anything he's babbling about.

Again, things don't go as planned. Faye doesn't let me skip lunch, "You need to put some protein in your diet, some power food, or an energy shot. You look like a Zombie, it's a wonder you're not dragging a leg."

"Ha-ha," I say humorless, following her into the cafeteria.

Maybe she's right, a snack might improve my mood. But instead of power food, I opt for two chocolate bars and a Mountain Dew. The lunch crew must have detected my grumpiness since they're not picking on me today. Either that, or they're afraid I might eat their brains.

I don't run into Ben at my locker on my way to Chemistry and arrive to class just as the second bell rings. Evidently, he's a no-show today. Michael is already at our station and has all the beakers pre-labeled. I take my seat self-consciously, wondering if he'll ask about my odd behavior earlier. But I should have known better, he's Michael, too preoccupied with his own thoughts to bother.

By the looks of it, he's completely forgotten the entire ordeal and seems ready to blow up the lab. I better start reading this stuff, before he actually does just that. He's dumping liquids in the beaker without measuring or even checking the instructions. I run my eyes quickly over the lines and look up at him. Beaker in hand, he observes the chemical reaction and gently swirls it.

"Don't swirl the beaker," I touch his arm to stop him from doing so. He looks up at me through his safety glasses, annoyed. I hold the page up for him to see and point out,

"The directions specifically say do not shake, stir, or swirl the compound."

"Perhaps we should add another drop from the pipet," he suggests, looking back at the beaker.

"*Perhaps*, we should not" I emphasize the word, wondering what's wrong with saying *maybe*.

Ms. Olson's plus-sized figure is moving from table to table supervising the experiments and approaches us at that moment, "How are we doing over here?"

Michael says politely, "We followed the procedure step by step, and it's not precipitating. Perhaps the concentration of the chemicals are not as precise as labeled."

He stares intently at the beaker as if he could make the reaction precipitate with the intensity of his dark blue eyes. All the while, he engages in a back and forth with Ms. Olson over the legitimacy of the experiment as written. I flip a few pages back and start rereading from the top.

"What's your opinion Ms. O'Neill?" Ms. Olson asks.

I'm clueless and just repeat what Michael said, "It should precipitate. I just rechecked the steps. We followed them exactly."

"Is that so?" Ms. Olson challenges. She's obviously not buying it.

Michael either doesn't notice or doesn't care that Ms. Olson is testing me. He jumps in, sounding sort of annoyed that the stupid chemical didn't form a clump, "Would you like us to write that the reaction didn't occur?"

A group at a table nearby is comparing their compounds and calls for Ms. Olson's assistance. So, she looks from Michael to me and says dismissively, "The important thing is that the two of you understand the concept. So just go ahead and write down that it precipitated and continue to the next one."

Ms. Olson walks away, leaving Michael looking perturbed and unconvinced. I hear Michael mumbling under his breath, "But, it didn't precipitate."

"She doesn't care, we grasped the principle remember? Just write it down," I tell him patiently.

He looks from the paper to the beaker, and then gives me an accusatory look that says "you can fool her, but not me. You didn't grasp anything."

Which makes me ask defensively, "You grasped, didn't you?"

He nods.

"So write it down," I say slowly.

He looks from the tube in his hand to the paper and then back at me. He repeats what he said a second ago, like a broken record, "This assignment is flawed."

This time, it's my turn to glare, and it works. Michael puts the beaker down and picks up his pencil. He places its tip on the paper as if to write the answer. Then, he lets the pencil drop in frustration, "I can't write that it precipitated when I know it didn't."

For a moment, I just stare as he sits back on his stool and runs his fingers through his dark hair. I don't see why all the girls are so mesmerized by him. He's eccentric and moody. I guess looks go along way. If I had to use a single word to describe Michael, "peculiar" would be it.

He lifts the pencil a second time and drops it instantly, "I can't. I just can't do it. Let's start over."

"Fine," I snatch the paper out from under his hand and slowly read the words aloud while I write, "When Iodine solution is added to ketone, followed by a sodium hydroxide solution to remove the color. The result is a pale yellow precipitate of triiodomethane." I slide the paper back to him, "And I'm pretty sure I'll never forget it."

I expect a wall of resistance when I look up, but instead he seems relieved. Yes, I decide. "Peculiar" would be Michael's defining characteristic.

From here on, we finish the assignment without further incident, and I'm grateful. This lab tested one's patience more so than their knowledge of Chemistry. Even Michael, who seems to be pretty focused, lost it with all the mixing, heating and observing. All for the sake of detecting the slightest reaction. Thanks to him. I'm still writing when the bell rings and we can't go until our station is clean.

All the other kids are filing out the door as Ms. Olson looks at the mess we've made and says, "I need to run to the teacher's lounge, but I doubt you two will be finished cleaning before I return. I can write you a note when I get back, but try to hurry."

Then, she walks out the door, leaving the two of us frantically cleaning. We're just about done when Spark enters the room for fifth period. Michael is carrying a tray to the side cabinet when she enters, and neither of them notice each other at first. They're practically shoulder to shoulder when they finally do.

They turn to each other, and their lips start moving. It looks like they're arguing, but I can't hear any words. Their entire bodies begin to distort, and they flicker like two holograms, on and off, on and off.

Am I hallucinating?

It's the only explanation for what's happening in front of me. Spark's face flickers from her familiar red spotted skin to a perfect porcelain complexion. Her eyes toggle from hazel to violet and back. The rest of her keeps blurring and contorting as if trying to change in form or shape.

Michael is awash in blinding white light that seems to curve around him. Light as bright as the driven snow. An array of colors I've never seen before illuminates the floor and walls surrounding him. It's like the air is sucked out of the room, the pressure drops, and my ears pop. All I hear is a muted hum, and my head starts pulsing. I cover my ears with the palms of my hands and close my eyes.

When I reopen them, nothing has changed. Both Michael and Spark stand in the same place, distorting and warping. Terror overcomes me, as my eyes keep dancing from Michael to Spark and back again. My legs give out, and I stumble, falling backward. I shut my eyes and wait for the impact of my head against the laminate tile. Instead, a pair of strong arms wrap around me from behind, gently lowering me to the floor.

Michael's voice shouts from above, "Get out, now!"

My head aches, and I think I'm blind. I blink, blink, but the darkness scares my eyes closed. Spark's combat boots sound loudly at a running pace without any hesitation, her footsteps fading off in the distance.

Michael's basketball jacket makes a swishing noise beside me, and he whispers something incoherent in my ear. Then, silence accompanies the darkness. I have the impression that I'm floating and will my eyelids to open, but they don't even flutter. I can't tell if I'm even breathing. I might be, my brain is still working. It'd stop if I weren't, wouldn't it?

An uncomfortably solid surface materializes under me, and I wish I could position myself more restfully. Maybe then I could sleep, and eventually wake up from this crazy nightmare.

I'm clinging to those thoughts when a familiar voice startles me back to consciousness, "Zoë said you wanted to talk to me... What happened to her?" Faye shrieks. "Is she alright?"

There's the sound of a door closing, followed by Faye's rushed steps approaching.

"She will be," comes a gentle reply. *Is that Michael?* "Don't touch her!" *Definitely Michael.*

"Why not?"

"Because I'm asking you not to."

"So... How about you answer my question first? What did you do?"

"It's irrelevant," Michael replies quietly. *"Why* this happened is what you should be asking. I–"

"Dude," Faye cuts in. "I can't just stand here and chitchat with you while my friend lies unconscious. Can't you just wake her up?"

"Not yet," Michael sounds patient, almost serene. "I need to do something first. Besides, I can't wake her, we need Zoë for that."

"Why Zoë? Why can't you do it?"

"I've already inflicted too much strain on her," Michael explains. "She won't survive if I awake her as well. Then again, it's irrelevant. I called you here because I need you to back off before Nathaniel notices what we're up to. Your intention is to protect her, but you won't be able to if Liz distances herself from you. Don't force her into seeing the true Nathaniel. Just be her friend and let her decide which path she'll take."

"But she needs to know what she's choosing," Faye groans.

"Ignorance is bliss," he points out calmly.

"Not in this case, it's not," Faye argues.

"Sorry Faye, but I have to disagree with you. As long as she's innocent there's hope. But if she knows and still chooses his path..." Michael lets his voice trail off.

"I see," Faye says in a small voice.

The door opens, and Zoë asks, "Are you done?"

"Just waiting for you," Michael replies simply.

"Michael, lapse her memory while I see Faye out. Then, I'll be back to wake her."

"I'm not going anywhere," Faye's determined voice is the last thing I hear before losing consciousness.

I wake up, and my head feels fuzzy. I'm no longer in the Chem lab. After rapid consecutive blinks, my vision clears up. I'm in a totally different room altogether, lying flat on some hard bed, like a stretcher or something. I prop myself up on my elbows and scan the room. At the foot of the bed, a skeleton hangs from a metal post. It appears to be smiling as it stares blankly at the wall. Startled at the sight I sit up and look around. I'm in a small room with powder blue walls. A stack of neatly organized pamphlets are on display, mounted to the wall. It's the school nurse's office. My head starts pounding at the abrupt movement and I close my eyes, flinching.

"You should lie down until your grandpa gets here," A woman's voice coming from somewhere behind me advises.

So I do. I close my eyes and try to remember how I ended up here. An excruciating pain tugs the back of my head, and I fail to stifle an audible groan.

Footsteps approach me at the same time Grandpa's voice calls from the door, "Where is she?"

I try not to think as I walk with Grandpa to the car, his hand on my shoulder leading the way. The pain is tolerable if I just zone out. Once inside, I buckle my seat belt and lean my head back.

"Must have been the chemicals," Grandpa tells me on the way home. "You probably inhaled some vapors in the lab. We'll take you to Dr. Huston if your headache doesn't let up."

I nod and rest my head on the passenger window, closing my eyes.

25

The persistent headache awakes me again this morning. It's my new alarm clock. It starts with a killing, throbbing, excruciating pain that compresses my entire brain and then hovers in the back of my head, never fully subsiding.

Nothing I do makes it go away. I've taken Aspirin, Ibuprofen, and Acetaminophen to no avail. It just adds grogginess and nausea to my state of misery. Now, I'm trying that little hand massage Faye did yesterday, pressing the pressure point between my index finger and thumb, but it isn't helping. I must be doing it wrong because the pounding just increases.

It's been over a week since my fainting episode in the Chemistry lab, leaving only an intractable migraine as a reminder that it ever happened. I recall next to nothing from that day. One minute I was cleaning the lab station, and the next I was waking up in the nurse's office. The worse part is every time I bring myself to remember, the headache becomes intolerable.

Everybody has been really worried about me since then. I've been trying to endure the pain in silence, hoping it would go away by itself. Unfortunately, It hasn't. It's Friday, and eight days of throbbing headache is as much as I can take. That's why, I've decided to do something about it. I'm telling Dad my headache is still around.

I sit down at my computer, flip my laptop open, then power it on. Neither Suri or Dad are logged in, so I email them both and make my way to the kitchen to boil some water for a mug of tea. If by the time I get back they're still offline, I'll call them. It's late afternoon in Japan. They're either just getting home from work or about to go for a business dinner.

Grandpa enters the kitchen and stares at me over a pair of reading glasses, "Feeling any better?"

So much for not worrying them.

I force a smile through the pain and reply in a small voice, "Apparently drugs don't work on me."

He notices the water I set to boil, "Go lie down, dear. I'll finish your tea and bring it to you."

"Thanks, Grandpa."

Back in my room I text Faye, telling her to go on to school without me. It's a quarter to seven, and my brain isn't up for another day of classes in its current state. Then, I grab my laptop, sit on my bed and lean back against my headboard. As I adjust a throw pillow on my lap my computer starts chiming, and I answer the video call.

Suri appears on the screen looking like a diva. Her black hair is beautifully styled, and her almond shaped eyes loom against the dark eyeliner. She's in a magenta chiffon dress with a ruffled front, confirming my assumptions about their agenda this evening.

"How are you, sweetie?" Suri sounds worried.

"Hi, Suri."

"Did you get my email? I replied from my phone the moment I received it."

"No, I didn't. I just got back from the kitchen, I was preparing some Kampo tea."

"Kenji is on his way to your place. He knows some mind-body therapy that might help you."

"Is Ken even awake this early? It's like seven a.m. here," I remark, muffling a yawn.

"Don't worry, Ken never sleeps," Suri jokes. " He should be there soon. I mailed some stuff to Ken from Japan a couple weeks ago and included a gift for you. It's an Omamori necklace that I designed to protect you against evil spirits. You've had some bad luck lately and could use some protection. It's very neutral, goes with everything."

"Thanks, Suri," I say, touched by the gesture. "I love your handcrafted jewelry."

A gentle knock on the door makes me look up. It's Grandpa. He walks in the room holding my cup of tea and a few bags of brown sugar, "I didn't know if you wanted sugar or not, so I brought some anyway."

"Thanks, Grandpa."

"You're welcome, sweetheart," Grandpa replies on his way out.

"Alright, alright," Dad's playful voice comes from the little laptop speakers. "Enough brainwashing my daughter." He appears on the video screen, "What's that I keep hearing about headaches? You've never had headaches before. What did you do?"

"Maybe I'm asking too much of my brain cells, and they've decided to protest," I attempt to make a joke, massaging my temples.

"Sounds legit," Dad dismisses and adds in a more serious tone, "I hope you're not staying up too late, or getting into trouble out there."

"Of course not, you know me," I reply abashed.

His expression softens, and he asks in a gentle fatherly tone, "What happened, kiddo? It really worries me you being so far away. You're all I've got."

He's clearly distraught, and there isn't much he can do from the other side of the world. I shouldn't have troubled him with my complaints. I take another sip of my bitter tea,

"I'm just being a baby, Dad. You don't need to worry."

"Eliza, I think you're forgetting a thing or two here. First off, I know you too well. Which leads to the second, we wouldn't be having this conversation if you were alright. This has been going on for over a week. Maybe you should see another doctor, have an MRI done."

"A dose of radiation exposure to complement the chemical fumes... Not such a good idea," I point out wisely.

"An MRI uses magnetism, dear," Dad sounds a bit disappointed.

"Oops, I might have been out the day they covered that in school," I attempt a joke. "Let's give it the weekend, Dad. I'll go see Dr. Huston again on Monday if I don't feel better."

Dad smiles, "If you say so."

"I do," I reassure him. "I'm starting to feel better. The tea is really helping, I should have thought of it last night."

He studies me some more and decides to drop it, "I ordered you a printer, Ken will set it up to work with your laptop when he gets there. It'll help you keep up with your homework."

"Thanks, Dad. But I don't think Grandma will be very pleased, Ken kinda scares her."

Dad laughs and pulls his phone out from his black suit pocket, "Maybe I should call Mom before he shows up."

Suri reappears on the screen, taking his place, "Let me tell you about the necklace. They say the longer you're in contact with it the more protection it provides. I've been wearing mine for almost two years. It's a small replica of the ones they use at the shrines. The amulet is made of embroidered fabric and the chain is real silver."

"Can't wait to see it, Suri. Heaven knows I've needed some kind of extra protection lately."

"Oh, your dad is back. I better finish getting ready," Suri excuses herself.

"All set," Dad informs and glances around, lowering his

voice to a whisper, "You don't need to wear the necklace all the time, just when she's around."

"I heard that," Suri's voice bellows from off screen.

Dad gives me a wink.

"It's fine, Dad. I love Suri's jewelry," I reply, siding with Suri.

"Did you hear that, Dave? She *loves* it. She has good taste," Suri's voice emphasizes smugly.

"You're encouraging her. Don't come complaining to me when she has you covered head to toe in charms," Dad teases.

"That would be unnecessary and unstylish," Suri points out, making me laugh.

"I see you're looking better, kiddo. Maybe your headache was a result of missing your dear old Dad," he says, smiling back.

Kenji's face pops in the doorway, "Playing hooky again?"

"Playing *what?*" I look up from my computer.

"Cutting school," Dad explains. "He's picking on you."

Ken enters the room, carrying a printer under one arm and a little dark green velvet pouch in his hand. He's wearing regular clothes for a change, his shoulder length black hair is pulled back, and his signature orange shades obscure his eyes as always.

"I think I scared Grandma off," Ken announces, walking up to me.

"She'll be back," Dad voices through the laptop speakers.

Ken puts the printer on the desk, pulls up the chair and sits down. Leaning over to get his face in front of my laptop's web cam, he says, "Hey there."

"Finally, what took you so long?" Suri asks, sitting beside Dad.

"It's *seven thirty a.m.* here," Ken emphasizes each word and adds playfully, "Cut me some slack."

"Did you bring the necklace?" Suri asks anxiously.

Ken drops the little green velvet pouch into my hands, and I open it, pulling out the Omamori necklace. It's lovely. The charm is covered with delicate details, and the loopy silver chain interlaces tiny pale green gemstones.

I turn to Ken, "Can you fasten it, please?"

Ken places the necklace around my neck and clasps it.

"The little green stones are jade," Suri notes. "Don't worry about damaging the fabric, it's waterproof. You can wear it all the time."

"Yeah, Yeah," Dad waves her off and half jokes, "Liz, take it off before you go to bed. I don't want my only heir choking to death."

"Dave, stop it. She won't choke. Bad spirits don't let up just because you're sleeping," Suri says reprovingly.

Dad shakes his head, "It's no use, decades of brainwashing."

"Ha-ha," Suri voices flatly.

"She will be okay," Ken reassures. "You're forgetting that I'm around to keep an eye on things. I'll play the big brother role, roughing up any low life with bad intentions."

Dad chimes in, "I guess that means any prospective boyfriends have already been neutralized. I appreciate that."

Ken pats my arm condescendingly, and I feel guilty not mentioning Nate. He's more of a guy friend, though.

Suri says, "Of course you can date, as long as he's a nice guy, and he's your age–"

"She most certainly cannot date," Dad interrupts. "She's too young!"

"Dave, don't be so overprotective," Suri rebukes. "I'm sure you had a dozen girlfriends when you were her age."

Dad scowls at her, "Yeah, but I'm a guy."

"I'm just going to pretend I didn't hear that," Suri replies. "Liz, we need to get going or we'll be late. Be good, sweetie."

"Love you, kiddo."

"Love you too, Dad," I log off and hand the laptop to

Ken.

"Is your headache gone?" Ken asks, getting to his feet.

"Mostly," I reply, taking one last sip of my tea.

He places my computer on the desk beside the printer and shuts it down. He plugs the printer into the USB hub and restarts the laptop. Bending over, he does a test print and taps his fingers on the desk as he waits. The printer clicks and buzzes, rolling out a sheet covered in colored squares and letters.

"It's alive!" He says maniacally.

"Perfect."

"Come on. Let's take care of what's left of your headache," Ken offers his hand, helping me to my feet. I follow him to the balcony.

Outside, the morning is crisp and cold. The sky is cloudy, and rays of light make patterns on the sand stone flooring. Ken walks me through a type of mind-body therapy called *Kiko*. It's supposed to help relieve migraines.

Twenty minutes later, I actually think it's working because my headache is almost gone. I'm beginning to believe these focused breathing exercises might be doing the trick. We run through the routine one last time, and then I walk Ken out.

Feeling much better, I choose to be responsible and ask Grandpa to drive me to school. After much convincing on my part that I'm no longer headachy, Grandpa agrees to take me. He walks me to the director's office to excuse my absence, and I'm immediately sent to class.

On my way to Calculus, I run into Faye in the hall, "What happened? I thought you were staying home for the day. Does that mean you're feeling better?"

"Yeah. Plus, I've already missed more than enough classes," I reply, following her inside the classroom.

We take our usual seats by the window, and I fight the urge to scan the room for Nate. Nate and I haven't talked much lately, I don't know why. It's probably because

Michael always seems to be around. Those two must have some kind of history, they don't get along. Mysteriously, Faye is being nice to him this past week, friendly even.

"Here he comes," Faye singsongs.

"Who?" I ask, turning my head to the door.

"Abe Kaur," Faye whispers, leaning in so she won't be overheard. "He's an exchange student from Dubai. He just got here."

I take in the guy walking through the door, he has a light olive complexion, jet black hair and thick eyebrows. He's also very lean and tall. He doesn't smile as he takes a seat three desks from the back on the exact opposite side of the room. He drops his backpack carelessly to the floor and looks straight at me. His eyes are disconcertingly pale blue, and I promptly turn away.

"Eerie, right?" Faye remarks quietly. "He's in AP French with me and kinda keeps to himself."

"How do you know so much about him then?"

"Mr. Neuville made him stand up and introduce himself to the class. Judy thinks his accent is totally charming. I don't know... There's something odd about him."

I frown and murmur to myself, "What's up with all the creepy blue eyes lately?"

She shrugs, and I steal another peek at the guy sitting across the room from us. He's staring straight ahead, lost in his thoughts.

The second bell rings, and Mr. Hathaway marches into the classroom, "Homework assignments on my desk."

By the end of class, my headache is lurking behind my ears. Three hours later, it's back in full force. I'm at the library with Michael and a few other students I've never talked to before. We're all working on page long equations, busy punching numbers into graph calculators. I catch Michael stealing worried glances at me several times, but I pretend not to notice.

When the bell finally rings, everyone gathers their stuff and leaves in unison. Except Michael, that is. He lingers behind, pointedly watching me now.

"Aren't you coming?" One of the guys from his entourage of googly eyed girls and basketball buddies calls out.

"Go on, I'll catch up with you," Michael calls back. He rests his hand on the chair back and asks, "Is there anything I can do for you? You don't seem okay."

"Don't worry about it. I'll live," I reply, forcing a smile on my face as I sit back, willing the pain to subside.

His expression is doubtful, but he doesn't argue, leaving the library with a simple, "Later, then."

I start on my Spanish writing exercise to distract myself while I wait for Faye. I'm on the tenth question when Nate's familiar teasing voice steals my attention, "What happened to you? You look kinda green. You're not about to puke, are you?"

Without looking up from my assignment, I reply, "Gee! Your ability to make me feel better is amazing. I would stay far away if I were you. Who knows when I might turn into that girl from *The Exorcist* and start spewing green bile all over the place."

"Thanks for the mental image," Nate puts his empty looking book bag on the table.

I look up, meeting his striking blue gaze. He's standing across from me, resting his hands on the chair where Michael sat just minutes ago. I didn't realize how much I missed having him around, until now, obnoxious remarks and all. Just looking at him in a pale blue shirt under his uniform jacket, which is against the dress code, makes my heart pound. It beats so fast that I break eye contact before I have an arrhythmia or something.

He leans over and whispers for the librarian's sake, "Faye said you're into classical piano," he pauses, and I look up at him, waiting for him to go on. He clears his throat, "Did you know that *Renshiro* is coming to Boston?"

"I had no idea. That's awesome."

"He'll be in town next Friday. I might be able to get tickets through Lill. Would you like to go with me?"

"I've always loved his music. It would be amazing to see him live," the words roll unintentionally off my tongue.

"It's a date," he declares. My smile seems enough of a reply because Nate goes on, "So, it's settled, I'll take care of the tickets. I'm meeting Lill later today, so I'll let you know. Can I call you?"

"Sure," I reply, still not believing the situation at hand.

Nate smiles widely, I smile back, and an uneasy silence falls. I start doodling on the bottom of my essay absent minded, feeling ridiculous just sitting here. He looks down at his feet, lets escape a little laugh and shakes his head before looking back up at me. If we were not talking about Nate Sinclair here, I'd say he's feeling embarrassed. The idea is just so ludicrous that now I'm the one to shake my head, laughing on the inside.

The movement triggers my dreadful headache, and I flinch, mumbling under my breath, "Not again."

Nate walks around the table and is standing beside me in no time, "You're truly feeling unwell, aren't you? What is it?"

"Headache," I reply in a small voice and gently massage my temples with my index fingers, wishing it would go away. *Please, I can't take it anymore.* I swallow hard, resting my forehead on the table as another wave of pain hits me more forcefully.

"Hey," Nate's voice sounds concerned, and he puts a hand gently on my shoulder.

Slowly, he lifts my chin up, forcing me to meet his eyes. His hands move up my face, tracing my temples with his fingers. I'm instantly more focused on his touch than the pain. A sudden relief washes over me as his thumbs run across my forehead, and the headaches starts to fade.

"When did it start?" He asks, his fingers following my hairline.

"Last Thursday, after I blacked out in Chemistry."

He drops his hands instantly as if he's been burned, mumbling something inaudible under his breath. I open my eyes at the abrupt movement, blinking in confusion. He rubs his eyes with his thumb and index finger. "How do you feel?" He asks, sounding a little uneasy.

Which makes me wonder why? I realize my headache is partially gone, but I can feel it lingering faintly.

"I sorta feel better," I smile gratefully at him.

He's looking through me and out the window, but my reply turns his attention right back to me. A serene expression touches his features, and he challenges, "Sorta?"

I smile at him shyly, and Nate pulls his iPhone out of his school uniform jacket, "This is the part where I ask for your number."

"Right," I reply, feeling my face blush and recite my phone number to him. He taps the numbers into his phone and brings it up to his ear. My phone vibrates inside my pocket, and I pull it out, looking up at him inquiringly.

"Go ahead," Nate nods.

I hesitate for a split second and then answer it.

"Hi," Nate says in a whisper.

"No phones in the library," The librarian calls out from behind her desk.

"Sorry. Gotta go," Nate hangs up, shoving his phone back into his pocket.

I try quieting my laughter without much success which earns me an angry glare as well, followed by a sharp, "Shh!"

Nate whispers, "I'll call you again tonight."

I nod, and he starts to take a few steps backward before turning on his heels. He stops short and spins around, "How late do you stay up?"

"Ten," I say quietly.

He doesn't reply, just flashes me a smile and starts making his way to the library doors.

"Hey, Nate," Faye says brushing by him.

"Faye," Nate simply acknowledges her.

She arches an eyebrow as she approaches and points over her shoulder with her thumb, "What's the matter with him?"

I just shrug, "That's just Nate being Nate."

"Ready?" Faye asks.

I nod and gather up my things, stupidly smiling as Nate disappears through the library doors. Faye snaps her fingers right in my face, and I raise my hands up laughing.

"Okay. Lets go," I stand up, swing my backpack over my shoulders and follow her out.

As we walk, the whole time I'm thinking, Nate Sinclair just asked me on a date and I agreed. I've never been asked on a date before. Sure, we had dinner together, but that doesn't count. We just happened to run into each other that evening. We skipped class and had a picnic a couple weeks ago, but this is different. It's official. Planned in advance, at night, a real date.

"Earth to Liz," Faye waves a hand inches from my nose. "Are you going to tell me what's wrong with you or do I have to guess?"

"Nate asked me on a date," I blurt out.

"A date with Nathaniel, huh?" Faye plasters a smile on her face. "You know what that means, don't you?"

I don't like the look on her face and shake my head.

She clicks her green bug opened and adds, "That means it's girls night. But first, we go shopping."

The instant we step foot into the mall, Faye drags me into a coffee shop wedged inside a bookstore. At the register, she blurts out an order that goes on and on like a freight train. I'm surprised when moments later the barista hands her a single cup of coffee. I order a hot chocolate, three vanilla scones, and a chocolate marshmallow sphere impaled on a stick which I've had my eyes on since we arrived. It seems like she has more difficulty taking my order than Faye's.

When I join Faye at the corner table by the window, she takes one look at my pile of treats and murmurs to herself, "I can't stand people with high metabolisms."

"Do you want to trade? I'll take your body, and you can have my metabolism," I ask in between bites of vanilla scone.

"I wish. You have no idea how hard it is to keep this body," Faye replies with a sigh. "I have my mother's genes, if I don't watch what I eat I'll pack on ten pounds of whale blubber in a week. Ian is more like my dad, he can eat whatever he wants and not gain an ounce. Between Pilates and keeping tabs on a low calorie, low carb, zero fat, sugar-free diet, it's a wonder that I still manage to have a social life."

I shake my head, smiling, "You know Faye, you should sign up for Drama." I regret my remark instantly, wishing I could take it back. I just remembered Mattie is in my Drama class, and Faye knows it. Regardless of how sweet he has been, Faye is just not used to rejection and Wellington choosing Mattie over her is still a sour subject.

To everyone's disbelief, Faye has been "boyfriend-free" since then. It's not because she kissed Wellington and left Ben out in the cold either. *Nope.* It's by choice. Guys keep asking her out and she turns them down left and right. I'm even starting to believe she actually has feelings for Wellington. She's respecting his decision for one and hasn't taken it out on Mattie. Faye knows how to twist the knife and Mattie would be obliterated by now. The conflicting part is that I know Wellington also has feelings for Faye. Even Mattie has noticed. Sometimes I feel like pointing that out, but I don't know if I should. Besides, I'm no cupid.

This past Wednesday, when Wellington drove Mattie and I home after Drama class, they got into another argument right in front of me. Entirely out of the blue, Mattie was like, "You're hung up on Faye. It's written all over your face. I'm making a fool of myself by staying with you."

Wellington's reply did nothing to help. He said simply, "If it makes you feel better, I don't want to be hung up on her."

They didn't raise their voices or anything, they just bickered, still it was a distressing situation to witness from the backseat. I wished then, I had taken the subway home. If it weren't for the lingering headache, I would have.

Now, Faye is making little circles on the lid of her coffee cup with her fingernail, looking all doom and gloom because of my stupid comment about her and Drama class. I take a tiny bite of my three dollar chocolate ball and the whole thing detaches from the stick, falls on the floor and rolls under the table.

"I saw that," Faye starts cracking up, and I join in, feeling defeated.

Two department stores later, Faye is overloaded with shopping bags. How much clothing does one person need? We have uniforms for crying out loud. Didn't she get all the shopping out of her system in New York?

At the third store, she talks me into trying on a pair of dark skinny jeans, a chocolate tee, and a cream winter coat.

"Look at you, Liz. You're hot," Faye remarks in front of the saleswoman to my utter embarrassment. "If I were a guy, I'd totally–"

"Ok, ok. I'll take it. Please, let's just go," I yank the curtain closed.

"Just sayin'," Faye *says.*

We stop at a drugstore on the way home. Evidently, Faye just remembered she's out of burgundy nail polish. She keeps opening the bottles to test the color tone on her thumbnail and asks my opinion each time, "This one, or this one?"

I shrug, "They look the same to me."

Faye rolls her eyes and picks up another bottle. I make my escape before her eyes roll back in my direction and spot a magazine at the cosmetic section register with Nate's sister on the cover. She looks glamorous and sensual, dressed in velvet, not at all like a teenage girl. The headline reads: *Lill Sinclair, only eighteen and she has more money than she'll ever spend.*

On the rack below there is another. In this one, she looks all innocent. It's a closeup of her face along with: *Lill Sinclair shares the secrets of her flawless complexion.*

I snatch up both copies and pay at the register. Faye buys four identical shades of nail polish, and we drive home.

As it turns out, Faye's idea of a girl's night is totally different from what I had in mind. Her itinerary seems harmless enough. First, a chick flick which Faye considers to be an instructional video on dating, followed by a rally of girl talk. So, we change into our pj's and start the movie.

I think I've seen this film before, several times actually, only starring different actors. The guy hooks up with the girl as a dare, they fall in love, she finds out, tries to leave and then the big finale at the airport. The end. I wonder to myself how these guys always manage to get through security.

As the credits roll, I start fixing the pullout bed for Faye while she chats about the latest gossip at school. It's all about the new guy Abe Kaur.

"You wanna hear the craziest thing?" Faye asks rhetorically. "Abe Kaur walked into our squad meet this afternoon right in the middle of practice."

"Did Ms. Johnson blow her whistle in his face?" I ask, unfolding her comforter.

"Nope. She just watched to see how it would play out. He walked right up to me."

"What?" I ask in disbelief. "And here I thought no one crosses Ms. Johnson."

"I know, right," Faye agrees, propping herself up in the bed I just made for her. "So, everyone was staring at us and giggling. Except for Zoë, to me it looked like she wanted to roundhouse kick him right then and there."

"What then?" I pressed.

"He said he wants to join the volunteer effort at the orphanage."

"That's it?" I ask in disbelief, touching my phone screen. It's nine fifty p.m., and Nate hasn't called yet.

"Yep," Faye confirms and catches me looking at my phone again. She lets out an exaggerated sigh, "Don't stress. Boys never call when they say they will, some kind of stupid three day rule. I swear, I might marry the first guy who does."

"Don't let that get out at school. One of your lovesick puppies might want to take you up on that," I remind her.

"Eww! I take it back," Faye exclaims, scrunching her nose.

"Faye!" I reprehend teasingly.

She waves me off, laughing, and I join in. Just then, my phone comes to life. It's Nate. My heart goes into double time, and I scramble for the phone.

"I'll give you some privacy," Faye stands up, grabbing her makeup bag on the way out.

"Hey," I answer the call, smiling widely.

"Hey right back at you," Nate replies. "Feeling any better?"

"A little. What have you been up to?" I ask.

"The usual," he replies vaguely. "I talked to Lill, she's getting us the tickets for next Friday."

"Cool," I let out in excitement.

"I thought you would say that," Nate says, laughing. "Sorry for calling so late, I have a lot going on these days."

I manage to suppress a laugh. Carefree Nate Sinclair with a full plate. *As if...* I want to ask what exactly he's up to, but I don't pry. Instead, I say, "It's okay." Then, I don't know what else to say.

After a prolonged silence, Nate says, "Alright then, I'll let you go."

I don't want him to hang up, but I have no idea how to engage in a conversation over the phone, so I say, "Night, Nate."

"Good Night. Sweet dreams."

26

I open my eyes to a pleasant starry night. I'm in the red velvet bench of an abandoned horse drawn carriage, facing the sky. Colorful flowers decorate the trim surrounding the lowered retractable roof. Two white horses tap their hooves, standing in place and nickering quietly.

As I sit up and look around, I recognize the park and the street lights. There are no cars in sight and not a single soul can be found on the sidewalks. The absence of people tells me that I'm in Raph's dream world. This time he's showing me a perfect replica of Boston Common Park. I slide to the end of the bench and cautiously climb out of the carriage. I feel a tug as my heels touch the ground. *My heels?*

Only then do I become aware of my attire. I'm in a pale blue sleeveless gown. The kind of dress only Grandma would make me wear. Double sparkling straps support the ruched bodice and the skirt culminates in layers of delicate fabric, adding a flowing quality to the floor length dress.

"Very funny, Raph! A carriage, white horses and an evening gown? This time you've gone overboard," I say aloud at the deserted night.

That's when it dawns on me, the darkness, the stars, it's

night time. *That's a first!* It's always been daytime in Raph's dream world. I start walking toward the park, putting some distance between me and the horses. Immediately I spot a silvery light glowing from deep inside the park. Something is off. The light is usually golden. I make my way toward it, turning one last time to the carriage, "Bye-bye pretty horses."

They huff in reply, and I cross through the park gates. I walk slowly, aware of each footstep I take. My heels make a clicking sound like a metronome, keeping time with my heartbeat. The half lit lamp posts appear to brighten in my proximity as I get closer to the silvery glow. Inhaling deeply, I let the fresh air and the scent of the red and orange oak trees fill my nose. I'm surrounded by the beauty of autumn, about to set foot into the silvery dome where Raph will be waiting to greet me.

As I reach the bridge, I stop and take in the shimmery light one last time. It's beautiful, so different from all the other times. It's like a swarm of glitter is swirling from its core. Then, the excitement of seeing him again takes hold, and I quicken my pace, smiling widely.

For the first time ever, Raph is nowhere to be found, making me wonder what he's up to. I take a few hesitant steps onto the platform, stopping midway and glancing down at the pitch black lake. A mirror image of the moon reflects on its surface, and where the light touches the water's edge a light blue glow shimmers. It's absolutely mesmerizing.

I begin walking again, my shadow getting longer and longer as I approach the light. I break through the glowing veil, but I'm met only with a fountain. *No Raph.* Then, footsteps come from behind, and I whirl around. There, standing in front of me, is Nate. He's wearing a button down white shirt with rolled up sleeves, black slacks and loafers. His tie is pulled loose and undone around his neck. He looks like the best man after a wedding reception.

"Nate?" I whisper in astonishment.

"I didn't think you were coming," he takes a few hesitant steps toward me.

It can't be, it's impossible. I've never dreamed with anyone else. The person standing in front of me is not Raph, it's Nate.

My face must show my confusion because Nate elaborates, "I've been waiting here for a while. You look nice by the way."

I'm glad he thinks so, considering he's the one manipulating this dream. But what if I'm wrong, what if he's not, Raph never gave me any straight forward answers about it. For all I know it might even be a *real* dream this time.

I smile at him, "Thanks. You too. But then again, you always do."

He laughs a brief laugh at my awkward compliment, "Thanks."

Nate takes a few steps closer, and a light breeze blows my hair into my face. It's not cold, not even a bit. I'm not certain that I feel the temperature at all. The park seems to be lit by the glow of the stars in the onyx sky.

"You're in my dream," I'm amazed.

He seems to be taken aback for a split second, but he quickly recovers and challenges, "What makes you think this is a dream?"

"I remember going to sleep for one. Also, this place is too perfect to be real," I reply, omitting my dreams with Raph.

"It looks like Boston Common Park to me," Nate points to the George Washington Statue.

"Yes, but it's just the two of us here. Well, there were the white horses, but they've probably run off by now. I'm pretty sure they were here just to lead me to you..." I let my voice trail off at the end. Stepping forward, I touch his face, run my fingers softly across his cheek and take hold of his hand, squeezing it slightly. Unreal, he's actually in my dream, just like Raph. Meeting his eyes, I ask, "How did you do it? How did you get inside my dream?"

"How do you know it isn't the opposite? What if you entered *my* dream?"

I look straight into his eyes and reply with certainty, "If I had walked into your dreams wouldn't you be the one finding me?"

"Maybe you're right, but neither of us have the answer. So, how about we just enjoy the moment?" Nate suggests, taking hold of my hands. "First, there's something I want to do. But I'll need your consent. May I?"

"Yes," I concede without a second thought.

"Close your eyes," he whispers, standing right in front of me.

I close my eyes, and his fingers gently trace a pattern on my head starting at my temples. Where his skin touches mine, the familiar tingling spreads, followed by a freeing sensation, and my entire body goes weightless. His hands trace behind my ears, softly curving to the back of my neck. I'm almost surrendering to unconsciousness when Nate whispers, "There. You're free of it."

A shiver runs down my spine at the sound of his voice, and before I have a chance to open my eyes, Nate speaks, "Keep them closed. I wanna show you something."

Nate guides me a few blind steps and turns me around. Seconds later, he whispers in my ear, giving me goose bumps, "Now, open."

I do, letting out a gasp.

The leaves are completely gone from the trees and the branches are dusted in a thin layer of white. The path and the grass is completely covered in blindingly beautiful snow. Above us, the stars are taking the shape of snow flakes and falling from space.

Nate pulls me close and gently moves my hair out of my face, lowering his head as if to kiss me. Our lips are centimeters apart, almost touching, when he vanishes into thin air, and everything goes black.

27

My heart is pounding out of my chest and my entire body convulses violently. It's like I'm laying at the epicenter of an earthquake. My eyelids flutter open, and I slowly realize what's happening to me. Faye is desperately trying to wake me, shaking me like a madwoman.

Through the corner of my eye, I peek at the digital clock on my night stand and groan in frustration, covering my face with a pillow. *It's four a.m. on a Saturday. No School.*

Of course, to expect that I could just go back to sleep is wishful thinking. Faye gets what she wants, and right now she wants me awake for whatever reason at four freaking a.m. on a Saturday.

Faye removes the pillow from my face, "Liz, we need to talk."

"At four a.m.? Can't this wait until the sun comes up at least?" I complain.

"No, it can't," Faye replies bluntly.

"Fine," I yawn, sitting up in my bed. I snatch my pillow out of her hands, and so help me, Faye rolls her eyes, at four a.m.

"Why are you even awake?" I ask, leaning against the

headboard.

"Because you were right," Faye replies simply.

"Good. I was right. Can we go back to sleep now?" I ask, wondering if I could still reach Nate if I fall asleep right away. Probably not.

"NO!" Faye whines. "You can't."

I groan, pulling my knees against my chest and hugging them. I look Faye straight-on and ask the question she's expecting, "What was I right about?"

"Vivid dreams," Faye replies with a knowing smile, absolutely sure that she has my full attention now, and she does.

"Did you dream of Raph?" I blurt out.

She frowns and asks, wrinkling her nose, "Who's Raph?"

"I guess not," I mumble to myself and give her a dismissive wave. "Tell me about your dream."

Faye doesn't need to be asked twice. She starts, "It began as soon as I fell asleep. I was wearing my cheerleader uniform, pompoms and all, laying on the bench in the girls' locker room when I opened my eyes. A glimmering light was streaming through the doorway, and I stood up to see what it was. I had to shield my eyes as I made my way toward it. The light was impossibly bright, blinding, pure white." Faye stops for a second, studying my reaction. Whatever she sees in my expression encourages her to continue, "By the time I reached the basketball court, my eyes were fully shut. I forced them open at the sound of a familiar voice, calling my name. When I looked around, I realized that we were surrounded by a dome of light. He was standing right in front of me–"

"Who?" I interrupt.

"Michael."

"Michael from school?" I ask confounded.

"The one and only... He told me to wake you. Therefore, my job is done. Night!" Faye says, going back to her pullout bed.

"Wait a minute... Why would he ask you that?"

"How am I supposed to know? You're the dream girl, not me," she lays down and tugs at the comforter.

"That's it?" I roll to my side and lean over the edge of the bed, looking down at Faye in disbelief. I really want to punch her pretty face right now. She woke me from the most perfect dream for nothing.

"That's it," she replies and rolls to her other side, facing away from the glowing lamp. Her voice is almost a whisper when she lets out, "You know that saying 'making a deal with the devil.' Well, let's just say I made a deal with an angel."

I groan, roll to my other side and shut off the reading light. Frustrated, I just lie on my back with my eyes wide open, thinking about my encounter with Nate and Faye's mysterious dream.

A few hours later, Grandma is waking us for breakfast. Thanks to Faye, I'm feeling groggy and tired. We spend the morning lounging on the balcony, reading the magazines about Nate's sister. Faye makes it pretty clear that she doesn't like Lill Sinclair, not even a little bit.

"She's a spoiled, self absorbed capital 'B.' That's what I think of her," Faye flips through the pages of the magazine. "She's all like, I built my empire with hard work and dedication. *Yeah, right.* She recites lines written by somebody else, shows some skin and poses for pictures. That's not hard work if you ask me. It's not like she's the only teen ever to become famous that way. I just don't get why everybody is so obsessed."

Okay. I've never seen Faye so annoyed over a celebrity before. I decide to change the subject and ask about her dream again, "So, why were you suppose to wake me up?" I've been bugging her to tell me more about it all morning, but she doesn't cave.

This time isn't different, she snaps, "Please, just drop it."

Her phone rings before I can argue. She looks at the

screen, frowning, "It's Kiara."

She answers it, and Kiara doesn't give Faye a chance to speak. Faye keeps nodding as if Kiara could see her from the other end of the line. The crease in her forehead deepens and she's on her feet, barking at the phone, "You listen to me, girl. I'll be there in ten. Don't you dare run off before I arrive."

She rushes inside and I follow suit, wondering what's going on. In my room, she hangs her bag on her shoulder and grabs her keys. Covering the mic on the phone, she whispers, "I've gotta go, or Kiara is gonna make the biggest mistake of her life. Catch you later, 'kay?"

"Okay," I say, just loud enough for her to hear it.

Then, she's out of my room, leaving only the scent of her fruity perfume behind. I put Faye's strange behavior aside and do my homework until it's lunch time.

After helping Grandma with the dishes, I head to my room and lie down in bed. My mind keeps going back to last night's dream, the white horses, the park, the silvery glow and Nate.

Why Nate? What did he mean by free?

I jump to my feet with a gasp. My headache is gone. It's been gone since I woke up. It wasn't just a dream, he healed me. I crawl across my bed, reach for my phone and unplug it from its charger.

Without thinking, I text Nate: *We need to talk. Can we meet somewhere?*

His reply comes immediately: *Sure, in NYC ATM. 6:00 ok? At the gates?*

I type a quick reply: *I'll be there,* regretting it the instant I hear the swooshing sound of the message being sent.

The phone vibrates in my hand with Nate's text: *Till then.*

What was I thinking? It's not like I can walk up to him and say, "I dreamed about you last night. What did *you* dream about? And by the way, my headache is gone. Your little trick worked." How awkward would that be? He'll think I've gone bananas. Come to think of it, maybe I have.

From what I've heard headaches are known to come and go. But then again, people also say dreams are just that, dreams. They're involuntary desires and emotions that one's mind creates while sleeping. *What am I supposed to do now?* If I'm wrong he might think I'm unstable and completely nuts. He'll run away screaming.

After hours of trying to distract myself with TV, games and homework unsuccessfully, I begin pacing back and forth. I still have no idea what I'm gonna say to Nate. I look again at my alarm clock and dart to the bathroom. I have less than an hour to get ready and leave. *Where did the time go?*

Exactly thirty-five minutes later, I'm standing in front of the bathroom mirror, brushing my teeth for about the third time. I'm still torn over the idea of mentioning the dream, maybe I'll just wait for him to bring it up. I dig through the drawers for my Chapstick, but it's nowhere to be found. Why do those things always disappear when you need them most?

At the bottom of the third drawer, I find the cherry-berry lip gloss Suri gave me last Christmas. It's still sealed. I've never opened it because the Japanese label with a berry character on it is way too cute. *Oh well, I need you now. Sorry, berry girl.* I glide my thumb nail under the clear plastic and pop the lid, applying a thin coat of gloss to my lips. My reflection stares back at me, ready to go. With too many things on my mind, I decide on the outfit I bought with Faye yesterday. My hair is impeccable for once, not a single curl out of place.

One look at my phone tells me I'm going to be late. It's five-fifty p.m. *Shoot.* I rush out of the bathroom and into the hallway, sliding my phone into my front pocket. I come to a halt and turn at the sound of Grandma's gasp. I walk up to her, concerned. She has one hand covering her mouth and the other on her chest. She looks like she's having a heart attack.

"Eliza, you look precious!" Grandma compliments me. Oh, not a heart attack then.

"Thanks, Grandma. I'm meeting Nate in ten minutes," I turn to leave.

"Bye, sweetheart," Grandma calls out. "Be back before curfew!"

I look over my shoulder and nod, smiling at her as I leave the apartment.

Downstairs, I push the front door open, and a rush of cold air hits me as I step onto the sidewalk. I speed toward the park gates, almost running not to be late. When I cross the street, I spot Nate coming from the opposite direction. He's wearing a dark blue winter coat, a graphite v-neck sweater and dark jeans. His hair is messier than ever, and he looks absolutely breathtaking. Just the sight of him is enough to give me goosebumps. There's no denying it, I've fallen for him.

We stop at the same time and in the exact spot we slammed into each other that day, only this time we see one another. Our eyes lock and neither of us look away. We just stand there, staring at each other, both completely out of breath.

I volunteer to break the silence, "This is the place."

"Shall we pick up where we left off?" is Nate's intriguing reply.

I want to say "yes," but I'm so nervous right now that I'm afraid my voice will crack. Instead, I nod in agreement, smiling at him. My hands are buried in my pockets, and they'll remain there, at least until I can get a hold of myself.

As if in conspiracy, a light breeze blows a curl into my face, and it sticks to my lip gloss. Nate takes a step forward, standing really close. He brings his hand to my cheek, making me keenly aware of the tips of his fingers gently brushing the hair out of my face. My heart flutters and beats wildly as I feel his other hand on my waist, pulling me toward him. He leans down and my eyes close, my entire body seems to vibrate in anticipation. I can feel the heat of his breath as he slowly lowers his lips to mine.

That's when my phone rings loudly, vibrating inside my coat pocket, and I take a step back. Sighing in frustration, I know the moment is over.

Just as I fish the phone out of my coat, Nate swipes it out of my hands, shuts it off, and puts it into his pocket. Nate places both hands on my waist and pulls me back toward him. I think I've not only lost the ability to speak, but the ability to breathe as well.

"Where were we?" Nate asks rhetorically, his hands sliding around me.

My heart thumps wildly, and his fingers interlace behind my lower back, pulling me even closer. Then, he leans down and kisses me, his long lashes brushing his cheeks as his eyes close. I close my eyes and can safely say that I'm holding my breath. My legs feel weak as if they can no longer keep me upright, and my heart might pop out of my chest if I don't pull it together.

Slowly, I start to calm down, leaving my insecurities behind. I begin kissing him back, letting myself go. Nate's lips feel soft against mine and his kisses are feathery gentle. Very deliberately, I lift my hands, letting them rest on his upper arms. All the while, his clasped fingers never leave the small of my back as our lips move in a rhythmic synchrony.

Suddenly, a single drop lands on my cheek and a hundred more follow. My eyelids flutter open at the same time Nate's do. Breaking the kiss, we find ourselves in the middle of a drizzly rain. I smile as Nate faces the sky, letting out an amused laugh. I tilt my head up, close my eyes and allow the light drops to refresh my flustered face.

"Come on, let's find some shelter," Nate says, his fingers still interlaced around my waist.

Unconcerned by the rain, I choose to prolong the moment. I get on my tiptoes, throw my arms around his neck and kiss him again. Unwavering, Nate brings my body closer to his and kisses me softly as the light drizzle turns into a downpour.

Eventually, Nate pulls back and unwraps my arms from his neck, keeping hold of both of my hands, "Come on, let's get out of here."

He leads me down the sidewalk, dragging me out of the rain and into the metro station. At the turnstile, he swipes his CharlieCard and motions for me to go on. I walk through and turn around to wait for him. Nate plants his palms on the top of the turnstile, kicks both legs over the bar in a swift movement and walks up to me.

I shake my head in amusement, and Nate pulls me toward him for another kiss. Our lips lock, and I forget all about time and space. Until I hear the sound of a man's exaggerated "ahem," and we break apart. A short bald man is standing between the rotation bar and us. To my utter embarrassment, we've been blocking his passage for who knows how long.

"I'm sorry," I apologize, stepping out of his way and trying to hide behind Nate.

Nate takes hold of my hand and leads me toward the Green line. There aren't many people around this evening. It must be the cold, or the rain, or maybe even the hour. I've never been at the station this late before.

"Where are we going?" I ask Nate as we step into an empty car, just before the doors close.

"Does it matter?" Nate retorts, leading me to the very last seat.

I sit beside him, just as the train departs with a jolt, making me tumble over Nate. He catches me, cups my face and leans down for another kiss. My eyes close, kissing him back. I lose count of how many stops we sit through. I'm lost in the moment and nothing else seems to matter. At least not until we finally pull apart, and I find out we have an audience. My lips are still tingling from all the kisses, and I swallow hard, ashamed of myself. I lean against Nate's shoulder, pulling my hair in a way it hides my abashed face.

He senses my discomfort and whispers in my ear, "We should get off at the next stop."

I nod without lifting my head from his shoulder, and the train screeches to a halt. We get to our feet and step out of the car. I look around, trying to identify where we are. But it's a completely unfamiliar place to me, I've never traveled this far in any direction before.

Nate moves toward the far end of the station, and I keep step with him, our hands woven together. We stop at the platform, and he places an arm around my shoulder, pulling me closer to him.

There aren't many people waiting for the next train. To Nate's left, two girls chat in a foreign language with their hands buried in their colorful jackets. On my side, a woman sits on a bench biting her lower lip as she reads a black book with a tie on the cover. A few yards away from her, a tall guy in a green jacket stands, playing with his phone.

As the train approaches, Nate lets his arm drop and takes hold of my hand. He steps forward, and a girl passes by us, walking fast to catch the train. She's in an olive sweater-dress, a dark brown jacket and matching knee length boots. A checker pattern umbrella hangs from her left arm, and she's holding a brown leather folder against her chest. Her black hair is shorter and spiked in all directions, but I recognize her instantly. She's the girl who tried to jump off the roof, her being here is further proof that my dreams are real. She's alive just like Raph said. That seems like such a long time ago. *When was the last time I had a dream with Raph? Where is he?* I just hope he's alright.

Keeping my promise to Raph, I dig my heels and tug Nate's arm with my free hand. He turns and looks at me quizzically.

"Let's take the next one," I suggest, softening my voice almost to a whisper.

He looks back at the open doors, but the suicidal girl is out of sight. She's already seated with her back to us, and the metro is departing. Nate looks back at me, his expression is unreadable as he shrugs and returns to my side.

His arm takes its place around my shoulder, and he inquires, "You never told me what it was you wanted to talk about."

I laugh, "It's not like you gave me a chance to speak."

Nate joins in laughing, just as a group of college students descend from the stairs and stop a few yards from us. The distant roar of the approaching train prompts all eyes to the left toward the dark empty tunnel.

My attention turns from the empty tunnel to a slow moving shadow emerging from the stairway. Following behind, a middle-aged man in a dark suit appears, carrying a black briefcase. His expression unnerves me, it's one that I've seen before. That same distant look the girl from the roof had on her face that night.

A stirring wave originates at the center of my spine, rapidly spreading through my limbs. He keeps walking at the same pace, eyes straight ahead and without conflict or hesitation. He heads toward the yellow waiting line, crosses it and steps right off the platform as if there were ground below his feet, falling face down across the tracks. The college kids run toward the oncoming train, waving their arms and shouting for the operator to stop.

My pulse races and I dash toward the man on pure instinct. But instead of moving toward him, I feel strong arms around my waist stopping me in my tracks. Then, I'm whirling around and being pushed in the opposite direction against my will. It's like I'm being torn in half, Nate is dragging me away while my instincts are screaming to go back.

I try unsuccessfully to free myself from Nate's grip and sprint in the opposite direction. But his hold is unbreakable, and we keep moving toward the stairwell. I wanna dig in, push back and refuse to go. Then, I realize my feet are off the floor. Nate is carrying me away effortlessly. He has one hand on my waist and the other pressing my right arm against my side. I know it's too late now. So I give up the fight as I hear the blast of the metro horn and the panicked screams coming from below.

Tears fill my eyes as I hear a male's voice shouting, "Somebody call 911!"

I turn my head to look, but Nate's body is blocking my view.

"Don't look back. There's nothing to see," Nate orders, his grip never loosening, probably afraid I might still attempt to get away. That's the last thing on my mind. It's too late, there's no way he survived. I would most certainly be dead as well, if Nate hadn't stopped me. This realization does nothing to suppress the devastation that overcomes me. Surprising even myself, I talk back in a cracking voice, "How can you say that? A man just died."

"You don't know that," Nate replies, his tone hinting at an exploding rage to come. So, I shut up, swallowing back tears. Even though, every single cell in my body wants to argue and tell him, "no one could survive that."

As we reach the top of the stairs, I see Abe Kaur of all people. He stares at Nate with mere disdain before turning his pale blue eyes to me and a sick smile twists in his lips. I look away, just as my feet make contact with the ground. Nate lets go of my waist and takes hold of my hand, picking up his pace. I'm forced almost into a run in order to keep step with him as Nate pulls me along with fearless determination.

My mind is in emotional turmoil, but something inside tells me that I should thank him for stopping me. Even though some inexplicable part of me disagrees and wishes he hadn't, so I might have saved that poor man. The other half is grateful since my dad, my grandparents and Suri would be devastated if he didn't.

After swallowing hard a couple of times, I blurt out, "Thank you for saving my life."

"You can say that again," he snorts sarcastically without looking at me.

Nate is emanating unclouded anger. I've never seen him like this before. He's outraged. I didn't know Nate could bother with anything enough to get so irate. His lips are pressed together in a thin line, his eyes are narrowed and his entire body is tense. He's leading me toward a line of taxi cabs in complete silence. Mad out of his mind, fuming actually, and I'm pretty sure its aimed at me.

More tears are forming, and my heart tightens inside my chest. Not only did I let a man die tonight, but I also just lost the guy I care for the most. Maybe I should explain that I'm helpless to control it. It's not like I have a choice. I can't stop myself from charging to the rescue of someone in need. It's as though my body goes on autopilot. For as long as I can remember, it's been there. It seems that the older I get, the stronger the pull. Tonight, however, is the first time I've ever failed, and it's killing me inside.

The fact that Nate is taking this personally is doing nothing to help me feel better about it. Something tells me that even if I open up to him and divulge the secret I've kept from everyone my entire life, it wouldn't do me any good. The opposite might be true, he might be even more frustrated, running away from me even faster.

I should at least try to apologize, it can't do any more damage in this case. So, when he opens the cab door for me, I say in a small voice, "I'm sorry."

He looks down at me for the first time since he started dragging me out of the station. His eyes are like laser beams, from up close he looks even more enraged than I thought. I swallow, bracing myself for the worst. But instead of admonishing me, he looks away and takes in a prolonged deep breath. He lets go of my hand, resting his arm on the car door. He stays like that for only seconds, but it feels like hours. From the looks of it, he's trying to summon patience with every fiber of his being and failing miserably. When he lowers his hand and his eyes reopen, it's visible even before he looks at me that my assumptions are correct.

He finally faces me, the rage shadowing his beautiful eyes as he hisses, "You made me cross a line that I've never stepped over before..." Nate trails off as if his own words burned him inside. He shakes his head in disgust and continues in a low voice, "You shouldn't try to change the course of things, the same way I shouldn't have changed yours. *It's called free will.* Now, get inside."

My tears threaten to come, but before they have the chance I climb into the back seat. I immediately face the opposite window, just in case I fail to suppress them. My heart seems to be compressing by some inexplicable pressure growing inside my veins. My throat feels closed, and it's getting hard to breathe.

"Keep the change," Nate tells the driver, bringing me back from my agony for a split second. I turn my face just as the door closes and then the driver takes off.

The anguish returns, ten times worse than before, as Nate walks back toward the station while I'm driven away in the opposite direction. My bruised heart threatens to jump out of my chest as the distance separating us grows.

Drops of rain roll down the glass as if the sky were crying for me. *Isn't it ironic?* Back at the park when the drizzle fell over us while we kissed I thought the same sky was offering its blessing.

The entire ride home, I dwell on the guilt of being unable to save that man's life and the confusion caused by Nate's reprehension. Is he right? Am I fighting against the universe, fate and the destiny of others? Why can't I stop myself then? Maybe I'm cursed. Maybe it all started when my mom died in that dreadful accident that I have no recollection of. Or maybe I caused my mom's death.

I press my lips together and fight back more tears as we

turn left onto my street. When we come to a complete stop in front of my building, I barely manage to choke out, "Thank you."

The driver nods and I step out of the cab, feeling the cool breeze against my warm skin. I gently close the door behind me and rush toward my building entrance, futilely trying to escape the rain.

As I enter the lobby a hand grabs my arm, forcing me to stop. I spin around, already knowing who it belongs to. Nate stands right in front of me and doesn't resemble perfection for once. He looks destroyed from inside out, as if he climbed out from under a steamroller. He's dripping wet from head to toe. He must have run to get here before me. My tears threaten to fall again, and I attempt to free my arm from his grip, not wanting him to see me cry.

His grip tightens in response, "I went overboard out there. I shouldn't have lost my temper the way I did. For the first time in my entire life, I found myself unprepared. I've always heard that I can deceive anyone, guess what? They were right, I managed to deceive myself. The joke's on me," Nate stops, his voice carrying a hint of sarcasm and laughter, but I don't dare look at him. If I do, I'm sure the tears will come. I won't be able to stop them. My eyes remain focused over his shoulder and out of the window as the rain falls relentlessly.

"Until tonight," Nate presses on. "I was going through the motions, living in denial. What happened tonight, it changed me forever. I can no longer lie to myself, pretending to be above it all. Truth is, I'm not. The consequences of what could have happened out there were more than I could bare. I saw you die, and it was too overwhelming to accept."

"I'm sorry," I apologize in a small voice and make the mistake of looking into his tortured eyes. The tears well up, and I immediately look down at my feet. But it's too late, a single tear escapes, falling down my cheek. Swallowing hard, I finish my apology, and my voice cracks, "I didn't mean to put you through that."

"I know," Nate's voice is filled with pain. He lifts my chin and cups my face, forcing me to look back at him. I lower my eyes, allowing a second tear to escape. His thumb gently wipes it away, and he says softly, "Hey, don't do that."

He bends down and touches his forehead to mine, as an attempt to meet my lowered gaze. But I just can't seem to do it. Everything is too fresh, and I'm crying inside.

He lowers his face, persistently, and a third tear escapes. This time, I feel the heat of his breath on my cheek as he gently kisses it and says in a merciful voice, "Hey, no tears. I'm not worth it." His words break my will and my teary eyes meet his blue ones. They're blue pools filled with agony, shimmering, almost as if he's about to cry as well. Nate whispers again, "I'm not worth it."

Now, he's the one who seems unable to keep the eye contact and leans his head on mine. He starts to repeat it a third time, "I'm not–"

I cut him off, managing to free my arm without a fight on his part. It's as if all the strength has left him. Instead of fleeing to the elevators like he expects me to, I wrap both of my arms around him, "You're worth my life."

He holds me so tight that I can barely breathe. But I don't try to break loose, I tighten my hold of him, wishing from the bottom of my heart that I'd never have to let him go.

I don't know how much time passes as we stand in each other's arms in the lobby. By the time Nate walks me to the door, it's way past curfew. He gives me a whisper of a kiss and hands my phone back to me, "Try not to torment yourself over what happened tonight. There was nothing to be done."

I nod to reassure him, but I'm not so sure it's possible to forget that easily. His lips curl into a half smile, it's visible he's unconvinced. He steps into the elevator and pushes the button. We stare at each other until the doors close.

Only then, do I turn on my phone. There's one missed call from Wellington, and I play the message, "Liz, it's Blake. Call me as soon as you get this. I think I figured out the Latin audio file from your iPod."

28

The night is a long battle between mind and body. While my mind doesn't wind down long enough to fall asleep, my body begs for some rest. The struggle ends in a draw just as the sun comes up. Feeling awfully tired, I roll out of bed and walk slowly to the bathroom, overly aware of the gravity pulling me downward. I step into the shower stall, not bothering to prime the pipes with hot water first. I gasp as the forceful stream of cold hits my skin, jolting me awake. It eventually warms up, or maybe my body gets used to it. By the time I leave the shower, I'm on full alert.

Back in my room, I throw on a pale green sweater and jeans, power on my laptop and towel dry my hair as it boots up. I sit down at my desk and load a web browser. My hands shake as I type the words "Boston train suicide" and click search. In a nanosecond lots of results appear on the screen, but nothing recent. I try several combinations of words, like "train incident," "death on the tracks," "man hit by a train," but find nothing. I search the online Boston news and still nothing. No articles, no blog entries, not even an uploaded video, and nowadays almost everything is caught on film. So, I head to the kitchen with the intention of borrowing

Grandpa's newspaper. If it's not on the worldwide web, maybe it'll be reported in something more local.

In the kitchen, Grandpa sits in his usual spot with his camouflage coffee mug propped up in one hand. He's in a brown wool sweater and slacks today, and his eyes lift from the newspaper to look at me, "You're up early."

"Morning Grandpa," I go straight to the pantry, grab a box of cereal and sit across from him.

"Your grandma and I didn't see you get in last night. Melody insisted on watching that documentary about the Amazon rainforest and we fell asleep," Grandpa informs me, shaking his head. "I keep telling her that my vision is too bad for subtitles, but she insists."

"It's alright," I chuckle politely and reach deep into the cereal box, popping a few chocolate and peanut butter pellets into my mouth. Noticing he's reading the sports section, I nod to the rest of the newspaper neatly arranged at his side and ask, "Do you mind if I take a look?"

He glances at me suspiciously, raising an eyebrow, "I see you're finally ready to unplug."

"You could say that," I shrug, tossing back another fist full.

"Suit yourself. I should warn you there's no cat videos in there," Grandpa replies, going back to his own reading.

I chuckle and try not to call more attention to my sudden interest in the news than I already have. I flip slowly through the pages and search carefully, paying attention even to the smallest columns. After going front to back twice and not finding a single line about the incident, I fold the newspaper and slide it back to him.

"Thanks, Grandpa," I say before leaving the kitchen, and he nods without taking his eyes from the paper.

My eyes go immediately to the alarm clock on my night stand when I walk in my room. It's only a quarter to eight, still too early to call Wellington. I tried reaching him the moment I set foot inside my bedroom last night, but his phone went straight to voice mail. I didn't bother to leave a message. I'd rather try calling again than have to wait for him to call me back.

I sit at my computer desk and start a new search, trying new combinations of words. I'm still unconvinced something that huge would be overlooked. With all the fabricated news and non-stories I came across this morning, I don't see why they wouldn't write about something that actually happened.

My phone starts ringing from my night stand, and I dash to get the call. Wellington's name shows on the screen. Whatever he found out it must be big, he's not exactly a morning person. I slide my thumb on the touch screen, answering, "Hey, I got your message. What's up?"

"Are you busy right now? I need to show you some stuff."

"No, not really," I reply, closing the lid of my laptop. "What did you find out?"

"I think this Latin audio file is about you," Wellington replies matter-of-factly.

Ten minutes later, I'm following Wellington down the hallway of his apartment to his bedroom. At the door, I suppress a shocked gasp. It's like Wellington's usual neatly organized room has been hit by an avalanche of colorful sticky notes. His bed is made entirely of books and papers. By the looks of it, he hasn't slept here for a while. The note board hanging on the wall above his bed is covered with fluorescent squares, instead of the usual calendar and the closeup picture of him and Mattie. But the pink, green, yellow, and blue squares of paper don't stop there. They're everywhere, closet doors, book shelves, walls, the back of his chair and the edge of his desk.

I walk up for a better look and catch sight of his cello, letting out a gasp this time. Wellington Blake has covered not only his cello case with sticky notes, but also his mahogany sheet music stand, while his precious cello lays abandoned in the corner of the room.

Leaning down, I squint my eyes to read what he's written. But Wellington's scribbled handwriting looks like hieroglyphics. It's unreadable.

"It's Latin. Most of the notes are," Wellington says, noticing my effort to read it.

I look from one note to the next, incredulous of what my eyes are seeing. I don't dare to touch anything in fear of disorganizing them. It's crazy. It's like he's bent on deciphering some sort of mystery. I kneel down, lifting the top book from a stack by his bed. It's called *Inferno* by Dante Alighieri. The next two are also from the same author, *Purgatorio* and *Paradiso*. Then, *Paradise Lost* by John Milton, and several others with similar titles.

I stand up and walk to his desk. There are open books that look like relics. It's like they might disintegrate in your hands. The titles are worn and barely legible. By the looks of it, they must be in Latin as well. I get the impression that this whole love triangle situation with Mattie and Faye has taken its toll on Wellington. He's become a shut-in.

"What is this?" I motion around. "When did you find time for all of this?"

"Sit down, please," he invites, piling up some papers carefully. He puts them aside and arranges some books neatly on the floor.

His actions calm me a little. Even deep in this chaos, my friend seems to have a system in place. I get the feeling I'm standing at the center of a very organized mess. I sit down and look up at him.

He lifts his cello bow from the bed and sits right across from me, letting it rest on his lap. He puffs his cheeks and lets out a breath, "Where do I even start?"

"How about from the beginning?" I suggest.

"It won't work, it's too confusing," he replies, shaking his head.

"How about telling me what the Latin recording is

about?" I ask, quickly adding, "And don't say *me*."

He gestures to the pile of books beside his bed and challenges, "Would you like to take a guess?"

I frown and shake my head, blurting out, "Are you sure? It's hard to picture Nate listening to a story about angels." Then, remembering the title *Paradise Lost,* I add, "Or fallen angels for that matter. It's so not like him."

"Hold on," Wellington sounds agitated, straightening up his posture. "What are you saying? Did Nate give this to you?"

"Not exactly," I press my lips together and let them loose, making a smacking sound. There's no other way out, but to explain how I ended up with Nate's iPod. "My first day back in town, I went out for a run and crashed into Nate. We accidentally switched iPods."

"You see him everyday. Doesn't he want it back?" Wellington cuts in, narrowing his eyes.

I shake my head, "He never asked, and I didn't bring it up since I gave it to you." I look up at him and press, "So the voice on the recording is talking about angels?"

"It sounds kinda like an audio book actually. It's about angels, ethereal beings, heavenly hosts and several other names they go by," Wellington confirms, smiling at my skeptical face. "I'm serious. I still didn't figure out the hierarchy, though. I don't even know if anyone can. It's all over the place with first, second and third spheres and which angels belong to which. Then, their categories, whether they are Seraphim, Cherubim, Ophanim, and so on. It's just too much. There are also the seven highest archangels of death, guardians–"

"Whoa, whoa, whoa," I cut him off. "Slow down, you lost me at *third sphere*. What on Earth are you talking about?"

"Right. Sorry," he apologizes. "I'm just frustrated that I can't put it together after all the research I've done."

I'm starting to get seriously worried about him. If my

friend gets tossed into the loony bin over this, it'll be my fault. I'm the one who gave him the stupid Latin audio book after all.

"Liz, are you with me? It seems like you're here in body, but your mind is on Mars."

"You're right. Sorry," I apologize. "So, are we talking fiction or non-fiction here?"

"I'll let you decide that," Wellington replies simply.

To speed things up, I ask, "Can you dumb it down a bit?"

"I'll try my best," he reaches for a pile of notes and checks the order. "For starters, I'll be referring to this Latin audio recording on Nate's iPod as File-X," he looks up at me for confirmation, and I shrug. Seeming satisfied, he begins, "Let's drop the spheres, categories and classifications. Let's put them into two groups: angels and archangels."

"That's better," I nod in agreement.

"According to File-X, there are gazillions of angels out there, but only fourteen archangels are mentioned in the story. Basically the archangels are like super-angels. Their traits are enhanced, and they have their own signature capabilities. We're talking here about kinetic abilities, like telekinesis, teleportation, invisibility, mind control, telepathy, and so on."

"Do they fly as well?"

Wellington merely shrugs, "I'm not sure. File-X doesn't mention it, and all the other books that I came across describe them differently. It's not like Math where two and two always comes out four. Some of these books are based on translations of translations from way back. Legends from a time where people drew on cave walls and carved in stone tablets. Folklore passed on from one generation to the next." He stops and something on my face amuses him because he adds, "In other words, it's hard to believe where the truth ends and the fantasy begins."

"What makes you think the Latin book from Nate's iPod is any different?"

"We'll get to that," Wellington replies vaguely. "So, back to File-X. It starts by mentioning the existence of two realms: The Earth and the upper dimension. Then, it jumps straight to 'the fall.'"

Here, he stops and looks at his notes before going on, "Whoever wrote this didn't take the time to explain why seven of the archangels recruited one third of the lesser angels to rebel. All it says is that they were banished to the Earth realm and the gates of the upper dimension were closed to them for all eternity."

He turns a page on his notes and picks up where he left off, "Condemned to spend their entire existence wandering the Earth realm, they became heavyhearted. Even though, they were free down here and kept all of their powers, they felt homesick. The fallen angels started turning against each other, placing blame for their misfortune. The fallen archangels joined forces and started plotting their revenge, a way to take down the upper dimension and reclaim it as their own."

"That's so stupid," I mumble to myself.

Wellington looks up from the paper he's reading, "What's stupid?"

"The fallen ones plotting to take the upper dimension back," I point out, starting to get into the story. "Didn't you say that only one third of them fell?"

"Right," Wellington replies, waiting for me to finish my line of thought.

"Can't you see? It's ridiculous, obviously a lost cause. They weren't only way outnumbered, but they were planning to take down a place they couldn't even get inside."

Wellington gives me a quizzical look, as if he's withholding information.

"What?" I ask intrigued by his odd reaction.

"I'm with you there," Wellington agrees. "But, let me continue."

I nod, and he goes back to his notes, his eyes searching

for where he stopped. When he finally finds it, he reads, "The fallen archangels being superior, more intelligent and persuasive, took the lead. The fallen archangel of death, Asmodeus, stepped in as their leader, and along with the other five started gathering the lesser fallen ones to do their bidding."

"Wait? That's six. I thought you've said seven archangels fell," I interrupt in confusion.

"Yes, I said seven. But one of them refused to join what he saw as a losing battle. Neither would he spend his days fighting and complaining about what they had lost. He opted to follow his own path, wandering the Earth realm alone."

"By the sound of it, he accepted his plight," I remark. "I think he was smart not getting involved in what would certainly be a massacre."

Wellington gives me a knowing smile, "Funny you'd say that."

"Why?" I ask in puzzlement.

"You'll see," he waves me off. "From what I heard and read his attitude was more like 'been there, done that. So thanks, but no thanks.' I do agree with you about the clever part, though. Because this book, file, or whatever... tags him as being the fallen one equivalent to Michael, the upper dimension's most powerful archangel of death, known as the highest of the seven."

"I've heard about that one," I blurt out.

"Yeah. This dude is famous. Every single book I've read mentions him," Wellington points out, making me laugh briefly. He looks over his notes and turns a page. "Dang! I left something out."

"What?"

"The 'soul carriers,'" he replies, and I frown at him.

What is this book? Archangels, angels, fallen ones, now soul carriers too?

"Let me guess? That's supposed to be us," I remark, still not buying any of this.

"More like the ancestors of our ancestors," Wellington clarifies. "We're talking about something that happened many thousands of years ago."

"Huh!" I exclaim.

"Where was I?" He mumbles to himself, scanning the page in his hand. He finds his place and goes on, "Soul carriers, aka the mortals that inhabited the Earth realm. They were fascinated by the fallen ones. However, Asmodeus and his followers couldn't care less about soul carriers at first. His main concern was evening the odds. That's where the demons come in."

"Demons?" I ask in disbelief.

"Children of two fallen angels."

"You've got to be kidding," I blurt out in exasperation. "Let me guess. They were deformed creatures with red eyes, horns, and long tails."

"Not really, no. According to File-X, they were just as perfect and beautiful as the fallen angels, but they always exhibited at least one disfigurement. Also, they were hollow."

"Hollow?"

"Yeah," Wellington confirms. "That's how they were mentioned in File-X, 'the hollow ones.' It calls the mortals 'soul carriers,' and the angels 'ethereal beings.' It's like each mortal had a unique signature which could be traced to its owner. Each angel, archangel, even the fallen ones, had their own unique spectrum which could also be traced. The demons, however, were hollow. They had no soul and no spectrum, making them untraceable."

"Did they inherit the powers of the fallen angels and archangels?" I ask, dubiously.

"Hang on there. I never said they were the offspring of fallen archangels. File-X is very impartial, almost like reporting instead of telling a story. But in my opinion the six fallen archangels seemed pretty arrogant. They saw themselves superior to the fallen angels. They kinda ordered them around with arms crossed, just dictating. The demons that were born on the Earth realm were the children of fallen angels. But to answer your question, they did inherit some of their powers. From what I understand, just the ones linked to their blood, but not the ones linked to their spectrum. I believe it's because demons are hollow. Unlike the fallen angels, they didn't get the invisibility, teleportation, telekinesis, or anything of the like. They inherited their strength, agility, and so on."

"Were they immortals too?"

"No," Wellington replies. "They only lasted around three hundred years before they started to decay. Hollow, remember?"

"Eewwww!"

Wellington points at a row of fluorescent green sticky notes with his cello bow and continues, "That's when a foolish ancestor of ours decided to seek the attention of the beautiful fallen ones."

"Oh brother," I can already see where this is going.

Wellington laughs briefly at my expression, "You think this story can't get any worse. Brace yourself, the sickening part didn't even begin." He turns a page, "The fallen archangels ignored them, but the lesser fallen angels started mating with soul carriers, bringing a dreadful race to the Earth realm. They were half human and half fallen angel. They were also hollow, no soul and no spectrum. Giant creatures with no regard for mortals. They would eat them alive, break them in two just to hear their bones snap and destroy their villages and families. The upper dimension was forced to step in by sending an army of their own to put a stop to it. This army was led by The Archangel of Death Michael." He flips a page and finishes with, "Michael and his army exterminated the halfbreed race, banishing Asmodeus and his followers to the underworld where they would remain until the end of time."

Here he stops to look at me and inquires, "One would

presume that would be the end of it. What do you think?"

"It's not?" I ask, considering it. "After that, wasn't the Earth realm void of fallen angels and archangels?"

"Not quite," he replies, going back to his notes. "Do you remember the seventh fallen archangel I mentioned earlier?" I nod, and he goes on, "He was nowhere to be found when all hell broke loose. Therefore, he wasn't banished and became the only fallen archangel to walk the Earth realm. There were a great number of fallen angels that were not involved with Asmodeus' scheme and avoided being exiled to the underworld as well."

Wellington turns a few pages and scans the room, not finding what he's looking for. Then, he reaches for a few loose papers on his night stand, and I hand them to him. He reads a few lines in silence and nods, "That's when the messenger stepped in."

"The messenger?" I interrupt. "Did I hear you right?"

"Yes. You've probably heard of him too, he's just as well known as Michael. All these books mention him," Wellington replies, motioning around. "The messenger archangel is known as Gabriel."

This info takes this story to a whole new level. Was Raph talking about Gabriel that day? If so, what does that make him?

I don't have time to process it. Wellington starts again, recapturing my attention, "The upper dimension sent Gabriel to impose a set of laws, some kind of code for the fallen ones who remained on Earth. They were granted the ability to cross between the under dimension and the Earth realm as long as they didn't break any of Gabriel's rules. If they did, they would either be destroyed or banished to the underworld."

He stretches and picks up another pile of notes, shuffling through the top few pages, "Now the real story starts. It mostly revolves around the fallen archangel of death Asmodeus–"

"Didn't you just say he was banished to the underworld just a second ago?" I cut him off, confused.

"Right. But being banished didn't stop him from bossing the lesser fallen angels around. It's not like he was doing any of the fighting when he was on the Earth realm anyhow," Wellington points out. "Asmodeus just relocated."

"It doesn't make any sense, though," I disagree. "It's one thing for the fallen angels to fight for Asmodeus when he's around to threaten and manipulate them, but another for them to actually follow him into the underworld."

He scratches the back of his neck, considering my input, and elaborates, "File-X doesn't use these exact words, but from what I gather the angels are weakened if not in direct contact with archangels. That's the only explanation I could come up with as to why Gabriel would allow them to transit between the Earth realm and the under dimension. Otherwise wouldn't Gabriel just throw the bad guys in the dungeon, leave the others be, and move on? But no, he allowed them free access to both realms, as long as they followed the rules."

"What are these rules?" I interrupt intrigued.

"File-X never goes into specifics. Like I said, it's more about Asmodeus and his evil deeds," Wellington replies with a quick shrug.

"Do any of the other books mention them?" I ask, referring to his little private library.

"Not really," he replies. "It's like I said before, they're all over the place. Although, now that you mention it, they do all agree on one point."

"What's that?" I ask

"Thou shall not interfere in the affairs of soul carriers," Wellington says theatrically, sounding a lot like a character in one of Ms. Campbell's plays.

I laugh, but stop abruptly when it sinks in. Nate's words from last night play back in my head, "You shouldn't try to change the course of things... *It's called free will.*" Nate must really believe in this stuff. It's like his code or something.

"What's the matter?" He asks, noticing that I've spaced out again.

I shake my head, "It's just something Nate said yesterday."

Wellington looks really interested now, "What did he tell you?"

"Never mind me," I reply. "Go on with the story."

He studies me a little longer before turning his attention back to his notes, "Asmodeus and the other five fallen archangels didn't see their imprisonment as defeat, but an opportunity to father immortal demons, born in the underworld. A new race, the pure blood children of two fallen archangels."

"*Gee!* This guy doesn't give up, does he?" I ask with a sigh.

"No, he doesn't," Wellington replies without looking up. "They were the worst kind of demons, extremely powerful. Although they were still hollow ones, they could absorb part of a soul or even part of a spectrum, being able to morph into an exact replica of their prey, like a clone. They were known as succubus and incubus."

He turns the page and continues, "These creatures were a threat even to Asmodeus. But, by the time he realized that, there were already dozens of them wandering the underworld. So, Asmodeus was determined to destroy each one of them. Unfortunately, most of them escaped into the Earth realm and immediately began preying on the ill-fated soul carriers who crossed their path. Needless to say that both Michael and Gabriel descended upon them. Michael had already wiped out two thirds of them when Gabriel put a stop to it as the creatures begged for mercy. The archangels agreed on letting them be as long as they followed the rules."

"Here we go with the rules again..." I let my voice trail off as something creepy crosses my mind. "I don't even want to know what happens when two demons get together."

"According to File-X, demons, succubus, incubus... none of them have the ability to reproduce," Wellington remarks. "But that doesn't stop them from trying."

"I'm sorry I brought it up," I change topics by asking, "So, did Mr. Evil give up after that?"

"Sadly, no," Wellington replies. "But this is where the story gets complex."

He picks up a blank piece of paper and starts drawing. I lean over to see what he's doing. He begins with one long rectangle at the very bottom of the page where he writes: *Asmodeus, fallen archangel of death.*

He draws another rectangle at the very top of the page and writes down: *Raphael, guardian archangel of light.*

He traces two lines, one coming down from the left corner of the top rectangle and the other from its right, drawing a circle at each end. Inside the right circle, he writes: *Michael, archangel of death.* In the other: *Gabriel, messenger archangel.*

Next, he sketches a squiggly design that comes from the middle of the top rectangle, passes in between the circles and ends at the center of the page. He writes down the words: *Flower of Light.*

He graphs a straight line across the center of the page, separating the top from the bottom and touching the pointy end of what must be a flower. Underneath each circle, on the line he just traced, he draws two squares. In the right square, he scribbles: *the prophecy.* In the left one: *Fallen archangel of death.* Where the line touches the flower, he writes: *Lillithiel, Spirit.* Then, making a circle, he writes down counterclockwise: *Air, Earth, Fire, Water.*

He looks at me and smiles at my confused face. I just wave for him to go on. He picks up his notes, turns a few pages and begins, "When all else failed, Asmodeus combined the 'elemental knowledge' he stole from the archives of the upper dimension with his sick twisted designs. His scheme was to incubate five mortal infants, one for each of the universal elements: Air, Earth, Fire, Water and Spirit. To accomplish this, he kidnapped pregnant women on their seventh week of pregnancy," he pauses, swallows a couple times, and his voice cracks a little when he finishes, "He drained the infants of their souls and infused part of his own immortal evil spirit into them."

Unable to contain my trepidation, I gasp.

Wellington leans against his headboard, "I know," his voice sounds disturbed.

"Why didn't the good angels stop him?"

"According to File-X," Wellington begins. "Some fallen angels that were sneaking pregnant women into the underworld were caught in the act and destroyed instantly. But, the ones that crossed through the gates of the underworld couldn't be stopped. Here is the thing, Michael holds the keys to the gates of the under dimension, but he isn't allowed to open them until the end of time."

"Couldn't he make an exception?"

"It's not up to him."

I scowl at Wellington, "How so? Didn't you say he is the highest of the seven? Plus, he holds the keys."

"From everything I've read," Wellington starts. "I can assure you that he'd be charging in there if he had his way. Hear me out, and you'll come to the same conclusion. The only reason Michael didn't descend in full force and destroy all of them for good was because Zophiel didn't consent to it. She's The Archangel of Wisdom, the counselor of the seven highest. Believe me when I tell you that she had a point. The upper dimension had no way to know if Asmodeus had succeeded or not. If he did and Michael opened the gates it would be the end of the world as we know it..."

Wellington is still talking, but I stopped listening to him when I heard the names Zophiel and Michael in the same sentence. A sense of Déjà vu washes over me. The bizarre conversation between Michael and Zoë comes back to me with clarity, as well as my failed attempt to confront Michael about it. *How did I forget all that?*

"Liz?" He calls to regain my attention.

"Keep going," I reply fully alert. "Please tell me someone put an end to all that."

"They did," he replies and turns a page. "File-X mentions an underworld archive called the A.O.T. What that stands for, I have no idea. But it's mentioned over and over in this recording. In this 'A.O.T. entry,' it's written that Asmodeus spent sixteen hundred years forming a single closed group of five elemental children."

He stops, but I keep quiet, waiting for him to go on. So, he starts reading again, "Of course, Michael and his archangels spent that same amount of time trying to find a way to cross into the underworld without opening the gates."

"Did they find a way?" I'm unable to stop myself.

"Yes, they did. Through a little girl, called Layla," Wellington replies. "But we'll come back to her, first I need to add something I forgot to tell you. From the fourteen archangels mentioned in File-X, there were seven who possessed the ability to reach out to mortals through their dreams. Of the seven, one fell and six remained in the upper dimension. Michael is counted as one of the six."

He looks straight at me, studying my reaction. I know what he's thinking and my thoughts are along the same line. But, I'm too curious as to what's about to happen to interrupt him with more questions. So I motion for him to go on.

He obliges, "Layla grew up in an orphanage and was fascinated by legends of the archangel Michael. Intrigued, he asked permission to visit her dreams, was granted and appeared in them sporadically throughout her childhood. You see, Michael is the only archangel incapable of lying. So when she asks his true name, he told her. Never would he guess she would be his key to the underworld," Wellington pauses for emphasis. "Now, here comes the loophole.

According to File-X, if you're pure of heart, and your life is in peril, you can summon an archangel by name and said archangel will come to your rescue. Layla was married and expecting her first child when she was kidnapped by one of Asmodeus' followers and dragged into the underworld. As she was being drained she summoned Michael by his true name, not for her own life, but for the life of her unborn child–"

"Does File-X actually mention Michael's true name?"

Wellington digs through his papers and produces a single index card. On it, a long Latin name is written in black ink. Then, he continues where he left off, "Michael came for her. He destroyed Asmodeus and every single fallen angel involved in his plot, saving Layla's baby. File-X never mentioned the child's name, or if he was able to save Layla's life as well."

Wellington stops, as if trying to solve a puzzle with missing pieces. I look at the chart, he still didn't explain about Lillithiel.

"That's it? Does it end like that?"

"No," he replies. "Michael accomplished his mission, but he never obtained the names of Asmodeus' elemental spawns."

"Why did he need their names?"

"Because they were hollow. Their souls were drained and destroyed. Asmodeus evil spirit granted his elemental children immortality, but they were still empty. They blended in with the demons, becoming untraceable. They were already released into the Earth realm and since none of Asmodeus' followers survived, their identity would forever be a mystery. Or so they thought."

"What do you mean? Did someone know their names?"

"Not at the time. This is where all these other books I found leave off. Fast-forward two hundred years after Michael destroyed Asmodeus and his minions, File-X continues the story. At the beginning of the twentieth century, a prophecy was revealed to Lillithiel. Aside from her, two other witnesses from the underworld were present, the sole remaining fallen archangel to walk the Earth, and the A.O.T. keeper. In the midst of all the death and destruction rampant in World War I, Lillithiel disguised herself as a nurse to cause more pain and suffering to those dying of their wounds, spreading infection and relishing in their pain. Not even the underworld knew who she really was. To them, Lillithiel was just another female demon that adored and served their cause. That changed when a dying maiden took hold of her hand and said:

You are the Spirit
Your evil is arcane, eldest of epsilon.
Your kin are unknown to you, and you to them.
But upon the horizon
the Flower of Light will shine like a compass,
and your true name will become plain.
And the same who destroy the creator will destroy the
creation,
The Flower of Light will be endowed,
And the guardian will dismount,
With their forces bound
Your soulless carcass will fall to dust."

Wellington puts down the paper he was reading and looks at me quizzically. I'm completely lost. Is that even supposed to mean something?

He continues, "As the prophecy echoed to all those standing by, Lillithiel panicked. Her identity reverberated for all to here. She was no longer safe in her anonymity, the underworld and the upper dimension knew she was the first of Asmodeus' elemental children. Even though the prophesier didn't reveal her by name, she revealed her as the Spirit. It would be just a matter of time before Michael came for her. Instead of retreating to the underworld, she chose to hide in plain sight, in the company of human shields. She knew Michael can only destroy her in his ethereal state, and he'd never assume his full form in the presence of a pure soul. So, Lillithiel recruited not one, but two pure of heart soul carriers to be always by her side, everywhere she went. Twenty-four hours a day, seven days a week. Then, she announced, shouting for all to hear, Earth, upper, and under:

> *I am Lillithiel, daughter of the underworld, heir to the throne of Asmodeus. The Spirit of the five elemental children."*

I wait for Wellington to go on, when he stays quiet, just staring at me, I ask, "Is that it?"

"Pretty much, yeah, that's it. File-X ends with the loner fallen archangel of death walking away, counting the days to Lillithiel's destruction," Wellington explains. "So, what do you think?"

I don't know what to think, except... "Why did you say this book is about me?"

"I thought you'd never ask," and that's when he drops the bomb.

29

"Liz, say something, anything. You're starting to freak me out. Leave the sticky notes alone. Tearing up my notes isn't going to change anything," Wellington insists as I toss the last of the colorful squares into the trashcan.

The ones I can reach, that is. Other than those, his eggshell white walls are visible once again.

"Liz, talk to me," he pleas for the tenth time.

I whirl around to face him, "Talk to you? You've clearly lost your mind if you believe in the stuff you just told me."

"You know my philosophy, nothing is coincidence," Wellington watches me carefully from across the room. "This unpublished book, recording, file, or whatever it is, well... it has too many similarities to be dismissed."

"*Unpublished?*" I inquire intrigued.

"Yes, I asked around." Wellington ticks off points by raising his fingers, "First, I asked Mom. Then, her friends, my old Latin teachers, and so on. I even asked Dad since he would know if this book were ever published."

"Then, maybe your translation is wrong," I remark, crossing my arms.

Wellington's phone vibrates on the night stand and he

reaches for it, texting a quick reply.

"Is it Mattie? Do you guys have plans or something?" I ask, looking for an excuse to leave. I need to be alone, it's the only way my brain can process everything.

"No. Just one of the guys. Nothing important. Mattie and I are sort of..." He trails off, catching on to my attempt to sidetrack him. "Never mind that. Liz, think about it," he pauses and waits until I'm done piling up and arranging his books neatly on his desk. It's only when I turn to face him that he continues, "You have to consider the facts. They all showed up the same week you arrived."

Right about now, I want to pull all my hair out. It's just too much. Swallowing hard, I look at him, unsure how to respond. My utter distress is palpable. Attempting to break the tension, he tosses a crumpled sticky note toward the trashcan, missing it entirely. Just then, my phone blasts loudly inside my pocket, and I jump three feet in the air at the sound of Ian's ringtone.

Ian's DNA theory suddenly sounds a thousand times better than Wellington's cryptic prophecy. Mentally crossing my fingers that Ian's assumptions are correct, I answer anxiously, "Hey, Ian. What's up?"

"O'Neill, I bare bad news," is his reply, deflating me instantly. He goes on, "Your DNA examination results were inconclusive. I found a defect in the genes that control the production of clotting factors."

"Um?"

"It's saying that you have hemophilia," Ian explains. "Which is impossible, since you didn't bleed to death that day we went climbing. Clearly, the test went awry."

"Oh!"

"Maybe we can try a blood test next time," Ian suggests.

"I don't do needles," I flinch at the thought. "It won't be necessary. Thanks for the update."

"No prob. Let me know if you change your mind."

"I'm pretty sure I won't."

"Okay then. Later, O'Neill"

"Bye, Ian," I hang up.

"No blaming the parents this time," Wellington remarks the moment I put my phone back into my pocket.

"I guess not," I agree sadly.

"Unless your mother is a direct descendent of Layla or something."

"Enough! Stop it," I growl at him indignantly.

"Just a thought," he throws his arms up in the air. "Even I must admit that's a tough one to prove since we don't have the genealogy to back it up."

"Gee, thanks, Wellington!" I blurt out in exasperation. "You've already accused my boyfriend of being 'The Fallen Archangel of Deceit.' And his sister, the supermodel, an eighteen hundred year old demon spawn called Lillithiel. You labeled my Chem lab partner Michael 'The Angel of Death.' And to top it off, you termed the newest cheerleader on the squad his counsel. Now, you're suggesting that my mom–"

"Wait! You're saying that 'The Archangel of Wisdom' is a cheerleader?" Wellington cuts me off quizzically.

"No. *You* are. I'm still not buying any of this," I reply defiantly.

His mother's voice sounds from the hall, getting closer with each step, "Wellington, do you have the car keys on you? You can use it this weekend, but I need to get some books from the trunk."

"I've got them," he calls out, standing up and digging his hand into his pocket.

She enters the room and seems taken aback. She doesn't even notice me standing there when she walks up to him and takes the keys. She motions around, "I assume things are back to normal between the clarinetist and you."

I chuckle despite myself, she reached the same conclusions I had when I walked in earlier. She turns around at the sound, spotting me. A genuine smile shows on her face, and she says in her Brazilian accent, "Minha querida, look at you, all grown up. I didn't see you come in." She pulls me into a hug.

"Hi, Mrs. Blake," I hug her back.

"How is Dave? Is he coming over for Thanksgiving?"

"Dad is fine, thanks," I reply when she releases me. "He'll be here, at least that's the plan. He's always busy."

"Tell your father I said congrats on his engagement and to stop by when he's in town."

"Will do," I reply, and she gives one last smile before leaving the room.

"Where were we?" Wellington asks when he's convinced his mother is out of earshot.

"We're at the part where I leave," I begin walking backward. As I spin around, ready to dash out of his bedroom, I collide with a girl holding a violin case.

"Ariel?" Wellington voices in surprise.

"Ariel," I repeat her name, almost in a whisper. I take a step back and look up at the owner of the hand carrying the violin case. It's the girl who was with Michael at the bookstore. Michael's sister, according to Faye. She's beautiful, the epitome of pure innocence.

One thing is certain, if anyone could be confused with an ethereal being, it would be her. Put a pair of wings on this girl and she's the picture of one. I shake my head to clear my thoughts, all this talk about angels is messing with my perception.

"Ariel, this is Liz. Liz, this is Ariel," Wellington introduces us.

She beams at me, switches her violin case to her other hand and extends her hand for me to shake. I take it, "Glad to meet you, Ariel."

"It's nice to finally talk to you," she replies simply, letting go of my hand.

Oh boy! She remembers me from the bookstore that day.

Ariel turns to Wellington, "Sorry for showing up

unannounced, but I need a copy of the score we worked on in Comp 2."

"Sure, sure. It's in here somewhere," Wellington stands up.

Even her voice is angelic, I think to myself. Okay, I definitely need to get out of here. One more second in this room, and I'll be seeing a halo over this girl's head.

"Sorry, but I was just leaving when you showed up, and I really, really have to get going. Really," I say idiotically and press my lips together after the third "really," not knowing what else to say. Then, I sidestep around her, trying to look apologetic.

Once in the hallway, I speed-walk out of his apartment without looking back. Cheeks burning, I mentally chastise myself all the way home. Seriously, could I behave in a more awkward manner than I just did? *What's wrong with me lately?* Ariel must think I'm deranged or something.

Back in my bedroom, I do another online search for yesterday's train incident and still nothing. I'm going insane with all the unanswered questions, all this mystery is killing me.

My brain is two seconds from exploding. I can't handle it anymore. I open a second search window, type "Nate Sinclair" and then click the magnifying glass. When nothing related to him pops up, I try his supposed full name, "Nathaniel Sinclair." Several links of people with the same name appears, but not him. He's not part of any social network. Not a picture, an article, or even a tag from his sister mentioning him is out there. The name "Sinclair" by itself, however, brings up site after site about *Lill Sinclair*.

Faye is right, people are obsessed with her. Kids all over the world follow her every move. From what I've read so far, her newest movie is a blockbuster, whatever brand she wears becomes the new trend and her perfume/makeup line "Sin" is all the rage. Unlike all the other celebrities out there, I didn't find a single picture of her caught off guard, looking less than perfect. Even on blurry cellphone camera shots, she looks divine.

It's sickening, no one is that flawless. *NO ONE!* Even Nate whose beauty is unmatched has his distressed moments, like yesterday night for instance.

It doesn't mean I buy anything Wellington said about the "Flower of Light" business, though. It's just too ridiculous to fathom. Leave it to Wellington to draw a chart in which the two most powerful archangels of death, Michael and the fallen Nathaniel, would be part of Saint Pete's student body.

Does he expect me to buy that?

I don't even think *he* believes it. I just don't. If those guys were anything more than a myth, they wouldn't be hanging out at a High School, would they now?

Unable to endure another picture of Nate's sister smiling at me, I shut down my computer and close it. I throw myself on my bed, face down on a pillow and let out a muffled groan.

"Is everything alright, Eliza?" Grandma's voice startles me, and I roll off the side of my bed, falling hard on my back.

"Oh dear!" Grandma gasps, rushing to my aid.

I take Grandma's hand and get to my feet, "I'm fine."

"I don't think you are," Grandma disagrees.

I try to reassure her and force a smile, but Grandma is unconvinced. After all those Wednesdays I spent in Drama class I should be able to smile on command by now, but no. *What a bad excuse for an actress I am.*

"Are you sure?" She presses for a third time.

"I'm just super tired, Grandma. That's all," I reply, sitting down on my bed.

Her face says she still doesn't believe me, but she'll let it pass this time. Grandma hesitantly turns to leave, but stops at the door, saying, "Sometimes things have to fall apart before they can fall into place." I blink up at her, and she adds, "Believe it or not, I was your age once. It wasn't all that long ago... I'll be on the balcony if you need me," and with that, she disappears into the hall.

Grabbing my phone from my pocket, I call Nate. Before the first ring, I chicken out, hang up and lean back on my pillow. *What if all of this is just a coincidence?*

Closing my eyes, I pointedly lie to myself. It'd be best if I postponed the inevitable questions for when we can talk face-to-face. Come to think of it, I'd never be able to know if he were telling the truth through the phone. It's a very reasonable thought. Besides, who can blame me for wanting just one extra day of ignorance and bliss? Not that I really have either right now.

30

"Can I talk to you?" Nate appears out of thin air as Faye and I walk across the parking lot.

How does he do that?

It's not like Nate blends in with all the other uniformed students. And certainly not if he happens to be leaning against his sunny side up yellow car.

"Sure," I reply, walking up to him.

Nate looks to my right, and I inevitably do the same. Faye has followed me for whatever reason and stands waiting, unconvincingly nonchalant. Her posture silently implies, "Carry on, I'm not going anywhere. Don't mind me."

"Maybe later," Nate hangs his book bag across his chest and walks away, leaving both of us standing in front of his car.

I keep my eyes on him as he heads to the building, admiring him. *I'm unable to believe that Nate and I had kissed. A lot.*

"*You kissed Nate?*" Faye screeches in such a high pitch that a group of girls a few yards away stop to stare at us. She makes a face and scrunches up her nose, making me realize I said it out loud.

I smash my hand over her mouth, and immediately lower it. *Why did I do that?* Now my palm is all sticky with a coat of glittery pink lip gloss.

Faye blinks at me, taken aback. And I'm positive that everybody, *EVERYBODY*, in the parking lot heard her. The entire school even, and now all eyes are on me. Double quick I spin away, my cheeks burning hot as I dash toward the main building.

Astonishingly, Faye, in her five freaking inch heels, gets into step with me just as I reach the stairs. She hands me a tissue, more aggressively than is necessary, "Here."

I take it, wipe my palm and crumple it in my hand, without slowing down.

"I'm sorry, okay," Faye grabs my arm, forcing me to stop.

"You know, you shouldn't be so judgmental. You act like Nate has a contagious disease or something. I like Nate, and he's nice to me." I can tell Faye is holding back an eye roll. Which takes a huge effort on her part, I give her that much, and she's instantly forgiven. I smile at her, "It's alright. I know you dislike him. Are you ever going to tell me why?"

"We're gonna be late," Faye dodges my question, turns and walks away. "See you in Calc, Liz."

I shake my head, smiling to myself, and head to English. The entire way to class, I keep contemplating, what did Nate want to talk about?

The first couple hours seem to drag, and I mostly space out. It's hard to focus with everything that has happened this past weekend. I was hoping to see Nate in Calculus, but he's clearly skipping. When he actually does show up to class, he's usually on time.

The second bell rings, and Faye walks in at the same time Mr. Hathaway does. "To your seat Miss Greenwood," Mr. Hathaway tells Faye.

"Yes, Sir," Faye replies mockingly, taking her sweet time

to sit down. She shoots me an apologetic glance, and I smile at her in reassurance as if to say, "We're cool, no hard feelings." She seems to understand, smiling back at me.

All the while, Mr. Hathaway's thunderous voice is explaining today's assignment, "I want you to pair up into groups of two."

A student in the front row starts inching his chair closer to his friend. Mr. Hathaway rests his hand on the guy's chair and stands over him, "Hold your horses, Mr. Clark. You'll be paring up in alphabetical order."

"Why?" A girl on the second row asks, sounding a little whiny.

"It's easier to grade," he replies bluntly.

Faye's last name is Greenwood which means she's paired with Zoë Fairchild. I sigh and turn to look at my partner, Samantha Parker, aka Spark. The good news is Spark seems just as thrilled about it as I am.

Spark shoves her desk against mine with an audible thud and says darkly, "It just keeps getting better."

We're half way through the assignment when Spark breaks her pencil in half from pressing it so hard into the paper. The result is a massive hole not only in our assignment sheet, but also the desk.

She curses under her breath and aggressively pulls a blank sheet from her notebook, copying the answers over. I'm reluctant to ask if she wants me to do it. So, I just continue on to the next equation.

When I can no longer take all the rage flaring in my direction, I ask, "Why do you hate me so much?" She looks up from the assignment, or should I say "glares." If she's trying to intimidate me, it's definitely working, but I don't let up. "What did I ever do to you?"

She doesn't answer and glares at me even harder. I lift my chin, clinching my teeth behind my closed lips to keep my face composed under such intense scrutiny. It seems like hours have passed when she finally replies, "I hate you because of what you are, who you are. People are always taking advantage of you, and you don't even realize it. You're so naïve, it's nauseating. I'm fed up with your Mother Teresa attitude. Do you want me to keep going, or do you think you got the message?"

My jaw hits the floor, and I force a reply, "Got it. I'm sorry you feel that way. I'll just shut up now."

Spark hisses, "There's only one person in this entire universe that I care about, and–"

"Nate," I interrupt in a whisper and regret it right away, because she's shooting me daggers of fire now.

"You've got that right. I've known him since before you were around. You're bad news. Tragedy follows wherever you go. If anything happens to him, I'll rip your guts out and shove them down your throat while you're still breathing. I don't give a crow about what happens to me afterward," Spark threatens. "Is that clear?"

"Yes," I say in a small weak voice.

"Good. Back to work then," she replies, making a linear cut from violently angry to docile. She starts writing again, ignoring me altogether, and we finish the assignment in total silence.

Spark's words haunt me for the rest of class and stick with me all the way to PE. I change into my gym clothes and put on my sneakers. I remove my necklace, hang it on the locker door and pull my hair up into a ponytail. I toggle my phone to silent mode and zip it inside my backpack. Then, I shove it into my locker, shut the door and head to the field.

Ms. Johnson is flirting with the varsity coach, while the boys are tossing a football back and forth. The cheerleaders are stacking up into a pyramid formation, which is making me nervous.

"Why aren't you with *Prince Charming*?" Kiara asks me as she passes by, not really waiting for an answer.

I scan the stadium and spot Nate sitting at the top corner of the bleachers. He's playing with his phone, unaware of his surroundings and disregarding the school rules, "No cellphones after the second bell."

"Yo, Mike! Over here," Ben shouts from the end zone.

Michael is passing through the front gates with Zoë. Just as they're about to part ways, Spark cuts between them, announcing in a singsong voice, "Here come the big guns!"

They both seem to ignore her, I should start doing the same. Michael joins in with the boys, and Zoë gets into formation. I make my way toward the bleachers, my heart beating twice as fast as I contemplate what it is that Nate wants to talk about.

"Hey, Liz! Look what I found," Spark calls out.

She's about twenty feet away, twirling Suri's necklace around her middle finger. I glance back at Ms. Johnson, but she's completely oblivious, chatting away. So, I turn and speed walk toward Spark.

She licks her lips, smiles wickedly and breaks into a reverse skip. She's enjoying herself, teasing me and twisting the delicate chain around her finger. I pick up the pace. She laughs, spins around and launches into a full sprint.

"You've got to be kidding me," I grunt audibly and give chase.

Just as I start gaining on her, she runs faster. Spark cuts through the football field and back on to the track on the visitor's side. I do the same, almost getting in arms reach. She glances at me over her shoulder and doubles her speed.

Man, I can't believe how fast she is. I begin running double-time, trying to catch up. I'm once again almost at arms length when she triples her speed, without even looking in my direction this time. I charge after her, not caring about who's watching us.

The familiar jolt of energy hits me like an adrenaline rush, and I harness the power, directing it to my legs and pushing well beyond my limits. I'm a nanometer from grabbing her shirt when my bad ankle snaps. It's almost like I can hear the bones cracking in my mind. Then, I tumble over, falling hard onto my shoulder. My right elbow scrapes the ground, tearing the fabric on my sleeve and breaking the skin below it. Blood spills down my forearm, and I cry out in pain as I slide several yards before coming to a stop.

Spark's face hovers over me, and she tosses my necklace carelessly to the ground, "FYI, this thing doesn't work." Then, she strolls off the track, leaving me stretched out in pure agony.

"Still breathing over there, O'Neill?" Ms. Johnson calls out from across the field.

"She's alright," Nate calls back, kneeling beside me.

"No, I'm not," I groan.

He picks up my necklace and gives me a once over, as if taking inventory of what remains intact. By the pain I'm experiencing, it's safe to say it's a short list.

"You will be," Nate slightly touches my ankle with his right hand and gradually starts rotating my foot with the other.

I tuck my lower lip under my teeth, bracing myself for the pain, but it never comes. A warmth spreads where his hands make contact with my bare ankle. The pain attenuates, slowly subsiding, and then the familiar tingling sensation pulses through me as he rotates my foot in small circles.

"I know you're still in pain, but we've gotta get you out of here. You can stand now," Nate says in a low tone.

He helps me up, and I notice the entire stadium is staring at me. That's twice in a single day. *I'm famous. Yay for me!*

The ball that was being tossed up and down the field, now rests in Michael's hands, and he's glaring at Nate. The cheer squad has broken formation, and Zoë starts in our direction. She steps in front of us, blocking our path. Neither Nate or Zoë say a word, they just exchange an unspoken hostility. Then, Nate tries to step around her, but she puts a flat palm into his chest.

"Excuse us," Nate says in a composed voice.

"Why don't you allow me to take Liz to the nurse's

office?" Zoë asks, looking at me.

"How about we let her decide?" Nate tightens his grip on my hand.

"It's okay Zoë. But, thank you anyway," I reply apologetically.

"There. You've got your answer," Nate says, looking past her.

Zoë squints at something over Nate's shoulder and I turn my head. Not something, but someone. Abe Kaur is slowly walking toward us, his expression giving nothing away. Zoë purses her lips as if making an agonizing decision on the spot. Then, she lowers her hand and steps aside, without saying another word.

Nate doesn't miss a beat. At once, he's walking easily around her and dragging me along by the hand. But instead of taking me to the nurse, he hurries me through the back gates. I look sideways at him as we cross the parking lot. He pops the doors of his car open as we approach, and helps me into the passenger seat. With hurried steps he walks around the car and climbs into the driver's side.

"Let me see your wrist," Nate reaches for my arm.

I switch positions, so he can take my left arm in his hands. He carefully rolls up my long sleeve gym shirt, and only then I notice that my wrist is visibly swollen.

I try to bend it, and a wave of pain restrains me, "It's broken, Nate. I can't move it."

He examines my wrist, touching it gently, "It isn't broken, only sprained."

"Has anyone ever told you that you're a terrible liar?" I scoff, flinching in pain.

"Beside you?" He asks, looking up at me.

I nod, and he applies slight pressure at the site with his fingers, like he's measuring the damage. I take a deep breath, burying my head in the seat.

At some point, I dare a glimpse as his capable hands wrap around my wrist. No pain, or anguish, just warmth and the usual tingling. I take in his face, his closed eyes, his perfect symmetry, and I no longer doubt Wellington's translation. Nate must be an ethereal being, he just healed me. The pain is completely gone. Not only in my wrist and ankle, but my entire body feels fully restored.

Looking down at my hands, I move my fingers fluidly and think to myself, "Thank you, Nate, my archangel."

His eyes open, and he brushes a curl off my cheek. An inexplicable impulse takes hold of me, and I raise both of my hands to cup his face, bringing my lips to his. I catch him off guard, and he stays still like a statue. I slide one hand around his neck, pulling him closer, and only then does he return the kiss. More intently today, but gentle nonetheless. My entire being surrenders to the feeling of his lips, delightfully warm pressed against mine. His fingers undo my ponytail and run through my hair gently, sending chills down my spine.

All of a sudden, he pulls away and turns the engine on. I blink at him, still a little dazed. Nate looks around surreptitiously, shifts the Lambo into reverse and peels out of the school's parking lot.

"What's wrong, Nate?" I buckle my seat belt. "Where are we going?"

"Somewhere we can talk in private," Nate replies, glancing into the rear view mirror.

"Are you going to tell me the truth?"

"I believe you already know," Nate says, switching gears. He gives me an almost imperceptible nod and makes a left turn, heading toward the freeway. Nate flips the sound system on, and I'm acutely aware of being trapped in Nate's moving car.

As far as I know we might be merging onto the highway to hell. I can picture a tiny Faye on my right shoulder chastising me, "How can you be so dense? You can't trust him. *ARE YOU OUT OF YOUR MIND?*" Along with a tiny Wellington right beside her, waving his cello bow, "Nate is the fallen archangel of death and deceit. It'd be wise to keep your distance." To my left sits Nate, a perfect excuse to disregard all of it.

Maybe I am being obtuse, or maybe it's the sound of violins playing softly in the background that's keeping me calm. *I am not afraid.*

About ten minutes in, Nate sucks in air sharply and curses under his breath. He looks up from the road and squints into the rear view mirror.

"What is it?" I'm startled by his heightened awareness and turn in my seat to look, but I don't see anything out of the ordinary.

"Abe is tailing us," Nate replies, scanning the highway for the nearest exit.

"Abe Kaur?" I ask confused. "Why would he be following us?" I try to spot his Kawasaki among the cars.

"He's behind the silver Prius." Nate notices me searching for his motorcycle. Abe Kaur's bike is barely visible behind the tiny vehicle, but his alien green helmet is unmistakable.

Nate pats his coat with one hand and then asks, "Can you get my phone from my book bag?"

I find his phone in the outside pocket and hand it to him. He touches the screen, "Siri, how far is the first exit toward U.S.1-South from here?"

"It is 5.2 Miles," informs the robotic voice.

"Thank you," Nate says, handing me the phone.

"It is nice to be appreciated," comes Siri's reply.

"That's not gonna work. I'll have to improvise," Nate says to himself.

"Please, don't tell me that you're finally going to test the horse power of your toy car."

"No, this is where I slow down," he replies, dropping way below the speed limit. The cars behind us respond with extended blasts of the horn.

"Shouldn't we get into the slow lane?" I ask, worrying that he'll cause a crash.

"Not yet," he replies, checking the rear view mirror.

I do the same, but probably not for the same reason. While Nate may be searching for Abe Kaur's motorcycle, I'm looking to see if we've caused an accident yet. I turn when I feel Nate's hand checking my seat belt.

Nate looks up at me and flashes an excited grin, "Hang on, Angel Girl." Then, he turns the wheel, swerving through three lanes of oncoming traffic, straight to the edge of the highway intersection. Speeding up like a psychopath, from forty to one hundred miles per hour in a matter of seconds, he drives onto the emergency lane, traveling the wrong way up an on-ramp.

Over my shoulder, I spot Abe Kaur on his bike, flying past us. Nate keeps driving against the flow of traffic until he's able to change lanes, performing another crazy maneuver. I hit my head hard on the roof and wince in pain. Before I can get a better grip on my seat, Nate makes a series of sharp turns, the momentum slamming me against the door panel. He slams the brakes, flicks the turn signal, and slowly blends back into traffic, just as a police car crosses the intersection.

Nate turns to me, "Are you okay?"

I nod, too shaken to speak.

Ten minutes later, we stop in the back of an abandoned brick building. A garage door opens as if a sensor has been activated by our arrival, and Nate parks inside. The door lowers behind us, and only the car's lights illuminate the pitch dark single space garage.

The Lambo doors' swing open, and Nate steps out, "Come on," not bothering to shut off the engine or lights.

I climb out of the car, following him. We approach a heavy looking wooden door, and Nate effortlessly pushes it open. The lights from the car blink off and the engine shuts down. I turn to Nate just in time to see him pocketing the keys, which seemed to have materialized in his hand. The old wooden door slams shut behind us, followed by a metallic clank, sounding frighteningly like a deadbolt. I stop on a dime, feeling locked in. Unsure if I should follow him any further.

"Still with me?" He asks, looking over his shoulder.

"Where are we?"

"Don't worry. We won't be found here," he assures and turns to face me. "You might want to close your eyes."

I shake my head. It's dark enough as it is. The outside light barely breaches the painted over windows. There's no way I'm closing my eyes right now.

"Are you sure? I don't want to frighten you."

I scoff at the sound of that and look him straight-on, managing to break out of my stupor long enough to point out, "I don't think it's humanly possible to be any more frightened than I am already."

"Suit yourself. I don't have the time or the inclination to argue right now," Nate replies, walking away from me.

I start to follow him, but the commanding tone of his voice holds me back, "Stay where you are." He opens his arms wide and closes his eyes. Slowly, he begins raising his hands, palms facing up. His lips barely move as he mumbles something incoherent to my ears. *Latin maybe?*

From the center of each palm, a silvery vapor starts to swirl, rapidly increasing in size. They pulse, like waves of visible energy. Blue fractals of spherical lightning emanates from their core, combining into a single vortex and passing through the high ceilings of the complex.

Nate slowly starts to turn counterclockwise, completely enveloped in silver light. His voice echoes louder and louder throughout the cavernous room with each rotation. My legs shake, and I cover my mouth with both hands, muffling any sound from escaping my lips.

Suddenly, the lights on the ornate chandeliers start flickering on and off, rattling. I turn around, wide eyed, letting my hands fall down from my mouth. Dusty paintings and crumbling statues blink in and out of sight with each flash. The whole dilapidated structure groans.

By the looks of it, we're inside an old abandon cathedral and fear hits me at once. I swallow hard and turn back around to Nate. His chanting gets louder and louder, booming throughout the chapel, and he's surrounded by a wild indigo blaze.

The sight of Nate engulfed in flames is too overwhelming to witness. I panic and run straight back to the door we came in, forgetting it's locked. A violent wind kicks up a storm of dust, blowing my hair wildly. I charge to another door situated across from the altar, but it's also locked. My heart seems to be pounding inside my throat. I desperately search for any low window that I can escape from, but they're too narrow and out of reach.

I'M TRAPPED.

If I don't die from the vortex Nate is summoning, I'll certainly die of a heart attack. *Or worse,* I'll die of third degree burns when this entire place goes up in flames. The only way out is the gigantic double doors at the front entrance of the old cathedral. To reach them, I must pass Nate in his circle of fire.

Against my better judgment, I dash toward them, my steps echoing loudly against the wood panel flooring. Light spreads like wildfire, forming a thin silvery blue coat upon the ceiling which crawls down toward the floor. The doors tower over me, and I grasp the giant cast iron handles with both hands and pull them with all my might. They don't budge, they don't even rattle.

I'm trapped in a dusty old abandoned cathedral in the middle of nowhere. My phone is back at school in my gym locker. No one knows where I am. I don't even know where I am myself. Leaning against the double doors, I let myself slide into a sitting position in surrender.

This is it. *I'm dead!*

31

The flames finally subside, and the old cathedral still stands. The hardwood flooring appears to be intact, and the ancient chandeliers slowly sway, casting an array of intricate shadows. An icy blue dome of glistening light forms an inner layer on the walls and arched ceiling, illuminating this abandoned sanctuary with a cerulean glow.

The vortex splits, diminishing back into Nate's palms, and he lowers his arms. His expression is serene which terrifies me even more, considering everything that just happened here. But then again, I'm still alive. Nothing raised up from the dust to swallow me whole as I expected. I have to admit that despite myself, I really believed Nate was conjuring some type of portal that would lead to the underworld.

Every fiber of my being trembles, I'm absolutely shaken. I lean back against the church's entrance door and wrap my arms around my legs, bracing them against my chest. I press my chin against my knees to stop my teeth from chattering.

Nate looks at me, taking in my state of shock. His eyes are once again painted blue, and his face is sad, shadowing anguish and disappointment. For what seems like a lifetime,

Nate just stands there, watching me. Then, something in my expression, or maybe the sight of my quaking body, makes him turn around. He slowly starts to descend toward the altar, increasing the distance between us. Everything about him screams magnificence, from the contour of his figure to the confidence in his stride. There's no denying it now. Wellington's assumptions are correct, and I must accept the atrocious truth. Nate is Nathaniel, the fallen archangel of death.

When he reaches the altar, he slouches at its base. He leans his back against it, facing me. Even a cathedral apart, I can clearly see him. For a change, he isn't trying to disguise what's in his mind. His face is an open book, implying that my fearful reaction is bleeding him from the inside out.

I swallow once, twice, but I still can't move or speak. I can hardly breathe for that matter. I'm petrified. Unsure of what exactly I'm afraid of. If Nate wanted to hurt me, he would have done so already. But he didn't. So, why can't I move? *Snap out of it.* He healed me today and saved my life not forty-eight hours ago. He won't harm me now, will he?

Nate finally breaks the silence, his voice echoing throughout the empty cathedral, "Part of me knew this would happen, the other part hoped..." He trails off and presses both of his palms over his eyes, seeming distressed. "Summoning the aegis before you," Nate tries again. "It was overkill. I should have known it would scare the life out of you. I didn't think it through. You're always so fearless. Death himself stares you in the face every single day, and you don't even flinch. *Hell!* You escorted him to the school nurse."

Is he talking about Michael? Of course he is, Wellington said he was The Archangel of Death. But if Nate means what I think he does, I should be afraid of *him*, not Michael. Nate is the fallen one. Michael is the good guy, evil slayer and all that.

Something else dawns on me, that day in the library when

Nate said he didn't expect me to be so friendly toward Michael. It wasn't jealousy, he expected me to fear the guy.

Nate is still staring at the floor, and I truly wish my tongue didn't feel so thick inside my mouth. I want to be able to say that I'm torn around Michael most of the time. That while part of me trusts him, the other half wants to run away screaming. My body, however, doesn't let me speak up. I'm still frozen in place.

"I thought you knew I'd never hurt you," Nate's voice is almost a whisper throughout this immense vacant cathedral. He goes on, "I'm sincerely sorry. It's new to me having a mortal knowing my true identity. I'm not too keen on spending time with mortals, period. I wish you wouldn't, but if you choose to leave, you may. The aegis, once complete, blocks intruders from entering, but those inside are free to exit. You can go anytime, and I won't pursue you. I interfered with your decision once. Trust me, I won't do it again."

I just stare at his cast down posture, willing him to look up at me. He seems devastated, like he's carrying the weight of eons. Come to think of it, most likely he is. I rub my eyes, trying to redirect my thoughts.

Evidently, Nate is done talking. He's just slouching there, his head lowered, sort of hanging. A light that seems to come from nowhere hovers over his form. It slightly shadows his profile, unveiling him as an ethereal work of art.

I inhale deeply, making up my mind. Enough is enough. I'm being absurd. I force myself to stand up on shaky legs, supporting my back against the thick wooden door all the way. I lean there for a moment and try to steady my stance, grasping for courage.

When I finally get a hold of myself, I deliberately make my way down the aisle, watching Nate with each step. He's looking down at his palms. His hands are earthly and godlike at the same time. They're capable of healing and manifesting shimmering tornadoes, but they're the same hands that tenderly touch my face. Through my eyes, I don't see the immortal fallen archangel he is, but Nate. The boy I fell for, my mocking, always at ease, devil-may-care, Nate. I seriously should stop using this expression, it's hitting too close to home.

Taking a deep breath, I continue to descend the aisle toward him. The floorboards creak and pop under my feet, compelling Nate to look up. His expression is one of disbelief, I've apparently surprised him once again. It's clear to me now, Nate expected me to bolt.

My steps are more confident than I truly feel, harnessing a bravery I never knew I had. Apart from the noise of my sneakers touching the floor and my breathing, the church is dead silent. Nate looks almost unreal, resembling a misplaced statue. He isn't blinking or moving, he doesn't even seem to be breathing.

I shake my head to clear my thoughts. If I let my mind wander in that direction, my legs will give out on me. And just like that, they begin to wobble. I don't dare to take another step. Instead, I sit down in the pew closest to me on the second row, a few feet from where Nate leans against the altar. He seemingly notices my moment of weakness and waits patiently for me to break the silence this time. Probably in fear he might scare me off otherwise.

I gulp and finally manage to utter a complete sentence, my voice cracking at the end, "That poltergeist thing you did, what did you call it?"

"The aegis," he supplies with a hint of a smile. "It's a dome of ethereal protection, to put it simply."

"Why did you do it?" I ask, my voice still a little shaken. "Were you testing me or something?"

Nate seems to relax a little, "No, I wasn't trying to test you. You want answers, and I want to give them to you. Within the seal of the aegis, no one can find or hear us. I don't know how long it will last, though. I'm out of practice. It's been awhile since the last time I used my spectrum to summon the aegis. It might hold for three hours at least, give or take a few minutes."

"Spectrum?" I inquire, recalling Wellington's vague explanation yesterday.

"The light you witnessed. That was a tiny glimpse of my spectrum you saw. It's the ethereal equivalent of a mortal's soul."

"The silvery blue light?" I murmur to myself thoughtfully. Then, it hits me. "The dream? It was real. You were truly there. The same light guided me to you. It was your spectrum, and then you healed me, didn't you?"

He shakes his head, denying it, and I frown in confusion. I'm absolutely positive that Nate healed my migraine. Any doubts I ever had about my dreams being real ceased to exist with his spectrum explanation. No matter what he says next, he won't convince me otherwise. It's so clear now, like pieces of a puzzle fitting together. Every time Raph visits my dreams there's that gold glow, and Faye mentioned that in her dream the light was blinding white. A flashback of memories bombard my brain, the forgotten incident at the Chemistry lab, Michael shimmering in bright light. How did I forget the chemistry incident until this very moment? Does it have to do with this "aegis" we're in?

"I didn't heal your headache. I unblocked your mind," Nate finally answers my question, jolting me from my reverie.

"Unblocked?"

"That day you passed out in Chemistry, he stifled the memory of what you had witnessed at the lab to keep you safe from me. Your mind fought back, hence the headache. I just undid Michael's work," Nate justifies himself. "I didn't know it until that afternoon in the library. I almost killed you, I could have. I thought you had a simple migraine and I was about to heal it, if I did you'd be dead."

I try making sense of this information. So, I didn't inhale any chemicals that day, Michael compelled me to forget. No wonder the headache didn't go away.

"You've been in a dream like that before, haven't you?" Nate asks straightforward. "With Michael?"

For a split second, I debate whether to tell him about Raph or not and decide on the truth, "Not Michael, Raph. He's the one who always visits my dreams. At least he used to."

"Raph?" Nate asks taken aback and answers his own question promptly, "Of course, Raphael. That sneaky dastard! No wonder he spent the past twelve years vacationing on the Earth realm," Nate says under his breath, sounding almost as if he's forgotten I'm still sitting right here. He goes on cynically, "Come on, Nathaniel. Lets see how long it takes to bore you into leaving me alone. Let's try Bora Bora, The Greek Islands, and Fernando de Noronha. You're still here, how about the Taj Mahal, Cancun, or better yet let's go back to South America."

"Oh my G–" I cover my mouth with both hands as the words escape my lips. Nate is Raph's shadow. I can't believe it.

Nate stops murmuring to himself and looks at me, inquiringly, "What is it?"

I let my hands drop into my lap, staring straight into his eyes, "Wellington's translation is correct, isn't it?"

"Come again?" Nate cocks his head to one side, studying me carefully.

"Your iPod," I clarify. "Wellington translated the audio file from Latin to English."

Nate looks me straight-on, "And it just so happens that Wellington Blake, seventeen, Cello Boy, speaks Latin. Why did you give it to him, instead of returning it to me?"

My cheeks burn, and I look down at my hands, letting my hair fall like curtains to hide my blushing face.

When I don't answer his question, Nate notes, "Curiosity killed the cat."

I look up at him, his face is a mixture of skepticism and

regret. Not knowing what to make of that, I say lamely, "So I've heard."

"Tell me," Nate starts. "How much was Blake able to translate?"

"Up until the part that says the fallen archangel of death Nathaniel walked away, counting the days until Lillithiel's destruction."

"Really?" Nate asks, still sounding dubious about Wellington's translation skills. "Do you mind telling me what the two of you have learned?"

"Angels and archangels rebelled, getting themselves cast down to the Earth realm," I begin. "There was a plot to reclaim the upper dimension, chaos ensued, and those involved were banished to the underworld. There was this fallen archangel called Asmodeus that started playing Doctor Frankenstein and created five evil spawns. When he was about to create the sixth one, Michael descended and kicked his butt, destroying Asmodeus and his minions. Centuries later a prophecy was revealed to one of Asmodeus' creations, Lillithiel. Something confusing about angel fusion, a glowing flower and Michael waiting to carve up the bad guys."

"Is that what he told you?" Nate sounds amused.

"That's all I can remember. He explained it with more details than I asked for." I stop and look up at the ceiling, trying to remember something important Wellington mentioned. Unable to conjure it up, I tell Nate the part about him, "You're mostly MIA the entire time. You're mentioned once in the beginning and then again at the very end as one of the witnesses to the prophecy."

"Is that all?" Nate inquires with an unreadable expression, dismissing my last remark.

"From your iPod? Yeah, pretty much," My brain works overtime to put the puzzle pieces together.

"But," Nate presses knowingly.

"You tell me," I reply, uncrossing my arms and throwing

them up in the air.

"Sorry, no can do," Nate remarks bluntly. "That would be against the rules."

"Yeah, yeah," I say in annoyance. "I've heard plenty about these rules. Wellington said they're mentioned over and over again. Except, nobody bothers to spell them out."

"It's a bunch of 'shall nots' and 'no-noes,'" Nate makes air quotes with his fingers. "Which can be narrowed down to a single rule: *Do not interfere in the affairs of mortals, allow them their free will.*"

"And he was right again," I let out in disbelief.

"Who? Blake?"

"Yes, Wellington Blake. I'm willing to bet his other assumptions are accurate as well, which makes me..." I let my voice trail off and press my lips together. I don't want to say it. Somehow, even after all I've experienced today, if I actually utter the words, it means I'm embracing my fate. I don't know if I want to. *Heck!* I know I don't want to.

"Please continue," Nate encourages me.

I sigh and offer, "Why not? I might as well. Wellington believes I'm the Flower of Light. Prophecy girl here," I point to myself with my thumb, attempting a joke to disguise my anguish. "Now let's do the GPS thing with Raph, go kick some demon butt with Michael and save the world."

"Wrong. Right. Wrong, and right again," Nate says thoughtfully.

"Um?" I let out at a loss.

"You may or may not be the human vessel mentioned in the prophecy. Every indication points to you, but the dates just don't line up. You're right about the spirit connection between Raphael and the Flower of Light. You can't defeat demons, they'll smash you before you can scream for help. But by choosing to join in with the celestial crowd, you'd be saving the world from Asmodeus' spawns," he rationalizes Wellington's wild theory.

"*Wait!* Is there a chance I'm not the prophecy girl?" I ask hopefully, missing everything else he said.

"No comment."

"Why?" I immediately guess the answer to my question. "Because I am."

"Not even under the aegis do I dare state my assumptions," Nate says. "Not even for you, Liz."

"But you said the dates don't add up," I say befuddled.

"The dates don't match, they're way off. You're sixteen, not twelve." Nate stops expectantly. When I just frown in reply, he spells it out, "The A.O.T. specifically registers the archangel Raphael descending to the Earth realm in the year 2000, not 1996. Which means you were four years old back then, and only a developing fetus could accept the transition. There are no records of him coming around before that, the A.O.T. is never wrong. Prior to then, Raphael hadn't set foot on American soil for over three centuries. And before you even ask, he hasn't been to Japan either for just as long."

"What is the A.O.T.?"

"The Athenaeum of Transgressions, where all the records have been kept in the underworld since 'the fall.' Any interference in the affairs of mortals from either side, upper or under dimension, is automatically documented in the A.O.T. The file in my iPod was Asmodeus' Chronicle narrated by the A.O.T. keeper by my request."

"You're telling me you have mp3 players in hell?"

"We had them before you guys ever did," Nate replies simply. "Eternity is a long time. It gets boring. We have technology you'd never fathom, wisdom retained from before the fall."

"The underworld doesn't sound so bad."

"Bad is an understatement. Once in, there's no way out. You're always surrounded by a mist of despair, no freedom, no personal growth. It's stagnant. And here, I'm talking about my kind. A lost soul becomes the fallen ones' play thing for all eternity," Nate pauses, allowing his words to sink in. "And like I said, eternity is a long, long time."

"Why did you need to make a copy in the first place?" I inquire bluntly. "You were there."

"You're right, I witnessed the prophecy. I knew about Asmodeus' scheme, but I wasn't around at the time, and I didn't have the full story. As it turned out, neither did the A.O.T.," Nate explains, starting to stand up. Half way, he changes his mind, sitting back down.

Looking straight at him, I point out the obvious, "Lill Sinclair isn't your sister, is she? Sinclair isn't even your last name. Do you even have a last name?"

"No to all."

"That day on the way to Yale," I swallow hard, considering my next words. "You didn't call your mother. You called Lill, didn't you?"

"Actually," Nate sounds bemused. "I called Spark."

"What? *Spark?* Is she...?" I trail off. I was about to ask if she's a fallen angel, but the question died on my lips.

"Spark is a demon, a succubus to be more precise."

"Spark is a *succubus*?" I blurt out, remembering what Wellington said about their immortality and the way they can morph into anyone they prey on. Nate suppresses a laugh with the back of his hand, and I try to hide my astonishment by quickly appending, "She's very protective of you. The things she said today... It sounds like she's known you forever."

"Not forever," Nate remarks. "We crossed paths when she was fourteen years old. Spark was only a toddler when Asmodeus attempted to destroy her kind, and they fled to the Earth realm. When Gabriel and Michael descended, destroying them and imposing the rules to the repentant survivors, Spark was one of the few who lived. She was too young to understand the law. The demon who rescued her from the underworld was destroyed and none of the survivors felt like taking care of a toddler in the new world they were in. They left her behind, lost and alone. A mortal couple found and raised her as one of their own without knowing she was a demon. She grew up unaware of her true nature. Until the day her needs awakened, that is. Having no idea what was happening to her, she mistook her impulses for lust and nearly killed the mortal boy she loved. Luckily for her, Gabriel was the one to descend instead of Michael, and I was able to advocate in her favor. I talked him into granting her a second chance, and Gabriel laid out the rules for her. She's been around more often than not since then, always having my back. Lots of times, like this one for instance, I wish she would take off and stay out of it..." He trails off, shaking his head.

"But," I press, urging for him to finish his thought.

Nate lets out a loud breath, "She refuses. She tells me that if I want her to leave, I'd have to command her to do so. She knows I'll never do it."

"Why not? It's for her own safety, isn't it?"

"If I ever command her to do anything, she'll be my minion for as long as I exist," he explains with a tone of finality in his voice.

Nate's lips form the beginning of a syllable, but I beat him to it, "Why did she steal my necklace? Just out of spite? Or what?"

"Oh, she had a reason, alright," Nate replies with a hint of sarcasm tinting his voice. "She was out of line and knows it. Why do you think she left the stadium so fast?"

"Because of you," I guess. "But why did she do it? It was so childish." I'm still annoyed by the entire ordeal.

"She was trying to expose you to Abe Kaur."

"*To Abe Kaur?* By making me chase after her?" I blurt out, understanding things the moment the question is up in the air. So, I throw him a new one, "Abe is one of you, isn't he?"

"Yes, he's a fallen angel, a lesser angel. Good enough to observe and report," Nate half jokes.

"Spark wants him to report on what? *How fast I am?* How does that expose me?"

"You don't realize how fast the two of you were running. I wasn't paying attention at first, only when Zoë told me to stop her did I look up. I could see the atmosphere around you start to yield. I've never seen a mortal outrun a demon before. Half a second later Abe stepped into the stadium. I was about to neutralize Abe with my mind when you tumbled," Nate replies, flinching at the memory.

"How did you hear her? She was nowhere near you."

"She directed her thoughts to me," Nate replies simply.

"You're talking about telepathy, like reading other people's minds?" I ask, wondering if all of this is an endless nightmare. *What happened with the peaceful dreams with Raph?*

"Some call it that. I'd say it's more like an exchange of thoughts. You communicate mentally, instead of verbally. You only share what's in your mind with the ones you want to. I can't hear your thoughts unless you open your mind to me. Like that day in the cafeteria, when your friends where bombarding you with questions and you plead to get out of there. Do you remember?" Nate asks watching for my reaction.

"I do. You came to my rescue." Only after the words are out do I realize what he's implying, *"Wait?* Are you saying I can do it?"

"I'm not sure," Nate replies. "Sometimes it seems like you can, others it's like you're just another mortal with loud thoughts. Regardless, you have no control over it."

"Is there anyway to find out?" I ask intrigued by the idea. *Now, that would be a cool power to have.* "Does that mean anyone can do it?"

"One question at a time," he laughs. "The only way to find out is by directing your thoughts to a mortal. I'm sensitive to mortals' thoughts, testing on me won't prove anything. And no, not everyone can do it. Not anymore anyways."

There were a few times people around me seemed to have

heard my thoughts. But, I can't be absolutely sure whether it was coincidence, or if they just read my expression. So, I ask instead, "Can I hear your thoughts?"

"Yes. But only when I direct them to you." Nate replies inside my head, making me flinch. Immediately, he apologizes out loud, "I'm sorry, I shouldn't have done that."

"It's okay," I reply, not so sure myself whether it is okay or not. "What else can you do?"

He lets out a long breath, running his hands through his hair.

I try a more direct approach, "I already know you can heal, hide us from the universe, compel, get inside people's heads, and invade their dreams. *Can you fly?* Disappear into thin air?"

Nate just stares at me, seeming exasperated by my mortal curiosity. I just look back at him expectantly. He inhales deeply and finally replies, "Yes to both. There's not much I can't do. I'm not bound to the laws of physics."

"Does that mean you can travel through time?" I ask, wondering if he could take me into the future for a peek.

"You had to pick the unattainable one," Nate half jokes. "Chrono-telekinesis is not on my list. I can't go back to the past or jump into the future. I can definitely manipulate time, slow down and speed up, only the current real time, though. But it's against the rules. It falls into the criteria of interfering with mortals."

"Can you change the weather, like you did in the dream?" I challenge.

"Not change. Again, I can manipulate perception and create an illusion," Nate replies, and I can tell he's grasping for patience.

I'm getting off point here, clearly testing his temper. I decide not to push it and steer back to a safer topic, "Why didn't Michael and Zoë send a thought to me instead? That surely would have stopped me."

"If they tried to emit a message to you, there was a

chance Abe could tune into it. Because of Spark, you see? At the field today, Spark was too close to you, any attempt on their part would be a shot in the dark. Spark is one of the most gifted succubi out there, her presence conflicts with their spectrum. Particularly Michael's, he's too powerful. When she doesn't conceal it, they clash. Just like that day in Chemistry."

"Do they know you healed me?" I ask, wondering if he's even allowed to do so.

"Yes. I can guarantee that both Michael and Zoë sensed your emotion changing from anguish to relief," Nate replies, seeming unconcerned.

Remembering Abe at the subway station that terrible evening, another question comes to mind, "Was Abe following us on Saturday too?"

"Yes. He's been shadowing you the whole time. The moment he's sure you are who they're looking for, he'll make his move," Nate informs. "That night, Abe orchestrated the whole thing to test you. He sent a shape shifter demon to jump on the tracks."

"*A what?*"

"A demon that can shift into an animal. The one in question changed into a rat. That's why you never found out anything about the accident, because it never actually happened," Nate explains. "That girl on the roof, the one you saved from falling –"

"What about her? Was she a shape shifter? I remember seeing a rat that night. Was that another of Abe's tests?" I'm dumbfounded. Abe Kaur wasn't even around when that happened.

"No. She's mortal, but she chose our path years ago. She belongs to us. Lillithiel compelled her to jump, not Abe."

"Was Abe chasing us today to find out if I'm the prophecy girl?"

Nate agrees with a simple nod.

"And Spark volunteered to help him," I murmur to

myself.

"No. She's just trying to get under my skin," Nate pauses and adds to my utter dismay, "She's giving you a hard time, because she believes you'll be the death of me."

"She kinda made that clear in Calculus this morning. I just don't understand how?" I ask with a scoff, still puzzled by the absurdity of it.

"She thinks if Michael goes in for the kill, I'll step in to defend you," Nate explains, sounding nonchalant. Not confirming or denying that he'd do such a thing.

"That's the second time you've insinuated that Michael is here to kill me. Nothing in Wellington's translation said anything about Michael being the grim reaper. From what I understand, he's supposed to protect humans," I remark confidently.

In the back of my mind though, I keep thinking about him blacking me out with only his words, the icy dark way he looks at me and the weird conversation with Zoë that I overheard.

"Sorry to break it to you, but it's most likely why Michael is here," Nate starts sarcastically. He fixes his piercing blue eyes at me and then continues in the most serious tone I've ever heard coming from his lips, "If it were up to him, you would be dead already. The only thing stopping him from killing you and taking you with him is his obedience. Michael will be Michael, selfless, incorruptible and loyal until the end. Also, Blake got it wrong if he translated that Michael is assigned to protect mortals because he's not. The only thing he's assigned to protect are the gates, and at the same time he's ordered to neutralize any threat. He isn't a guardian archangel like Raphael, nor an archangel of wisdom like Zophiel. He's an archangel of death, just like Gabriel. Except Gabriel is the messenger which obliges him to apply his own discretion. Michael, however, is sent to destroy. No one can defeat him, The Archangel of Death Michael in destruction mode is unstoppable."

His words give me goosebumps, and I grasp for anything that might oppose his logic. All I come up with is, "What happened to human's free will? Or does that not apply to them, only to you?"

"It applies to all of us. That's why he can't take you yet. As long as you're not a threat to the gates, you're allowed to live," Nate explains. "He could invite you to come with him. If he did so, chances are you'd go. Michael would give you a glimpse of paradise and you'd go willingly, any mortal would. However, there's the slight possibility that you would decline, and they would never risk it."

"If I said no, I'd be joining your team by default," I say, fearing his answer.

"Maybe, or maybe not. It all depends on what you decide in the end. Either way, the underworld would be sure of your identity, and he'd have to end your life. It's a lose-lose situation," Nate replies sincerely and then adds with a knowing smile, "They also know you're into me."

I know he's trying to sidetrack me, lighten up the tension. But for once, his beautiful eyes and smile can't do the trick. Not after just finding out that both upper and under dimensions are out to get me. Without smiling back, I ask, "Why?"

To his credit, Nate replies without asking me to be more specific for a change, "If you're the girl from the prophecy, and so we're clear, I'm not saying you are. It makes you 'wanted.' Lill wants you dead, just for good measure. She sees you as a threat to her existence, and has been set to destroy the Flower of Light since the prophecy was revealed to her. The underworld wants you because somehow you're linked to Raphael, which makes you the key to the upper dimension, and that's all they've sought since 'the fall.' Michael wants to take you with him before you have a chance to make the wrong decision. I shadowed Raphael for twelve years and have no idea of his motives for being on

Earth, other than enjoying the sun and salty air, that is. Zophiel, Ariel, and Gabriel want you to locate Asmodeus' evil spawns, otherwise they'll be forever lost."

"And you?" I brace myself for the answer I fear.

"Lillithiel assigned me to you. She withdrew me from my prior assignment after you saved the little girl in Japan," Nate replies dismissively.

"What exactly is your assignment?" I press, watching him closely.

"To put it simply, I'm supposed to ascertain if you're the prophecy girl, persuade you to come with me and drop you off at the gates of the under dimension," sarcasm drips from Nate's voice.

As outlandish as it may sound, the cynical tone in his words somehow assures me that he'd never do it. Every fiber of my being confirms my hunch and I challenge him further, "Why didn't you? You know I would follow you anywhere."

"You didn't learn the most important lesson," Nate gets to his feet, his eyes never deviating from mine as he makes his way toward me. "Be careful with your words. You just gave me permission to take you to hell, Angel Girl."

"Angel Girl," I scoff, shaking my head in disbelief. *How did I miss that?* He does believe I'm the girl from the prophecy. "You knew it all along."

He sits sideways at the pew right in front of mine, facing me, and finally admits, "I wouldn't say all along, just for a long time."

"You never answered my question," I press on unashamed.

"I never answer most of your questions," Nate mocks. "Do you want to know why I didn't do it?" He rests his chin over his stretched arm.

I nod once.

"You know the answer."

"No, Nate, I don't," I say softly, grasping for patience.

"I wanted you to live before you die," Nate replies,

almost to himself.

His answer hits me like a ton of bricks, a confirmation of my fate, and the bitter retort is out before I can stop myself, "Why do you care?"

Nate does not dignify me with a reply. He turns around and slouches in his seat, facing the altar. So, I shoot off another question, "Why did you get involved? Wellington and I, well..." I trail off, swallow hard and go on, "We thought you were a free agent."

He spins around so fast in his seat that I recoil. Nate says in a low voice, "You're wrong." He closes his eyes, and it's obvious he's trying to get a hold of his temper. I don't dare to breathe, suddenly aware that I've crossed the line. After a tense moment, he speaks in a more composed tone, "When we fell, we were all bound as one. I can refuse to do their bidding, but can't escape what I've become, truly fallen. I'm the sole fallen archangel allowed up here, but there are others like me imprisoned behind the gates. Let's just say the upper dimension is not the only one with the power to confine me to the underworld. If I'm still free to come and go, it's because at times I'm called upon by the fallen archangels and I oblige."

"I see," I say quietly, standing up. I jump over the pew's back rest and sit beside him, wondering if I can make a deal with death. If I allow Michael to take me, would he agree to free Nate from the grips of the underworld in return.

Nate shifts in his seat to face me as if straining to hear my thoughts. I try to clear my mind and focus on his face, it doesn't take long until my fascination with his eyes overtakes me.

How could I have mistaken him for a mere mortal? He has *divine* written all over him. Sitting so close, I can see the slight movement of his shoulders and abdomen as he breathes in and out. So he *does* breathe. Of course he does, I should have remembered from when we kissed, not only his breathing, but his heart beat when we held each other at the lobby.

How? What makes him immortal?

Nate makes a sound between a scoff and a laugh, breaking my line of thought. He answers my unspoken question, "It's attributed to my ethereal soul. My spectrum makes me an eternal being, immortal."

There must be a way to silence my thoughts. Something tells me that if it's possible, Nate won't be the one teaching me how.

"Why did you choose to seclude yourself from the others, to be the loner fallen archangel?"

He smirks, "Loner fallen archangel?"

"That's how the iPod, I mean, the A.O.T. file thing, describes you," It's so frustrating. Most of the time, he knows everything I'm thinking. I can't even tell if he's annoyed or about to crack up. "It pretty much sounds like you kept to yourself, to me at least. Wellington however had another opinion."

"Oh?" is his only reaction.

"He thinks you're okay with being stuck here and don't want to go back."

His face turns upward as if looking through the ceiling, beyond the aegis and into the sky. In a disconnected voice, he declares, "Truth is, Eliza, there was no longer a choice to be made. I'm damned, just existing, until Michael comes to destroy us once and for all. Whether we like it or not, that's how it ends. All their effort and schemes are in vain. It's like I said before, Michael is unstoppable. My kind has this preposterous idea that they can unite forces, get the key and take down Michael before the end of time. I'm too much of a realist to gamble on that. Michael was created for that purpose. No one can change fate, you can try to postpone it, but it eventually catches up with you."

Once again curiosity gets the best of me, and I ask, "What made you join the rebellion?"

"I was from the original hierarchy of the fourteen

archangels in the upper dimension, and seven of us rebelled. No noble cause behind it. I didn't fall for love, or sacrifice. My reason was completely selfish, freedom, to no longer live in servitude. Even though, I knew how it would end," Nate looks at a broken sculpture behind the altar, not really seeing it.

"Do you have regrets? Would you choose differently if you had a second chance?" I ask in a soft voice.

"Now you're romanticizing it," Nate scoffs, stretching his arms and legs.

I don't push it. Instead, I ask him another question, my voice almost a whisper, "Does your kind actually have wings?"

He stops stretching and looks at me, "What was that?"

"Never mind," I reply, refusing to repeat the question. Chances are the answer is no. *Where would they be hidden?*

Nate's eyes don't leave mine, waiting for me to repeat the question. But I don't. Instead I reach out with my hand and touch his arm, and move my hand to his shoulder. As if doing so reaffirms that he's tangible and actually exists. Placing his hand on my neck, he pulls me closer and kisses me. In response, I entwine my fingers in his hair, kissing him back.

Gingerly, he shifts us, pushes me onto my back on the pew and leans over me. He breaks the kiss and props himself up to look at me. I stare back at him and trace his perfect features with the tips of my fingers. He closes his eyes in response to my touch and brushes his lips gently against mine, softly at first. Then, he deepens the kiss passionately, our bodies pressed together, making me forget the world and its complicated ways. Until a surge of energy hits us, that is.

A blast of cold air sweeps mercilessly over the cathedral, and I open my eyes. Nate sucks in a breath, helping me to my feet so fast that it gives me a head rush. Pinching the bridge of my nose, I shut my eyes and allow him to support my weight. His protective arm wraps around my shoulder, and he pulls me closer to him.

The sound of footsteps rapidly approaching us forces me to open my eyes, and I blink in confusion. Ken is standing right in front of me with Ariel at his side.

"You're coming with me, O'Neill Junior," Ken announces, reaching for my arm. Before he even touches my shirt sleeve, Ken is thrown up and back.

"Nathaniel, STOP!" Ariel shouts in a commanding tone, mismatching her fragile appearance.

By the rage plastered in Nate's eyes, he'll just ignore her protest and fling Ken across the cathedral, letting him crash against the double doors. But he surprises me, by freezing Ken midair and leaving him suspended. It's only then, I take notice that Nate's arm is still around my shoulder and his other hand is in his coat pocket.

Nate exhales loudly, "Here I am, waiting for Michael to kick the door down, sword in hand..." Nate lets his voice trail off and finishes sarcastically, "And what do I get? *His sidekick*, and a Tengu demon tag along."

Wait? What? Does he mean, Ken? My Ken? A demon? No freaking way!

I'm astonished. We've known him forever. I look up at him in utter disbelief. He's floating in midair, looking annoyed. *Ken can't be a demon, he just can't.*

"Oh, but he is. Take your glasses off," Nate orders to a hovering Ken.

"Don't do it," Ariel retorts.

Ken crosses his arms, looking affronted. He's suspended upside down, and above him, the silvery blue dome is completely gone. It's safe to assume Ariel broke the aegis.

"Nate, put him down!" I cut in. "I know him, he's like family."

"*Family?*" Nate scoffs. "He's not what you think he is, he's a six hundred year old demon."

Whoa! Six hundred?

Ariel narrows her eyes at Nate, "You told her

everything." It's a statement, not a question.

"Come on, Ariel," Nate antagonizes. "You're smarter than that. Do you see Gabe anywhere around? No, you don't. I didn't break any rules. The aegis can't hide me from Gabriel's law, and you know it."

An image of Nate having his head cut off pops vividly into my mind, and I jump to his defense, "I already knew."

"Of course you did," she's obviously talking to me, but her eyes never leave Nate's. "That was your plan all along. Wasn't it, Nathaniel?" Ariel challenges and then turns to me, "He gets the file from the A.O.T., loads it as audio into an iPod and drops it right at your feet."

She can be terribly convincing. Her words get me thinking, while the back of my mind tries to rationalize my fears.

Nate sounds unfazed and caustic as ever, "Yes, Ariel, because interfering in the affairs of mortals is how I get my kicks. I won't bother defending myself. You've already labeled me as the master of lies throughout the millennia. So, why bother?"

Even Ariel seems to be taken aback by his statement, her expression changes from all-knowing to doubtful, as if trying to decide whether or not he is telling the truth.

In the end, it seems like she decides to go with her gut, "Wrong again, Nathaniel. I'd never say you lie, but you manipulate the truth in your favor. Besides, last I checked you were under Lillithiel's command, and this sounds precisely the kind of idea she would come up with."

"Give me some credit," Nate sounds annoyed. "Do I look like one of Lill's lap dogs, doing as I'm told?"

Ariel looks determined. It's impressive how intimidating she can be for someone dressed like a fall collection *Barbie*. Her long blond hair is down, seeming to have a life of its own. She has a pale pink over coat, tightened neatly at her waist with a belt, a pair of white pants and matching ballet flats. So, yeah, impressive is an understatement.

I observe their conversation like one watching a tennis tournament. The way they keep talking about me as if I'm not even here is starting to get on my nerves. They go on back and forth for a couple more minutes before Ken's voice coming from above us breaks in, "Hey Ariel, can't you use your celestial lie detector on him? I'm not the biggest fan of heights."

Ariel turns and looks up, as if she had forgotten he was still suspended there next to the dusty chandelier. Ken now lies down on his back as if he were lounging on an invisible couch, using his arm as a pillow. Ariel shoots Nate a look. She hasn't made a move since she entered the room.

Either she can't take him or she's afraid he'll hurt me.

"Both," Nate whispers into my ear, attune to my thoughts.

"What was that?" Ariel squints at Nate.

"Must you celestial crowd always know everything?" Nate inquires cynically. He *tsk-tsks* at her and lets Ken drop without a warning.

I gasp, but Ken lands on his feet with catlike reflexes.

Nate looks at me, "Let's go, I'll drive you home."

We barely take two steps before Ariel is blocking our path. A split second later, Ken is standing next to her, at the ready.

Ariel advises in a authoritative tone, "No, you will not. *We* will drive her home."

I'm more than ready to leave and don't really care who's behind the wheel. Nate, however, doesn't share the notion, "She came with me, she'll leave with me." He's so confident, so sure about himself. He doesn't even seem tense.

There's a brief stare down during which Ariel decides, "Fine. She can ride with you, just know that we're following close behind."

Nate shrugs, as if he couldn't care less about Ariel shooting him daggers. Neither Ken or Ariel make a move, and Nate lets out a deep breath, "Are you planning to step aside anytime soon, or are you waiting for me to move you?"

They choose the former, and I follow Nate through the door we came in. When I get into Nate's car, Ken apologizes meaningfully, "I'm sorry O'Neill junior, but it's for your own good."

What does he mean by that?

I expect something untoward to happen, but nothing *does*. We leave the cathedral and pull into the late afternoon traffic. A split second later, Nate shakes his head at the rear view mirror, bemused, and I shift in my seat to take a look. Michael's black Mustang is right behind us with Ken at the wheel and Ariel riding shotgun.

I turn back and look at Nate, "That day at the park, you asked me about my beliefs. Do you remember?"

"I do," it's his unassuming reply.

"I've changed my mind," I inform him. "I can safely say I believe in angels and demons."

Nate lets out a brief meticulous laugh and shakes his head. I just stare at his beautiful profile until he finally turns to face me, "It's too late now to call it faith."

32

"Where have you been, young lady?" Grandma chastises the moment I step inside.

I gulp, coming to a halt. Grandma doesn't usually wait for me by the front door. I look around in bewilderment, Grandpa is sitting in his reading chair with a sports magazine. He doesn't seem worried over my whereabouts at all. Grandma, however, looks me from head to toe and frowns.

Self-consciously, I look down at my attire. After everything that went down today, I totally forgot that I'm still in my gym uniform. I'm covered in dirt from rolling down the field. There's a giant hole in the left knee of my gym pants, surrounded by grass stains and dried blood. I don't even want to know what my hair looks like right now. I try to smooth it down with my hands, and my pinky finger gets stuck in a tangle.

"I'm sorry. I know I should have called, but I left my phone in the locker room," I explain embarrassed, squinting at the clock on the far wall.

Is it only a quarter to five? *Wow!* It should be much later than that. Why all the panic then? I didn't miss dinner or anything.

"I received a phone call from director Layton's secretary," Grandma reprimands. "She informed me that you skipped PE and left campus with Nathaniel Sinclair."

"I didn't. I mean, I fell, and Nate, he..." I bite my tongue, not to dig the hole any deeper. No matter what I say, it's just going to be used against me. It's my fault, I never stopped at the school nurse like I was supposed to. Therefore, no note, no proof. Besides, what am I supposed to tell Grandma anyway? Hey, Grandma, I fractured my ankle again. Not only that, I also broke my wrist as well. But no worries, Nate healed me. By the way, since we're having a heart-to-heart here, my boyfriend is actually a fallen angel, and his fake sister Lill is an eighteen hundred year old abomination that wants me dead.

Yeah, right! The truth is not a viable option. Grandma wouldn't even bother asking what I've been smoking. She'd just send me back on the first flight to Japan and let Dad deal with me.

"What were the two of you doing all this time?" Grandma presses, raising an eyebrow.

I measure my words carefully, "Nate was gonna take me to the nurse after I fell. But since I started feeling better, we just hung out and talked. I'm really sorry, it won't happen again."

Grandma studies my face for any trace of a lie before adding, "Your father was also notified."

"They called Dad in Japan?" I'm in complete shock.

"Not the school," Grandma pauses at my horrified expression. "Don't look at me like that. I didn't tell your father, that Kenji character did. David phoned here a few minutes ago asking about you and why you were not answering your cell. He said that Kenji woke him up with the news of you cutting class and your dating adventures. Your father said he's very disappointed in you."

Grandma turns to face Grandpa who's not paying

attention whatsoever. He's still focused on his sports article. She clears her throat, prompting him to look up. He immediately straightens, closes the magazine on his lap and removes his reading glasses. Then, he directs his gaze at me and declares under no uncertain terms, "You're grounded."

I blink back tears, nod and spin on my heels to leave. But, Grandma's voice stops me short, "Faye Greenwood was kind enough to bring your backpack home. I'm confiscating your phone," Grandma states plainly with my iPhone in hand, as if making a point. "You'll be going from home to school and back. No concert date with Mr. Sinclair this Friday, no basketball game, no Halloween dance either. Do I make myself clear?"

"Yes, Ma'am," I reply meekly.

"Good. Now, go do your homework until dinnertime."

"Yes, Ma'am." I repeat, leaving the room before Grandma adds anything else to her list of restrictions.

Bummed out, I make a beeline for the bathroom to wash the filth off my skin. As I impatiently untangle my hair, I think about Dad being disappointed in me. I get that Ken is just looking after me and all, but really? He's a Tengu demon for crying out loud, whatever that means.

In my bedroom, I close the door behind me and walk to the closet, putting on the first pair of jeans and sweater I come upon. When I remove my Calculus notebook from my backpack, a note falls to the floor. I pick it up, unfold it and read Faye's rushed hand writing.

OMG, you're in so much trouble!!!

Kiara told me what happened. Prozac chick went haywire this time... maybe she forgot to take her meds?!? I tried to tell your grandma that you fell, that Ms. Johnson saw you leaving and didn't say anything. But I don't think she bought it. You're probably grounded now, but I need to talk to you. Try to get on Skype, if you can, :(TTYL.

XOXO,

Faye

I fold the page in half, and put it inside my notebook. Then, I power on my tablet, log in to Skype and put my headphones on. Faye isn't online, so I leave the app running while I check my email.

Before I even open my inbox, Wellington is video calling me. When I answer, he bombards me with questions, "What's this I heard about you skipping class with Nate? Where did you go? I was worried sick. You weren't answering your phone, and I didn't want to call your grandma—"

"I'm fine, *Blake*," I cut in.

"So what happened? Did you confront him?"

Gee! He doesn't even go to my school, and Mattie is not talking to him lately. *How the heck does he know all this?* Kiara probably told Dwayne who told EJ who told him. I think I'll never get over how fast stuff like this spreads.

"Well, did you?" Wellington presses.

I adjust the volume, so I can hear if someone comes down the hall. The last thing I need is to lose my online privileges as well, "'Confront' is a strong word, and I'm not that brave."

"What are you talking about? You're the bravest person I've ever met. You can tell me what happened. Please, don't leave me hanging, Liz," Wellington presses expectantly.

His words conjure up the memory of Ken hanging from the ceiling, and despite my frustration, I open up to him, "You were right, you know?"

"Really?" He asks, seeming genuinely surprised. As if he'd never been right before. "You mean about the translation?"

"That and everything else," I pause, considering what I just said. "I mean, almost everything. Do you remember Ken?"

"I do," Wellington sounds confused. "What does he have to do with it?"

"He's not just one of Dad's best programers, he's a six

hundred year old Tengu demon. And Spark is a real-life succubus that survived the escape from the underworld."

"Now, I won't feel so jealous of Ken's six-pack," says Wellington wistfully. "Tengu? Does that mean he can take the form of a bird?"

"I don't know," I reply in puzzlement. "How do you even know that kind of stuff?"

"It's just a wild guess, Liz. Some video game lore. It's probably untrue, though. Are you sure about Spark being a succubus? Maybe you got it mixed up or something. It doesn't make much sense, you know?"

"I'm positive. It's hard to get it wrong when your boyfriend's partner in crime is a possessive and extremely jealous demon. I heard him loud and clear. Why?"

"Succubi are supposed to be these super attractive female demons that entice men, so they can drain their souls," Wellington explains. "They can assume any form they want to."

"Let me guess, you learned that from a video game as well," I tease.

"No, that's from comic books," he informs to my annoyance. "So, either she wants to look like that, or the comic books are wrong. But never mind, get to the good stuff already."

"You're not going to believe it..." I begin, detailing what happened today. I start with Spark, Nate's healing power, Abe Kaur being some sort of underworld spy, and him chasing us on his motorcycle. I explain about the A.O.T., Nate's summoning the aegis, and all the answers he offered.

"Wow!" Wellington exclaims once I'm finished and asks, "Zoë and Michael, then?"

"Yep. You were right," I point out, remembering something else. "You know who else is an angel in disguise?"

"Faye?" He half jokes.

"No. Not Faye," I let out a laugh, "Ariel. She was the one

bursting in on us at the cathedral."

"Ariel? *My* Ariel?"

"Actually, as it turns out, she's *Michael's* Ariel. She's here to make sure no one approaches you with the pretense to get to me."

"How did they find you guys?" Wellington asks, sounding intrigued. "I thought you said he summoned some sort of shield to hide the two of you."

"Yeah," I nod. "The aegis. And it worked, that's why Abe never found us. None of them could, actually. That's where Ken comes in. He hacked Nate's phone signal and found us. Apparently, aegis doesn't shield GPS signals."

"So, Zoë is in fact The Counsel Archangel of Wisdom and Michael is The Archangel of Death... Spark is a succubus, Abe Kaur is a lesser angel, Nate is The Fallen Archangel of Death, and *you* are the prophecy girl... Oh man! Are there any *normal* humans at your school?"

I laugh and begin naming off the cafeteria crowd, "Judy, Alexis, Fran–"

"No," Wellington cuts me off. "Being human requires a pulse, and those girls are heartless. Try again."

"Hey, Mattie has a heart. Therefore human. Oh, wait? You broke her heart, what does that make her?" I half joke.

"Very funny," Wellington says, not laughing. "FYI, she hurt me too. Who else?"

"Faye?" I suggest.

Wellington cracks up, "*Faye, human?* She's cyber woman. I'm not even kidding. That girl has a photographic memory or something. Robot brains. She'll roll her eyes at you if you point it out, though."

"You noticed it too?" I jump in. "I'm always wondering how she pulls that off. She's top of the class and has four college level courses. She's on the newspaper, yearbook, and let's not forget she's the head cheerleader. To top it off, she manages to look impeccable every single morning."

"Don't forget she takes vocal lessons at my school too,"

Wellington reminds me. "It makes me wonder why she puts up with her wannabes. Apart from you and Kiara, of course."

"Of course," I play along. "There! Kiara is human."

"Nah, she's a saint to put up with Dwayne," he disagrees.

I laugh, "Running out of choices here, you might have a point."

Faye starts calling me then, and I ask, "Can we talk more later? Faye is online, and there's something she has to tell me."

"Ok, but call me back, Liz. We're not done talking. We have to figure out some sort of escape plan for you."

"I think I'm safe for now. I'll call you back ASAP," I touch the screen to switch to Faye.

"Where were you?" Faye blurts out, sounding worried. "Are you alright? Kiara said you took a dive from one end zone to the other."

"Kiara is exaggerating. I'm fine."

"You're not grounded then?" Faye asks. "I was sure your grandma wouldn't let you off so easy."

"She didn't. I *am* grounded."

"They must have no idea you're online," Faye points out.

"I better not stay on too long, though. I found your note. What did you wanna tell me?" I ask.

Faye begins, "Michael said that–"

"No, let me guess," I cut in. "Nate is a fallen archangel of death that's out to get me."

"Um...Yeah," Faye sounds dumbstruck. After a moment of silence, she blurts out indignantly, "I can't believe Nate told you."

"He didn't. Wellington and I figured it out. Nate just confessed."

"Wait? Blake knew?" Faye asks in disbelief.

"Yeah, it's a long story. *Literally*," I say, attempting to sidetrack her. "What about you, Faye? How did you know?"

"It's a long story," Faye parrots cynically, "*literally*."

"I know it has to do with Michael, doesn't it? He told

you. You said yourself, you made a deal with an angel."

"What can I say? Subtlety is not my thing."

"You fooled me," I snort.

"How do you feel about all this?" Faye asks thoughtfully. "What's in your mind?"

"Are you really going to psychoanalyze me right now, Faye? I'm grounded, probably until graduation. I can't go out, the concert is off, and Grandma confiscated my phone. So, I guess everyone got their wish. I'm safe from Nate's evil influence," I blurt out in the heat of the moment, regretting it immediately as always.

"Wow. Harsh much?" Faye complains. "I'll get out of your face."

"Faye, I gotta go. I think I hear footsteps," I say, watching the door. I power down my tablet and tuck it under my pillow just as someone knocks on my door.

"Come in."

Dominika opens my bedroom door halfway, and her face pops in, "Mrs. Melody asked me to come fetch you. You have a visitor. Miss Lill Sinclair is here."

33

How am I supposed to get to Nate's balcony from here without falling? It's impossible. Just because I can climb a giant rock doesn't mean I can scale the wall of my building. It's not like I can jump to the fire escape stairs of the adjacent building and climb onto his balcony.

What was I thinking?

Too late now, I should have thought about that before lowering myself onto the ledge outside the rail. Now, I'm completely stuck. My balcony is too high up, and Nate's is too far away. They didn't seem that far apart from where I was standing a minute ago.

The chilly air isn't helping either. As if it weren't bad enough that I'm stranded up here with my back against the wall, now I'm starting to shiver uncontrollably. Maybe I have a death wish or something. Then again, if I had a death wish I'd just stay inside where Lill Sinclair is having a sit down with Grandma.

I take a deep breath and mentally measure the span between the two buildings. If I jump and miss the fire escape, I'll fall to my death. If I stay here much longer, a neighbor might see me and call 911. Then, I'll end up in an asylum for attempting suicide.

Should I scream for help or jump?

I look down, calculating my odds.

"Close your eyes, Liz," Nate's voice utters inside my head. I let out a sigh of relief and do just that.

My body goes weightless, and a gust of cold wind blows past my ears. When I dare to reopen them, my feet are slowly touching down on his balcony floor. Nate stands in front of me, his face is unreadable. He looks winded, his hair is shooting off in every direction.

"Get inside," he orders, scanning the evening sky suspiciously.

I rush in, and he follows, sliding the glass door closed behind us. His place is spacious with a minimalist design. A contemporary white leather sectional sofa occupies the center of the room, facing a sixty inch TV mounted to the wall. Interestingly enough, there's a purple shoe lodged by its heel into the fractured flat screen panel. *Odd.* To the left of the sofa, a stainless steal and onyx marble counter, along with three tall matching stools, divide the living area from the kitchen. On the ceiling, inset lights are spread out symmetrically, brightening the ivory walls and the white marble flooring.

Concerned that I might get the floor dirty, I reach down to take off my shoes. But Nate stops me, placing a hand on my shoulder, "Don't worry about it. Take a seat and tell me what's going on."

He slouches on the sofa, and I sit down at its edge, placing a black and gray pillow on my lap. Nate is watching me intently, and I fidget a little before beginning, "Lill showed up at my place. She's in there right now with Grandma, and I think she's manipulating her mind or something. Because as I was sneaking out from the balcony, I overheard part of their conversation. By the sound of it, Grandma agreed to let me attend her birthday party. I'm not allowed to see you. Why would she let me go to your sister's party? Ken told Dad that I cut class to make out with you. Therefore, I'm grounded."

"I kind of figured that out when I saw that you were trying to jump to my apartment instead of using the door," Nate teases.

"Is Lill a threat to my grandparents?"

"No, they're safe," Nate assures me. "She got what she wanted."

"Are you–" I begin, but Nate places his index finger to his lips in the international gesture for silence, and I stop mid-sentence.

He's on his feet just as abruptly, pulling me by the arm and dragging me to the corner of the room, between the TV and the glass doors.

"Stand right here and close your eyes," he orders inside my head. I blink up at him, wondering what's going on, but I do what I'm told. Nate spouts off a rhythmic chant. It sounds different from what he said in the Cathedral, but a gust of wind hits me violently all the same. I squeeze my eyes closed, fearing a replay of his terrifying light show. I have the sensation that I'm being sealed in a thin layer of plastic cling wrap, and then Nate mentally whispers, "You can open your eyes, Liz."

There's nothing visible coating my skin, and I lift my hand to touch the transparent veil surrounding me.

"Try not to move," Nate stops me with his words.

"What is this?" I let my hand drop.

"You're under the protection of my spectrum," Nate explains in a rushed tone. "No one can see or hear you."

"What's wrong?"

"Someone's coming," Nate says bluntly. "I'll get rid of whoever it is as fast as I can."

"I can't be here. Grounded, remember?" I blurt out in distress.

"That's the least of your worries," Nate's voice is inside my head. "Just stay calm and trust me."

I nod.

There's a knock, and he takes his sweet time to answer it. The door is barely cracked open as a lightning fast mist of darkness flies in, and Nate slams it closed with a bang.

"I don't have time for this," he lets out in a loud irritated voice. "Let's just talk, Ken."

Ken?

A throwing star flies straight toward Nate's head. He dodges out of the way with time to spare, and it sticks right in the middle of an abstract painting.

"Seriously, Ken? Are you gonna throw shuriken at me now?" Nate exclaims indignantly, crossing his arms.

The mist flies around the room, sticking to the walls like a shadow. The throwing stars buzz all around, ricocheting off the marble floor. Nate dodges every last one with the slightest movements.

Unlike me, he isn't freaking out about getting hit. He appears more aggravated with the destruction of his modern looking apartment. Not until a throwing star hits the wall two inches from my head, that is.

Do not freak out, do not freak out.

If I'm invisible, maybe I'm also intangible. I hope this cloaking shield is shuriken proof. *It's not.* Otherwise, Nate wouldn't throw his body and pin me against the wall to block a second star coming in my direction. He knocks the air out of my lungs with the abrupt pressure of his weight, catching it with his bare hand.

The sharpened edge sizzles as the hot steel penetrates his flesh. Nate tosses it aside, and it clanks against the marble surface before falling flat. A trail of red follows Nate's every step. It's his blood, looking exactly like that of a human.

I cry out, but neither seem to hear me. The shuriken steams on the floor, and Nate stands over it. Blood drips from the cut on his hand like a leaky water faucet. Ken assumes his physical form and appears as baffled as I am.

"Why did you do that?" Ken asks in bewilderment.

Nate's response is a drop kick straight to Ken's chest, sending him flying across the room and into the adjacent wall. Before Ken hits the floor, Nate is above him ready to deliver a body slam. But, Ken's fast reflexes and agility allow him to slip away. In a swift reversal, Nate is the one being lifted above his head.

In a movement too fast for my eyes, Nate pivots and rotates around, landing on his feet. It's like Ken's counter attack was nothing but a minor inconvenience. Nate tries taking Ken's back, but he slides out of reach, rolling into a somersault. He immediately pops up and delivers a deep kick to Nate's sternum, sending him against the wall with a powerful thud.

A haze of white pulverized dust fills the room, partially obscuring my view. Sounds of violent impacts and objects crashing to pieces are the only indication the fight continues. Their footsteps and thuds come from all directions. My anguish escalates with each blow, and I wish with all my might for them to stop.

Looking like an avenging angel emerging from the clouds, Nate bursts in to view. Ken lunges at him, but Nate sweeps his legs from under him. Ken rebounds off the floor, spins, and his shin makes contact with Nate's temple in a swift roundhouse. Nate collapses onto his side, and I gasp.

Without pause, Ken follows up with a heavy knee drop that would mean instant death for any living thing. Somehow, Nate seems barely fazed. He manages to get back to his feet and promptly dishes out a stiff side kick to Ken's throat, pinning him against the wall. It doesn't hold. In a heartbeat, Ken is free. He flips onto the center table and takes a defensive stance. Instead of neutralizing Ken with his mind, like he did at the cathedral, Nate jumps in with an air attack. Ken parries it, catches Nate by his shirt collar and slams him to the floor with the sound of cracking bones.

I cry out again, just as Ken lifts him with his left arm and holds him against the wall. One hand compresses Nate's windpipe, and the other curls into a tight fist.

Why isn't Nate rag dolling Ken around with his telekinesis? Why is he taking such a beating?

It doesn't make any sense. Then, it clicks. He can't. He's focusing his power on me, keeping me protected and invisible here in the corner. He's going to get himself killed because of me, and there's nothing I can do to stop it.

The sound of Nate's choked laughter forces my eyes open, and Ken puts a voice behind my question, "I'm about to crush your skull and you think it's funny?"

"I do, actually," Nate chokes on his words. Ken eases his grip, and Nate elaborates, "We both know you can't really kill me. Not even with your enchanted toys. You can beat the hell out of me. But you don't have what it takes to end me."

"I can still pulverize your pretty face and leave you to suffer," Ken replies, preparing to swing.

"Certainly, you can incapacitate me for a few hours or so. As you might have noticed, I'm not stopping you. I'll let it happen."

"Let me?" Ken scoffs.

"Have at it. Enjoy yourself," is his reply. Almost imperceptibly, Nate glances straight at me, a wicked gleam in his eyes, and repeats my thoughts to Ken, "Before I change my mind and start tossing you around like a rag doll."

Man, he's a good liar.

I can sense how spent he is right now, the invisible wall flickers with his weakness. His hand still carries the deep gash caused by the throwing star. His entire body is visibly injured, and he must be in agony. And yet, he's lying through his teeth convincingly.

Ken lowers his fist and releases Nate from his grip. Then, he takes a step back and says, "Look at you, Nathaniel. You're a mess. Go get yourself cleaned up, and then we can talk."

With staggered steps, Nate walks slowly out of the room

and disappears down the hall. Ken raises a hand, and all his stars dislodge from the walls and furniture, flinging back to his grasp. I remain as still as I can, barely breathing. The last thing I need is for Ken to find out that I've witnessed this entire encounter.

Nate comes back in a pair of dark jeans, buttoning up his wrinkly red shirt. He looks too good, considering the punishment he has just absorbed. He'd been gone for no longer than three minutes, but he looks like he just stepped out of the shower. His hair is wet, and his face is mostly healed.

As he rolls up his long sleeves, I get a glimpse of an open wound on his palm. It's the hand he used to stop the shuriken mid-flight. The cut looks raw and downright painful. Ken raises an eyebrow, walks up to the sofa and slouches down with his back to me.

"Red," Nate takes a seat facing the shattered flat screen. "Just in case you change your mind and decide to beat the life out of me again." He sounds better, more like himself, and I let out a sigh of relief. Ken remains silent and Nate asks, "What's in your mind, demon?"

"You don't wanna know."

"Oh, but I do," his lips curl up as he stares down at Ken. "Please share."

Ken motions to the TV, "Is that some kind of interpretive modern art?" He bends a little for a closer look. "By Jimmy Choo?"

"A little parting gift from my fake sister. Evidently, she doesn't like the word 'no,'" Nate replies simply. "Anything else?"

"Do you know why the devil's assistant chose you of all people?" Ken shakes his head. "No offense."

"None taken," Nate says dismissively. "She's Lillithiel. No one knows how her mind works."

"You know what I think?" Ken leans forward. "She knows exactly what she's doing, and so do you. Who better than the primary witness to the prophecy? Particularly when considering, he's also the same one who pursued The Guardian Archangel Raphael for the past twelve years."

"I'd personally send one of the lesser fallen. They're better with the mortals," Nate suggests nonchalant.

"Except I don't think Lillithiel had seduction in mind. She was aiming for the power of persuasion. And who better than the great deceiver, The Fallen Archangel Nathaniel and his manipulative dreams?"

"I'm not sure if you're underestimating or overestimating Lill here," Nate sounds bemused.

"I honestly don't know myself," Ken runs his hands through his black hair. "You'd be the smartest choice, except you're the most unreliable one."

"No argument there. But enough about me. I see someone has been hacking the A.O.T. records," Nate replies. "No wonder it has more holes than a slab of Swiss cheese where Eliza O'Neill is concerned. The question is: *Why?*"

Nate waits, watching Ken closely. Ken slumps, puts his arm on the seat-back and settles for saying nothing at all.

"Silence is admission of guilt," Nate prompts.

"You can always compel me," Ken pauses as if reconsidering the idea and then mocks, "Oh, wait? You can't, you might end up compelling yourself."

I don't get their private joke, and Nate doesn't seem amused, shooting him a forceful glare.

Ken raises his hands in surrender, "Sorry. Just telling it like it is."

"Since you're not talking, and being that you've already beat me up tonight," Nate sounds frustrated. "Is there anything else I can help you with?"

"You let me win," Ken says with a shrug. "You're not a fighter, hand-to-hand you'll lose every time. But I can't fight against your *Hocus Pocus.*"

Nate scoffs, "Since you won't give me a straight answer about the A.O.T., tell me, when did you start taking jobs?"

"I don't do anyone's dirty work, if that's what you're asking. I work a real job," Ken stretches out. "How do you think I can afford my opulent lifestyle?"

"So what's your angle?" Nate presses. "Why get involved with Eliza?"

"You won't get answers from me. I didn't stop by for an inquisition–"

"Duly noted," Nate waves his wounded palm for emphasis.

Ken leans forward, "Just so we're clear, I'll do whatever I can to keep your kind away from her. None of you have any business in her life."

"You're a demon," Nate retorts. "What is she to you?"

Ken inhales deeply, laying his head against the seat-back. His black hair contrasts deeply against the white leather.

Nate goes on, "I know you work for David O'Neill, but that doesn't explain your actions in the modification of the A.O.T. I don't believe you're so in debt to your boss that you'd put your life at risk for his daughter's sake."

"Not to him," Ken replies flatly. "I owe a debt to an old friend. She lives in Sendai. Her granddaughter happens to be Dave O'Neill's fiancé, Suri. I vowed to protect Eliza from your kind, and I intend to keep my word."

"I'm no threat to her," Nate counters.

"Who are you trying to deceive here?" Ken scorns. "Your presence alone is harmful enough."

Nate doesn't bat an eye, "It can't be worse than delivering her into Lill's clutches."

"I don't buy it. Why get involved? You usually just look the other way. It makes no sense, unless..." Ken lets his voice trail off, lowering his orange shades. The entire room brightens intensely, as if we're on the surface of the sun.

Nate shields his eyes with his arm, "Put your shades back on, Cyclops. Are you trying to blind me?"

"Come on, Nathaniel. Let me see your eyes. I need to know your intentions. It's impossible to believe a word from your mouth, but the eyes don't lie."

Nate throws up his other arm and buries his face. Ken sighs and puts his glasses back on. I blink at the sudden change from bright to dim, seeing a black spot in the center of my vision. Nate rubs his eyes with the back of his hand. The gash where the shuriken struck is still wide open. It looks worse now, as if the wound is spreading.

"The archangel of deceit is in love," Ken slaps his hand on the couch. "Well, I'll be damned!"

"Undoubtedly," Nate avows, still adjusting to the light.

Placing a hand to his chest, Ken feigns an overly dramatic voice, "You're dashing my dreams of an eternity in paradise."

"Yeah right, keep the faith," Nate replies sarcastically.

"Sure thing," Ken stands up. "So you're sticking around for a change."

Nate gets to his feet, but doesn't reply.

"That's rich," Ken shakes his head. "I'll be watching you."

Ken makes his way to the hall leading to the door, and Nate sees him out. He locks it and rests his back against the wall, letting his head drop. A heavy pounding on the door startles me, and Nate whirls around, mumbling under his breath, "Does anybody call anymore?"

"Open up, it's me," a familiar voice is shouting from the other side of the door.

"Spark?" Nate sounds as surprised as I am. He unlocks and opens the door wide.

"Are you going to invite me in?"

"You don't need an invitation, you're not a vampire," Nate points out, stepping aside.

She walks graciously inside, taking in his destroyed apartment. "What happened to your place? Did you lose your cool? Or are you renovating again?"

Nate casually sits on the couch, and she takes a seat on a high stool at the bar, crossing her legs. My jaw hits the floor.

The girl in the room sounds like Spark, has the same name, but she's *so* not Spark. *No way.* This version of her looks like a sci-fi action hero in one of those super tight black outfits, every curve of her body on display. Gone is the spotty red skin, replaced by an immaculate fair complexion. Her violet eyes accent the blue highlights in her jet black hair, which falls straight to the center of her back. Nothing like the girl always scowling at me in class. Save for the combat boots, that is.

She points a long blue fingernail at the flat screen, "Lillithiel?"

"What brings you here?" Nate inquires, ignoring her remark.

"Evidently, Zoë has never heard of texting," Spark replies insolently. "She sent me here to pass along a message."

"Let me guess," Nate mocks. "Stay away from Liz, blah, blah, blah. Or you'll be annihilated and more blah."

"No. You're invited to join the celestial crowd's meeting at Michael's place in an hour. *Alone.* She said you'd know the place." There's a hint of concern in Spark's voice.

"Pardon me?" Nate exclaims puzzled.

"You heard right," Spark folds her arms. "Let me emphasize the word 'alone.' I'm here to stop you from going. It's obviously a set up."

"Please," Nate waves her off.

"He's here, you know?" She uncrosses her arms and makes an air circle with her index finger. "Not here, here. He's in Revere Beach, twenty minutes away, and that's too close for me."

"Just so we're clear, by 'him' you mean Gabriel."

"Who else?" Spark asks, lifting both hands in the air.

"Running into almighty Michael in the school hallways, not a problem. Playing mind games with The Archangel of Wisdom, no sweat. But, the fact that the messenger is a few miles away gives you a panic attack?" Nate looks amused.

"What can I say? Last time we met, he tried to separate

my head from my body with a burning sword," she points out aggravated.

"Oh, yeah," Nate feigns to recall. "I almost forgot about that minor incident. I tend to live in the actual millennium we're in."

"It's hard to get over almost becoming dust. If you didn't step in..." Spark lets her voice trail.

Nate shrugs, "What can I say? I enjoy messing with Gabe's mind. I live for it."

"I really don't get you," Spark shakes her head. "Unlike the others, you don't see us as abominations, or minions from the underworld. You don't blame us for what we are. It's almost like you blame your own kind for our existence."

"It's not my place to pass judgment," Nate remarks simply. "They have a full department for that. Besides, I thought having one of you in my debt would be resourceful along the way, and I was right as usual."

"And yet, I'm still the boss of me," she arches an eyebrow. "You've yet to give me any commands."

"Not just yet."

"Well, I've got one for you. You're not going to that celestial *shindig*. I won't let you walk into a trap."

He laughs sarcastically, "Spark, Spark. Do you really believe they would need a trap? We're talking three of the seven highest here. If Michael, Zophiel and Gabriel wanted to end me, there would be no invitation. Formal or otherwise."

"It's irrelevant. You have no reason to collude with them. *None.*"

"They won't destroy or banish me without a cause," Nate reassures her, "I already know what they want. They won't try anything. Now, I have something to ask of you."

Spark tilts her head to one side, "Are you commanding me?"

"No. I'm asking nicely."

"Go on."

"Keep out of sight," Nate requests. "Drop school and stay off the radar for now."

"Seriously? No more Saint Pete's High? You just made my night," Spark sounds animated for a change.

"Don't get too excited, it's temporary," Nate reminds her.

"It sounds like you have a plan. Let's hear it," she says tentatively, switching her crossed legs.

"Not tonight, but you'll know soon enough. For now, keep an eye on Abe and tell me if he attempts to approach Faye or Blake. Just try to be inconspicuous."

"I don't think Abe will be bothering either one of them. Lillithiel ordered him to follow you and Liz around, since you're not doing your job. He doesn't have a mind of his own, if you know what I mean. Anyways, I'm more than happy to keep both eyes on Wellington Blake. I'll let him play me like his cello," Spark pauses, waiting for a reaction before pressing. "You wouldn't mind that, would you?"

"Careful there," Nate cautions. "Gabe wouldn't be so keen on you preying on innocents."

"Where's your sense of humor, Dark Angel?" She stops abruptly, her eyes fixed on Nate's palm. A deep furrow appears on her forehead, and she gets to her feet, "What happened to your hand?"

"It's nothing. It's already starting to heal," Nate stands up, making a fist.

"You're so full of it, Nathaniel. It looks like demon poison, let me see," she's at his side in a blink of an eye, grabbing his arm. She unlocks his fingers one by one and runs her thumb gingerly over the open gash in his palm.

Nate's shoulders tense up, and she lifts his wrist higher for a better look. The cut appears to have doubled in size.

Spark looks up at him, "Ken, huh?" Nate remains silent, and she presses on, "Well, that explains the blood red color scheme of the décor. Were you trying to restore her honor after he caught the two of you going at it in the cathedral?"

"Whatever you say, Spark," Nate dismisses, looking past

her.

"It's not the first time I've detected Liz's aura on you," she shoots him a knowing look. "What would Lillithiel say if she knew you were corrupting her one and only chance to set foot in the upper dimension?"

"Back off," Nate tries to free his arm from her grip, but she doesn't let go. She lifts it up even higher, pressing his palm to her lips.

What is she doing? It looks like she's kissing his hand. *Is she sucking out the poison?*

Her eyes close, and Nate lets his head fall back. The scene unfolding before me appears so intimate that I'm not sure if I can keep watching. But at the same time, I can't take my eyes off them.

All of a sudden, her eyelids flutter open, and Spark tilts her head to one side, peering over Nate's shoulder. For an instant, it's like she's looking right at me. Then, she smiles almost imperceptibly and sinks her teeth hard into her lush lower lip. It's a wonder she doesn't draw blood. It's obvious now, she knows I'm here.

Nate stands motionless like a granite statue. His back is to me, so I can't see his expression. But when he lowers his arm to his side, his hand is entirely healed.

"That's better," she says, her violet eyes turning back to Nate. "You really need to unwind." Spark takes a step forward, closing the distance. Her eyes never leave his as she places her hand behind his neck and draws him to her in a swift movement, kissing him. She starts gently, enticing him almost imperceptibly.

I'm stunned. He's not pushing her away. He's not resisting at all. *Is this her succubus power in action?*

Nate pulls her close, wrapping his arms around her.

I want out of here. Put me back on the ledge.

She lets her hand slide down the back of his head to his collar. Then, in a single tug, she tears his shirt in two, each half falls to the white marble floor. Their kiss intensifies, their hands are a blur, all over each other.

Claustrophobia hits me hard, it's like I'm in an invisible straightjacket. I'm getting sick to my stomach, and I can't breathe.

Nate, please! You're suffocating me.

A pair of dark wings violently erupt from the center of his upper back, and I gasp. The invisible shield dissolves into a silvery blue mist, disappearing into thin air in a flash, and a gust of air washes over me.

I'm free.

In a single movement he backs her up against the wall. His hand finds her wrists and pulls them together, tightly pinning them over her head. He presses his knee into her stomach, and reaches for a sword that materializes from nowhere. Then, he rests the blade against her neck just close enough so she's trapped.

"Give me a reason not to end you," He speaks in a low threatening voice.

A lazy smile forms on Spark's face and she looks a little too calm for the situation she's in, "This is a familiar scene, but look who's wielding the blade now. Are you starting to regret your decision, Dark Angel?"

"Next time you pull a stunt like that, you won't live to see another day," Nate threatens, driving the edge of the blade closer.

Spark stares back at him, as if daring him to do it.

"I'm letting you go now," Nate studies her for several seconds before lowering his knee and letting go of her wrists. His dark wings cast a shadow over her and his sword is still against her neck. "And that was a four hundred dollar shirt," Nate remarks, sounding annoyed.

She blinks up at him and pushes his sword away from her neck with the tip of her index finger, "Well, now you have two. You should be more appreciative. I just siphoned the poison out of your hand. It would have consumed your entire arm."

"Consider us even," Nate shoots back.

"You're not getting rid of me that easily," Spark says, showing herself out. She stops midway and looks over her shoulder at him before adding, "I'm still your bitch." And with that, she disappears into the hall, and the door closes behind her.

Nate lets out a breath, and I look back at him. His wings and sword are gone. He doesn't speak, looking completely spent. I move my neck from side to side, working the stiffness out of my body. Torn is an understatement. There are so many conflicting thoughts spinning inside my head, that I don't even know which way is up. *What just happened here? I'm not even sure if I want to know.*

Nate senses my distress and approaches me. Before I can protest, he hoists me into his arms and holds me tightly against him.

"It's okay," I volunteer in a small voice. "I understand."

"I don't think you do," he looks down at me.

"She's a succubus. You were under her spell."

"And yet, you're still hurt," he says quietly.

"It was just hard to watch," I admit.

"I'm sorry you had to," he pulls me closer against his chest. His heart pounds against my cheek, rhythmically in time with mine.

Standing here like this with Nate, it'd be easy to believe everything that transpired tonight happened in an alternate reality. My arms wrap around his waist, and I close my eyes.

34

"Eliza O'Neill?"

"Here."

"Samantha Parker?"

"Samantha Parker?" Mr. Hathaway scans the room and repeats once again, "Samantha Parker?"

All eyes turn to the back corner where Spark's desk sits empty. Mr. Hathaway looks down at his attendance roll, saying, "Moving along then. Nathaniel Sinclair?"

There's no reply, but Mr. Hathaway doesn't call Nate's name a second time, jumping to the next one on his list, "Joshua Tyson?"

"I'm here."

"Hannah Zurowski?"

"Here."

Mr. Hathaway puts his attendance sheet aside and gets to his feet, "Pairs of two, please. I have another handout for you."

There's a commotion of moving desks, and a cacophony of complaining voices. A girl in the front row pulls her chair with a high pitched screech, the sound giving me goosebumps. Mr. Hathaway approaches her and places a firm hand on the back of her chair. She blinks up at him visibly confused.

"Lets try something different today," Mr. Hathaway announces. "Pair up with the pal to your right."

More commotion and sighs. The wall is on my left side, and to my right sits Zoë Fairchild. We inch our desks together and peel open our text books.

Mr. Hathaway hands out the single page assignment and we busy ourselves solving the ten equations. We get stuck on the last one. Well, I do anyway. I'm pretty sure Zoë knows the answer. But instead of sharing, she opts to pass along the necessary steps to solve it, "Now do the root test."

I stop writing for a brief moment and peek over at her out of the corner of my eye. She's in uniform, just a student like the rest of us. Her pale blue eyes fixed on the Calc book, and her long black hair is clipped back out of her face. Does she look like that for real? Maybe she's different in her dimension, a shimmering talking light or something of the like. A floating apparition, kinda like you'd see in a movie.

"We really need to do something about your telepathy," Zoë declares inside my head. I drop my pencil, not expecting to hear her voice so clearly in my mind. Zoë picks it up and places it back in my hand.

"Here you go," she says aloud. In my mind, she adds, her lips unmoving, "As if undoing Michael's work wasn't bad enough, he had to reveal everything to you."

"He didn't," I jump to Nate's defense and then add in a whisper, "Not really. I sorta figured it out. I mean, Wellington did."

She gives me a quizzical sideways glance, and I go back to finishing the equation, unsure of what to say. As I circle the final answer, the conversation I overheard at the nurse's office pops clearly to mind. I blurt out in a rushed voice, "Besides, Faye was in the loop long before I was, and she has nothing to do with any of this. Apart from being my friend, that is."

Inside my mind, she relays, "Michael revealed just enough in order to protect you. She's your closest friend, and you trust her. We didn't hand her an iPod loaded with the secrets of the Universe," she offers me a reproving look. "And Liz? *Be careful*. You can't control your thoughts, but you can control what you say aloud. There are rats everywhere. Besides, Nathaniel's succubus is no longer around to stymie your thoughts from the likes of Abe Kaur," she alines the two pages and staples them together.

Nate's succubus.

The way Zoë says it brings the events from last night front and center. The kiss, Nate's dark wings and his veiled sword. I shake my head, disturbed by my own thoughts.

Zoë's eyes widen, and she says aloud, "That changes everything."

What does she mean by that?

She stands up and walks to Mr. Hathaway's desk, placing our completed assignment on the top of the pile just as the bell sounds. I slowly gather my things, not in any rush to head to the cafeteria all by myself. Faye is absent today, and I'm dreading lunch with her wannabes. I zip up my backpack and stand. Before I can put it on, Zoë is dragging me out by the hand.

"Where are we going?" I ask, trying to keep up.

"To meet with Nathaniel," she pulls me down the staircase.

We're moving so fast I'm afraid I'll roll down the steps, "I don't think he's here today. He'd be in Calc if he were."

"He's home," she notes at the bottom of the stairs.

I dig my heels and grab the rail with my free hand, scarcely managing to stop her, "I have Chemistry next and then Spanish. I'm already in too much trouble as it is. I can't skip any more classes."

"Liz, come along for your life's sake. I'll explain on the way."

I shake my hand loose. If I get caught ditching class the

day after I was grounded for skipping school, my life *will be* over. There's no doubt in my mind that Dad would send me to an "all-girls" boarding school in Switzerland.

"Please, come with me," Zoë pleads.

On the other hand, I'm not exactly among friends here with Abe Kaur and Lillithiel after me. I let go of the rail with a sigh and follow her into the parking lot.

Outside, it's a cold October Tuesday. The sun is hidden behind the clouds, and the sky is mostly gray. Zoë pulls out the keys to Michael's black Mustang and clicks it open. I reluctantly climb into the passenger side and buckle my seat belt.

Once we're out in traffic, I finally ask, "Okay, why are we going to Nate's?"

"Because he kept an important detail from us last night that he shouldn't have," Zoë replies without looking away from the road.

I'm suddenly aware I inadvertently leaked said detail, "What's that?"

"You saw Nathaniel in his ethereal form and didn't burst into flames."

Does she mean the wings?

I shake my head, "Maybe that's because I was under the protection of his spectrum."

"No aegis could shield a mortal from instant death at the sight of an archangel in full form," Zoë explains, making a right turn.

"But–"

"Why do you think Michael has yet to destroy Lillithiel?" Zoë cuts in.

"I thought," I shake my head, trying to make sense of things. "I don't know."

"Human shields, several of them," Zoë clarifies. "For over a hundred years she has always managed to have at least two humans by her side at all times, along with an army of fallen ones at her behest. She knows Michael can only destroy her by brandishing his sword, and he can only summon his blade in his ethereal state."

I gulp, "You're saying I don't have a soul."

"Of course you have a soul," Zoë insists and parks directly in front of Nate's building.

I'm at a loss, "I don't understand. Why didn't I burn up in Nate's apartment last night, then?"

"I have a hunch, but Nathaniel has the answer," she states confidently, shutting down the engine.

I get out of the car and follow her, "How can you be so sure?"

Inside the elevator, she pushes the button for Nate's floor and faces me, "He wouldn't assume his ethereal form otherwise."

The elevator arrives on Nate's floor and the doors slide open. We step out, and Zoë looks sideways at me as we walk down the hall. She knocks at his door, and we wait and wait. She knocks again. *If I had my phone I could have texted him on the way here to give him a heads up.* Zoë knocks a third time. Just as I'm about to suggest that maybe he's not home, Nate opens the door. He looks like he just fell out of bed, barefoot, disheveled hair and dressed only in a pair of flannel pajama pants. It's visible on his face that he's taken by surprise.

Zoë doesn't wait for an invitation, sidestepping him, "Get dressed, Nathaniel. She's taken by you as it is."

Nate leans in for a kiss, but I look down at my feet, too embarrassed by Zoë's comment. He straightens up and ushers me inside, "Not as taken as you think, Z."

She tosses a white shirt at him, and he catches it behind his back without turning. He hangs it over one shoulder and disappears into the hall, calling out, "Kick back, relax, make yourself at home."

Zoë and I both look around, taking in his destroyed décor of busted furniture and cracked marble tile, accented with a touch of blood splattered on the walls. Lill's orchid stiletto is still impaled in the flat screen, and there are narrow holes everywhere left behind by Ken's shurikens. The sight of which doesn't seem to faze Zoë at all. She brushes some broken glass from the sofa and sits all ladylike. I take a seat beside her on the opposite end and tap my fingers, peeking at the corner where I was trapped last night.

Nate returns in a pair of beat up jeans and a black v-neck shirt, sitting across from us, "To what do I owe the honor of your presence this pleasant afternoon, Zophiel?"

"Save your breath, Nathaniel," Zoë says straightforward. "What else are you hiding?"

Nate looks at me as if searching for clues, and I jump in, "I don't think he knew."

"Knew what?" Nate looks from Zoë to me and back again, letting out, "Enough with your mind games. I thought we cleared this up yesterday. I'm not the bad guy. The threat lies with Abelec, Lillithiel, and whatever minions she might summon. We're on the same page here, to protect her and sidetrack them."

Nate must be referring to the meeting at Zoë's place last night.

"That's been established," Zoë agrees. "Except you neglected to mention that a few hours earlier Liz saw you in full form and didn't die."

A laugh escapes Nate's lips, but he immediately composes himself, "So that's what this is about." His bemusement seems to irritate Zoë, but being Nate, he doesn't seem to care. "So what? It doesn't change anything. She's *still* not going."

"It's not your decision to make," Zoë points out.

"Where am I not going?"

"Don't you see, Nathaniel?" Zoë presses, dismissing my question completely.

"No, I don't," Nate cuts in louder than is necessary, ignoring me as well. "What's your brilliant plan? Use Liz as a decoy? It's time for you to admit that we fallen ones rule the Earth realm. Your set of laws works both ways, you're just as tied to them as we are. Only the mortals are free here," he runs his fingers through his hair. "It all comes back to their free will. If they fall you can catch them, but if they jump..."

"Try to be reasonable," Zoë says calmly. "It's a chance to take Lillithiel down. She'll never see it coming. We can end this."

Nate gets to his feet, "I don't give a damn about your agenda. Liz is not gonna be your bait, and that's final."

"I'll do it," this time they both turn to me.

Nate looks like he wants to bite my head off, and Zoë smiles genuinely, revealing perfect white teeth. He drops into the couch, burying his head in his hands. His distress makes me second guess my impetuous decision.

"Don't worry," Zoë speaks up. "Michael will escort you. We'll make sure you're safe."

"Hell, no!" Nate fumes, and Zoë winces at his choice of words. "Are you out of your mind? Just put a neon sign on her saying 'I'm the one.' Better yet, give Michael the thumbs up to kill her already. You're supposed to be wise, you being the counselor of wisdom and all," Nate shakes his head. "If she's signing up for this, I'll be the one taking her. And I demand that she's in on the plan."

"I'll leave that to you," Zoë stands up. "Get her to control her thoughts, and it's fine by me." She turns in my direction, "I'm going back for Michael, are you coming?"

I glance at the cracked clock that hangs tilted on the wall, and yet still ticks off the seconds, "School is almost over. No point in going back now."

"Go get Mike, I'll keep Liz," Nate appeals, but Zoë hesitates. He inhales deeply and lets out cynically, "She already agreed to be your sacrificial lamb, what else do you want?"

Zoë nods and puts a gentle hand on my arm in reassurance as she passes by, "I'll have Michael stop by to drop off your backpack."

"Ok, thanks."

She stops at the door, "One more thing. Liz has a human soul. How did you know she wouldn't die?"

Nate shrugs, "I took a chance. Something told me she could take it, and I was right."

Zoë nods and closes the door behind her.

"Why Liz?" Nate looks me straight-on.

"I just want this over with," I reply honestly. "So I can get on with my life."

"Did you stop to consider that your life may not go on after this?" Nate seems to be grasping for patience. "I said I'd protect you, but you're not making it easy." He stands up slowly and offers a hand to me, "Come, we have work to do. Let's go to your place."

I take his hand, and he pulls me up, "I'm still grounded, you know," I look at him expectantly, Nate just stares back at me, so I add, "You won't get past Grandma, and I'm supposed to be in school."

"Fair enough," Nate consents. "We'll just have to hang out here then." He motions for me to sit and explains, "We need to get a handle on your thought transference. You need to harness the ability to direct and block it at will. This comes as second nature to us, but you'll have to work for it. Your mind is vulnerable to me when you're nervous or upset. Sometimes when you space out, as well. I'm gonna ask you a question, and your job is to not think of the answer."

"Ha!" I blurt out. "You're joking."

"One plus one, Liz," he tests me.

The number *two* pops in my mind instantly.

He tries again, "Your father's name is..."

David, no George.

Nate shakes his head, "What's your favorite color?"

His car comes to mind first, followed by *my yellow hoodie.*

"That's the idea, using associations. But try to be more vague, think about something else completely. In what city were you born?"

"Concentrate, Liz. Where did we first meet?"

"How old are you?"

"What's your favorite flavor of ice-cream?"

"What's Faye's middle name?"

"Are you jealous of Spark?"

I blink and blurt out aloud, *"What?"*

"Focus, Liz. Who is Ariel?"

The Little Mermaid.

"Perfect! Now, who is Michael?" Nate asks in excitement.

"You're wasting time," Michael's voice comes out of nowhere. Then, he blinks into existence at the doorway.

I yelp, and Nate faces him, looking annoyed, "Do you have a better idea, Pretty Boy?"

"I do actually," Michael drops my backpack at my feet. "Let the grown ups handle it. She's better off in the dark."

"Not gonna happen," Nate turns back to face me. "You guys need me to get in, and my condition remains."

"What's at stake here is the element of surprise," Michael rationalizes. "If she's in on the plan, she'll unwittingly broadcast it to any demon or fallen within a ten mile radius."

"She needs to know what she's getting herself into," Nate retorts. "So please excuse us, Your Highness. We have a lot to cover."

"Save your futile attempts for later," Michael stretches out, cracking his back with a twist at the waist. "For now, I'm taking her home. She has a human life to tend to. We have a lab report due tomorrow and a quiz in Spanish." Michael starts toward the door, "Come along."

Nate stands up with me and places a hand on my shoulder, "We're not finished, Liz. We've got ten days to figure this out. Try to recruit Blake to join us tomorrow after school, so we can work on a different approach."

I nod, and follow Michael out of Nate's apartment.

Back in my room, I pull my Chem text book out and Michael starts, "Page seventy-eight, Solvents and Solutions."

I flip to the page and we begin reading from the top.

"*Hey Liz, five times five?*" Nate's voice pops clearly into my mind.

I let out a long sigh and start reading aloud.

35

My alarm goes off at seven in the morning. I hit the snooze button and turn onto my back, eyes wide open. My mind is swimming with random trivia. I fell asleep to Nate's voice inside my head last night. We must have gone through five hundred questions, and I don't think I'm any closer to rewiring my brain.

Ten minutes pass in a matter of seconds. My alarm sounds again, this time I turn it off. I roll out of bed, making a beeline to the shower. My morning ritual beats its all time record, seven minutes. Yeah, I'm sorta cheating today. I just towel dry my hair and let it down. I'm too wound up to deal with it right now.

"Can I come in?" Grandma asks, standing in the doorway, and I nod. Like always, her blond hair is perfectly styled into a smooth bob with highlighted strands. It's seven twenty in the morning and she's all made-up. I realize just then, I've never seen Grandma without makeup.

How early does she get out of bed?

She enters the room, hands me my phone back and informs all casual, "I've cleared up my agenda for this afternoon. I'm taking you to Talita Keys to have you fitted for a dress."

"Why do I need a dress?" I ask confused. "I thought I was grounded. Are you letting me go to the concert with Nate?"

"No. You're still very much grounded. But I am making an exception for his sister's birthday party. She's a very fine young lady. That's the type of company you should keep. Perhaps you'll make some new friends and stay out of trouble."

"Are you feeling okay, Grandma?" I'm suddenly concerned. "What did she say to you?"

"I'm fine, dear. I just think Lill Sinclair is a very fine young lady. That's the type of company you should keep. Perhaps, you'll make some new friends and stay out of trouble," and with that, Grandma leaves my bedroom.

I'm in complete shock, and immediately power on my phone to text Nate: *What on Earth did Lill do to my grandma? Whatever it is, undo it.*

I know he won't read the message until he wakes up, so I should hear back around noon. It's almost seven forty and Faye will be downstairs a quarter to eight as usual. She needs to hit the drive-thru at the coffee shop for her "Regular, non-fat, sugar free, *Mocha-laka-taka* with light foam," So, I grab my backpack, and head out.

On the drive to school, Faye talks in detail about her dentist appointment yesterday morning. For an instant, I believe I'm off the hook, and maybe she won't get on my case about Nate.

"What's the point of dating a fallen angel anyway?" Faye starts as we leave the coffee shop drive-thru.

No such luck.

"You're giving me dating advice?" I scoff. "*You?*"

Faye does her signature eye roll, "I'm just saying... A couple should have common interests. The two of you are from different planes of reality."

"What are you talking about?"

"What I'm saying is," Faye draws out the words. "You

date a guy that you can see yourself growing old with...."

I can tell she's not gonna let it go. She's truly getting on my nerves. About a block and a half down the road, I snap. I grab her pink phone from the center console, scroll down her contacts until I locate the name Blake, and touch call.

It rings several times until he finally picks up, "Hey, Faye. I have my hands full here, can I call you back in two seconds?"

"Sure," I hang up.

Faye gives me a questioning look, but doesn't have a chance to ask what I'm up to, because exactly two seconds later Wellington is calling back. The pink cellphone starts pulsing in my hand, blasting a pop melody, *"Cause you're hot then you're cold, you're yes then you're no, you're in then you're out, you're up then you're down..."*

Interesting choice of ringtone. It's my turn to shoot her an inquiring look. She reaches for the phone, knowing exactly who's on the other end, the only one with a personalized ringtone. But I pull it out of her reach just in time, answering, "Hello, Wellington."

"Liz?" He asks confused.

"Don't sound so disappointed," I tease. "Here's the thing, Grandma is taking me to buy a dress after school, and I have to cancel on you. So, I'm sending Faye in my place."

"Are you crazy?" Faye mouths with an expression of disbelief, apparently I managed to catch her off guard for once.

"Sure," Wellington hesitates, but quickly recovers, "Yeah, yeah. Of course. My place or hers?"

I consider briefly before replying, "Yours."

"Great! I'll be waiting for her after school," he says meaningfully with excitement in his voice.

"Bye-bye," I singsong.

Faye's glossed lips are in an "oh, " and she asks, "What did you just do?" She shakes her head as if to clear her mind. "It's official. Nate's evil scheming side is rubbing off on you."

"It's more like your wannabes are," I reply, unable to disguise the smile forming on my face.

My classes go by in a blur. I've been so focused on coming up with the wrong answers that I'm pretty sure I just flunked my physics pop quiz.

During lunch break, I observe first hand the extent of Lill Sinclair's fandom. Not only at our table, but all around the cafeteria. Everybody is laser focused on their smart phone displays, following Lill's Twitter feed. She's listing the celebrity RSVP confirmations for her birthday bash, one at a time. I'm amazed to find out that most of the students here would die to attend her party. *Ironic, isn't it?*

The commotion over Lill's party spills over into Chemistry. One thing is consistent among all the chaos, Michael's brooding personality. At least now, I know why.

He looks up from the experiment, indicating he just heard my thoughts. He leans closer and whispers, "Tell Nathaniel, the clock is ticking." Then, he goes back to his notes, his dark blue eyes a million miles away from here.

In Spanish I get a text from Nate: *Meet me at the library after sixth period.*

I don't reply. I shouldn't have even looked, but curiosity got the best of me. I put my phone inside my backpack pocket, fearing I'll get caught with it.

I don't dress out for PE for once. Mainly because I want to get a head start to the library. In the meantime, I just sit in the bleachers, trying not to draw any attention to myself. At long last the final bell sounds, and I rush to the library.

Nate is already there. He's engrossed in his reading, his blue eyes quickly tracing the words across the page. I put my backpack on the table and sit down across from him, "I got your text."

He looks up, "Don't worry about your grandma. She'll be fine. It'll wear off in time."

"Do you even hear yourself?" I chastise. "Lill has my

grandmother under a spell."

"She's been compelled, and I can undo it anytime," Nate says a little too calmly in my opinion.

"Why haven't you already?"

"I thought it best to check with you first," Nate fixes his eyes intently on me. "Lill actually did you a favor, if you really want to go through with it, that is. The moment I undo her spell, your grandma won't let you leave the house. It's your choice."

I drop my forehead to the table, "Why do I have to keep making choices?"

No teenagers should be allowed to make life altering decisions.

Nate laughs, "Ex mero motu."

I look up at his bemused expression, and just drop my head back down with a thud, "*Ow.*"

"Come on, Liz. Save the drama for Ms. Campbell," Nate stands and holds my backpack. "I'll walk you."

I let out a long deflating sigh and go with him, dragging my feet. The door is already closed when we arrive, and Nate opens it quietly, handing off my backpack. Instead of taking it, I pull him by the wrist into the classroom with me.

"And here she is," Ms. Campbell announces. "Our Helen of Troy."

Half the room claps and whistles. Michael stares down Nate who looks just as uncomfortable as I am. Even my ears are burning hot, I must be the color of Ms. Campbell's vintage red dress.

Ms. Campbell clasps her hands enthusiastically, "And you brought Achilles with you."

Oh, no.

"I brought *who*?" I whisper to Nate.

"Achilles, the Greek hero from the Trojan War," Nate replies telepathically.

"This fall's production will be *Helen of Troy*. We will be performing at the 50th Annual Thanksgiving Festival," Ms.

Campbell clarifies, her face shining with excitement. She turns back to me, "You, my dear, will be playing the part of Helen."

"Ms. Campbell," I croak. "That's not a good idea. I've never acted before. I'm not an actress."

"That's why you're here, Miss O'Neill, to learn how to act," Ms. Campbell points out, her mind entirely made.

"I don't even know who this 'Helen of Troy' is," I say in a small voice, sounding pitiful and whiny even to my own ears.

"Take a seat please," Ms. Campbell gestures to two open seats. "Mr. Sinclair, will you be joining us?"

"As a matter of fact, I was just leaving," Nate tries to twist his arm loose, and I tighten my grip. He surrenders, "Or not." Inside my head, he adds, "You owe me."

Ms. Campbell summarizes the play, "The story takes place around 1200 B.C. The Greeks are plotting an invasion to steal the treasures of Troy. Meanwhile, Prince Paris is sent by his father, the King of Troy, to travel to Sparta and negotiate peace with the Spartans. In the midst of his journey, he nearly drowns at sea during a ferocious storm, and the Queen of Sparta, Helen, rescues him. Believing she's only a slave, and struck by her beauty, Prince Paris falls in love with her."

A laugh escapes my lips, and Ms. Campbell stops to look at me, arching an eyebrow inquiringly.

I blush and mouth the word, "Sorry." When she turns away, I whisper to Nate, "And she wants me to play Helen? Yeah, right."

He cocks his head to one side studying my face. To my surprise, Nate offers telepathically, "Ms. Campbell is on to something. You do remind me of her."

I scoff before I can stop myself, and Ms. Campbell shoots me another look. I press my lips shut and try to compose myself. *Since when did I start getting reproving looks from school faculty?*

"I should know, I was there," Nate adds inside my head.

I just stare at him, unable to tell if he's joking or not. He just nods in Ms. Campbell's direction, trying to deflect my attention.

Ms. Campbell continues, "Upon his arrival at the Spartan palace, he is arrested by the King of Sparta, Menelaus. Once again, Helen comes to his rescue. Together, they travel back to Troy. The king accuses the Trojans of kidnapping Helen, declaring war against them. A war fought for a solitaire young woman which would lead to over a decade of blood shed and despair. The Spartans fight a losing battle, until Odysseus derives an ingenious subterfuge; To withdraw their one thousand ships from the Trojan waters and leave behind a parting gift at the gates of Troy, the legendary Trojan Horse."

Ms. Campbell hands out a stack of scripts and we spend the next forty minutes reading through key excerpts from the story.

Since Grandma is picking me up, Nate and I go our separate ways. He walks to the parking lot, and I head toward the school's main entrance.

Faye gets into step with me as I pass the stairwell, "I just got a text from Blake. I'm meeting him at the coffee shop across the street from his dad's bookstore, isn't that exciting?"

"Uh-huh."

Faye steps in front of me, "What's wrong with you? Why do you look so gloomy?"

"It's nothing, " I sigh.

"Liz, it's me. I know we've been butting heads lately. But I'm still your friend," Faye says meaningfully.

"It's just something Nate said that got me thinking, like really thinking for the first time, and it finally sunk in. It's crazy that it never crossed my mind before, but with everything else, it didn't occur to me until now. "

"What did he say?"

"Ms. Campbell chose me to play Helen of Troy, who apparently was some beautiful goddess from over three thousand years ago. Nate said that I reminded him of her, and since he was there, he's qualified to say so."

"Huh! I thought the whole Trojan Horse story was a myth," Faye says thoughtfully.

"Apparently not. *Hey?*" I ask intrigued. "How did you know about Helen of Troy? Have you read *The Iliad*?"

"No," Faye rolls her eyes. "Hello!? Haven't you seen the movie *Troy*? It's considered to be Brad Pitt's artistic nude."

"Eewww! Brad Pitt is like my dad's age." I reply grossed out by the idea.

"Said the girl who is officially dating the oldest man on Earth. Besides, Brad Pitt is still hot if you ask me," Faye points out, shaking her head. "You sure know how to pick them, girlfriend."

I nudge her with my shoulder playfully and stick my tongue out at her before rushing to Grandma's car.

"You know I'm right," Faye calls out, laughing.

36

I spend the next nine days on edge. To top it off, all the teachers are overloading us with reports and assignments. Even Ms. Campbell, who usually doesn't give us homework, isn't cutting us any slack. I have page after page of lines I need to memorize for the play. Knowing what to say is not enough, you need to know how to deliver the ridiculous lines.

Who talks like that anyway?

As if that's not enough, I have to remember when to say them, how to say them, where to stand, when to turn my head, when to blink, when to breathe... Every little detail seems so crucial. It's like one missed step and it'll be the end of the world, which hits a little close to home.

The more I read about Helen of Troy, the more I realize we're nothing alike. Not in personality or appearance. At least not the Hollywood version, that is. I streamed the movie on my laptop last night. Yeah, she's tan with curly blond hair, but that's where the resemblance ends. The actress is this beautiful German model, the curvy type with a full D-cup.

But let's say for argument's sake, that Ms. Campbell and

Nate have a more historic vision of her. I might resemble an old painting, sculpted bust, or something. *I* say, "I'm nothing like her." She's promiscuous and selfish. If she didn't run away with Prince Paris that war would never have happened, and I wouldn't be playing her part in front of the entire school at the 50th Annual Thanksgiving Festival.

At home, I divide my time between homework and getting a grip on my thoughts. We're still no closer to mastering my so-called *telepathy* than we were when we started. Nate attempts a new strategy every day, but it's no use. Even in the dream world our efforts are futile. Nate is being nothing but patient, going overboard in what Michael calls a losing battle. His efforts are certainly earning him brownie points with the angel gang.

That's why tonight I'm walking blindly into the lions den. All I know for sure about the plan is that Wellington and Faye are in on it. Nate isn't thrilled with any of this to put it mildly, but he's going along with it at my request.

I inhale deeply and step in front of the mirror, the girl staring back looks anomalous to me. She looks uneasy, nervous and haunted by uncertainty. I touch a lock of my hair and the reflection does the same. It's half up and half down, Grandma spent an hour getting my hair to stay like this. My gown is pearl white, cascading in a full length skirt and embroidered with light shades of iridescent beads. My Garland two-tone glitter gold heels put me right at six feet. The entire outfit costs more than a one way trip to Japan. Considering I might be buried in it, I figured it would be okay to splurge for once.

Grandma places a kind hand on my shoulder, "Come on, my dear. Nathaniel is waiting for you in the foyer."

Nate stands up when we walk in, and I do a double take. The word handsome doesn't do him justice, he looks absolutely breathtaking in a black suit and tie. His expression is warm and appreciative. All my worries decimate for that spellbinding moment in which our eyes meet. He holds my gaze, and despite the evening still to come the smile forming on my lips is genuine. His smile mirrors mine, reaching his blue eyes.

Nate offers his hand for me, "You look beautiful."

"Thank you," I squeeze his hand. "You too, I mean, you look great," I try disguising the fear growing inside.

I let go of Nate's hand and pull Grandma into a tight hug, "Thanks Grandma, thanks for everything."

"You're very welcome, my dear."

I repeat the gesture to Grandpa, "Love you."

"Go. Have fun," Grandpa pats my back.

I take hold of Nate's hand. If he notices my nervousness and odd behavior, he doesn't give it away. He says good night to my grandparents, promises to have me home before midnight and leads me out of the apartment.

In the elevator, he pulls me against him and wraps his arms around my waist. I mean to say something, but words fail me. A sharp nervousness builds up inside me, and my shoulders tremble.

"Hey, it's okay," Nate whispers. "Do you hear me?"

I nod against his chest, trying to get a hold of myself. The ding sound of the elevator announces our arrival at street level, and Nate guides me outside, helping me into his car. Try as I might, it's tough to keep a positive outlook. It's like I'm seeing everything around me for the last time.

We stop at a red light, and Nate turns to look at me, "I can take you anywhere. To your family in Japan, to your friends back in California, to the Florida Keys, you name it. I can take you beneath the aegis where none of them will ever find you. Just give me the word."

The light turns green, and I face him, "Take me to the party."

Nate gives me an almost imperceptible nod and makes a left turn. About two blocks down the road, we're pulling up to the valet. The doors raise, and I hesitate, running my fingertips along the yellow and black dashboard one last time.

"Come on," Nate extends his hand with a sad smile on his face. I take it, stepping out of the car, and he leads me through the glass doors.

We walk into a hugely bright lobby with black and white checkered marble floors. The doorman nods to us, and I force a nervous smile at him. Nate places his hand on the small of my back, guiding me to the last elevator on the left. The newest Calvin Klein model holds hands with a stunning brunette in a black dress, and they both greet Nate by name as we approach.

Once the four of us pile inside, the elevator operator presses for the thirty-third floor and the doors slide closed. Retro music plays in the background, and no one speaks the entire ride up.

Why did I agree to come here?

I'm feeling more and more unsettled with each blinking number. The doors finally slide open, and we're in another humungous lobby; again all glass with black and white checkered marble flooring. We walk toward a set of tinted glass doors, my high heels clip-clopping all the way. They slide open the moment we draw near, like they have a motion sensor or something, closing behind us the instant we pass through.

I gasp, and take a step back. A few feet from where we stand, two panthers sit atop a pair of short pillars that look a lot like the Greek Doric columns from Drama. Except these aren't made of Styrofoam.

The panther sitting on my right is pure white with pale blue eyes. The one on my left is velvet black with golden yellow eyes. They sit up at attention, looking like living statues. It's almost like they're guarding the entrance. On second thought, they're on the inside so maybe they're guarding the exit.

"What on Earth? Those can't be real," I blurt out, frozen in place. As if on cue, one of the beasts yawns.

"Apparently so," Nate replies, admiring the animals. "Smart girl," Nate adds in a voice so low that I'm not sure if I heard him right.

I deviate my eyes from the panthers and look quizzically at Nate. Inconspicuously, he positions himself right in front of me with his back to the animals, obscuring them from my line of sight. I frown at him, confused.

He sweeps the hair from my left shoulder, leaning in, and quietly elaborates, "Eyes on me, don't react to what I'm about to say."

I take his hand and give it a gentle squeeze to show I got it.

His lips curl up, "The cats are bound to Lill. They're her eyes tonight. She'll know who walks in and out." I gulp, and he whispers, "There's no turning back now."

I swallow hard and tighten my grip on Nate's hand. He studies me a second longer before turning around and leading me inside. I walk warily as we pass the two beautiful beasts, praying that neither of them so much as look in my direction.

Immediately, we are immersed into the sound of pulsing EDM music. At the exact opposite side of the venue, on an elevated platform, a DJ stands nodding to the music behind his turntable. *DJ Rack* must be someone famous and edgy, because if I were to throw a party of this sort, I would choose a DJ with better taste in music.

The atmosphere is just the extravaganza I expected. Everything looks awe-inspiring and highly breakable. The interior is bright with a modern and exotic décor. From the ceiling hangs a delicate drapery resembling the inside of an enormous tent. It's replete with black and white chandeliers, causing the light to diffuse throughout the fabric and the entire setting glows. The center of the room is a dance floor with dining tables arranged around the perimeter.

To our left, a glorious staircase rises to where I expect Lill Sinclair will descend as part of her grand entrance. To our right, there are two rectangular tables, one holds a champagne tower, and the other a bejeweled black and white birthday cake. Behind them, the fairy light curtains resemble shimmering waterfalls.

Lill's guests seem the exact type one would expect a celebrity super model would have. There are more guys wearing white suits than I expected. Oddly enough, the guys in suits don't look all alike as I thought they would. They look exceptionally distinct from each other. Maybe it's because a majority of these guys are from the fashion world.

Nate's entire body tenses beside me, and I peer up at him. He's looking straight ahead, his eyes speculative. I turn and search around conspicuously. Then, I have to fight the urge to crack up laughing. I think I might be having a nervous breakdown. It's not like I can spot a demon by its tail. I could eliminate the celebrities, but then again Lill is a celebrity herself.

"Relax," Nate brushes his lips to my cheek, probably sensing my distress. Either that or he's hearing my thoughts, and that's not good. He tilts my chin up with his thumb and index finger. "Think about snow flakes, baby ducks, chocolate covered cherries."

If he's trying to distract me, it's working. I'm intrigued, "Chocolate covered cherries?"

"My favorite," Nate smiles down at me.

A catering server stops in front of us, brandishing a silver plate of *hors d'oeuvres*, and offers, "Honey Walnut and Brie Tartlettes."

I raise my hand to grab one, but Nate karate chops my arm down, saying, "No, thank you." The server strolls away, and Nate adds, "We're not taking any chances."

Super. This party is going to be fun.

I look around in search of any celebrity I actually like, maybe Milla Jovovich is around somewhere, or P!nk, or Joseph Gordon-Levitt. No such luck. I keep an eye open for any sign of Abe Kaur, Ken, or Zoë, but so far they're nowhere to be found. I spot Wellington in a black suit, walking arm in arm with Ariel.

Ariel?

I knew Wellington would be here, but I thought he'd be here with Faye. Ariel's dress looks so much like mine that it can't be a coincidence, especially since her hair is half up half down. As if sensing me staring, Wellington turns and spots me. He sends a subtle wink from across the room and looks away again. Any thoughts of coincidence I had diminish just then.

Ariel is clearly part of the–

I jolt out of my reverie, losing balance as I twirl into Nate's arms. He lowers his face to mine. Before I can gather my thoughts, he's kissing me.

A series of bright flashes break us apart, and I blink to erase the black spots in my vision. A short bald man with a goatee in a black tuxedo points a camera the size of his head right at us. It flashes once again, before he lowers it, asking, "Mr. Sinclair, who's your plus one?"

At first, I get the impression Nate is going to shove the guy all the way across the room. But he just inhales deeply and plasters a full-teeth smile onto his face, "My girlfriend."

"Do I get a name?" The photographer presses.

"You're about to miss the grand entrance," Nate points to the top of the staircase.

DJ Rack announces through the loudspeakers right on cue, "Here comes the birthday girl, and she's a vision in Valentino!" The man scurries away through the crowded dance hall, his camera held high.

A weird birthday song remix kicks in, and Lill Sinclair steals the scene. Rapid fire camera flashes brighten the entire room, and a wall of smart phones raises overhead, all aimed at the balcony. The music transitions to a mashup of old 80's tunes given the dub-step treatment. It's official. *DJ Rack is the worst Disc Jockey EVER.*

The flashes die down, and Lill Sinclair pauses at the top

of the stairs with a dazzling smile on her face. It's only then I realize she's breaking her own black and white dress code. Her gown is scarlet red, flattering her perfect silhouette by its sheer design. It brings out her red hair. She's wearing it down, in beautifully arranged natural curly style. Her look is bold, daring, and suitable for dragging me straight to the underworld.

Lill starts to descend and the flashes kick up to full blast, stopping only when she reaches the bottom of the stairs. It's a wonder she isn't blind yet. Nate puts a protective arm around my shoulder, pulling me closer as she makes her way into a swarm of guests. She poses for photos and delivers warm "thank yous," smiling radiantly all the while.

My fears intensify as she makes her way toward us, greeting guest after guest. I try to conjure up chocolate covered thoughts to keep from having a panic attack. My body is rigid as a stone, and my heart thumps in my throat. Nate squeezes my shoulder ever so slightly, a clear attempt to calm me down. I turn my face to look at him, waiting to hear his reassuring voice. But the only reassurance I receive comes from his eyes.

"Little brother and Eliza O'Neill, I'm so happy you guys could make it," Lill flashes a wide smile at us. Her words are sweet, but the threatening tone hidden behind her words are not lost on me. "I knew I could count on you, Nathaniel."

"Happy birthday, sis," Nate replies and returns her smile, seeming unfazed. To my surprise, he lets go of me and pulls her into a hug. The photographers following her around don't skip a beat, catching the moment on camera. Lill turns to me, but I'm sure as heck not going to hug her.

"Thanks for inviting me," I touch the fabric of her dress. "Happy birthday, you look gorgeous." *There.* All those drama rehearsals have finally paid off. I'm almost as cordial as Queen Helen.

To my relief and Lill's annoyance, the photographer saves me from any further contact by shoving a camera in our face. Lill positions herself between us, and a few shots are taken. She switches places, facing us once again. Nate pulls me closer against him, and I have a feeling her pretense of a gracious party host ends with us. I get a queasy sensation in my gut, just as Nate's phone vibrates against me.

I'm fighting with all my might to keep the smile on my face, when Lill abruptly turns around and looks toward the main doors as if anticipating someone, or maybe "something." For the first time tonight, the panthers seem restless. Their growls resonate over the loud music, triggering a collective stir in the crowd.

Just then, Michael steps into view. Lill sucks in a long drag of air, and I grip Nate's hand. For once, I'm forced to agree with the rest of the school girls. He's striking. Michael suits up in head to toe black. His hair isn't falling in his face as usual and his dark blue eyes are discernible even from this distance. He looks dark and deadly, dignifying his title.

Faye steps out from behind him and takes his arm. She's in a silver gown, which brings the number of dress code deviants to two. Her hair is glamorously down and her makeup is serene, accentuating her beautiful features. Her strapless fitted bustier outlines her figure and cascades into a beaded tulle full-length skirt. Lill doesn't seem extremely pleased with Faye's color selection, and even less so with her choice of plus one.

"Now that's what I call a vision in Valentino, Lill," Nate says just loud enough for her eavesdropping press to hear, undoubtedly an attempt to provoke her even more.

Lill gives us a menacing smile, and a chill runs down my spine. She excuses herself, "I need to mingle, but I'll be back." She strolls toward the next guest and the words "so don't even dare try to leave" remain unsaid, but there they are loud and clear.

The moment she's out of sight, Nate pulls his phone out of his pocket and lets out a brief laugh of pure disbelief,

"That explains this horrendous circus tent theme."

"What is it?" I ask unable to suppress my curiosity.

Discreetly, he puts the screen in sight for me to read. The message is from Faye, *"Michael says 'aegis alert.' Whatever that means..."*

Nate is scanning the party, and I do the same, having no idea what we're looking for. Nate shakes his head in disbelief, and my eyes follow his to the top of the stairs. Dressed all in white, like a chameleon blending with the décor, Abe Kaur stands. Eyes like a hawk, he appears to be aware of everything that's going on in here.

Nate kisses my cheek as a pretense to say, "Don't stare. He'll sense it. There's nothing to worry about." Maybe I heard wrong, but I could swear he said "yet" under his breath.

As the events of the night unfold, my anxiety grows. Each minute that passes feels like one less I have to live. Lill does not approach us again, but I know it's just a matter of time. The party goes on, regardless of my distress. The dance floor fills to capacity, and the entire building seems to move to the beat. Lill is constantly surrounded, but it's like nothing gets by her unnoticed. It's a quarter to eleven and I don't know how much longer I can stand this.

Nate's phone vibrates again, and this time I jump. I'm so tense that it's getting hard to maintain the "enjoying myself" facade. I'm terrible at this kind of thing.

He lifts his phone to check the message. Without a word, his arm slides from my shoulder, and he takes hold of my hand. He starts to pull me toward a set of glass doors leading out to the balcony, and I follow searching for any sign of Wellington or Faye. Just as fast, Nate comes to an abrupt stop, checks his phone again and curses under his breath.

"What's going on?" I'm unable to refrain my uneasiness any longer.

"Good question," Nate sounds on edge as he looks straight across the dance floor. "I'm giving them ten more seconds."

That's when I hear Michael's voice inside my head, loud and clear over the grinding dubstep patterns, "Faye, what are you doing?"

I follow Nate's eyes and spot Faye and Michael near the staircase at the edge of the dance floor. Still clueless, I turn to Nate, but he's still peering fixedly in their direction. Just as I look back, Faye places her left hand on Michael's neck and pulls him gently toward her. Next, she's kissing him. Faye is kissing Michael. Are angels allowed to kiss? I kiss Nate all the time but that's different.

What's happening right now?

Their kiss lasts for a full minute, and Lill Sinclair is watching them instead of me for a change. As the kiss ends, Michael lifts her up and twirls her around, capturing the interest of the media. When Faye's feet are planted on the floor, another unexpected thing happens. Wellington suddenly appears, his hand is balled up in a fist and he throws an arching punch at Michael's face.

At first I thought, well, *the obvious.* But now, I'm not so sure. Michael was plainly not expecting the blow. He loses his equilibrium, bouncing against the table that serves as the base for the champagne tower. Faye reaches to steady him a second too late, and the damage is done. The tower crashes down in a cascade of broken glass, and the shattering sound breaks through the music. Every single photographer in the room starts snapping pictures of the unfolding chaos.

That's when I panic, Michael is going to kill Wellington instead of Lill now. *What was Wellington thinking?*

I start making my way in their direction, but a gloved hand pulls me forcefully back and starts dragging me toward the balcony. I have one last glance at the chaotic scene and catch a glimpse of Nate leading Ariel quickly up the stairs, his hand on the small of her back. It's the last thing I see before being enveloped by darkness.

37

It's devilishly dark, the air is crisp and chilly. The wind blows my bare arms to goosebumps, and fear overtakes me as the red gloved hand drags me toward the ledge of a humongous open balcony. The scarlet edges of her gown flap in the wind, whipping against the white organza of my cascading skirt. I try to shake loose and free my arm over and over again. She's stronger than I am, a thousand times stronger.

My lips part, screaming for help, but no sound comes out. Lill laughs with menace and lets go of my wrist. I'm not expecting it and topple backward, losing my equilibrium. I stumble before managing to regain my footing and force myself to stand unafraid.

Lill cocks her head to one side, giving me a once over, "You're just what I expected you to be. Even your appearance resembles his."

What is she talking about? Who do I resemble?

Lill squints, as if trying to look through me, "I can see your soul, shimmering yellow like the Sahara sun. Nathaniel must have sensed it at first sight as well," she moves forward, and I instinctively take a step backward. Her lips curl into a smile, "Scared little girl! You're smarter than I gave you credit for. You *should* be scared."

I stop. It's not like I can run. We're on the balcony at the top of a highrise. *If I jump, I'll die. If I don't, I'll die.* Inside, the party is in full effect. My best chance is to stall her until they realize I'm gone. There's only one flaw to this plan, I can't speak. Lill has stricken me mute somehow.

"What?" She mocks. "Looking for a way out? Flower of Light or not, I don't think you'd survive a fall from this height. You'd be a splash of red on the concrete. I kinda like the visual, maybe that's how I'll kill you," she laughs, and fear courses through my veins.

What do I do now?

Lill takes another step, "Do you want to know a secret? Contrary to popular belief, I am not immortal. Not yet, anyway. Your very existence impedes me from becoming so. That's how we find ourselves in this predicament," she shrugs. "You and I can't exist on the same plane. The Earth realm needs me more than it needs you. Take this party for instance, all these people crawling over each other for a mere glimpse of my essence. I'm the Spirit of this realm, the very lifeblood of the planet. One of us has to die, and I choose you. 'Why?' You may ask... because you're worthless. You're hardly a blip on the radar, a drop in the bucket, less than nothing. And above all, you will never make an impact on this world. You'll be forgotten. Now, by killing you tonight, I'll be granting you a worthy death. One that will change the world as we know it. You'll be surrendering your life for a grand cause. You should be grateful to me. How many can claim that honor?"

Gee! She's completely deranged. This tirade sounds disturbingly well rehearsed.

"The problem is... I'm undecided on how to go about this. It's my party, and killing people can be messy. But if I simply toss you over the side, I won't have a good view of the impact from up here. And I've been waiting so long to see you die. A century prior to your birth even. So you can understand why I'm torn. I think we can both agree that a girl deserves a little fun on her nineteen hundredth birthday. Considering I'm short on time, I'll split the difference by torturing you here, then down you go."

Good. You do that. Give them time to come for me.

"What was that?" Lill tilts her head to one side. "I can assure you that no one is coming for you. Anyways... Tell me, do you feel that?" Lill asks mischievously, but I don't feel a thing.

If I can keep her talking, maybe I could–

My chest compresses, and I let out a high pitched wheeze. The air is knocked out of my lungs, and I bend at the waist, gasping. Lill puts a red gloved hand on my shoulder, her voice lowers, and she whispers in my ear, "The air is thinning, barely enough to breathe. How is that for torture? Being outside, feeling the cold air against your skin, and yet you can't breathe it. That's been my curse, and now you know how it feels. It appears your little friends' plan to distract me backfired. It's laughable even. They failed to consider one important factor: *I see everything*. It's great to be always underestimated."

I cough, my throat feels raw, and my lungs burn. She forces me to straighten with an upward shove, and I cough mutely. My eyes watering, tears escaping from each corner. Lill's lipped smile becomes a full grin, "Thanks to their slight miscalculation, I'll be eternal, free to roam the Earth realm. Indestructible, forever nineteen. Not even your precious keeper, Michael, will be able to touch me."

I have no idea what she's going on about. I'm in too much pain, wishing she'd just shut up and get it over with.

Lill just keeps talking, "How foolish do they think I am? Did they really believe I'd be thrown by Michael's presence enough to be oblivious to their scheme? What was the plan exactly? I might let you speak one last time, so you can lay it out for me."

They never let me in on the plan. But if she allowed me to speak, I'd be able to take a breath. If only I could think loud enough for them to hear me. Where are my loud thoughts when I need them?

"Or not," she thinks better of it. "I just don't care enough to endure hearing your sweet girly voice. I'd rather cast you off this balcony and become immortal," Lill continues in an alarmingly serene voice. "The underworld needs you so they can reclaim their precious upper dimension. I have no interest in that. I believe that's the one thing Nathaniel and I have in common. Neither of us could care less about the upper dimension. It's unfortunate that he chose to betray me. It would be nice to have an ally of his caliber to rule the Earth realm by my side for all eternity. But no, he had to fall for you instead. It's a pity!"

I suck in a lungful of cold air with all the strength I can muster. All it does, however, is scrape the inside of my throat, deepening the pain in my chest. I seriously consider throwing *myself* off the side of the balcony. Would that count, or does she have to kill me to become immortal? I don't know how much longer I can take it.

"You look confused, which is understandable. So let me spell it out for you. Neither the upper nor under dimensions have heard the final piece of the prophecy. The secret I just divulged to you. That part of the prophecy, she conveyed to me alone through touch. After tonight, I'll be truly alive, no more hiding behind the weakness of mere mortals. But first, I need to be absolutely sure you are the Flower of Light. It wouldn't do me any good to kill the wrong girl, would it now? Nathaniel would not be happy, and he can get pretty cranky at times. Worst of all, I'd be back to square one. So before we go on, I need to taste your blood. Bleed for me!"

Oh, great. That's why she's stalling. She isn't sure I'm the one she's been looking for.

Upon her command, hot liquid fills my mouth, and I swallow hard. No proof for you. If you want me dead, you'll have to take the risk. A little voice in the back of my head cheers, "Yeah! Now, we're talking. Fight back! Whatever she's doing isn't real, it's all in your mind."

I inhale deeply, filling my lungs with air. I can do this, I'm strong enough to fight. Then, realization dawns, and I stop myself, coughing for air. If I beat her at her little mind game, she'll know I'm the girl from her prophecy. Then, nothing will stop her from killing me. If only I'd nailed down how to control my thoughts, I could summon Nate to come to my aid. Now, If they don't find me soon, she'll torture me to death.

I stop resisting, and Lill's eyes widen with pure uncertainty and despair. She's hesitating, visibly unsure now. She was bluffing before, she knows nothing.

"I thought you'd at least put up a fight," Lill's voice proves my assumptions. "The Flower of Light wouldn't accept her demise so easily. It'd be a shame to end yet another innocent human life, so young. But you know what they say, better safe than sorry."

From nowhere, Wellington takes a running jump onto her back, but Lill doesn't even flinch. Fresh cold air fills my lungs, and I look up, wheezing, sobbing and gasping for air. He wraps his arm around her neck, gripping his bicep and sinking in a choke hold. Lillithiel seems unfazed and launches Wellington across the balcony with a wave of her hand. He lands hard on his left shoulder and slides a few yards back before coming to an abrupt stop against the brick.

Faye appears, brandishing a tall white vase over her head. In a downward motion, she cracks it on Lill's skull, and it shatters into a million pieces. Lill seems only mildly inconvenienced, apart from a drip of blood that traces a thin line down her forehead. She whirls around to attack Faye, edging her to the ledge of the balcony.

Out of the blue, I suddenly recall words from the translation, "If you're pure of heart, and your life is in peril..."

"Mikha'el, Princeps Militiae Caelestis!" I scream Michael's true name at the top of my lungs with all my might. The sound of my voice startles my own ears.

Lill collapses into a pile of red silk fabric and hair right at Faye's feet.

"The two of you, out! Now!" Michael's voice shouts.

Wellington pulls himself up and limps toward Faye, taking a detour around Lill who lays inert in a heap. He helps Faye stand, and they quickly exit the balcony through the glass doors. I lean against the rail, unsure of what to do.

In a heart beat, a flurry picks up. Michael is blown backward in a blast of wind, and Lill stands upright. He lets his body drop out of the current of air right before the balcony's edge, landing on his back. He rolls over his shoulder into a sprinting stance and dashes toward her.

Lill launches a focused gust from her left palm, and he dodges it, still advancing. She throws a second with her right, and he slides down fast, sweeping her legs from under her. Lill falls forward, catching herself, and in a swift motion kicks her legs up into a front hand spring.

A surge of extreme wind comes from all sides, it feels like we're in a typhoon without the rain. Lill's red hair whips about like a crackling fire. The wind hits me then, and my body lifts up. I have to lock my arms onto the rails to keep from flying away. Michael stands before her, unmoving like he's made of stone. Right foot forward, his left slightly pivoted and planted firmly on the ground, only his black tie flutters in the violent wind.

The glass starts to rattle, and the wind kicks up in the opposite direction. I'm like a flag, held only by my hands, fighting to get my feet back on the ground. Now, the wind is pushing me away from the ledge and into Lill's direction. I honestly don't know which one is worse.

Michael remains static, absolutely motionless, and Lill doubles down the ferocity of the wind. An awning breaks loose and flies like a missile out of sight. Michael doesn't move an inch, his fists clinched at his sides. Lill is enraged and juts forward, hands extended toward his neck. In a fluid motion, Michael steps his back leg forward and uses Lill's momentum against her. He grips her by the jaw, lifts her up and then drives her headlong into the ground. The wind diminishes straight away, and I fall into a sitting position.

Michael stands, casting a shadow over Lill. Wide blue eyes stare up at him. She's paralyzed, like a deer in the headlights. A shimmery white glow slowly surrounds him entirely, and he extends his right hand to the night sky. Shafts of light pierce through the clouds and illuminate the balcony.

This is it. Should I close my eyes? Can I really survive the sight of the highest of angels in his true form?

"Michael, STOP!" A female voice shouts out.

Ariel is crossing through the glass doors. In front of her, a familiar looking brunette in a knee length black float dress is frozen in place, her eyes fixed on Lill's unmoving body. She's one of the two girls I saw escorting Lill into Nate's building before. The same who came to my apartment the day Lill paid a visit. She's one of her human shields.

The glimmering light surrounding Michael flashes out and fades away. Behind him, Ariel shouts, "Get out of here, girl. Run."

A maniacal laugh issues from the ground, and Lill blinks, "She's deaf, you simpletons."

"I'll take Rebecca out of here," Nate announces, one step behind Ariel. He grabs the girl's arm, but she crouches down and wraps her arms around a support pillar, impeding his effort. Nate lowers to lift her bony body off the ground, just as another girl enters the balcony.

Lillithiel gets to her feet. She straightens her dress, adjusts her heel and carefully removes a shard of porcelain from her hair. Confident she's no longer in danger.

More party attendants file in, and Nate's voice utters inside my head, "Get out of the corner, go to your left."

With quick steps, I follow his instructions. In my peripheral vision, a commotion of party guests begin to form.

"Let's see it, Michael," Lill taunts. "Don't hold back on their account. Let them enjoy the light show. I want to see the real you." Camera phones raise up, ready to capture what they might believe to be a dramatic breakup. Lill speaks again, her eyes never leaving Michael's, "Abe, go get the girl."

A hand covers my mouth and another grabs my arm, pulling me aside, and a male voice whispers in my ear, "Time to run, Blondie." He releases me then, and I spin around.

"It's you," is all I manage to utter.

"It's me," is his reply.

By the looks of it, he came from the party since he's in a suit and tie. In a swift move he vaults over the concrete rail, and a metallic thud resonates a few feet below. I lean over the balcony, my heart beating out of my chest as I look down. He's standing on a fire escape platform, grinning up at me, way too cheery for the situation at hand. He throws his arms out, motioning for me to jump. I don't hesitate, adjusting my skirt so I can climb over. I carefully sit on the rail and swing both legs simultaneously to the other side. Then, I let myself fall into his waiting arms.

He catches me, alright. But not without the both of us crashing down to the metal grate.

"I hope falling on me is not becoming a habit, Blondie."

"I'm sorry, Dwayne," I get off him, adjusting the many layers of my gown.

"Lets get the heck out of here," Dwayne stands up, and we quickly begin our descent down the infinite flights of stairs below.

Curse these stupid heels! It's impossible to keep up without tripping over my dress. We keep a good pace until Dwayne stops at a platform and starts pounding on the window. Before I can ask why, the window slides open, and another familiar face pops up.

"EJ?" I ask in confusion.

"Hi, love. Get inside," EJ helps me climb in.

"Do you live here?" I ask abashed, taking in the room.

"No. My grandfolks do. Faye said you might stop by, but I assumed you'd be using the front door," EJ explains, sliding the window closed.

"That's been happening a lot lately," I murmur quietly.

"No time, we need to get going," Dwayne ushers us to the front door. "You can come visit him another day and chat."

"Right," EJ replies in agreement, and we're out of the apartment through the front door and into the stairwell.

"Is it time for me to be clued in on the plan yet? How did you even get in the party? It's RSVP," I ask, lifting the ends of my skirt with both hands as we race down the stairs.

"I wasn't invited, I crashed," Dwayne calls back from below us. "I don't know about any plan. Faye just told me to show up and bring you to EJ's if you were in trouble."

"I'm supposed to show you to the parking garage," EJ comments from behind, sounding out of breath.

"Dude, you really should stop smoking," Dwayne points out.

After twenty-five flights of stairs, we reach an exit door leading to the underground garage. I'm even more surprised to encounter Ian in a pair of dark jeans and leather jacket, waiting for us by his black BMW motorcycle.

I look down at my full-length skirt. *Are they expecting me to ride wearing this?*

"Get on, O'Neil, I'm plan F," Ian confirms to my horror.

"*Plan F?*" I repeat taken aback, wondering what happened to plan A through E.

"She'll freeze to death," EJ points out, sounding concerned.

"Can they take your car?" Dwayne asks EJ.

"Sure," EJ replies, patting his front pockets. "Blimey, my keys are upstairs–"

"That's okay. I'll be fine," I cut in. Right about now, freezing to death is the least of my concerns.

Ian tosses me a helmet and I put it on, squishing flat my two hour hair do.

EJ gets into step with me and removes his dark blue jacket, handing it to me, "Here, love. Take this."

"Thanks," I say gratefully, putting it on over my dress.

I roll up my cascading skirt and manage to straddle his bike easily. For once, it pays off being tall. I adjust my heels on the foot pegs and rest my hands on either side of his waist.

"You better hold on tighter than that," Ian advises and kindly pulls my hands around his waist.

Before I have a chance to say bye to the guys, we're speeding out of the garage. Coming across no traffic, Ian accelerates and we fly forward. The cold wind freezes me to the core, and I shiver, holding Ian tighter. I lean my head sideways against his back, watching the city lights go by.

The bike races down the streets, turning right, blasting through a stale yellow signal. The roar of the engine reverberates between the buildings as we race through the freezing night. We approach a line of cars as we enter the downtown area, and Ian splits the lane, maneuvering onto the center line. He takes several bends before entering the tunnel. The speedometer glows sixty mph, as we launch through the covered passageway. He maintains his speed as we continue onto Massachusetts 1A North highway.

Down the expressway, the bike fires up even more. Ian lets out a low chuckle when I squeeze him harder, tightening my grip around his waist and clutching my fingernails into his jacket. The motorcycle speed keeps increasing, as does my adrenaline. We just hit eighty mph. It's like riding a roller coaster on a winter day. We exit the freeway, and I'm completely numb from the cold. At a traffic circle, we slow down and Ian exits onto a narrow street, turning right and right again. Eventually, he pulls over on Michael's street and puts the kickstand down.

Zoë is there waiting for us, wearing a pair of skinny jeans and a pale pink hoodie with the words "I'm no Angel," stamped on it. A sense of relief builds inside me at her sight as I dismount the bike.

I'm alive.

I take my helmet off and hand it to Ian, throwing my arms around him and giving him a grateful hug, "Thank you."

"Any time," he replies with a smile and straps the helmet down. He twists the throttle, and the bike roars to life. Then, Ian gives us a little wave before taking off down the road.

"Lets go inside," Zoë invites politely.

I start heading to the building's entrance, but she takes hold of my arm, stopping me. I turn around, confused. Before I have a chance to say anything, Zoë gets hold of me, and we're shooting upward fast. In a matter of seconds, we're landing gently on the balcony of the top floor.

"*Wow,*" I let out in a whisper.

Zoë smiles, lets go of my arms and slides the door open. Following her inside, I'm welcomed by the warmth of their heated apartment.

"Zophiel, summon the aegis," a gentle low voice orders.

A blond guy, probably Ian's age, slouches on a sofa. His piercing blue eyes are gentle and intimidating all at once. There's no other way to say it, he's dressed like a drifter. He's sporting a faded Red Sox hat, and his golden blond curls stick out around the edges. His jeans cross the line between fashionable to plain old ragged, and his Converse sneakers look as though he has walked across the country in them.

Who is this guy?

He has to be one of them, he just mentioned the aegis. But he sure doesn't look the part. Only his t-shirt under his beat up unzipped hoodie looks fairly new, it has some words across his chest, but it's partially hidden by his faded green jacket. I squint, trying to make out the words. He extends his arm across the edge of the backrest, offering a full view. My eyes jump up in embarrassment, absolutely certain that he just caught me reading his shirt. But his attention is still turned to Zoë, so I quickly glance down and read, "Don't shoot the messenger."

He's Gabriel. *Him?* No freaking way!

My skin prickles, and I look back to his face. This time, his piercing blue eyes are on me, and his mouth curls into a closed lip smile.

Great. He read my mind.

"I'm sorry," he apologizes and then adds, as if I already didn't know who he was. "I should have introduced myself. I'm Gabe."

"I kinda figure that out," I gesture to his shirt. His smile widens, and he turns his attention back to Zoë.

Zoë nods, "Please, have a seat."

I walk to the loveseat on my left and sit down. Only then, do I take notice of their place. It's almost entirely empty, but cozy somehow. Everything in here looks neat and unsophisticated. The walls are slate gray and the tile flooring matches it perfectly. The room is evenly illuminated by contemporary white ceiling lamps in uniform intervals. The couch set occupies most of the room, positioned in a half circle. It could probably accommodate at least ten people. I run my fingers across the soft vanilla fabric and reach for a sepia colored pillow, resting it on my lap.

The only other piece of furniture in the room is a dark chocolate hardwood center table, and nothing else. No paintings, no pictures on the wall, no decorative lamps, no flat screen TV, no sound system, no fireplace, no nothing. Their place smells fresh, like the salty sea breeze.

Zoë is barefoot and stands on top of the center table. She closes her eyes and spreads her arms with her palms facing up, just like Nate did at the cathedral. She starts chanting words in Latin, but I can't really tell if they're the same. They certainly do sound to be. Except they don't come off as formidable in her soft musical voice.

From the center of each palm shimmering purple glitter starts to twirl. It's completely different from the silvery blue vapor that came from Nate's palms. They're like waves of palpable energy. Lilac fractals of spherical lightning emanate from her hands and unify into a single vortex that passes through the ceiling.

An inexplicable wind blows her long black hair back in dark ripples. Her voice quickens in pace and she slowly turns clockwise, entirely enveloped in lavender light. The sight is breathtaking. Zoë resembles a glowing Japanese anime fairy with her serene expression as her lips enunciate each word. Instead of recoiling, I lean forward, mesmerized. Until, Zoë bursts into violet flames, that is. Gone is the spellbinding unearthly shower of particles. The lights flicker on and off, and I thrust back, bracing myself. Gabe is calmly studying me, and when our eyes meet he winks.

Light spreads like fire, forming a thin lilac coat upon the ceiling which crawls down toward the floor. Zoë's lips stop moving, and the flames immediately subside. The violet glitter dissolves back into her palms, and her eyes blink open. To my amusement, Zoë playfully throws herself backward into the couch with a short leap. Her features are a picture of pure delight. Gabe seems as gratified as she does. I, however, feel unease about the whereabouts of Faye and Wellington, wishing there were a clock on the wall to tell me the time.

"It's eleven fifty-six. Only four more minutes until they arrive," Gabe replies, addressing my unspoken concerns.

Note to self: I MUST learn how to control my thoughts.

Gabe raises a questioning eyebrow. *He's doing it again.* It's infuriating.

Zoë chuckles from the couch and tucks her long black

hair behind her ears, "Even if Nate manages to teach you how to control your telepathy, you still won't be able to keep your thoughts from Gabe."

"Huh?" I let out in conflicted hesitation.

"Gabe is the messenger," Zoë notes simply, as if that explains everything. I must look confused because she elaborates, "He delivers the message and collects the truth. No one can deceive Gabe, the same way Michael can never lie."

I blink, suddenly intrigued about how loud it must be inside Gabe's mind with all the people on this planet.

"Not every single being, only the ones carrying an ethereal soul. Angels and fallen ones alike," Gabe clarifies simply. "Which makes the Earth realm much quieter than the upper dimension."

"Huh?" I repeat, and as it clicks I add, "So, does that mean–?"

Gabe nods before I even finish the question, "It means you are Raphael's vessel. Part of his ethereal soul resides in you. Yes, I'm talking about *Raph* from your dreams."

I gulp, "I've always believed he," I pause to gather my thoughts. "I just–"

"You assumed he was only a dream," Gabe cuts in. "Raphael is real. A guardian archangel gifted with the ability to enter dreams, just like Nathaniel."

"Is he a fallen one like Nate?"

"Last I checked, he's still one of us," Gabe sounds bemused.

"Where is he? He just disappeared. I haven't heard from him in over a month. Is he alright? He sounded worried last time we talked, something about circles closing, and the messenger..." I trail off, realizing Raph meant Gabe.

"He's alright," Gabe reassures. "He's just keeping his distance at the moment."

"Why is that?"

"If he enters your dream, the underworld can locate him,"

Gabe explains. "And at this point, it's important that he stays out of sight. I informed Raphael that three of us were descending to the Earth realm to protect you and advised him to stay off the radar. He agreed as long as I reported on you. He worries a lot, the same way you worry about him. The two of you are linked by spirit. You're connected."

"How?" I blurt out, recalling the story of Asmodeus and his failed attempts to infuse his spirit into infants.

"That's where the difference lies. Asmodeus sought destruction while Raphael aspired to save your life," Gabe explains, studying me closely.

Suddenly, everything makes sense. How I ended up surviving the accident that took my mom's life when I was a child. Raph saved me. Also, the dates. They finally match, it was twelve years ago because I was four.

"Is that why Raph lives on Earth, to protect me? Is he my guardian angel?"

"Raphael was your mother's guardian angel," Gabe replies. "He was unable to save her, and felt compelled to rescue you."

"What do you mean?" I ask at a loss, my words choking up.

"Your soul was shattered, and Raphael bestowed upon you his own ethereal spirit to restore it. His spectrum is entwined with your soul. That's why he's confined to the Earth realm and unable to return to us," Gabe pauses, allowing his words to sink in. "It's also why you feel the urge to save others, you carry his guardian tendencies."

The front door bursts open, and Michael walks in with Faye and Wellington following suit. They appear to be unscathed which is a relief. I stand up and rush to hug them, both at the same time.

"I was so worried," I begin. "You're both okay."

"And so are you," Faye replies studying me.

"Let's all agree to skip Lill's twentieth birthday," Wellington half jokes.

"Deal!" Faye and I say in unison.

Zoë walks past the three of us, rushing toward Michael. She places a palm on his cheek, and the purple bruise where Wellington's hay-maker landed slowly fades away, healing before our eyes.

"Thank you," Michael sits down right in the center of the couch as if he owns the spot. His eyes appear to read Zoë's shirt and then Gabe's, "Where did you get the shirts, 'Cliché's-R-Us?'" His tone is as serious as ever.

"Here. We got you one," Gabe tosses a dark charcoal t-shirt to Michael.

Michael unfolds the shirt, one side of his lip sort of curls up. He shakes his head and drapes it over his shoulder, "I'm glad you guys had time to buy souvenirs, but I hope you kept the receipt because we failed."

"Ariel here," Nate's familiar voice fills the room when he crosses the threshold. "Well, let's just say she has the wrong profession in the upper kingdom. She should join the death angels' crew."

"*Oh?*" Zoë voices inquiringly.

"I managed to survive Lill's soiree, but almost died with Ariel behind the wheel," Nate elaborates, squeezes in beside me and puts his arm around my shoulder.

"Since we're all here now, can anyone tell me why Liz arrived on the back of a motorcycle?" Zoë asks to no one in particular.

"Yeah, about that," Nate lets his voice die out.

"Ian said he was plan F," I blurt out, not knowing what it even means.

"Plan F?" Zoë looks confused for a change. "What happened to the original plan?"

"For starters, we were under surveillance the moment we walked in. It's like her party was staged for us," Nate begins. "The place was crawling with demons, minions and lesser fallen angels, only her guests were actually mortals. Apparently, I'm not as deceiving as everyone paints me to be. Lill didn't buy into the notion that I'd be presenting Liz to her as a birthday gift."

"Telepathy was out," Michael contributes. "Abe had summoned his aegis and was listening in."

"What was the plan?" I blurt out, unable to hold back any longer.

"It was as simple as breathing," Zoë begins, and I immediately think, *nice choice of words.* She looks at me inquiringly, and I motion for her to go on. She does, "Nathaniel was to convince Lillithiel that he'd bring you to her party and take you upstairs at exactly eleven o'clock. The idea was to isolate Lillithiel from her human shields long enough for Michael to destroy her."

"And how did you persuade Lill to invite Michael to her party?" I ask Nate directly.

"I didn't," Nate deadpans. "I got Faye an invitation. Michael was just her plus one."

"And Ariel was Wellington's," Zoë clarifies. "That's where the tricky part comes in, switching Ariel and you unnoticed under Lillithiel's watch—"

I frown, interrupting, "Wasn't I supposed to be the bait? Why not take me upstairs instead? It couldn't go wrong that way. Why switch us?"

"Too dangerous," Nate answers. "That was their plan, but I never agreed to it. In the end, we compromised by bringing you to the party and using Ariel as a proxy."

"Either way," Zoë cuts in. "It was a risk we weren't willing to take. The other half of the plan was to create a distraction in order to make the exchange. That's where Michael comes in."

It's all she manages to say before I jump in again, "Are you saying Michael kissing Faye was part of the plan?"

"Michael kissed Faye?" Zoë's voice is almost inaudible.

I guess that's a "no." Maybe I should have kept my mouth shut.

"I thought it was part of the plan," Nate mocks. *I'm so*

sure. He looked as surprised as I did. He shrugs, "That's how the switch happened."

"The angel of destruction kissing a human girl," Gabe remarks bemused. "It'd definitely distract me. To any fallen angel or demon that would mean the Apocalypse is off."

"Holy sh–" Faye starts, but manages to stop herself, finishing, "Shoes! I didn't just mess with the end of the world, did I?"

"Michael is incorruptible," Nate lets out a laugh. "He's all about the greater good."

Zoë ignores Nate's remark and picks up where she left off, "We believed Michael's presence alone would do it. That Lillithiel would take her eyes off Liz and focus on Michael instead. Once they made the switch, Nathaniel would lead Ariel up the staircase into a private area. Wellington would be at his post ready to get you out of there via the fire escape and drive you here in Michael's Mustang, which was parked in the alley."

"Except this monkey-head strayed from the plan and punched Michael instead," Faye snorts.

"Good thing he did," Michael announces to my utter surprise, considering he can't lie and all. That's what I call turning the other cheek. He elaborates, "Lillithiel didn't take the bait. If Wellington were anywhere near Liz at that moment, she'd have killed him for standing in her way, and who knows where Liz would be."

"Dead," I say quietly at the same time Gabe asks, "How did that happen?"

"She didn't fall for it," I reply. "She came after me. She wanted to kill me to become immortal."

"If she didn't want to surrender you to the under dimension," Gabe cuts in. "Why didn't she kill you?"

"Wellington and Faye fought her off long enough for me to summon Michael."

"How did you know where to find her?" Zoë asks, looking from Wellington to Faye.

"I could hear your voice," Wellington jumps in to explain. "It's like you were standing right beside me. I heard you thinking about leaping from the balcony."

"Wait," I let out, not believing my own ears. "Did you just say you heard my thoughts?"

"You were inside my head," Wellington replies. "There's no other way to put it."

"I still can't fathom why she let Liz live," Gabe says thoughtfully. "She hasn't been so hesitant in the past."

"I keep asking myself the same question," Michael says under his breath. Then, he looks at Nate and adds with conviction, "All I can come up with is *you.*"

Nate seems taken aback for a heartbeat, but recovers just as quick, "Care to elaborate?"

"Come on, Nathaniel. Do I really need to spell it out for you? The only reason she tested her before ending her life is you. If she killed Liz, and it just so happened she was not the girl from the prophecy, what would you do?"

Nate doesn't reply, meeting Michael's gaze evenly.

Michael's lips curl up slightly, "You're not me, Nathaniel, and Lillithiel knows it. If Liz weren't the girl from the prophecy, Lillithiel could still be destroyed and you would kill her along with her legion of human shields."

No one speaks right away, processing Michael's conclusion. It's hard to disagree with someone who never lies. I'll never see him as my gloomy Chemistry lab partner ever again.

Zoë is the one to break the silence, "And yet, my question remains unanswered. Where did Ian and plan F come in?"

"Oh, that," Faye waves her hand dismissively. "Your plan was brilliant, don't get me wrong. I just kinda like having a back up," Faye explains sheepishly. "I knew the rules, no one else beside us could know about it. But I happen to know a few people that wouldn't mind helping Liz out, no questions asked."

Considering my angelic body guards, there can be no

doubt left in Lill's mind that I'm the one she's looking for. She won't hesitate to kill me next time.

"Right now, Lillithiel is the least of my concerns," Gabe addresses my inner thoughts, grabbing everyone's attention. "Abe is the biggest threat. He'll report to the underworld who you really are."

"No, he won't," Nate replies. "He's Lillithiel's lap dog. He and her minions will do or say whatever she orders them to."

"She has no interest in taking over the upper dimension," I offer, remembering her endless monologue. "She has her own agenda. Lill wants to rule the Earth realm." I meet Nate's eyes, "And you were supposed to be some sort of king, until you betrayed her, that is."

Michael makes a noise that sounds a lot like a suppressed laugh, but his expression gives nothing away.

"Good thing I made the right decision, then," Nate half jokes.

"But that's not all," I continue. "She truly believes that if she kills me, she'll become immortal."

Nate, Michael and Ariel turn to Zoë for confirmation. To my chagrin, she nods, "She's correct, killing Eliza will render her eternal. The prophecy works both ways."

"Huh?" Faye blurts out. "Are you saying that Liz will become immortal if she kills the evil skank?"

"That's not what she meant," Gabe replies. "Zoë is talking about the elemental children. Lillithiel's half siblings. She's the Spirit of them all. As long as they live, she can utilize their ascendancy of the elements: Air, Earth, Fire and Water. She doesn't know who they are, or where they are, but she's always able to tell if they're alive. If one is destroyed, she'll lose her affinity with that element. The Flower of Light can locate them in the midst of darkness. In the same way Liz is the light to Lillithiel's end, she's also her immortality."

Zoë adds quietly, "Not only would Lillithiel be eternal,

but also her siblings."

"I don't get it," Faye blurts out. "Does Lill want to kill Liz or give her to the underworld?"

"When this all started, she'd lure girls who fit the description straight to the gates of hell and back," Nate explains. "Nowadays, she's gotten cocky, just killing them left and right. She knows she's untouchable."

"*What?*" I let out in shock. "I'm not the first? How many others before me?"

"Finding you has been her obsession for a hundred years," Gabe replies in a serene tone.

"What are you saying?" I choke the words out. "Those girls died in my place. I should just kneel at Michael's feet and plea for him to take me away right now."

"No," Nate, Wellington and Faye voice as one.

"It's an option," comes Michael's reply. He ignores the glares and presses on, "But after tonight, I'm wearing the team colors. I'm determined to keep you alive."

"Yeah!" Ariel pumps her fist.

Michael shoots one of his dark looks at her for the interruption before continuing, "We're ending this." He leans over and rests his elbows on his knees, looking me straight-on. "And what do you say we start with Air?"

38

Zoë, Nate and Gabe stay behind to discuss my fate without me once again. Michael is the designated driver. He's driving us home through the empty streets of Boston at three in the morning. Wellington, Faye and I are compressed into the backseat while Ariel is riding shotgun. She keeps flipping through stations of the satellite radio to Michael's dismay. He drops off Wellington first.

"Thanks for the ride," Wellington turns to us. "I'll call you guys tomorrow."

He steps inside of his building, and we're off again. Faye is spending the night at my place, so we're next. It's only a couple blocks apart, and we're all real quiet until Michael pulls over in front of my apartment. We say goodnight and head upstairs.

Not wanting to wake my grandparents, we tiptoe inside the apartment. Grandpa is fast asleep on his brown leather reading chair. I grab Grandma's blanket from the sofa and cover him. Then, I quietly follow Faye upstairs.

Dominika is a true angel. She prepared the pullout bed for Faye. I'm exhausted. All the anticipation, the stress, the running and the revelations got me beat. So it's only a matter of how fast I can step out of this dress, get into my pajamas and hit the sack.

As it turns out, not as fast as I thought. Giving up on unzipping this thing, I drop face first into bed, dress and all. Faye comes back from the bathroom just then, forcing me back up, "You can't sleep in it. Your grandma won't like that."

She helps me unzip the gown, and I step into my comfy pj's, ready to fall back into bed. But Faye has other priorities, and they include me. She insists I remove my makeup, wash my face with some special soap from her pink toiletry bag, and do "the three steps." Since arguing with Faye is futile, I just do what she says.

Once my face has been washed, exfoliated, rinsed, drenched with toner, and moisturized. I'm allowed to brush my teeth before being dismissed. I throw myself into the comfort of my bed, pulling the blanket over me. I hear Faye's voice, but my eyes close before I can make sense of her words.

Next, I'm walking through what I sincerely hope to be a nightmare. I'm back in my dress with hair and makeup in place. The tinted glass doors slide closed behind me, and the two panthers stand right ahead. They roar, and I spin around. I attempt to pry the doors open with my fingernails, but they don't budge. The two tinted glass panes begin to fuse together, forming a solid wall of glass before my eyes.

Slowly turning around, I face the two beasts and gulp. They don't move, just sitting there. A bright light is coming from inside, but I'm too scared to walk past them. I let myself slide into a sitting position, still watching the panthers breathe in and out heavily a few feet away. The white panther yawns, and I get a glimpse of its long ivory fangs. The black one licks its gigantic paw with its enormous pink tongue. I shudder in fear, knowing well enough what I have to do. There's only one way out, and it's to follow the glowing light.

Hoping that I'll simply wake up, I wait and wait. If I

choose to stay put, never following the light, I'll eventually wake up in the morning, won't I? It's not like I can sleep forever. Is this how if feels to be comatose? Trapped in between? Maybe Lillithiel found her way into my dream world. That would be the worst kind of nightmare.

Just sitting here, watching the panthers watch me, it's like the hands of the clock have stopped entirely. I'm stuck in limbo. Frustrated by my cowardice, I stand up and one of the beasts blinks, the other yawns again. They must be as bored as I am.

"Good to know I'm not that interesting to you," I regret the words the second they leave my mouth. Now both animals are growling at me. Slowly, I take hesitant steps forward, studying the animals closely.

As I slip by the panthers, their hot breath hits me from both sides. I don't need to look at them to know they're facing me. My legs tremble, but I just keep walking. The distance I cover can't be more than ten feet, but it feels a lot longer.

Once I cross the threshold, I spot Nate sitting sideways at the very top step of the staircase. His back against the slats, one of his legs propped up. He's looking away, lost in his thoughts. Lifting the ends of my skirt with both hands, I quickly climb the steps toward him. Weirdly enough, my heels don't make a sound.

"Nate," I call out, when he doesn't seem to acknowledge me.

He turns his face in my direction and stands up when I reach the top. Without a word, he lifts me into a hug, and I wrap my arms around his neck. He lowers his lips to mine, kissing me softly.

"What took you so long?" Nate puts me down on my feet and takes hold of my hands.

"This place," I reply, following him back down the stairs. "I still don't know how I talked myself into coming back."

"Tell me about it. It's a black and white nightmare," Nate

agrees, leading me to the balcony. Outside, his eyes scan the empty night, and he asks, "Why here?"

"I thought you…" I trail off in confusion.

"No, Liz. This is your dream. Maybe you needed closure," Nate says, leading me down the stairs and out to the balcony.

The night is starry and the half moon appears to be smiling at us. Completely different from the dark and cloudy night I experienced earlier. A brisk breeze brushes the bare skin of my arms, invigorating and comforting me at the same time.

I turn to face him and hesitate, looking down at my feet. I want to see him in his true form once again, but I don't know how to ask.

"Liz," Nate whispers.

I lift my head and pull in a breath. Nate stands before me, arms hanging at his sides, and shirtless with his wings folded behind him. I blush and look away, embarrassed.

"I can't change the way I am," he says sadly. Whether to me, himself, or the universe, I can't assuredly tell.

I look back at him, "I wouldn't change a thing."

Nate tucks his hands in the pockets of his pants. He looks down at his feet and stands perfectly still as I walk around him. My eyes on the iridescent feathers of his dark wings, I stop behind him and take a step closer. Hesitantly, I lift my right hand to touch them, pulling it back fast as they slowly spread open before my touch. They're so beautiful, reminding me of the wings of a dark swan.

Nate looks at me over his shoulder, "Go ahead."

I take another hesitant step forward and run my fingers through his light velvety feathers. They're softer than I expected they would be. His body remains absolutely still, but his wings appear to have life of their own. They move involuntarily in a slow motion flap.

"Does it bother you?" I ask, pulling my hand away.

"Not a bit," he replies in a low soft voice. "I'd compare it to touching the ends of your hair."

"So, you can't feel it," I pull a feather out.

"Ouch!" He lets out, and I don't know if he's kidding or not.

"I'm so sorry," I step back. "I thought –"

"I'm just messing with you," Nate spins around with a huge smile on his face.

He pulls me firmly toward him and kisses me like never before. Our bodies compress, lips longingly entwined. Nothing matters anymore, but being here lost in his gentle kiss. His fingers caress the back of my neck, interweaving with my hair. I wrap my arms tighter around him and he responds by holding me firmly, his hand moving gently up and down my back. I could keep kissing him forever. Breathing in comparison becomes a distant second priority. I wish we could live within this dream, our kiss never ending.

But wishes are rarely granted and eventually we break apart. My heart is overwhelmed, and his eyes appear to reflect my feelings. He leaves his arms around me, keeping me pulled close. I rest my head against his chest and let my eyelids fall shut, wanting nothing more than to prolong this moment.

"We've been here too long," Nate whispers against my hair. "It's a wonder you're still here with me. I keep waiting for you to vanish from my arms."

He pulls me closer, kissing me again. When he tries to let me go, I cling to him.

I don't want to wake up.

"You have to," Nate voices inside my mind.

My eyes open, "Do I really?"

"Staying here is not an option. Life happens when you're awake," Nate says quietly. "Besides, I need to check on something, and I'll be gone for awhile."

"Where are you going?" I pull back to look him in the face.

"Down," Nate replies flatly. "I need to do some damage

control after Lill's public scandal."

"How long will you be gone?"

"Not long. It'll fly by," Nate reassures me. "You'll have a lot to keep you busy. Now close your eyes and let your mind drift back into your body," he whispers in my ear in his hypnotic voice, giving me goosebumps.

The scene goes black, and my eyelids flutter slowly open. I'm hugging my pillow and immediately push it away. With a yawn, I sit up in my bed.

Faye navigates the internet with my tablet, sitting with her legs crossed on the corner chair. She's fully dressed, makeup applied to perfection. She looks up at me, "Finally!"

"Morning, Faye," I lean back against the headboard.

She stands up and squeezes beside me, forcing me to inch over. She holds the tablet for both of us to see and touches play, "Watch this."

On the screen, Lill is in Michael's face: "...crashing my party is low even for you," she announces overly dramatic for the benefit of the onlookers.

"I couldn't miss the party of the millennium," Michael stares daggers at her.

"Aw, how adorable. After all these years, you're still obsessed with me," she lifts her right hand to touch his face and he abruptly grabs her wrist. Her other hand swings to slap him, but he catches it with his left. She tries to shake her arms free unsuccessfully, her eyes fuming in rage. A wave of red swings up as her knee thrusts upward, Michael checks her kick with his own knee. She hisses at Michael, "I want you and your friends out of my party this very instant."

"That's just what I was waiting to hear," Michael gives her a cavalier smile.

Just then Ariel steps in, pulling Michael away by his tie. "We're out of here," Ariel announces, dragging him through the crowd.

Lillithiel shrieks, "Security!"

The video stops and twelve little preview squares appear

as related videos. It's the same scene recorded from a slightly different vantage point. I glance down at the title: *Lill Sinclair kicks out party crashers.*

Just this one angle has thirty-seven thousand views and five hundred and nineteen likes. I scroll down to read the top comments. It's amazing how even when she's clearly humiliated, there's nothing but love and compliments for her.

I look out the window, "What time is it?" It's raining and dark outside.

"It's five p.m. You slept the entire day," Faye rolls her eyes.

"You're kidding, right?" I sit up straight. "Where's Grandma?"

"Your grandparents left early this morning, but you were still asleep. She said we could order pizza, and they'd be back late from their charity event."

"Why didn't you wake me up?" I ask politely, happy that she didn't.

"You had this cute smile on your face. I didn't want to bother you," Faye shrugs. "Besides, you deserve some rest. You've been through a lot, and there's a lot more to come."

"What do you mean?" I ask intrigued. "What do you know that I don't?"

"There's another plan in the works. But, I can't talk about it. You know why," Faye explains, tapping the side of her head.

Not again...

39

When Faye said two weeks ago there's more to come, she wasn't kidding.

Wellington is trapped, and so am I. They're coming from all sides, some of them have little ugly monsters bursting up out of their heads. Wellington and I are surrounded, standing back to back. I keep shooting and missing. Wellington is taking forever to reload his guns. That's it, we're doomed.

I shout in despair, "Faster, faster... We are about to die here."

"I'm doing my best. It would help if you quit kicking and shoot instead, you know."

At that exact moment, one of them grabs me and I can't free myself from his hold. Before Wellington has a chance to help, my phone starts vibrating. A split second distraction that makes the screen go black, and bloody letters appear, "*You are dead.*"

I sigh, pick up my phone and answer, "Thanks a lot Faye! You just got us killed."

"What are you talking about? Who died?" Faye asks from the other side of the line.

"Leon and Jill," I reply.

"Who?" Faye asks confused.

"Never mind that, it's just a game Wellington and I were playing," I explain dismissively. "What's up?"

"It figures. You two need to stop being such geeks, you're ruining my reputation," Faye jokes. "We're meeting at Michael's apartment. I'll be downstairs in five to pick you guys up."

"We'll be there," I reply, hanging up the phone.

"Be where?" Wellington asks.

"Downstairs, Faye is giving us a ride to Michael's place," I reply.

Thirty-five minutes later we're at Michael's apartment on Revere Beach Boulevard. Gabe sits there right where we left him two weeks ago. Same hat, same faded clothes, same beat up sneakers, different shirt.

Just as we sit down, Nate strolls in and tosses a manila envelope on the center table, announcing, "Just so we're clear, I don't approve of this strategy."

"I think we got the point the first twenty times you said that," Zoë's voice sounds tired.

"And yet, the plan is still in motion," Nate retorts sarcastically.

"The only reason you don't like the plan is because it doesn't require your presence," Ariel points out.

"That's not why," Nate disagrees. "I don't approve because it doesn't have a safety net."

"I like it. It's ingenious, if you ask me," Ariel contests. "Besides, it's totally different this time. She won't be walking into a trap. She'll be the one setting it."

Gabe does a head count, "Where's Spark?"

"Feeding, she'll be here soon," Nate informs bluntly.

"And Ken?" Gabe's question is directed to Ariel.

"He's not coming. He's back in Japan," Ariel replies. "He's keeping a close watch on Mr. and Mrs. O'Neill, just in case Lillithiel has any ideas."

"Just like last time, the plan goes awry before it even starts," Nate murmurs cynically under his breath.

"And yet, you're still on board," Zoë remarks pointedly at him.

"And he will be. As long as Liz is involved he will stick around. He loves her," Michael voices out of the blue.

"Look who is feeling talkative today," Nate says sarcastically.

"Can we bring Liz up to speed now?" Zoë asks, nudging the conversation back on topic. "Or should we wait for Spark?"

"Spark is already in on it," Nate shrugs. "And I'll be here to keep her in line."

"Alright," Zoë begins. "Before we start though, I want to know how things went with your sister, Nathaniel."

"You of all people should know Lillithiel is not my sister," Nate points out in a low annoyed voice.

"She's not?" Faye asks with fake surprise.

"Do you see a resemblance?" Nate shoots her an inquiring look.

Faye studies him, as if really considering it. Then, she shrugs, "You're both easy on the eyes."

Nate ignores her and turns back to Zoë, "Lillithiel is on probation. The underworld isn't very keen on having to clean up after her. She has a month to prove her theory or they'll drop it. While I was there, I checked the A.O.T. for any entries linking Raphael to Liz and found none. It's as if he hadn't been to North America for centuries. All of which made for a compelling case against Lill. They ate it raw."

"I guess we're in the clear," Ariel beams.

"I wouldn't say that. Lill is bent on proving me wrong," Nate doesn't sound as confident as Ariel.

"But she won't get the chance to because our plan will work," Ariel reassures.

"You guys didn't even ask Liz if she's up to it. I have a feeling she won't be," Nate points out simply, and all eyes turn in my direction.

"I didn't know I had a choice," I say amazed that they

even suggested it.

"There's always a choice," Miss Wisdom, aka Zoë, informs me.

Gee, let me think. Go along with the plan or stay and wait for Lill to kill me. There's not much of a choice if you ask me.

"I'll sidetrack them. I'm good at it. You don't need to do anything," Nate assures me, tuned in to my thoughts.

"Nathaniel," Gabe reprehends.

"It's okay. I want to do it," I reply and squeeze his hand.

He looks away, seeming vexed by my decision yet again. But I don't have time to dwell on it because Zoë starts without missing a beat, "Liz, you'll be traveling with Ariel to Bora Bora to meet Raphael." She stops, studying me closely.

"And how is she gonna pull that off?" Faye asks, voicing exactly what I was wondering.

A knock on the door interrupts our discussion, and Gabe calls out, "Come on in, Spark. Perfect timing."

She's in her ultraviolet form, gorgeous and lethal. Faye squirms beside me, taken aback. Until now, she had no idea Spark was a demon. Wellington squints at her, as if he's trying to see Saint Pete's Spark beneath the glamor.

"Spark will play a pivotal role in this," Gabe says, gesturing in her direction.

Spark shifts her weight from one combat boot to the other, not seeming exceedingly comfortable under the spotlight.

"You said she's a succubus, didn't you?" Wellington whispers.

I nod, and his lips slightly curl up with understanding. I frown at him and ask, "What?"

"She will be you," he explains in a rushed tone.

"What?" Faye and I ask at the same time.

"He's right," Gabe informs us. "Spark will play your part while you're away."

"How did you know that?" I ask Wellington, leaning over Faye.

"Yeah, how do you know all this stuff?" Faye inquires.

"RPGs," Wellington whispers with a shrug.

Spark hears him and chastises, sounding a lot like the Spark we know, "Hey there, *Cello Boy*. Just so we're clear. I don't have horns or a tail. This is my true form."

Wellington's eyes widen and his lips part, followed by the barely audible words, "You're the girl from Dad's bookstore."

Spark smiles, apparently pleased to be recognized. I study her closer just to realize he's right. She's the same girl, porcelain skin, violet eyes, and dressed all in black. How didn't I put two and two together? *"Probably because she was smashing face with your boyfriend,"* a little voice inside me points out. I'm awestruck. Was she after me back then? Or was she trying to get close to my friends?

Wellington leans forward, resting his elbows on his knees, "I guess it's safe to say you do know Aramaic then."

Spark winks at him and turns back to Gabe, "So lets get this over with."

Understanding dawns, I blurt out in disbelief, "Let me get this straight. While I'm in Bora Bora with Ariel, Spark will be taking my tests, doing my homework and playing Helen of Troy in my place." I face Nate and half joke, "Tell me again why I wouldn't like this plan."

"How about the part where I'll be making out with your boyfriend?" Spark asks cynically. "Do you still like the plan?" Leave it to Spark to burst my bubble.

"Easy, Spark," Nate reprehends, and she crosses her arms with a scowl.

Zoë turns her attention to Wellington and Faye, "The two of you will keep her company to maintain the facade. Just hang out with Spark as if she were Liz."

Faye nods, but Wellington looks conflicted, a furrow forms between his eyebrows.

"What is it?" I ask him.

"He figured it out," Spark replies with a menacing smile on her face.

"Blake, what is she talking about?" Faye asks narrowing her eyes at him.

"Shall I explain? Or will you do the honors?" Spark inquires to no one in particular.

"It might be unpleasant," Zoë clarifies kindly. "But not damaging."

"There's nothing unpleasant about a kiss," Spark bites her lower lip. "You might find it quite pleasurable."

"Forget it. I'm not kissing her," I shake my head vehemently.

"It's just a kiss," Spark taunts.

I cover my mouth with both hands, still shaking my head.

"Fair enough," Spark points out and turns to Gabe. "Leaving now," and with that, she's out the door.

"Nathaniel," Zoë looks him straight-on, and they commence in one of their staring contests, a dead giveaway that they're communicating via telepathy.

Nate heaves a sigh and stands up, "I'll talk to her," rushing outside.

After the door closes, the room falls silent. You can hear a pin drop, it's so quiet.

Did I just ruin everything?

Just then, Nate returns alone, taking his place beside me. He squeezes my hand with a solemn expression on his face. "I guess the plan is off," I remark, squeezing his hand back.

"Now what?" Nate asks to no one in particular.

They look to one another and Wellington asks, "I have a question, is there a way Raphael can come to Boston without appearing in the A.O.T.?"

Gabe raises an eyebrow, before explaining, "It'd be too much of a giveaway..."

Nate starts playing with my hair, and I take hold of his hand. I want to hear Gabe's reasoning, but Nate's caress is very distracting. I turn to shoot him a look as if to say "not here" just as he leans over and sinks in a kiss.

I drift off, and a shiver runs down my spine. His kiss deepens, making me self-conscious since we're not alone. Try as I might, I can't seem to pull away. The kiss feels odd, though. *Different.* Something is wrong.

Then, he breaks the kiss abruptly, saying in a raspy voice, "Now, that wasn't so bad, was it?"

My eyes open to find Spark's face a few inches from mine. By reflex, I push her away with such force that she flies across the room and lands hard on her butt near the hallway.

"*Whoa!*" Wellington exclaims, his voice tinted with surprise and concern.

Startled by my own violent outburst, I stand up and rush toward her, offering my hand, "I'm so sorry. I didn't mean to..." I trail off.

Spark takes my hand and gets to her feet. "It's okay, Angel Girl. I like it rough."

I turn to see Nate leaning against the wall, but I just look away. For once, I'm not in the mood to see his face.

"I owe you an apology," Zoë steals my attention. "It was my idea. You wouldn't do it any other way, and we're running out of time."

"Did it hurt?" Faye asks in concern.

I shake my head. It didn't hurt, it just felt weird. That's all.

"So, what now?" I ask.

"Now, I do this," Spark says smugly. Her face changes shape, her hair shifts from straight black to curly blond and her eyes fade from violet to green.

Suddenly, I'm staring into a mirror. Faye gasps audibly, and Wellington just blinks nervously. I, however, might never be able to speak again.

I have a real-life clone.

40

Before today, I've never even considered going to Bora Bora. It's one of those surreal places that seems perfect, but out of reach. Not entirely beyond the bounds, but entirely out of the way. Thirty-three hours. Give or take a few. That's how long it will take us to get there.

Ariel and I will fly to LA where we'll take a connection to Papeete, French Polynesia. From there, we'll take another connecting flight to Bora Bora.

I let out an exaggerated sigh.

"Not so thrilled anymore, I see," Spark comments sarcastically, her voice exactly like mine, but in a tone I never imagined coming out of my mouth.

She's right, of course, but not for the reasons she may think. I'm nervous about turning my life over to her. Spark will be living in my room, a succubus demon under my grandparent's roof. Not only that, I'm handing her the power to ruin my life. The more I think about it, the more torn I become. But then again, I wouldn't have a life to be ruined if Raph hadn't saved me. In a way, I'm living on borrowed time. So, it's the least I can do.

Staying here is not an option, I'll be a sitting duck and

everyone around me would be targeted. I turn to Nate, "You know, people will realize that she's not me sooner or later."

"Well, you better hurry back then," says Nate.

"That's it. I need a cigarette," Spark stands up and makes her way to the balcony.

"Hey," I call out, standing up to follow her. "You can't smoke in my body."

"FYI, Angel Girl. It's my body, and I'll do whatever I want with it," Spark looks over her shoulder at me.

I'm too annoyed to argue and just blink at her.

"Spark. Stop tormenting her," Nate reprehends in a tired voice. He's still keeping his distance, probably sensing I haven't gotten over the stunt they pulled on me.

Spark ignores his remark and strolls out just the same.

Wow! She can make even my tall awkward body look sensual.

"Patience is a virtue," Nate murmurs under his breath and adds for my benefit, "Don't worry. She'll be on her best behavior. I won't let her out of my sight." He walks to the center table and takes out two passports from the manila envelope. He hands one to me and the other to Ariel.

She opens it and reads aloud, "Aria Ellenore Smith," she looks up from the document. "Really, Nathaniel? Was that the best you could come up with?"

"Smith is a common name," Nate replies defensively.

I open mine, and it reads, "Elizabeth Claire Smith."

"Why do they even need tickets and passports? Can't you just teleport Liz to Bora Bora? You read minds, invade people's dreams, learn how to drive stick in five seconds... You're angels for crying out loud, don't tell me that teleportation isn't on your long list of abilities," Faye inquires, crossing her arms as if making a point.

"I think it has something to do with the Athenaeum of Transgressions," Wellington half whispers.

"Correct," Zoë confirms simply.

"What the flip is that?" Faye asks. "And how do you

know about it?"

"Blake knows too much for his own good," Nate replies. "But he's right. Whenever ethereal powers are used in this realm, it's a huge red flag. Therefore, a traditional mean of travel it is."

"If we hope to reach Raphael anytime soon, we better get going," Ariel points out, wheeling in two hot pink carry-on size suitcases.

"We're leaving right now?" I blurt out. "Can I stop and pick up a few things for the trip?"

"No, you can't," Gabe replies. "You have to leave your life behind. Don't forget, you'll still be here while you're away."

Ariel hands Nate the keys to the Mustang, "Care to drive us to the airport? I'm sure you'd like to see Liz off."

Nate nods once, and my heart tightens inside my chest. Will Nate still be around when I come back? He'll have no reason to stick around once this is over. Michael said Nate loves me, and he can't lie. Still, there are different kinds of love. It doesn't mean that Nate is *in* love with me. What does the archangel of destruction know about love anyway? For all I know, he'll just go back to whatever he did before Lill dragged him into her obsession. Either way, I shouldn't be mad at him for tricking me. It was Zoë's idea, not his. I should savor which might very well be our last moments together. Besides, I don't want my last kiss from him to be from Spark. I give him a conciliatory smile and he nods in accord.

Gabe stands up and we all follow suit. I look down and play with the zipper on my powder blue hoodie out of sheer nervousness. Faye approaches me and throws both arms around my neck, pulling me into a hug. Wellington does the same. They both seem at a loss for words.

"Are we done here?" Spark asks, returning from the balcony, summoned by the commotion.

"Leave your phone with Spark," says Gabe.

Reluctantly, I pull the phone from my pocket and run my fingers across the screen. Then, I take a deep breath before handing over the last connection I have to my world.

Nate tosses his key fob in her direction, and she catches it, "What do you want me to do with this?"

"Drive the car straight home," Nate instructs.

"Whatever," she replies, shoves my phone in her back pocket and starts toward the door.

"And Spark, don't forget to be at the O'Neills before curfew," Nate says as an after thought.

"Shoot me now," Spark groans.

Ariel puts a hand on my shoulder, "Come on, travel buddy."

I take one last look at my friends and force an assured nod. Then, I follow Ariel and Nate out the front door, wheeling my carry-on behind me. We pile into the elevator, and Nate pushes the G button. Hesitantly, I hook my pinky to Nate's, and he responds by interlocking his fingers to mine with a squeeze. A ding sound announces our arrival at ground level, and we gather around Michael's black Mustang. Ariel climbs into the back seat, allowing me to ride beside Nate. Then, we're off, driving to the airport at sunset.

The traffic is intolerable. It's rush hour on a Friday, and everybody wants to get somewhere. It takes us twice as long to reach Logan International as it would by metro. By the time we arrive, we've got less than twenty minutes before the flight departs. Not nearly enough time to say a proper goodbye to Nate.

"Go on, Angel Girl," Nate says quietly when I cling to him, unable to let go. Knowing that when I do, I might never see him again. Nate leans over and brushes his lips to mine. I kiss him back, just as Ariel returns with a stack of boarding passes.

"We really have to go," she announces when we break apart.

"Don't worry, you'll be back before you can even miss

me," Nate runs his hand against my cheek.

"Liar. You know I miss you already."

"The only thing you're gonna miss is the flight if we don't get moving," Ariel tugs my arm, breaking us apart. "Come on, Liz."

Torn and holding back tears, I grab the handle of my carry-on and rush to catch up with Ariel. Over my shoulder, I take one last look at Nate, trying to capture a mental picture to remember him by. Then, I follow Ariel through security after throwing Nate one last kiss.

We're flying first class, courtesy of Nate and his no limit credit card. Apparently, being the fallen angel of deceit has its monetary perks. Still, there aren't enough movies, magazines, books, or snacks to make the hours pass faster. I wish I could have brought my tablet, a game or something. Three words are enough to describe myself right now: anxious, lovesick and bored.

Some people can sleep on planes. I'm not one of them. Ariel, however, is. *So much for being my travel buddy.* Ever since take off she's been sound asleep, waking up only for our connection in LA, then right back to sleep. The only practical advantage of traveling with a real life angel thus far has been the enthusiastic assistance. Not even once have we had to wrestle our luggage in or out of the overhead compartment. Men step on each other to lend a helping hand. Women stare at her shamelessly, some with admiration and others feeling sour grapes. There is also the look of puzzlement as if they were trying to remember which movie or magazine they might have seen her in.

She wakes up just as we touch down for our final connection and happily stretches her arms, looking refreshed. Now that she's all revitalized and blissful, I'm hopeful she'll stay awake through our next flight so I'll have some company. But, she doesn't. Her eyelids fall closed in mid-sentence the moment the plane breaks through the clouds, and she's fast asleep once again. *Sigh.* I guess it's back to browsing the SkyMall.

When we finally land in Bora Bora, my legs are stiff. My head is swimming and my feet are probably stuck inside my Converse permanently. I'm completely zapped of energy. We departed Boston Logan International on Friday at six thirty-seven p.m. Now, it's eight thirty-four a.m. on a Sunday. "Beat" is an understatement.

Just as we step outside, I realize we're not driving to Raph's via taxi. No, we're catching a freaking launch boat, which means another fifteen minute ride across a lagoon to reach Raph's over-water bungalow. But even feeling drained, I have to admire how beautiful Bora Bora is. It's warm, about eighty degrees, and a refreshing breeze moves over us. The people here are hospitable and speak English with a unique accent. As we board the boat, however, Ariel takes the opportunity to practice her Tahitian, speaking to the crew like a native.

It's no wonder Raph chooses to take residence here. Paradise can't be much different from this. If I had to pick one word to describe this utopia, it would be "blue." From the cloudless morning sky above to the deepest lagoon, shades of blue saturate the scene.

As we dock, Raph is there waiting for us. He looks no different in my waking life than he does in my dreams. As always, he's dressed for the setting, wearing a white shirt with rolled up sleeves, white beach pants and sandals. His smile is welcoming and familiar. His eyes are as blue as the water surrounding us. He's golden tan under the sunlight, but still ethereal somehow. I can't help but smile back at him. Raph opens his arms wide, and I run to his embrace, abandoning my luggage on the dock. Hugging him in real life feels a lot like hugging my dad, safe and comforting.

"And so we meet," are his first words to me.

"It's been a long time, stranger," Ariel greets, right before he pulls her into a gentle and caring embrace.

We walk with Raph across the sundeck to his island flat.

The place is open and airy, sparsely decorated with mahogany furniture that looks as sturdy as it does heavy. The view is astounding, and the calm breeze moves quietly over the turquoise water, flowing through the sliding doors and windows. There are three bedrooms, including Raph's. They're all identical and mostly empty, apart from the canopy beds.

I turn to Raph, "It's so beautiful. The prettiest place I've ever seen. From now on, I'll meet you here in my dreams."

"I particularly enjoy the peace and quiet," Raph replies smiling at me.

"So, what now? How does that GPS thing work?" I ask, taking a seat on a wooden chair.

"First, you need some rest," Raph sounds amused. "It's not as easy as you may think. We both need to be fully rested and clear of mind. That's why I chose this place."

"Great choice, by the way," Ariel comments, sitting down in the chair next to me. Then, she looks me straight-on, "And you *really* need some sleep. You've been up for two days."

"Go rest, Liz. Tomorrow we begin to prepare," he pauses as if recalling something and then goes on playfully, "For the GPS thing."

I toss the little beige pillow I had in my lap at Raph, and it bounces off him without a blink, "What do you mean by prepare?"

"We need to get your soul in synchronicity with my spectrum," he explains in his familiar calm and collected voice. "Nothing else can occupy your thoughts. That is the only way. But don't worry about it. I'll guide you when the time comes."

I nod and head to my designated bedroom, leaving the angels to do whatever it is that angels do. I refresh for a nap and lie down. Before even feeling the soft pillow under my head, I'm out.

When I wake up, the sky behind the palm trees is purplish

gold, the colors of the evening reflecting in the lagoon. I wander around the bungalow and find Raph and Ariel sitting outside precisely where I left them. I guess when you're immortal time doesn't mean the same as it does for us mere mortals.

"Hey, look who's awake?" Ariel jokes, looking up at me.

"What time is it?" I ask, feeling groggy and disoriented.

"Don't worry about the time. How do you feel?" Raph studies me carefully.

"Rested, I guess," I reply, and my stomach growls to remind me that I'm also hungry. So, I add, "Starving."

While I nibble on some tropical fruit, they explain what the coming days will involve. It's called "cognitive diffraction," not "GPS thing," by the way. Basically, I need to reset, reboot, or as Raph put it, "To achieve mental tranquility through requiescence." And we will be starting when the sun rises.

At dawn, I find myself once again being asked to clear my mind. One might think that would be an easy task. What's there to do? You just sit there and don't think. Not quite. It's a tall order for me. I can't sit still for extended periods of time. I'm even worse at regulating my thoughts. I'm so bad in fact that we're going on, by my mental count, three days with no progress at all. Mostly, I'm irked by Spark assuming my identity. Try as I might, it's hard to forget a succubus is hanging around my family and friends.

Raph does his best to comfort me by pointing out, "The more you torment yourself, the longer it will take."

I gulp, well aware of what he means by that: Spark's tenure as me will be extended.

It's just the motivation I need. After a few more days of sitting and staring at the turquoise waters of Bora Bora, I clear my mind just enough to be in harmony with Raph's. I seem to be finally tuning into the same wavelength as him, like we're reaching a harmonic balance.

In the morning, Raph suggests we give it a try. But any

hope I had that it would work is swiftly swept away, just like a sand castle at high tide. After a full day of attempts, all we manage to do is exhaust Ariel's aegis. Nothing happened. *Nada.* I never thought you could exert yourself by simply attempting to keep a clear mind. But it's possible alright. I'm exhausted. It's like I've run a marathon, opposed to spending an entire day sitting around.

We keep trying one morning after another. It takes us countless frustrating attempts until we finally make the slightest progress. Ariel appears to have it the worst. It can't be easy to summon all that energy to shield us day after day. By now, I've lost track of how long we've been here. I'm in a timeless paradise, getting a glimpse of what it means to be eternal.

The following day, I wake up before dawn to a light breeze coming from my opened window. I stretch, roll out of bed and step out onto the deck to watch the sunrise. Taking a seat outside, I inhale deeply and enjoy the gradual blend from night to day.

Raph arrives with the sun and takes the empty chair beside me. Without a word, he takes hold of my hands, and I close my eyes. The golden rays of morning light flash orange behind my eyelids and something different happens. An overwhelming warmth emerges from my pores, engulfing every inch of my skin. My eyes remain shut, but inexplicably a transparent yellow shield covering my body is visible from behind my eyelids. The translucent fibers within the light emanating from my skin begin to entwine with crystalline strands emerging from Raph. Together they bind into a blindly golden cocoon as if sheltering us from the universe.

Then, it starts. Luminous blocks build into walls, quickly assuming distinct shapes. All of a sudden, it's like we're right in the middle of a three dimensional holographic simulation of a claustrophobic bedroom. There are books all over the place, ashtrays filled with bent cigarette butts, and two empty bento boxes with the chopsticks inside them. An unmade futon bed occupies most of the room, on it a pile of clothes, more books, and an empty Saké bottle. There is a laptop computer on a desk hooked up to an external monitor. The screen is blank and a little green light blinks on its bezel. Beside the computer, more books are piled up, but I can't read their titles. They're written in Kanji. It looks like a very disorganized college kid's bedroom.

As soon as I reach that conclusion we're outside. People traverse down the sidewalk in a rushed pace without paying us any notice. They must know we're standing here, as no one has walked through us yet. The glow of neon signs illuminate the street, and we're right in front of a golden Shinto statue with English words written at its base, reading, "Billiken Things-As-They." A yellow paper lantern hangs right above us, and it's safe to say we're somewhere in Japan.

Suddenly, we're observing from sky level, and almost immediately I know where we are. I'd be able to recognize the Green Mall in Osaka from any angle. Dad, Suri and I came here right before I moved to Boston. Its architecture is so unique and elaborate that it's impossible to mistake it for any other place.

Next, we're floating over the entire country, looking down from orbit, like a satellite. In the blink of an eye, we're floating away from Earth into the aether. Then, it's like we're pulled into a black hole. I open my eyes startled.

Raph opens his eyes much more calmly than I did and looks up at me with a serene smile, "You did it, Liz. We know where to find Asmodeus' spawn."

"Osaka, Japan," I smile back, feeling energized. I'm overtaken by a feeling of triumph, which is new for me. "Now what?"

"We're going to Osaka," Ariel says, joining us outside. She sits at Raph's feet and finishes, "Once we're there, we'll wait for Michael and Raphael to arrive."

"How will Michael know?" I ask, considering we are to remain in isolation.

"My mind is connected to Gabe," Raph explains. "He knew the moment I did."

A thought crosses my mind, and I frown.

"Is there a problem?" Raph's smile leaves his face.

"I didn't see a picture, a name, a face... All I know is how to get there," I elaborate my concerns. "How can we be sure that Asmodeus' creature lives there?"

Raph's smile returns just as quickly, and his voice is almost a whisper, "Trust me, we'll find her."

Her, not him. I follow Raph back inside, wondering how on Earth he knows that?

41

About thirty-two hours later, Ariel and I are landing in Tokyo, Japan. Once again, she slept the entire flight. Now she's all bubbly and excited, talking the entire time as we head to buy our tickets to Osaka.

I follow close behind her, dragging my feet all the way. I'm so tired that I don't see my dad and Suri walking toward us until it's too late. Lucky for me, Ariel does and gives me a little push out of the way. She distracts my dad with an Oscar winning performance while I duck behind a pillar. I brace myself for them to notice me, my ears on high alert. Suri complains under her breath in Japanese, and I suppress a giggle.

"Oh my goodness, it's you, isn't it? You're Dave O'Neill. I'm your biggest fan. I simply could not live without your genius contribution to our systematic computational world," Ariel babbles. "May I have your autograph? I know I have a pen in here somewhere..." She trails off, digging through the outer pocket of her carry-on.

"David, sweetheart, we need to get going," Suri cuts in, taking the opening.

"Here," Ariel straightens up and hands Dad a pen and a

magazine. "Would you mind signing this for me?"

I wish so darned badly that I could see their faces right now. I don't think anybody ever asked for Dad's autograph before. I'm fighting real hard not to crack up and blow my cover.

"Sure," Dad replies awkwardly, his voice full of uncertainty.

"Thank you so much," Ariel takes the magazine and pen from Dad's hand. "You're too kind. And you're much more handsome in person. Did anybody ever tell you that you look like Christian Bale? Because you really do."

"Oh, thank you," Dad says with uneasiness tinting his voice. "We just landed from an international flight, and we need to get going. But it was nice meeting you ..." He lets his voice trail, not knowing her name.

"Nice meeting you too, Mr. O'Neill," Ariel calls after them since Suri is pretty much dragging Dad away. Suri is obviously steaming. Dad waves back over his shoulder, laughing to himself, probably wondering where this girl came from.

"That was hilarious. They must have just returned from Boston..." My voice trails off in sudden realization. Dad and Suri just got back from Thanksgiving with my grandparents and my succubus clone. I just hope Spark didn't do anything outrageous.

Ariel notices my sudden change of mood, "What's wrong?"

I shake my head, not wanting to talk about it. No reason to dwell on things I can't control. I need to focus on what's to come, destroying this evil spawn and reclaiming my life.

If Michael is right, and he usually is, once this is all over my family and friends will be safe. No one can say for sure Lill won't be searching for another Flower of Light. From the few minutes I spent with her, I can guarantee she won't give up that easily. Nate disagrees, however. He says Lill isn't as menacing without her backup army, and she'll lose

435

them the instant the underworld finds out she was wrong about me. I'll be safe, and so will everyone else.

If only there were a way we could end this once and for all. No other innocent girl would be at risk ever again. But, the idea is impossible even inside my head. Spark couldn't be me for several months in a row. From what they told me, Spark won't last a month disguised as me full time. They gave us twenty-five days tops. Succubi need to shift back to demon form to feed, and there's only so long Spark can assume my identity before it starts to fade. Even so, Spark wouldn't stand for it.

The flight to Osaka is short compared to our last one. It's an hour and a half, and we easily make our way out of the airport. The weather on the street is dreadfully cold. Especially after all the time we spent at a place with almost double the temperature. It's forty-three degrees and windy here. So when we finally manage to secure a cab, I can't get inside fast enough.

On the way to the hotel, I take in the streets of Osaka. It's almost night time, past rush hour. We stop at a red light, and my eyes follow the people speed walking across the pedestrian crosswalk. As usual, I'm amazed by the tempo change between different places.

It takes us about fifteen minutes to reach the hotel we're staying at, and the cab driver pulls over. He kindly helps us with our luggage and slightly bows before taking his place behind the wheel and driving away.

One of the uniformed doormen steps up to assist us. He places our luggage onto a cart and wheels it inside. He waits while we check in and then guides us to our room. Ariel hands him a tip, and he quietly bows before leaving us to our own devices.

Our room has a classic décor in shades of yellow, and it's so high up that we have a splendid view of Osaka. The position of the beds allows us to look out the window at the city lights. After almost forty hours awake, any flat surface is a welcomed luxury, and it's becoming difficult to keep up with Ariel's conversation.

When her soft voice calls my name, I open my eyes to a sunny morning. The day light pours in the window and illuminates the entire room. I must have fallen asleep while she was talking to me last night. I don't feel as bad as I should about it, though. She certainly had no qualms about sleeping countless hours while I sat talking to myself on the plane.

"Are you hungry?" Ariel repeats, probably for the second or third time since I awoke.

I yawn, sit up straight in bed and nod.

"Great," she pulls her hair up with a clip, looking more like a celebrity in disguise than ever. "Michael and Raphael are already downstairs for breakfast. If we hurry, maybe we'll still catch them."

"*They're here?*" I inquire. "When did they arrive?"

"They showed up in the middle of the night," Ariel relays. "You were sleeping. So we decided to wait until morning. There wasn't much we could do then anyways."

Just the knowledge that Michael is in the same building prompts me to jump out of bed. I can't get ready fast enough. I've never been so anxious to talk with someone as I am now. I've had no updates from home since I left, and Michael has been there the entire time. I have so many questions, I don't even know where to start.

Downstairs, Michael sits alone in an isolated corner. As we approach he looks up, and I smile so widely that he does a double take, saying, "I can safely say that no mortal has ever been so eager to see me before."

Michael in a good mood? That's new. I take advantage and ask, "How is everybody?"

"Everyone is fine," he replies simply. Using chopsticks, he skillfully brings a Tamagoyaki bite to his mouth and takes his time chewing the tiny rolled omelet. If it were Nate instead of Michael, I'd say he's testing my patience. But since it's Michael, he's clearly enjoying his breakfast. He catches me staring and quickly takes a sip of water before saying, "I'm sorry. I should elaborate a little. Spark is doing well enough. I stopped by at your place the day after Thanksgiving to touch base. I met your father and Suri while I was there." He stops and shakes his head.

"What is it?" I press, filled with anticipation. I'm fighting the urge not to grab him by the collar of his dark blue shirt and shake it out of him. Even though, I saw them just yesterday, the question blurts out of my mouth, "What happened?"

"I can assure you that everyone is in perfect health," he replies as calm as ever.

"And he should know," Ariel remarks in a bemused voice. The two of them exchange looks as if sharing an inside joke. For once, I get it.

The waitress stops at our table to take our order. But I've been too distracted to even check the menu. So, I order what he's having: Tamagoyaki, rice bread and water. When the waitress scurries away, I ask, "If everything is fine, why did you react so oddly when you mentioned them?"

He breaks a piece of rice bread and shoves it into his mouth. Again, he calmly chews and takes another sip of water before finally replying with a question, "Did I act weird?"

I just glare at him.

"I did then," he concludes, shaking his head again at the memory.

The waitress returns with the food and distributes it across the table. I'm dying to know what happened, but too annoyed to press the issue. He clearly doesn't want to talk about it. I'll ask Grandma when I get home. Better yet, I'll email Suri. She'll tell me.

"I'm curious now," Ariel surprises me by asking. "What happened?"

"Suri is a very perceptive person," Michael replies

between bites. "She picked up on some things. But there's nothing to worry about. I'm not so certain Suri approves of you and Nate."

It's my turn to bite and chew. I always joked about Suri having some sort of sixth sense, who would guess that I was right after all.

"Interesting," Ariel says thoughtfully. "It makes me wonder how she reacted to your presence."

"Intriguingly, she seemed to like me well enough," Michael replies simply.

I have a thousand more questions, but Raph joins us then, putting an end to the small talk. He jumps right in, bringing Ariel and I up to speed. We keep our voices low as to not call attention to ourselves, speaking vaguely to prevent any eavesdropping. Once we're all done eating, Raph suggests that we should gather to talk specifics in privacy.

"How do you know for sure it's a female spawn? All we saw was a cluttered bedroom," I inquire the moment we're alone.

"Neither of us gets the full picture," Raph patiently explains. "If you see the location, I'll see the subject, or vice-versa. In this case, I saw *who* she was while you found out *where* she was."

"What's her name?" Ariel asks curiously.

"She goes by the name Hideko," Raph replies with a hesitant tone in his voice.

"What's wrong?" I press, suddenly anxious.

"We're in the third most populated city in Japan," Michael's voice drips with frustration as he continues, "I have to destroy her without lighting up any innocent bystanders. It'll have to be fast and private."

This is starting to feel real. I was more worried about how exactly we would locate the thing. It never crossed my mind how to eliminate it. Now, that they're calling "it" a "her," and *she* has a name…

"So what do we do now?" Ariel asks, looking from

Michael to Raph.

Raph shakes his head, and Michael exhales deeply, mumbling to himself, "If only we could reach out to Zoë."

It's not an option. Gabe was very clear about us being on our own here. An idea pops up, and I immediately share, "Can she be lured to some deserted area or something?"

"In Osaka?" Michael asks, sounding amused by my question.

"Yes, in Osaka," I reply, a little frustrated by his constant belittling. "Somewhere in the middle of the night or before dawn. A place that's closed to the public during the night, like the Osaka Castle Park for example. They have standard operating hours. If only there were a way to lure her there–"

"It would be over quickly," Michael cuts in, finishing my sentence.

"How exactly do we plan to reel her in?" Ariel inquires, not putting much faith in my idea.

"She may come voluntarily, if it's me," I suggest in an exceptionally soft voice, waiting for Michael's scoff, but it never comes. The opposite is true. He seems to consider it, but after some thought he shakes his head.

"What are the chances of Hideko getting the drop on us?" Raph challenges. "Between the three of us, we can keep Liz safe from harm. Ariel can summon the aegis around the park so no human can enter until we're finished. It's a good idea. We just need to be sure the grounds are clear first."

"I don't like anything that involves a 'what if?' It's risky. She might escape, and then what?" Michael asks, alluding to the obvious. His unspoken words are loud and clear. If Hideko escapes the trap after seeing me and Raph together, all of this will have been for nothing. It's the death of me as far as Michael is concerned. I'll become a liability to the gates. They'll have the five elemental children and the key. It'd be like handing the underworld the launch code to their own nuclear weapon. I'd be their Trojan horse.

"Hideko doesn't need to know who I am," I point out.

"Liz is on to something here. She can confide in her," Raph offers in agreement.

"Won't she sense that Liz has no affinity to the elements?" Ariel jumps in.

"No," Raph replies. "Hideko is Air, not Spirit. She won't be able to sense Liz's affinity or lack thereof. She'll have to ask Liz to prove it. That's all the time we need to close the aegis and destroy her. She won't see it coming."

"Now that's something to consider," Michael agrees.

"I second that," Raph notes.

For the rest of the day, Michael and Raph study satellite maps of the park in search of the best place to ambush her. While Ariel and I search the social networks for her phone number. It turns out, that even demon spawns are on Facebook. It's just a matter of time until she appears online.

At nine p.m., her name lights up and I send her a private message, "I want to meet you."

The reply is instant, "Who is this?"

"You and I are the same," I write back.

An extended pause follows before Hideko replies, "Where?"

"By the fountain at Osaka Castle Park at one a.m."

"Why so late?"

I don't know how to reply to that. So I shout for help. Before any of us can come up with anything, Hideko messages back, " I'll be there."

That's how I find myself standing alone by the fountain in the Osaka Castle Park. It's almost two a.m., and this place is as dim as it gets. I'm freezing to death, and there's been no sign of her so far. Hideko should have been here like fifty minutes ago.

Without warning, Ariel's crystalline aegis closes above us. Its surface is iridescent with tiny swirling strands glimmering like diamonds inside. Back in Bora Bora, sunlight refracting through her aegis would disperse rainbows all around us. In the darkness of night, it's nearly invisible.

The presence of the aegis is an indicator that Hideko must be nearby. I just hope she's oblivious to Ariel's ethereal dome. Just then, a slim figure finally emerges from the shadowy trees. It must be her. My stomach does a little flip and my heart drops. I take a deep breath and keep my hands in my pockets, forcing myself not to look away.

The closer she gets, the more uncertain I feel, but for all the wrong reasons. The figure approaching me is just a girl in a pair of jeans and blue jacket. She stops in front of me and lowers her hoodie.

I do a double take. She's an ordinary girl a few years older than me, a sweet looking one. Her hair is dark black and cut shoulder-length. Her face is pale under the dim park lighting and her eyes are jet black. For some reason, I expected them to be pale blue like Abe's. She doesn't have Lill's menacing poise either. Nothing about this girl comes off as being evil.

She nods politely, and I do the same. Then, she says in Japanese, "Hi, I'm Hideko."

"I'm Clarisse," I use my middle name.

"You're from America," Hideko immediately identifies my accent, and I nod. She gives me a closed lip smile, snowballing my uncertainties. She can't be one of them. She looks and sounds human. Maybe Hideko sent someone else in her place. She speaks again, "I got your text message. What makes you think you're like me?" Her voice is soft and delicate, sounding concerned. It's as though she genuinely cares what may happen to me. It's unnerving.

Oh, no. It's the wrong girl. Even if she's Asmodeus' elemental child, how can they be so sure she's evil? She could be like Ken, or Spark even. Why should she have to die? Lill should be the one to die.

I look past her, Michael is already charging forward. In a blink of an eye, a pair of pure white wings flares out of his back and a smoldering sword appears in his right hand. My eyes widen, and I suck in a deep breath, *"Michael, DON'T!"*

Hideko spins around and slides away just in time to dodge Michael's slashing blade.

"RUN!" Michael shouts, dashing out for her.

My brain doesn't process his command, I just stand there mesmerized. Michael in his full form is devastating, all-powerful and graceful. He blazes in a spectrum of light, suddenly illuminating the entire park. I never thought death could be so beautiful. If he were the one coming for you when your journey ends, dying wouldn't be all that bad.

"ELIZA, RUN!" He shouts even louder, breaking me out of my daze. But it's too late, a blast of wind lifts me up, and I'm spinning fast. I'm trapped in a spiral of air about five feet above the ground. Just as sudden as it enveloped me, the wind stops, and I fall flat on my back with a thud. All the air from my lungs is knocked out of me, and I struggle to get to my feet. This time, I don't hesitate, I run.

"GET DOWN!" Michael shouts from above.

At the sound of his voice, I let myself drop, but it's too late. Before touching the ground, I'm sucked in by a tornado. I scream at the top of my lungs as my body swirls faster and faster, quickly shooting me upward about thirty feet in the air, high above Michael. This time, I spot Hideko hovering way above the tree line, just below the apex of the aegis. She's controlling the wind with her fingertips, as though the massive cyclones are the strings of a marionette.

"RAPHAEL!" Michael calls out, launching toward Asmodeus's Air spawn.

"I'M ON IT," Raph shouts back over the deafening howl of the wind.

I'm spinning so fast that I can no longer scream. I press my eyes closed, and extreme vertigo kicks in.

Raph's voice calls out from nearby, "ARIEL, NOW!"

Instantly the tornado dies off, and I'm falling fast. I squeeze my eyes shut, screaming my throat raw all the way. Two arms coming from nowhere swiftly catch me in midair, and I dare to open my eyes.

"Gotcha," Ariel's voice cuts through the rushing air, and relief washes over me. I'm inside a blur of icy white light and feathers, no longer falling.

She lowers me safely to the ground and immediately launches skyward. I blink in confusion. Black spots move across the sky, and I rub my eyes as if to wipe them away. When I look again, they're still there, and multiplying. The twitching shadows take the shape of dark winged creatures. Their black pointy wings flap wildly as they fly in a swarm, hissing and screeching. They remind me of giant bats, only with distinct human traits. *Demons?*

A blast of wind throws me backward, catching me by surprise. I struggle to keep my footing before falling on my butt.

"STAY DOWN," Michael's shout sounds far away.

And I do, rolling on to my back for a better view of what's happening above.

"ARIEL, BEHIND YOU!" Michael warns loudly, fending off blast after blast of wind directed at him. His wings rattle like a kite in a typhoon, chasing Hideko to the perimeter of the aegis.

Ariel is a scintillating light at the center of a violent flock of ghostly shadows. She skillfully fights them off in their multitudes, her blades piercing and impaling them. Instantly, they dissolve into what looks to me like viscous charcoal, dripping from above. A horde of demons charge at her from behind, and she gives no indication of having heard Michael, but dives downward at the very last second, letting them fly overhead. Then, she's right back to sinking her twin sai into creature after creature.

"LIZ, GET OUT OF THERE!" Raph calls out, fighting off a mass of gooey creatures of his own. They try to encircle him as well, his golden wings overshadowed by distorted human silhouettes with flapping bat wings. He shoots up, stopping half an inch from the glimmering dome, and then descends in a spiral slicing them asunder with the sharpened edge of his open wings. The creatures burst into charcoal ash on contact and dark particles rain from above.

"ELIZA, MOVE!" Michael's commanding voice gets me crawling out of the way, just as a thick boiling substance surfaces from the turf, shooting straight up into the sky. It adheres to the glassy dome, like a two ton leach slowly moving and drinking its energy. The shield flickers as if fighting it off.

"MICHAEL," I scream for his attention, frozen in terror. "THE AEGIS."

He looks up at the yielding dome and then over to Ariel. As if sensing his gaze, she calls out, "BETTER HURRY, MIKE." Her hands are a blur, dispatching demon after demon to the earth below.

The scent of burning sulfur fills my nose as a haze of soot envelops my surroundings. I crawl on hands and knees, stopping at the edge of another black lava puddle pooling up in front of me. My first instinct is to get to my feet and run, but that would be suicide. Michael, Raph and Ariel are too preoccupied to catch me this time. I turn and go to my right, coming to a halt just in time to avoid digging my hand into the hot bubbly sludge that begins to emerge. I shriek and roll backward.

The revolting smell makes me sick to my stomach. More black goo is inching toward me, I'm surrounded. There's nowhere to go. If I stay here, I'll burn up for sure. If I stand up, Hideko will just toss me in the air again. I get to my feet and jump over the bubbling puddle, deciding I'd rather fall to my death than burn to ashes. Then, I run as fast as I can, putting some distance between me and the dark substance before dropping down again. I roll on my back and peer up, curious as to why Hideko didn't send me flying this time. Michael is giving chase and keeping her occupied.

Hideko moves lightning fast, dodging Michael's attacks one after another. It's like she's the wind herself, becoming almost invisible in her speed. All her energy seems to be focus on Michael, she sends powerful gusts of air at him each chance she gets, as if building a barrier of wind between them. Michael recoils, deviates and then charges in again at different angles.

What happens if the Aegis breaks? Will the creatures that Hideko summoned from the underworld escape into the city? What then? All the innocent people, my Dad, Suri, my friends...

Things are looking grim. The highest peak of the dome is blackened with sludge, and it appears to be caving in. Ariel and Raph are way outnumbered. It's like forty to one, and the demons just keep coming. Michael's blade nearly makes contact, and Hideko lets herself drop a few feet. She gets close enough for me to hear her audibly summoning the demons to help her. Chances are, she'll escape and take the knowledge of my true identity with her.

All of a sudden, light spreads brighter than anything I've ever seen. It's like the sun itself is crashing through the atmosphere straight at us, but without the heat. I shield my eyes with my hand and squint at Michael, believing at first that *he* is the source of such a powerful light. But it's not coming from him. His battle with Hideko continues apart from the light.

A crack has formed from the center of the aegis' dome all the way down, and I gasp in terror, anticipating its impending failure. Just when things can't get any worse, the pulsing leach at the center bursts into a shower of black mire. A glob of black sludge drops right on my chest and I yelp, sitting up and shrugging out of my jacket. I throw it as far away from me as possible, and it corrodes before my eyes. I stand up to take cover, and that's when I see him; *Ken*. His eyes are the source of the sudden brightness. It's like they're amplifying and reflecting the three archangel's brilliance; rays of golden, white and silver projected as parallel beams of luminance.

A splatter of gelatinous muck hits the ground half an inch from my feet, and I reflexively jump back. Ken's light beams shatter the dark creatures the same way the archangel weapons do, but with greater efficiency and without prejudice. The scene quickly becomes a downpour of rocky charcoal ooze.

In my moment of distraction, I'm caught inside a tornado once again. But this time, it only lifts me five feet in the air before I'm released to fall face down on the ground. I groan in pain and crawl to the shelter of a nearby tree.

Directly above, Michael's attacks are a flurry of light, feathers and blades. As if in slow motion, I catch a glimpse of Michael's sword coming down on Hideko. His blade splits medially down her center, and she falls into two symmetrical pieces, instantly dissolving into light purple particles of ash.

Michael wastes no time and joins Ken, Ariel and Raph in battle against the winged beasts. Together, they eliminate each of the remaining demons ten at a time. Raph is the first to descend when all the creatures have been wiped out. He approaches to check on me, and I ask, "What were those things?"

"Trust me, you don't want to know," He replies, spinning me around to examine my clothes for any signs of the acidic sludge.

Ariel joins us, "That's what I call improvising."

Michael descends a short distance from where we stand, and Ken stops beside Ariel.

"Why?" Michael stares down at me. He's the only one who remains in full form, sword in his right hand, white wings folded on his back.

When I first met Michael, his dark gaze alone made me uneasy. Add wings and a sword to the equation back then, and I would have runaway screaming. I don't know what really changed since then. Maybe it's what he said the night of Lill's party, or maybe I've faced death too many times to still fear him. His intense black sapphire eyes no longer intimidate me, and I surprise even myself by answering his question without omission for a change, "I was wrong. She looked human. I thought Hideko sent a decoy. I made a mistake."

He takes a step closer to me, his eyes hardening, and yet I don't have the urge to step back. Michael's voice is low and icy, "Didn't you learn anything in the past three months? I'd know if she were a human, any of us would–"

"Michael, don't." Ariel cuts him off, pleading. "It's not her fault. She saw a girl her age and perceived her as harmless. She carries Raphael's spectrum, but she's not one of us. She couldn't know that Hideko was hollow."

"She grew up in Japan," Raph supplies. "Hideko might have reminded her of an old friend."

My gaze is affixed to Michael. He closes his eyes and lets his wings dematerialize behind him before turning on his heels. On his shoulder blades, two identical parallel lines remain. They're the same glowing white of his wings, like two rays of dim light.

He looks over his shoulder at us. I'm absolutely sure Michael either sensed me staring at his bare back or read my thoughts. If he did, he doesn't give it away. He simply says in a tired voice, "Drop the aegis, Ariel. We're going home."

What does he mean by "home?" Boston, or the upper dimension?

Apparently, my thoughts were loud enough for him to hear this time. He replies without turning around, "Raphael is going back to his post. Ariel and I will drop you off in Boston before returning to our dimension, and Ken is on his own."

As we reach the main gate, Ariel undoes the aegis. The cracked dome dissolves before my eyes, blowing away like a shimmery cloud. Looking up at the sky, I can't help but wonder about the other four elemental children.

Ariel puts her arm around me, "Everything in its right

time. We want you to lead a normal life from now on."

"In other words, you need to quit playing 'guardian angel,'" Michael murmurs ahead of us. He doesn't seem remarkably content with his victory.

"He never does," Raph informs, tuned in to my thoughts. "He has the hardest task of us all, the most excruciating. He is the archangel of destruction."

42

Michael drops me off with a simple, "Here we are."
"Thanks," I reply and delay a moment, giving him room to speak again. But he doesn't. He just stares narrowly down the street.

I want to ask "a penny for your thoughts," but I'm not sure if I truly want to know. So, I pull the handle and step on to the sidewalk. Michael drives away, and the black Mustang disappears down the street one last time.

It seems like nothing has changed around here, apart from the weather, that is. It's as if time has frozen in my absence, patiently awaiting my return. At the front entrance the door opens before I reach for the knob, and Spark sidesteps me on her way out. She's back to her true self, beautiful and dark.

As if sensing my eyes on her, she pauses and whirls around, "You know what, Angel Girl? Sucks to be you!" And with that, she descends the steps and turns left at the corner, walking away in my favorite yellow hoodie.

Upstairs in the apartment, Grandma looks confused, "You're back already, what happened?"

"Changed my mind. I'm staying in," I smile widely at her.

"In that case, perhaps you should take a moment to straighten up your bedroom. It's chaos in there. Dominika is not your personal maid, young lady."

"Yes, Ma'am," I reply, and Grandma looks taken aback as if wondering what's gotten into me. I step closer, bending to kiss her cheek. Then, I exit the room, leaving Grandma completely baffled.

Chaos is putting it mildly. Not a single thing I own is in its place. It's like a tornado tore through my bedroom. *Unbelievable.* This is gonna take forever to clean up.

I grab my phone from my night stand and slide my thumb on the screen. It comes to life, and immediately a blue box pops up, "Low battery." I touch dismiss and dial Nate. Instead of ringing, an automated voice message announces, *"The person you are trying to reach is not accepting calls at this time."* I hang up, my heart deflating in my chest. Nate is gone for good.

My legs suddenly feel tired, as if they can't support my weight any longer. But there's nowhere to sit, the place is a complete mess. I start gathering my things, putting them away. Then, I collect the dirty clothes spread all around the room and throw them in the hamper.

An hour and a half later, I can see the floor again. I grab my tablet, sit on the bed and check my email. My inbox is filled with unread messages that have accumulated since I left. I open the latest email from my dad with the subject line: "Back in Shinjuku."

Hey, kiddo.

We made it home alright. But, we're missing you already. I hope you're well. You seemed a bit on edge. Suri says it's a teen phase. Let's just hope that she's right. Take care and write your old man when you have some spare time.

I love you, kiddo.

– Dad

P.S. Suri says you can do better than Nate. He gives her a bad vibe, ROFL.

I click reply and type:

Hi, Dad.

Sorry I didn't write before. Things have been a little crazy. I'm really sorry about my behavior on Thanksgiving, I wasn't myself. No need for concern. Tell Suri not to worry about Nate, I don't think he'll be sticking around.

Love you too, Dad.

Liz

P.S. What's this I hear about you signing autographs for groupies, Christian Bale? LOL.

I reread my message and press send. Standing up, I set aside my tablet and go back to putting things in order. With everything in its place, I carry the clothes hamper back in to the bathroom. I turn on the tap, throw water on my face and look at my reflection in the mirror. Drops of water fall from my eyelashes onto my cheeks as I blink, and I wonder how my life will be from now on.

Dominika's foot steps sound from down the hall, and I quickly dry my face with a hand towel. I turn off the light just as she reaches my bedroom with Wellington and Faye in tow. They're dressed all elegant, looking ready for the winter dance. Faye is in a pale green gown, and her hair is in a messy updo. Wellington is in a black suit and his hair seems a little longer than usual, purposely disheveled.

"Are the two of you finally together?" I ask when they approach me.

Faye rolls her eyes, "We're going to the winter dance at his school *together* if that's what you're asking."

"I'm too much of a geek for Faye," he jokes.

They look cute together, sort of balancing each other out. Hopefully after tonight they'll be a thing. At least someone gets a happy ending.

"Do you want to come?" Faye invites. "Dwayne, Kiara and EJ, will be there."

"No. Not this time."

"Come on Liz, it'll be fun," Wellington presses.

I shake my head in reply. "How did everything go while I was away?" I inquire almost afraid to ask.

"We want to hear your side of the story first," he says before Faye can answer.

I haven't had time to work it all out in my head yet, so I give them the short version. When I finish, Faye supplies, "We knew you guys did it, because Abe walked out in the middle of class the day before yesterday and never came back. We drove to Zoë's place to ask what was going on, but they were gone."

"Their apartment was empty," he picks up where she left off. "There was no sign that any of them had ever lived there. Spark let us know that you were on your way home. Nate left these for you," Wellington hands me an envelope along with my long lost sketch book and iPod. "He gave them to me the day after you left for safe keeping. He said I should return them to you once you guys got back."

I trace my finger over the iPod screen before putting it down. A lump forms in my throat, I swallow hard and open the sketchbook. Flipping fast through the pages, looking for the only portrait I've ever drawn, but as I expected, it isn't there.

"He took it," Faye states in a distant voice.

I look up at her, blinking.

"Mind if I see?" She asks for my sketchbook and I hand it to her. She turns page after page, absorbing each drawing intently. When she reaches the back cover, she says, "You're very good, like great actually. You should consider studying architecture in college."

"I'll think about it," I force a smile.

"So, do you want to know what Spark was up to while you were gone?" Faye asks, changing the subject.

"Tell me she didn't flash the entire school in the middle of Helen of Troy," I half joke.

"Where to start?" Faye considers.

I cover my face with both hands and groan, leaning back

on my bed expecting the worst.

Faye laughs at my expense and so does Wellington. I take a peek at her between my fingers, and she says, "She did okay. Don't worry about it."

"She's actually kinda cool," Wellington grins, and Faye gives him a perplexed look. He throws both hands in the air in surrender, "Come on, Faye, admit it. You liked her too."

Faye lets out an exaggerated sigh before consenting, "She's alright, you just have to get to know her. You'll like her too when I tell you she aced all your tests."

Something in my expression prompts Wellington to jump in, "The thing is, she looks and acts so human, we sort of forget she's not. It can't be easy being nice when you're a demon, you know?"

Faye bites her inner cheek and nods in agreement.

I frown, "Ken is a demon, and he's nice."

They exchange a look, and Wellington speaks again, "Ken keeps to himself. He doesn't hang around with a bunch of teenagers, pretending to be someone else."

"She didn't need to do it, you know?" Faye looks at me straight-on. "All I'm saying is regardless of her motives she put her life on the line to save our mere mortal butts."

They're probably right. I should be more grateful to Spark. Voluntarily or otherwise, she did help save my life. If it wasn't for her, Lillithiel and her minions would still be watching my every move.

"Maybe you're right," I agree meekly.

A ding sound comes from Faye's pale green clutch. She opens it, pulling out her cell.

Silver? What happened to her pink phone?

"It's Kiara. She wants to know if we're coming or not," Faye informs Wellington.

"We should get going," he suggests. "Are you sure you don't want to come, Liz?"

"Too tired. You guys go and have fun. Thanks though," I smile at them.

Faye gives me a hug and whispers, "I'm so glad this is all over."

"Me too," I whisper back.

Then, they're off, walking down the hall, side by side, hands slightly brushing with each step. I watch until they disappear into the foyer and then return to my bedroom.

I pick up the yellow envelope with my name on it. I open it, removing a sheet of paper folded into three. For a moment, I just stare at the paper not wanting to read his goodbye. Tears are forming in my eyes, and I try to hold them back.

My mind made up, I put the paper back in the envelope and close it inside my sketchbook. Then, I walk to my closet and put on the first coat I find. It's a new one, Grandma must have bought it while I was away. It's cashmere and has a hood. It's beautiful, but not in a color I would ever pick myself, a shade of peach. The tag says: "salmon." I put it on, tie the belt around my waist and tuck my hands into the pockets. There's a note inside, and I unfold it.

It's official, Angel Girl. I canonize you Saint Eliza. 'Coz only a Saint could tolerate life in your shoes. Consider the boots a farewell gesture.

Hope to never see you again,

Spark

On the floor sits a pair of Spark's signature combat boots. I guess it's a fair trade. I smile despite myself and place the note safely inside the Japanese manga that I bought when I first arrived. Faye and Wellington were right as usual, Spark wasn't that awful after all.

Grabbing my iPod, I turn off the lights and head to the balcony. I pause at the kitchen door and find Dominika emptying the dishwasher. She sees me watching her and commands, "Miss Liza, I trust you'll be joining us for dinner tonight. You need to put on some weight. One of these days the wind will blow you away."

A smile crosses my face, if only she knew. I give her a

single nod and spin on my heels. Passing the living room, I turn back and stop at the door. For a few seconds, I just stand in silence admiring Grandma and Grandpa as they sit together, side by side, watching TV. Grandma voices one of her usual critical observations about the news, and Grandpa pats her hand indulgently. A tear escapes, and I wipe it away, stepping out of view before they spot me.

I traverse the dining room with a few quiet steps and slowly slide the balcony door open. Snow flakes float in the wind, and it's a quiet cold evening. I bury my hands in my pockets, walking up to the rail. My fingers touch my iPod, and I pull it out, putting the earbuds in. As I power it on, I think about Nate.

Was he curious about what I was listening to as well?

A melodic familiar song starts playing in answer to my question. Not the same upbeat song it was playing the morning it all started. This one is from my latest playlist, and I turn the volume up. I *love* this song. The way the instruments join in one at a time, followed by Chris Martin's soft and melancholy voice, the lyrics matching my despondent mood perfectly.

I take in the park, already covered in white. Two lively figures catch my attention, a blonde and a brunette, throwing snow balls at each other like little kids. A third figure approaches, and I recognize him by his clothing. All in black, his hands tucked inside his coat pockets. It's Michael.

Ariel ruffles his hair, and Zoë takes the cue to playfully throw a snow ball at his chest. He's patient as usual, tolerant to their attempts to cheer him up. Eventually, he surrenders and shapes a snow ball of his own and throws it lightly at Zoë, letting the burden of his title aside for the briefest instant.

The two girls lie down flat, sweeping their arms and legs back and forth across the driven snow. Then, the three of them slowly fade into thin air, leaving a pair of snow angels behind.

My eyes water up and a warm tear escapes, rolling down my cheek. I wipe it away and let myself drift into the lyrics, trying not to cry, *"through chaos as it swirls, it's us against the world."*

A hand touches my shoulder, and I'm not startled for once. I turn around, meeting Nate's painted blue eyes. My first instinct is to throw my arms around him. But instead, I pause the song and remove the ear buds.

"You're here," my voice is almost a whisper. He gives me a quizzical look, and I elaborate, "I thought I'd never see you again."

Nate takes a step forward and asks knowingly, "You didn't read it, did you?"

I shake my head, "I didn't. I wasn't ready to say goodbye."

"You won't be getting rid of me quite so easily," His eyes telling me more than his words, just like the first time we met.

"Does that mean you'll be around?"

Nate smiles and brushes his lips to mine in reply, "I missed you, Angel Girl."

I get onto my tiptoes and kiss him, lingering a little longer than he does.

"I'll be around," he finally replies. "For now, I'm still subject to the underworld. But don't worry, I'll be off-site from time to time," Nate grips the iPod and my hand simultaneously, "What are you listening to?"

He restarts the song, placing the device inside his right coat pocket. One bud in my ear, the other in his. Then, he puts both arms around my waist and pulls me closer. I lean my head against his chest, enjoying the warmth of his embrace, as we slowly move to the rhythm of the song.

"Liz?" Nate voices in my mind, and I tilt my head up to face him.

His lips meet mine, not quite touching, brushing a tiny tender kiss and letting it build. My hand slides from his shoulder to the back of his neck, and I gently bring him closer, returning his kiss. I lose myself in the swirl of emotions fluttering inside me and relish each one intently.

As we break apart, I realize the light snow has ceased and tilt my head up, letting out a gasp.

"What is it?" Nate asks, touching his lips to my cheek.

"We're floating," I reply, latching my hands onto his shoulders.

"You're right. We're floating away," Nate says carelessly.

We're inside a bubble hovering about five feet from the balcony. Meeting his amused eyes, I ask, "Can we go higher?"

"Only if we lose the aegis sphere," Nate looks bemused as he advises, "Whatever you do, don't let go."

The bubble dissolves, allowing us to fall a few feet down. But before we touch the ground, Nate's dark wings snap open, ripping through the back of his coat, flapping as we shoot upward. We soar up and above the buildings, the freezing wind rushing by us. I'm captivated by the beauty of the city covered in white, and the speed in which we're piercing the evening sky. I'm even more mesmerized by Nate and his dark wings glistening almost blue.

We cut through the clouds, leaving the city behind. Against my best efforts, I shiver with the cold and my jaw trembles. Nate's wings move in slow motion, and he shields us in a bubble once again. He wraps his wings around us both, "This is the highest I can take you."

"It's perfect," I look up at him.

"You're perfect," Nate complies and kisses me softly.

When my eyes open, snow is falling inside our bubble as we float above the clouds. Snow flakes swirl and dance all around us, as if we were on the inside of a snow globe.

From up here life seems infinite. I find myself right in between, where the city hides beneath the clouds and the world blends into the universe. For better or worse, everything is different now. I can't change my past or my plight. Nor can I disregard all that has transpired. Tomorrow, everything changes, but tonight I'm letting myself drift into Nate's embrace. In this moment, I'm just an ordinary girl in the arms of the one she loves.